ANATOLY KURCHATKIN

TSUNAMI

A NOVEL

Translated by Arch Tait

ИНСТИТУТ ПЕРЕВОДА

AD VERBUM

Published with the support
of the Institute for Literary Translation, Russia.

GLAGOSLAV PUBLICATIONS

TSUNAMI

by Anatoly Kurchatkin

Translated by Arch Tait

Published with the support
of the Institute for Literary Translation, Russia.

© 2017, Anatoly Kurchatkin

© 2017, Glagoslav Publications, United Kingdom

Glagoslav Publications Ltd
88-90 Hatton Garden
EC1N 8PN London
United Kingdom

www.glagoslav.com

ISBN: 978-1-911414-29-2

A catalogue record for this book is available from the British Library.

This book is in copyright. No part of this publication may be reproduced, stored in a retrieval system or transmitted in any form or by any means without the prior permission in writing of the publisher, nor be otherwise circulated in any form of binding or cover other than that in which it is published without a similar condition, including this condition, being imposed on the subsequent purchaser.

ANATOLY KURCHATKIN

TSUNAMI

A NOVEL

'Rus! Where are you careering to? Answer comes there none.'
Nikolai Gogol, *Dead Souls*
'Turning, he saw the sea.'
Joseph Brodsky, *Post aetatem nostram*

CHAPTER ONE

Radislav was no habitué of the Conservatoire, but it was there his path first crossed that of Andronicus Tsekhovets. Rad was preoccupied with pursuing a glamorous young Helen of Troy evidently predestined for a career as a Soviet diplomat. His campaign of many months was currently in a limbo of interminable phone calls. He had piqued her interest but the citadel was not yielding to siege tactics. He needed a ploy, a secret weapon.

His Trojan Horse presented itself in the shape of Vladimir Horowitz, a 'celebrated American pianist of Russian descent,' as Rad learned from the *Greater Soviet Encyclopaedia*. In the last years of Soviet rule, many ex-Russians who had found success in that very different world beyond the ocean hastened back to tour the Soviet Union, so soon to take its place in the history books. Among their number was Horowitz.

His name rustled through the less than numerous Conservatoire aficionados of Moscow University's Faculty of Mechanics and Mathematics, generating so much excitement and awe that Rad pricked up his ears. He discreetly approached one aficionado, who owed him a favour for supplying a crib sheet for an exam.

The aficionado not only briefed him, but provided a secret password securing access to insiders who alone could secure him the impossibly sought-after tickets to a Horowitz recital. The password was to be whispered in the ear of those who owned the queue at the Conservatoire and kept outsiders out. At the head of their tightly knit team was Jan, an illustrious Polish aristocrat who, a few years later, effortlessly transformed himself into a Jew and went to live on welfare in Germany. He was a round-shouldered individual who had taken a battering from life. Despite his age, he had the demeanour of a late-developing sixth-form student playing truant and intoxicated by the first gusts of the air of freedom. Jan pulled from his jacket a much-thumbed exercise book, ran a ball-point pen down a list, and picked a number and a name he awarded to Rad. One immediate condition was that he must be on duty that night, keeping vigil with a notebook until eight in the morning, noting applicants for tickets and preventing anyone else from setting up a rival queue. 'You can't fish a bird out of the pond without effort,' he counselled Rad, providing him with telephone numbers to call for backup in case of need. 'A fish,' Rad corrected him. 'You can't pull a fish …' 'Any fool can catch a fish in a pond,' Jan retorted.

As a new recruit Rad had to stand sentinel not for one night, like the others, but for three, and then also during the hours of daylight a couple of times for a few hours. His reward, however, when the tickets went on sale and a thousand-headed monster snaked the length of the street from the Conservatoire's colonnaded rotunda, was to be only forty-fifth in the queue. Half an hour after the box office opened, he emerged the victorious possessor of two tickets.

On learning of the treasure he could lay at her feet, the beauty from the Institute of Foreign Relations flung open the gates of her stronghold as if they had never been barred. 'How on earth did you get them?' she asked incredulously over the phone. 'I tried through Daddy's account and even that didn't work.' 'Daddy' was the Soviet ambassador to a Latin American country, and his status conferred access to sought-after cultural events in his homeland whether he was actually there or defending its interests far beyond its borders. 'What it takes,' Rad told her smugly, 'isn't corrupt official perks, but initiative and a turn of speed.'

He had no recollection afterwards of what Horowitz played or how. Something by Chopin, no doubt, or maybe Liszt. He had read that Horowitz was a great virtuoso of the Romantic school but Rad had little interest in the genius of his celebrity: he was too busy savouring his victory. Troy had all but fallen. *La belle Hélène* was squeezed against him on a crowded red bench in the gallery, so tightly he could feel the hardness of her hip bone through his trousers and jacket. He could feel a hardness in his trousers painfully confined within an incommensurate space. When Yelena, who preferred to be called by her westernised nickname of Nellie, took the opera glasses from him to peruse the great pianist's features, and when she gave them back, her fingers caressed his and the constraint became all but unbearable. When next he took back the opera glasses, he retained her hand in his for an infinite moment as it tensed, considered which way to go, and then surrendered to his power.

In the interval they went to the buffet. 'Nellie' was not that keen but Rad insisted. A poor victory it would be that was not celebrated with a feast. In the buffet, champagne was poured into tall flutes, open sandwiches with smoked salmon and caviar were served, and tea and cakes were also available. Rad ordered champagne and sandwiches and tea and cakes. To pay for it he plucked from his pocket a crisp new 100-ruble note, readied for this moment in exchange for all the cash he had managed to scrape together at home. Whipping a 100-ruble note out of the recesses of your jacket hints that there may be plenty more where that came from, and out of the corner of his eye, Rad detected it had produced the desired effect on his Hélène.

That the barmaid might be unable to change it, he had not foreseen. Although Rad had piled up quite a feast, he needed change in the region of eighty-five rubles. The barmaid may just have been reluctant to plunder her float of smaller denomination notes, but, 'You'll 'ave to change that for something less,' she announced in a tone that proclaimed her a bastion more formidable than Troy.

Rad turned to the crowd behind him and immediately recognised the features of Mironov, star of both the silver and the television screen.

'Can anybody change this?' he enquired, waving his crisp note with its sepia portrait of Lenin in the air. The question was addressed to no one in particular, but his eye was on Mironov.

The actor, as if addressed personally, delved into the inside pocket of his elegant grey jacket, so familiar from television, and pulled out banknotes: a ten, a ten, another ten, a fifty, a hundred, another hundred. Hundreds he had aplenty: lower denominations he was short of.

Realizing this, Mironov froze for a moment, transferred his sad Judaeo-Slavic gaze from Rad to his lady companion and then, with a lithe movement, whisked Comrade Lenin out of Rad's hand and, raising him even higher, scanned the crowd in the bar. It seemed he could read from people's faces how much they had in their pockets.

'You, young fellow! Do the community a favour and facilitate the forward movement of the queue. Change this note!' He had singled out a youth of Rad's age, remarkable only for a grey checked suit no less elegant than the actor's jacket and the fact that he had the bulbous nose of a circus clown.

The young fellow harrumphed, pulled out his wallet and, with the aplomb not of a clown but of a conjuror, flourished note after note: a fifty, a ten, another ten:

'But I expect a glass of champagne as commission,' he stipulated, holding the money up in the air but not yet passing it to Mironov. 'Deal?' He looked at Rad.

'Another glass of champagne,' Rad instructed the barmaid.

Still harrumphing over what he evidently judged a profitable transaction, the young man handed Mironov a colourful fan of banknotes and the sepia Lenin disappeared into the folds of his illusionist's wallet.

'My pleasure,' Mironov said as he passed the notes to Rad, glancing at him cursorily before lustfully devouring *la belle Hélène* with his eyes.

Rad saw clearly enough what had motivated the celebrity's altruism, or rather, who. Standing next to Nellie, he could feel the radiation of her beauty. She was a chalice brimming with precious elixir and knew it, as anyone could tell from the way she inclined her head, her deportment, the way she walked.

He bridled. How could he have allowed another male, no matter how famous, to encroach on his triumph? He beckoned the youth with the wallet to help carry and, turning his back on the great actor, obliged his lady to do the same. 'Let's take everything in one go. Carry as much as we can.' He loaded her up and gave her no opportunity to glance back at her admirer, who was doubtless still rapt in his contemplation of beauty.

The youth with the bulging wallet, seemingly frozen in mid-harrumph, also collected glasses, cups, saucers and plates from the counter and carried them wordlessly to the table Rad had found. When they were seated, he introduced himself.

'My name is Andronicus,' he said. 'Sorry about that. Dron to my friends.'

'Never mind,' Rad said graciously. 'We share that misfortune. My name is Radislav.'

'Radislav, Radislav …' their unanticipated table companion mused. 'Are you a Czech?'

'Jewish, of course,' Rad said, in no hurry to deepen their acquaintance.

'Oh, come off it. You can't be!' their companion expostulated. 'A Jew with a name like Radislav? Impossible.'

'Evidently not!' Rad replied curtly.

Their companion tempered his boisterousness. Indeed, he fell silent and, like a prodded snail, withdrew into his shell.

No less suddenly, however, Hélène came out of hers. Her eyes sparkled, she became animated, her voice beguiling; she seemed to glow.

'You have a seat in the stalls? That's just amazing!' she said. 'How on earth did you get the tickets? Rad here could only manage the gallery.'

'Eagles fly. Theirs is a place in the sun,' the snail, immediately emboldened, emerged from his protective shell. 'To listen to Horowitz from up in the gods, oh dear! Positively *mauvais ton*.'

'*Mauvais ton*? It's nothing of the sort,' Nellie retorted, nettled. 'Do you even know the meaning of the expression?'

'Vulgar. Will that do?' The snail, its body fully re-emerged, now sat at their table, guzzling their sandwiches and cakes and drinking their champagne with a gusto that implied this had all been laid on specially for him.

'No, vulgarity will most certainly not do,' Nellie responded, enjoying the cut-and-thrust and splashing her elixir everywhere. 'Vulgarity is the privilege of the plebs.'

In this disputation Rad found himself entirely superfluous, an empty chair at the table, a spectre at the feast.

The Achaean, having all but taken impregnable Troy, felt a surge of righteous wrath.

'I propose a toast,' he said, abruptly breaking off the inane banter of his lady and the rampant mollusc. He raised his glass of champagne and proposed, 'Let us drink to Homer!'

'What has Homer got to do with anything?' Nellie and the snail demanded in unison.

'Homer tramped round Greece in sackcloth and sang in the squares,' Rad said, 'while the Greeks sat on their bums in the dirt and listened.'

'Sounds marvellous,' remarked the bulging wallet with the egregious nose and ridiculous name.

'What on earth are you talking about?' Nellie again demanded. 'You want us to drink to sitting in the dirt? No thank you!'

A presentiment of loss wafted over Rad, as bitter as the scent of wormwood.

'Well, we can't just drink to nothing, can we?' he said in a more conciliatory tone. 'Homer, Horowitz ... There would be no Horowitz if there had been no Homer. Here's to beginnings!'

'That I can drink to,' said Helen of Troy, proffering her glass.

'Fine by me,' their guest, whose glass was by now all but empty, acquiesced.

The clinking of flutes of Soviet champagne heralded the beginning only of the end of the taking of Troy. Shortly afterwards, their importunate companion left them, dissolving into the interval crowd. Rad and Nellie returned to their gallery and sat, periodically transferring the opera glasses, through the second part of the concert. It culminated in a half-hour ovation for the trans-Atlantic celebrity. Rad delivered his intended prey to the door of her apartment, and she fluttered away from him: for a day or two, he supposed, but in fact for much longer than that. Hélène, having raised his hopes, once more retired to her citadel. The interminable phone calls resumed until, suddenly, the battery which had kept him dialling her number went flat. He found he had not phoned her, not just for a day or two but for much longer, and also that he no longer had any wish to.

This was facilitated by the appearance of someone new who, perhaps not entirely unexpectedly, strayed into his orbit and was far more inclined to fling wide the hospitable gates of her citadel. She might not have appeared had Hélène not retreated into hers, but at all events, he withdrew his troops from her bastions and grass soon grew on their approaches. A little more time, and la belle Hélène was gone from his life as if she had never existed. The famous Mironov, who had crashed into it with all the subtlety of a cannonball to poison the joy of his victory feast, never re-appeared. A few years later, however, Andronicus Tsekhovets did.

* * *

'They'll have your guts for garters,' said the round-faced geek with high cheekbones. Around thirty-five, he looked like an over-inflated pink ball, except for the heavy spectacles weighing down his nose. 'It's just instinct with them. They don't stop to think. They're guard dogs: let them loose and they bite your balls off.'

'What makes you think they'll go for our balls rather than yours?' another geek, also wearing heavy spectacles but with a thin pike-like face, rounded on him.

'Because I have not the least intention of involving myself in this escapade!' the first geek retorted. 'One should undertake projects which have some prospect at least of a positive outcome. Collective suicide is not for me.'

'Well, great! Why didn't you say at the outset that you're a coward?' Pike-face exclaimed. '"I'm scared, my lips are trembling, my knees are knocking," instead of pretending to be so concerned for everybody else?'

A girl skinhead wearing a bright red scarf and crushing a cigarette between her fingers as if about to light it but constantly putting off the moment, pointed a finger at Pike-face and gestured in the air. 'There's no denying it, Roman is absolutely right. They regard any organization they haven't sanctioned themselves as a crime against the Russian state. Article 72 of the RSFSR Constitution. Penalty: anything from ten years to the death penalty.'

'With confiscation of property,' interjected Round-face, pleased to have found an ally.

'Gentlemen, this is not moving us forward,' the lady who had invited them all intervened. She was a big woman, built, in fact, like an elephant, with fleshy, elephantine features and a derisive voice which brooked no contradiction. Her tone implied that, while everyone should be free to say whatever they liked, she had a monopoly on insight and knowledge. 'The Communists are finished. They are no longer capable of anything. They are impotent, gentlemen, impotent! They may still manage a wank but they can't get it up for a thorough-going fuck. You have nothing to fear, gentlemen, nothing!'

'Who says anyone is afraid? Did I say I was afraid?' Round-face protested. 'That's who was talking about being afraid!' he added, pointing at Pike-face.

'Look, just don't bother pointing!' Pike-face protested in turn. 'Always trying to shift the blame to someone else. You need to stop doing that. Times have changed!'

'Oh, gentlemen, do stop bickering!' their hostess again interrupted. 'Even if they can still give us grief, that is beside the point. The times have thrown us a great opportunity and we have no right to pass it up. We've not come here to talk about danger: we are here to agree a party constitution and outline a plan of action. A plan of action, gentlemen, action!'

Their hostess's extraordinary way of addressing people, not as 'comrades' but as 'gentlemen', the casual way she bandied words like 'wank' and 'fuck', the very fact of this gathering in her apartment to discuss establishing a democratic party to oppose the Communist Party, was all so unbelievable that the top of Rad's head felt cold and his teeth ached with the excitement.

He did not himself know the lady who owned the apartment, the argumentative round-faced and pike-faced 'gentlemen', or any of the thirty or so other people crammed like herring in a barrel into the apartment's only room. He knew Sergey, a fellow student who had brought him here. They had happened both to be standing in the corridor earlier in the day looking at the faculty timetable, had exchanged a few words and got on to the hot topic of the small co-operative businesses to which the Party had first given its blessing but now, when they were proving only too successful, was trying to strangle. Rad told him a joke about a Party secretary whose former subordinate set up a co-operative and pulled in stacks of money. It was a very pointed joke, with the Party secretary represented as a bungling idiot. Sergey fell about laughing, before unexpectedly inviting him to come that evening to a certain event. Where? What was it about? Rad enquired. 'You'll find it interesting,' his new friend assured him.

Actually, there was one other person in the apartment he recognised, and that was the possessor of the bulging wallet who had changed his 100-ruble note at the Conservatoire. With his hyperplasic nose, it would have been difficult not to recognise him. Rad could not remember his name. As for his surname, that he did not know, yet.

Were they acquainted? Rad decided that drinking champagne together in the fifteen-minute interval of a concert did not constitute an introduction. His Conservatoire drinking companion, however, evidently thought differently and was making a beeline for him through the crowd.

'Hello, there. Decided to join the revolution?' he enquired jauntily. 'Democratic greetings. What brings you here?'

'Probably the same as you,' Rad replied non-committally.

'I hardly think so. Did someone invite you?'

'Yes,' Rad confirmed. 'What about you? Are you one of the organisers?'

'What, me?' he retorted, as if Rad had just said something funny. 'That really would be something. I'm here as an observer. You've heard of UN observers? Well, something along those lines.'

'That's pretty much my position too,' Rad admitted.

'A UN observer?'

'No. More an outside observer.'

'Ah, I see, I see,' his companion nodded. 'Well, nothing wrong with that. Are we going to join the revolution, then?'

Rad looked at him uneasily. Sergey had no sooner brought him to the apartment than he had rushed off to shake hands with this one and that, including the hostess, who gave him a motherly pat on the shoulder. The discussion had yet to begin and Rad was far from certain what kind of activity he was being drawn into.

'What if we don't?' he asked.

The other man shrugged. 'It's a free country now. No one is going to force anyone to do anything!'

A little later they found themselves on different sides of the room and Rad mentally confirmed his earlier view that they had not been introduced. An acquaintance is someone you know something about, Here he could not even remember the man's name.

No sooner had he thought that, than the name popped into his mind. Andronicus. Dron. Not a common name.

It was nine at night before they moved from their various private conversations to debate the matter for which the meeting had been called. Midnight came, the metro stations closed. Two o'clock came and went, and they had yet to agree either a constitution or a plan of action. Rad's teeth had stopped aching, the top of his head had stopped feeling cold, and instead his jaw was aching from yawning. This was no longer interesting. The sense of new initiatives and extraordinary happenings which at first had made his head spin, had dissipated, and the fare on offer seemed unappetizing without it. He felt no urge to join any party, neither the one that had ruled Russia for seventy years nor this one, which aspired to oppose it. He just wanted to get his degree, get taken on as a postgrad, and then see the lie of the land. There was little to complain about, and if he was not a member of an elite which effortlessly procured tickets for Horowitz concerts, well, there never would be enough to go around. He would make do with someone less famous.

Rad looked around for Sergey, whom he had not met up with since he went off to shake hands. There was no sign of him. The room seemed to have become noticeably more spacious. People, many people, had left and he could see it was time for him to be off too.

Out in the hallway he decided, before venturing into the night, to go to the toilet. It shared a room with the bath and the door was bolted. When it opened his Conservatoire companion emerged.

'We meet again!' said Andronicus. 'Are you thinking of leaving? I am. I'll wait for you. Everything's more fun with two.'

Given the lateness of the hour, it really would be more fun if there were two of them.

'I'll be right with you,' Rad said.

Night was assaulting the streets with the ferocity of Achaean troops storming a fortress. The February wind slashed their faces with a finely honed bronze sword. The street was deserted as far as the eye could see. It was only a five-minute walk to Profsoyuznaya metro station, but there would be a three-hour wait outside before it would re-open.

'*Oh, where's my white Mercedes now?*' Dron sang quietly to the tune of Vysotsky's 'Oh, where is my black pistol now?'

'*On Greater Carriage-Makers' Row*,' Rad continued automatically.

'Not quite, but nearly,' his companion agreed from inside the warm cocoon of fur surrounding his face. 'On Stoleshnikov Lane, actually, where I reside. It's the building with the fur shop on the ground floor. Do you know it? On the corner of Stoleshnikov and Pushkin Street.'

Rad gave a silent whistle on hearing Dron's address. The corner of Stoleshnikov and Pushkin Street was a five-minute walk from the Kremlin.

'I know the fur shop,' he said.

'And your own residence?' Dron enquired.

'Oh,' Rad drawled, 'far from your neck of the woods. Out by Pervomaiskaya metro station.'

He lived with his parents on Lilac Boulevard, in a substandard Khrushchev-era five-storey block on the opposite side of Moscow from where they were now.

'And how did you imagine you would find a driver to take you from this backwater to your backwater?' Dron exclaimed. 'Unless, of course, you had a hundred rubles to spare,' he added.

'A hundred rubles?' Rad responded, as if to say that would hardly have been enough. 'I just couldn't stay in there any longer,' he went on, in an attempt to justify his rash departure in the middle of the night.

'You did well to leave,' his companion replied from the depths of his warm hood. 'The lads will be clapping them all in irons just about now. Well maybe in half an hour. Or an hour at most.'

'Who will?' Rad halted. They were walking towards the city centre along the edge of the road, ready to yell if a car should appear, but suddenly it was as if he were in a car and someone had slammed on the brakes. 'The KGB, do you mean?'

They were exchanging confidences.

'Who else?' Dron replied, impatiently shifting from one foot to the other in front of him. 'Wasn't that why you left too?' he added, deepening their complicity.

'Is that why you left?' Rad asked.

'Too right! Do you think I would wait for the doorbell to ring and try to dart out under their armpits? They don't let you get away that easily, and once they've got you, just try proving you're not a camel if the KGB says you are.'

'How come you know the KGB will be turning up?' Rad asked, starting again to walk down the road.

'Some of their guys told me, of course,' Dron said, as if it were the most natural thing in the world to be hobnobbing with agents of the state security service.

'You mean, you knew there would be a raid and you still went there?' Rad was aware of a note of grudging admiration in his voice.

'It's not a big deal,' his companion replied with a quick, smug laugh. 'The guys actually said to me, "Go and listen if you want to hear what they've got to say, only don't leave it too late to clear off." They aren't brutes, you know, and they don't want to make extra work for themselves either. They can pull in fifty people and give themselves a lot of hassle, or pull in twenty instead. That's quite a difference. If some get away, who cares? And if some people choose not to keep their heads down, they've only themselves to blame.'

This conversation was becoming more interesting by the minute. Rad had gone to the meeting purely out of curiosity, with no inkling that the KGB might be taking a close interest, but his companion, fully aware of the risk, had gone along anyway.

'So why did you want to listen to them?' he asked.

'Why not?' he replied with that same smug chuckle. 'Who can say how everything is going to turn out? For all we know they may really take power. It's not a bad idea to make friends with a future regime before it's in power, while the clay is soft. After it hardens you could beat your brains out and still not get inside.'

Like a blow from an Achaean sword, a sudden gust of wind blew Rad's hat from his head. He caught it in time and put it back on. The top of his head felt cold, but it had already been chilled as it had been at the beginning of the evening. Never had he given a thought to the kind of things his companion was talking about.

'What, did someone send you there?' he asked.

'What do you mean?' A note of resentment was to be heard in Dron's voice that anyone could think that of him. 'I chose to go there. Your destiny is in your own hands. Of course, if my Dad knew I was planning to go he would have blocked the road with tanks. They really do believe their monolithic Party will be at the helm for the next thousand years.'

'Who do you mean by "they"?'

'Our daddies. Their generation.'

For a moment Rad was thrown. His own father was no Party member, so he asked,

'Who is your father then?'

Now it was his companion who was on the hop. 'My dad?' Dron was clearly reluctant to answer. 'Oh, he's just a good guy. That's all,' he said and changed the subject. 'So you left because you'd had enough?'

'Yes.' Rad did not press for an answer. 'But really we ought to go back and warn them to break it up.' He stopped in the road again.

'Should we?' his companion asked mock-conspiratorially. 'Suppose you get back just after the KGB turn up. You've had the luck to get out in time. Why not keep it that way?' He took Rad by the arm and pulled him on down the road. 'You don't need to worry about them. They're not going to be exiled to the labour camp at Solovki. As to whether they might ever amount to anything politically, I'd bet my life that isn't going to happen.'

They had been deep in conversation for fifteen minutes or so when they heard an approaching car. It was driving towards the centre, pushing 120 km an hour, but their flailing arms and leaping about in the roadway caused the driver to brake and then stop. He agreed to give them a lift, but only as far as Stoleshnikov Lane.

'Lilac Boulevard?' He spat it out like an expletive. 'I wouldn't take you there for a hundred!'

'Well, of course, I can't give you a hundred, I don't have much on me, but from Stoleshnikov to Lilac Boulevard for another two tens is good money,' Rad persisted, leaning towards the partly open window.

'I wouldn't take you out there for two hundreds!' the driver said bluntly.

'Okay, chief, take us to Stoleshnikov,' Dron said, propelling Rad in the direction of the rear door and himself opening the front one. 'If you don't want to be rich, you might as well be honest.'

'Is that me you're calling not rich but honest?' the driver asked, offended.

'Oh, it's just a saying,' Dron reassured him, plonking himself down in the passenger seat. He turned and said to Rad in the back, 'We'll go to my place. You can crash there till the metro opens.'

The apartment they entered a quarter of an hour later seemed infinite. The ceilings were unimaginably high, and the room where they sat whiling away the time was bathed in light from a crystal chandelier which appeared to be suspended from a sky-hook. They sat there, sipping palate-searing Beefeater Gin from a square, litre-sized bottle, drinking dizzyingly aromatic Brazilian coffee that tasted of almonds, and smoking Havana cigars from which they snipped the ends with a special, dazzling chromium-plated cutter. These were luxuries unheard of at the time, as if he had been miraculously transported to a realm which lived by rules quite different from any he knew.

Rad finally learned the surname of his acquaintance.

Dron Tsekhovets was studying at the Military Translators Institute. He was in his final year and had the privilege of living at home and not having to wear a uniform.

'It would have been quite something if the KGB had arrived and put me in chains,' he chuckled between puffs on his cigar. 'I would be out of the Institute as fast as shit off a shovel and into the army as a conscript. I'm already an officer, but not commissioned yet.'

'That was some risk you were taking then,' Rad said, genuinely impressed.

'Do anything you like, just don't get caught,' Dron counselled sagely, blowing cigar smoke out of the corner of his mouth.

He was looking forward to joining the secret intelligence service of the KGB and travelling the world as a tourist. Rad expressed doubt that working for that department would involve travelling as a tourist.

'Of course not,' Dron said seriously. 'When you come back you have to draw up a report. If you're travelling you have to collect information.'

'But how much information can you collect as a tourist?' Rad felt sure Dron must be having him on.

'If I didn't know what I was talking about I wouldn't have said it,' Dron retorted tartly. 'The father of a friend of mine has driven all over Europe. Private motoring tourism. He brought back piles of cool gear and electronics.'

'What makes you so sure you'll get to travel as a tourist?' Rad asked. 'Man proposes but God disposes.'

'God has already agreed.' Dron was lounging in an armchair, the ankle of one leg resting on the knee of the other, and his whole languid posture expressing a sybaritic pleasure in the moment.

Rad recollected his evasiveness about his father's identity, and again asked who he was.

This time Dron opened up. Here they were, sitting in his home, drinking gin and coffee, smoking cigars. Their relationship had moved to a new level, and now he could reply. So, at least, thinking back to that night, Rad concluded.

His father, he told Rad, was a deputy minister in one of the Russian Republic's ministries. If it was not Mount Everest it was certainly Communism Peak, which at 7,495 metres was high enough to give you a crick in your neck if you looked up at it.

'How about you? Have you got a job? Are you still studying?' Dron asked.

'Mechanics and Mathematics at Moscow University.' It was the first time Rad had felt embarrassed about revealing where he studied.

'Ah, so you can look forward to sweating it out in some research institute for the rest of your life,' Dron remarked feelingly.

'What makes you think that?' Rad was offended. 'I may go on to postgraduate research. It's very much on the cards.'

'And after that you'll be explaining $a2 + b2$ to all your students!' Dron continued relentlessly. 'Are you looking forward to that?'

'Well, not "$a2 + b2$", something a bit more difficult than that,' Rad tried to fend him off.

'I can believe it will be something a bit more difficult,' Dron conceded, washing down a drag of cigar smoke with a sip of coffee from a narrow purple cup which resembled an inverted cone. 'It's going to be shit, though, isn't it? Admit it!'

'No it isn't,' Rad responded instantly, feeling like a fencer parrying the thrust of an opponent.

'Well, fair enough. To each his own,' Dron conceded, seemingly lowering his rapier, but then pointing his finger at Rad and shrieking, 'Zat voss written over zee gates of Buchenwald! *Jedem das Seine!*"

Drinking gin and coffee and smoking cigars, then adding something more substantial for the stomach in the form of bread with smoked sausage and hard 'Swiss' cheese, they talked not until the metro opened but until dawn, until it was time to set off to their respective alma maters. By now Rad was able to look Dron straight in the eye without being distracted by his egregious nose, something he had not been able to manage at the meeting of would-be democrats, as Dron had evidently been unpleasantly aware. Rad felt they had known each other forever, for years and years, and that each had a place in the other's life, and that from now on they would be phoning each other and hanging out together.

With declarations to this effect, and the ironical suggestion that they should take in another concert at the Conservatoire some time, they said their goodbyes and descended into the metro at Marx Prospekt, which a few years later was to be renamed Hunter's Row.

And so it was for a time. They phoned each other, and even met up once because Rad wanted to read Ivan Bunin's *Cursed Days*, published for the first time in the Soviet Union but impossible to obtain. Needless to say, Dron had a copy. They met in the spring, after Victory Day in May 1990, when life had taken off for both of them, and indeed was out of control: defending dissertations, taking the national examinations, being allocated jobs. Rad was recommended for postgraduate study, but would he be accepted? After the coup attempt in August 1991 it was difficult just to stay in the saddle. For a while Rad remembered he had not returned Dron's Bunin, which was plain bad manners. He meant to call and meet him somewhere, but did not, and later had other things on his mind and forgot the book.

Neither did Dron phone. When Rad did occasionally think about him, it was to register that he had not called, and that seemed partly to excuse his own passivity. Indeed, if Dron had phoned it would have been a surprise. All they really had in common was a long night of confidences which had had no continuation. The seed had fallen on stony ground and withered. If Rad had suddenly taken it into his head to phone, Dron would probably have been no less surprised.

CHAPTER TWO

The wall clock opposite the window was showing half past eight.

Rad turned and saw it was still dark outside, although it would doubtless be light soon. Even in December, dawn would be waiting on the threshold. Six weeks ago, by this time in the morning he would have been at his fitness club for half an hour already, in a suit, a clean shirt with razor-sharp creases which still retained a memory of the iron's heat, and a tie. In the middle of the day the boss can afford to absent himself for an hour, or even two or three, but at opening time he must be at his post without fail, even if there is not yet a soul around intent on busying themselves with their body.

'Arise, Monsieur le Comte, for dawn is breaking!' The words of the song came back to Rad, a memory from his youth when he had felt, if not an aristocrat, then at least a free spirit with no bonds or obligations to anyone. The words of the song had held no hint of irony and promised a life unblemished by failure.

He threw back the blanket, sat up in bed, and lowered his feet to the fiendishly cold floor of Swedish oak. A few seconds of contact with its icy varnish dispelled all somnolence. Now what remained of the night was only the oval of yellow light cast on the ceiling by the standard lamp. Since his old life had collapsed and he had found himself banished to this village of Semkhoz, strangely named, apparently, in honour of a seed farm, Rad had taken to sleeping with the light on. What was that about? Was he afraid of something? Was it just a kind of claustrophobia caused by darkness?

He stood up, shambled over to the lamp and pressed his heel on a button on the floor. In the ensuing gloom he shuffled to the wall switch, light poured down from the chandelier, the gloom was banished to the corners and the day had begun.

Rad dressed and did his rounds of the house. It was a big villa, with five rooms on the first floor, four on the ground floor, a kitchen, halls, corridors, a toilet and bathroom downstairs, a toilet and bathroom upstairs, a sauna and swimming pool in the extension, and a basement. He spent the next fifteen minutes opening doors, switching on lights and inspecting windows. If the house had been his, Rad would never have gone to so much trouble, but since it was not, and since this morning round was a condition of his residence here, he took it in his stride and even quite enjoyed it.

In the basement, which had a probably permanent smell of cement dust, Rad clicked the dial of the thermostat on the white enamelled AGW control panel with a practised hand, raising the water temperature in the radiators by a few degrees. He liked to have the house a little cooler at night and warmer during the day.

To his morning workout of press-ups, sit-ups, and bodybuilding exercises for his biceps he devoted some forty minutes, more than he had ever been able to afford in the past, even as the owner of a fitness club. Fierce jets of steaming water blasted down on him from an Italian showerhead with a curved, swan-like neck. Now the water pressure was all you could wish for, all the time, not just at night. In October, when Rad had first moved in, only a spiral of sparkling water had trickled from the showerhead during the day. At that time the surrounding area was still full of summer visitors who lit smoky bonfires of leaves in their gardens, and from dawn to dusk watered their fruit trees to prepare them for winter, with ridged hoses snaking over the ground which they pulled from one place to another. Now, no one was burning or watering anything and all around was silence and solitude. A never-thawing white blanket covered the ground, although it was still only the beginning of the first month of winter.

Since he had been living here, Rad's breakfast had remained immutable: three fried eggs, preferably with the yolks unbroken and sunny side up; three slices of toast from a Borodino loaf, two with ham and one with cheese; and a large cup of coffee. He brewed fresh coffee in a German cafetière with a piston which pressed the grounds down to the bottom, and for the Borodino bread he made a special trip to a nearby town, whose renowned monastery had withstood siege by the Poles in 1612. He had discovered a small shop near the railway crossing which sold bread from the monastery bakehouse. The coffee from his cafetière was entirely passable, and the bread was excellent and, in its plastic bag, kept for a good week and a half.

Rad's room was adjacent to the kitchen, and he moved back to it to drink his coffee. Here he slept and spent his day. He would have preferred the first floor, which afforded a broad view of the surrounding countryside and sometimes gave an illusory but agreeable sense of being elevated not just above ground level but above life itself. The master of the house, however, wanted him on the ground floor in the belief that from there he could guard the property more effectively, and he had had to choose a room from those he was offered.

His mobile phone rang after Rad, sipping his coffee, had connected his computer to the network and started downloading emails. He subscribed to some thirty mailings and it could take the computer ten or fifteen minutes to download them all. During that time the landline was engaged, and not infrequently for quite some time afterwards. Having downloaded his mail, he would cast off and circumnavigate the globe on the great pacific ocean of the Internet. There really was little else for him to do. He surfed the Internet for hours at a time. Indeed, he resided in this house, but lived in the Internet.

'Hi,' the owner greeted him. 'Again the skull and crossbones is flying from the mast despite the earliness of the hour?'

'Earliness?' Rad glanced out the window. The chandelier was still lit but its light was no longer needed. Outside was the full light of day. The fluffy snow which had fallen the day before was sparkling gold in the sunlight.

'Well, I don't know when your morning begins,' the owner joked with an undertone of grumpiness, before getting down to business. 'How are you? Everything okay?'

'Everything is in order. The frontiers are sealed and, as you hear, I am still alive,' Rad replied.

'I do,' the other said, 'and despite the early hour already active. You had quite some snowfall there yesterday. How are you coping?'

'I've cleared it all,' Rad reported. 'You could dance in the courtyard, only it might be chilly.'

'If it's chilly, turn up the heating,' the owner said solicitously. 'Have you been down to the basement to check the boiler?'

'I have, and everything is working well,' Rad replied a little shortly.

This conversation was repeated every day, varying only with the weather; sometimes, indeed, twice a day, when the owner arrived at his office in the morning, and in the evening before moving from a vertical to a horizontal position. The conversation was an essential part of the conditions for his living here and Rad accepted that uncomplainingly, although he found his patron's inflexible conscientiousness wearing.

'I'll be invading your solitude this evening,' the owner said. 'Is that agreeable?'

As if it were for Rad to decide whether or not to allow the man to visit his own house!

'With an extensive retinue?' Rad asked, in the light of past experience.

'The usual.' The master of the house sounded pleased with his formulation. 'Seven or eight guests. Polina needs to network with some of her people.'

Polina was the owner's wife, and if he said seven or eight people, that might mean ten or fifteen if the past was any guide. Polina occupied her days by taking painting lessons and socializing with people in the art world. Her unreliability and unpredictability were the ugly sisters of her talent.

'Please remind her not to introduce me to anyone,' Rad requested.

'Shall do,' said the owner.

'And not to accidentally bring anyone who knows me.'

'You can check them all out through the spyhole in the door before you let them in,' his patron repaid him in the same coin. 'See you this evening. Over and out.'

'See you this evening,' Rad said before throwing his phone down on the table and exploding, 'Bloody hell!'

He had no wish to see anyone. Every intrusion into his clandestine existence breached the delicate equilibrium in which he forced himself to exist. He thought of himself as a fragile crystal sphere magically suspended in the air. The least draught could destabilise it and send it crashing to the floor.

Meanwhile, the email program had been performing dutifully while he was talking on the phone. In a line at the bottom of the screen it reported completion of its task and how many emails had been received. Rad ran the cursor down the list of downloads. There were only mass mailings which, as he never emailed anyone himself, was only to be expected. People were probably still emailing his old mailbox, which must be full by now, and he sometimes felt tempted to forward the messages to here so he could at least look at them, but always suppressed the urge. He wanted nothing to link his former life to his present phone number.

The owner's announcement had disorientated him and he lost all desire to read the mailings. Rad abruptly clicked a succession of multiplication crosses, closing windows, and switched off the computer.

When he went out on to the verandah he was greeted so jubilantly by light, snow and frosty air that he stood for perhaps a minute, rooted to the spot. He needed time to get used to this brash, stunning symphony, to adapt to it like an amphibian moving from breathing through its gills to respiration using its lungs.

After walking out to the main road, which bisected his village like a knife slicing lengthwise through a loaf, it was a ten-minute bus ride to the monastery town. Buses, though, were few and far between, and enterprising capitalists, their lust for gold no less than that of Pushkin's covetous knight, had re-equipped their vans as minibuses, which passed the bus stop with the frequency of film frames. As a result, half an hour after leaving the house Rad was alighting at the stop near the bread shop. His supply of Borodino bread was almost exhausted, but there was never any guarantee he could replenish it, because the schedule of deliveries to the shop was incomprehensible to the secular mind. Today, however, he was in luck, arriving just after the trays of loaves. The bread was still warm.

He bought four, as many as would fit into the twin partitions in his black bag, zipped it up, threw it over his shoulder and left the shop.

Red Army Prospekt split the town in two, just as the main road bisected his village. Along it, the adapted minivans sped even more frequently in both directions, their windscreens displaying the numbers of the bus routes they were supplementing. Within a few minutes he could be at the monastery in the town centre, but Rad decided to walk.

He looked around as he went. Winter had not yet piled up snowdrifts; the roads and pavements were as yet unlined by banks of snow, and everywhere the white expanses shone immaculate and virginal. His destination was the public call centre at the foot of the monastery hill. He could have phoned from the post office diagonally across the road from the bread shop but always phoned from the centre, and always walked there. To phone from the post office would mean his expedition was over before it began, whereas walking through half the town made it more purposeful and significant, more meaningful. The extensive always seems more significant than the curtailed.

The cavernous hall of the telephone centre, a honeycomb of wooden cubbyholes with glass doors, was as desolate as the Arctic. Only in one of the booths with 'Moscow' in large letters on the glass, looking like a bee stuck in honey, was the figure of a young woman in a grey fur coat. Rad went to another booth labelled 'Moscow', the one furthest from the bee in the fur coat. He went in, closed the door tightly behind him, undid his anorak, took out a card with a magnetic strip and put it in the slot. At home his mother picked up the phone after the first ring, as if she had been sitting by the telephone waiting for him to call.

'Hello! Hello!' he heard her anxious voice, as tense as a string at breaking point. Perhaps she really had been sitting by the phone or, more likely, dragging it around the apartment with her.

'It's me, Mum,' Rad said, hastily adding, in order not to give her time to complain that he had not phoned for a long time, 'I'm okay. Everything is fine.'

His ploy did not work.

'Oh, well, thank heavens, at last!' she said. 'Can you really not phone a bit more often? As it is, I don't know what to think. God knows the things I imagine!'

'You don't need to imagine anything, Mum. I've already explained, but I'll say it again. If anything happens to me someone will phone you. If nobody phones, including me, it means everything's fine, I'm doing all right!'

'You're doing all right! But what about me, waiting here to see if this wretched phone is going to ring or not, trembling all the time. Do you think it's easy for me?'

'Sure, Mum. I've explained the situation.' Rad moved the receiver away from his ear and stood for a while not listening to his mother's reply. It was a necessary tactic if he was not to lose his temper. After a while, he brought the receiver back to his ear. She was still talking. 'I'm alive and well and everything is fine. How are you?' he broke in.

The line was silent for a while.

'Thank God, I am well enough,' she resumed. 'It's just this waiting. I am taking valocordin by the bucketful. Can you not at least tell me where you are?'

Rad did lose his temper.

'Not again!' he exclaimed. 'I'm safe and well and the reason I'm not telling you where I am is so things stay that way! Speak to you again soon. Goodbye!'

He slammed the phone down without giving her time to say goodbye herself. The receiver crashed down in its cradle as if crying out in pain. He instantly felt remorse. It was no way to treat a telephone, or his mother, come to that.

For a time he stared unseeing at the panel of buttons on the blue of the payphone in front of him, struggling with feelings of guilt. His father had died three years before and he was their only child. How sad his mother now was in her old age, alone in her fifty-square-metre concrete cell in the outer suburbs at Pervomaiskaya, and how she worried about him! What a pig he was not to have shown more patience and understanding.

Perhaps it would be perfectly safe to call her on his mobile phone, but Rad simply did not know whether the connection would be secure. He suspected her phone might be bugged, which would make it easy to work out where he was calling from. He was not tethered to the public telephone, but his mobile was always on him, and the village was much smaller than the town. It would not take long to locate him there.

When he finally opened the door and stepped out of the booth with its payphone privacy, the bee in the fur coat was just doing the same. Rad instinctively sized her up. She turned and glanced at him too. He detected no particular invitation in her eyes, but there was no doubting her interest. He had never had any trouble being liked. It just happened. 'It's because you look like Gregory Peck,' a school friend had told him after another of Rad's conquests at a dance in a neighbouring school. Afterwards, he made a point of going to the classical film cinema at Nikitsky Gate to see *Roman Holiday* starring Audrey Hepburn and Gregory Peck. Back home, he stood in front of the mirror and looked closely at his face, but if he did look like Gregory Peck he could not see it, and could only take the word of his friend for it, who had suffered a crushing rejection at the same dance.

Noting the bee's interest, Rad's first impulse was to rush after her, but he slowed down and began descending the long staircase which led out of the telephone centre to the street only after the door down below sent up a sliver of light as it opened and then closed. He wanted no honey from anyone. Perhaps just a spoonful of real, pure honey in his mouth, to enjoy the taste. But as for going out to get it, coming to the hive and getting past the entrance block, no. Right now he had not the energy for that.

When he came out onto the porch, the bee had already flown a good twenty metres away. The door slammed noisily behind Rad and she looked round, evidently not spurning his attention, but Rad declined to meet her gaze or quicken his step. Fly away, bee. Take your honey to a safer hive than this one.

His hive had been devastated, burned to ashes. There was no other way to put it.

Even now he could not understand how he was supposed to have run up nearly a quarter of a million dollars of debt. He had not borrowed that much: he simply had not needed that much credit. Most likely he had been set up by his company's bookkeeper. She must have been bought by the gangsters who worked out at his club, and falsified documents for them. Or perhaps she had not been bribed but simply intimidated. For him it made no difference. She was a pretty, twenty-five-year old airhead with long brown tresses who, he knew, couldn't wait to be sexually harassed by the boss. He probably should have obliged; then at least she might have warned him what those close-cropped neanderthals were pressuring her into. 'Nice place you got here ... really had a blast ... makes your heart sing like a nightingale,' the bruisers would say as they emerged from the shower after circuit training to rehydrate themselves with a couple of beers at the club bar. They had even said with a snigger, 'We'll have to take it off you, re-register it as ours.' He had thought they were joking, but he was wrong.

Rad had little recollection of the eight hours he spent on the wrong side of two Kalashnikovs. Evidently some psychological defence mechanism had blurred his memory of the ordeal, but there was no defence against the hard fact that his fitness club was no longer his.

In the end he signed all the papers they waved in his face. 'Just sign it, asshole. Take the pen, do it! How long ya gonna keep the lady waiting? She's worn out, she needs to get home to her kids!' yesterday's customers derided him, making obscene gestures and jabbing him in the ribs with their assault rifles.

The lady was a tough-looking, whiskery Armenian notary with a hoarse voice who seemed to have a permanent cold she had brought with her from the chill winds of the Caucasus. She sat patiently outside his office, opening the door now and again to ask in a disturbingly male bass, 'You need me yet?'

He put his signature to a statement that, in addition to the fitness club which he was making over in settlement of debts, he owed the gangsters a further $100,000. His options at the time were to surrender his money, or his money and his life.

The 'unpaid' dollars were the reason he was now lying low in another man's country residence, hardly daring to stick his nose outside. He had no way of satisfying the appetite of his ex-customers. He could not have raised $100,000 even before, when he was working at a bank, manipulating millions (not, of course, his own millions). And after the bank, there was no chance.

In early 1994 he had a stroke of luck, of the kind you only appreciate in hindsight. His daughter had just been born and they had started taking her out in the pram, when one day his wife got talking to another young mother. Only this young mother was the daughter of the director of a bank whose name at the time was unknown only to babes in prams. There were no privately owned country villas then, like the one Rad now guarded. Moscow had yet to sprout expensive mansions segregated from the rest of the city by high wrought-iron railings. Everybody was mixed in together and you could still bump into a banker's daughter strolling down the street. 'He graduated from Moscow University in Mechanics and Maths?' she exclaimed. 'But Daddy is desperate for people with good mathematical brains! He even asked me if I knew anyone who might be suitable.'

In the two years before his job at the bank, Rad had felt he was in a giant mortar, with a giant pestle pounding him relentlessly. He had been accepted for that postgraduate degree but not destined to complete it. The year 1992 rose like the sun over a Russia liberated from the yoke of communism, but a sun so fiery that under its scorching rays everything went up in flames. In the next two years he had so many jobs that, if he later tried to count them, he would invariably overlook a few. His first was as a schoolteacher, but on the money that paid he could afford only a diet of bread and water. For a couple of months, remembering romantic tales heard at the University of intellectuals who retained their dignity in grim times, Rad took to shovelling coal in an antediluvian boiler room. He failed to discover any higher meaning in the occupation, or to earn enough to feed himself. After that he worked his way through a succession of the computer companies which sprang up like toadstools after rain, effortlessly transforming himself into a programmer, but without exception they went bankrupt, and without exception failed to honour their financial obligations to their employees. He worked as a porter in a shop, sold books in the street, and even tried his hand as an apartment tout, as estate agents were known at the time. He made nothing at that either. Within three days of that chance encounter, however, Rad had been sent to study at a financial college and was mastering the arcana of Western-style banking.

There was always the option of going abroad. Rumours would reach Rad that someone in their year had found a job as a software engineer in America; someone was doing the same in Australia; someone else in Canada. Anyone Jewish headed for Germany where, to expiate their sense of guilt over the crimes of Nazism, the Germans had passed a law granting Jews asylum, providing free German lessons and, until they found employment, paying a substantial allowance. Rad mulled over the possibility of going abroad himself. He made contact with foreign employers, but his wife objected. 'So, you will go off as a *Gastarbeiter* and I get left behind? You have affairs while I am stuck here holding the baby?' They already knew she was pregnant and Rad had to abandon the idea. How it would have worked out abroad if he had managed to take her with him, there was no telling, and he felt he had no right to leave her alone in Russia. In any case, he did not much feel like travelling abroad on his own.

His wife stopped him going abroad, his wife got him his job in the bank, and it was his wife who called the shots when the bank collapsed after the Russian government defaulted on its loans in 1998. It was little help that the bank was a bubble pumped full of virtual money: when it collapsed it crushed depositors and employees alike as murderously as any building collapsing in an earthquake. They were left to drag themselves out of the rubble as best they could. In retrospect Rad believed he had almost gone out of his mind at the time, and supposed that was what had made his wife leave him, but that was not when she took a lover. When he was lying in a state of collapse under mental rubble for days on end, getting himself off the sofa only to make his way to the toilet, that was only when she regularised the situation, turning her lover into someone she could legally rely on, a breakwater to shelter her from the storm. It was Rad's wife who left him to 'rot on the sofa,' as she herself put it.

Who knows, perhaps that was precisely why he pulled himself together. Solitude, it transpired, inhibits the process of degeneration. His only mistake, as he crawled out from under the ruins, was to suppose that the worst was behind him. The fitness club was not what he had hoped for in life. It was hardly a grand aspiration, but he was making a success of the business and with that he had to be content.

The bee in the grey fur coat, as she was turning the corner of the red brick building which housed the telephone service centre, looked back one last time. Rad was tempted to wave to her to fly away from him. He was on the verge of pulling his hand out of his jacket pocket, but stopped himself. The bee might interpret his gesture as an invitation and, if she really did not mind his attention, could be placed in an unfair situation. That was something Rad was not going to wish on her.

'Fly away, bee, fly away,' he said, but only to himself as he thrust his hand back deep into his pocket.

* * *

In the minibus on the way back, Rad met an acquaintance from the village store, a local war veteran called Pavel Grigorievich. He was an old man who looked like a gnarled stick seasoned by time, with rickety legs and arms which looked like driftwood, and whose weary, earth-brown face too seemed sculpted from driftwood. In general, Rad did his best to avoid meeting people here, but Pavel Grigorievich was an exception. Back in his very first days of living in the village, standing behind the old man in the queue, he had been happy to help him out with paying for his shopping, contributing the five or six rubles he was short. Since then, when they met they would say hello, and sometimes he had to stop and talk.

Now, too, he had no option but to talk to him.

'I've been to buy paraffin,' the old man said, pointing to a large can blackened by time with a narrow neck which lay on the floor at his feet. 'Whatever next, eh? You have to take the bus to buy paraffin, seven versts you have to travel. What a waste of time!'

'Did you not have to in the past?' Rad asked out of courtesy.

'Nah. We used to have three stores selling paraffin in the village. Then one was closed down, but that still left two. I went to the nearer one. But now you have to take the bus, and when you get there they haven't got it. I've only bought it now, this third time! Three times I went, just wasting my day.'

'Can you not get by without paraffin?' Rad asked. 'What do you need it for? Are you cooking on a paraffin stove? Why not use gas?'

'What gas would that be?' Pavel Grigorievich enquired. 'I use a paraffin stove, of course I do. I couldn't afford gas under the Soviets and I still can't. It's not like in the cities, you know, where they bring it to your door and you can just turn it on. Here you have to pay for everything yourself. They lay a metre of pipe for you and that's a thousand rubles gone. Another metre, another thousand rubles. And I would need seventy metres. I'd need to buy a cooker and a boiler, and put in central heating. I'd have to not eat or drink or spend my pension for ten years to get that much.'

'What about your children?' Rad already knew Pavel Grigorievich had three children, and that his younger daughter and son-in-law lived with him. 'I expect your children could help?'

Pavel Grigorievich paused for a while.

'A fat lot of use children are!' he said. 'Do you help your parents a lot? All of them just want you to give, give, give. Do you help a lot, I'm asking?'

Rad remembered his phone call.

'What help could I give?' he said.

'Well, there you are, talking about children!' Pavel Grigorievich grunted.

The minibus had already come to the village, stopped at one stop to let passengers off, then at another, and Rad stopped talking to his local acquaintance and started looking out the window so as not to miss the place where he should get off. He didn't go to the city all that often, and at speed the familiar has a way of becoming unfamiliar.

The highway took a turn, and from behind fences and skeletal trees there appeared the glass and concrete, single-storey building of a shop painted pale yellow. Some distance from it, sixty metres or so from the highway, behind a scrawny, ill-kept park, stood the grey, two-storey building of the old House of Culture. Even further, beyond the House of Culture, on a slight rise a new, unexpectedly rose-red replica of an old steepled church pointed heavenwards. Rad was relieved to find that, despite his problems with orientation, he had not overshot his stop.

'Pull up by the road beyond the House of Culture,' he requested the driver.

Pavel Grigorievich came to life, his driftwood face registering joy.

'We'll be getting off here together. Would you be able to help me get my can of paraffin out? It's a terrible weight.'

'No problem,' Rad assured him.

'Well, thank you, Slava, thank you kindly,' he rewarded Rad by using that name.

'Rad?' he had repeated that time they first met, when they were already coming out of the shop on to the porch. 'What sort of name is that?' And learning that it was short for Radislav, decided on the spot, 'Well, I'll be calling you Slava. Rad, indeed. That's no name for a Russian.'

Rad took Pavel Grigorievich's can and got it down from the minibus for him. It held 10 or 12 litres and was itself solidly constructed. Pavel Grigorievich emerged from the bus behind him. Rad gave the door a shove, it slid shut, and the adapted minivan, its motor cheerily puttering, sped on its way down the highway.

'What way would you be going from here then, Slava?' Pavel Grigorievich enquired. 'Perhaps you could help me to carry this canister of mine a bit. I've been greedy: filled it right to the top. I've been dragging it along and my hernia's been bulging. I'm afraid it'll come out and get strangulated, you know? The last two times I took a trolley, but then today I didn't, thinking there would be no paraffin again. But of course there was. I knew I should only half fill it, but I was greedy. You know how much paraffin cooking takes! You have to use such a lot.'

Rad lifted the can off the ground, very conscious of its liquid mass.

'Show me the way, Pavel Grigorievich.'

He was not in a hurry to be anywhere. Even if the old man had asked him to carry the paraffin to the far end of the village, he would have helped to lug it there.

They turned off the highway up the asphalt road which branched off towards the centre of the village, past the House of Culture set in the ornate black script of its park in winter, past the startling carmine of the church behind its arrow-head iron railings, and Rad, to pass the time as they walked along, asked,

'If your hernia hurts so much, would it not be best to have an operation?'

'It wouldn't help at all, whether I went for the surgery or no. A new one would only pop out,' Pavel Grigorievich responded, striding briskly along beside him. 'I have to do heavy work all the time, there's no escaping it. How can I do without it. They already cut out one hernia for me, they did. And what? Here I am, suffering again. I'll carry on for as long as it doesn't get strangulated.'

'And if it does, will you know that in time?'

'Well, if I miss, I miss it and die. What kind of life is it anyway? Call this living? You never know how you're going to get through tomorrow. What sort of pension is that they pay? So there you are with your hernia, digging your plot to plant potatoes. Four hundred square metres to be dug over with a spade. Do you think that's easy?'

'Let's face it, Pavel Grigorievich,' Rad allowed himself a little irony, 'Even if they did pay your pension, even if you were flying off to a resort every month, hernia or no hernia, you would still be planting potatoes. Am I right?'

'I would,' the old man agreed, 'but not 400 square metres.'

'Only 300, eh?' Rad enquired in the same ironic tone.

Pavel Grigorievich, striding along beside him, not falling behind, in turn looked at Rad but this time did not answer.

'And what brings you to these parts, Slava? Have you a house here, or are you spending the winter in somebody's dacha?' he asked after a pause.

The canny old man was a bit too near the truth for comfort.

'I'm just living here,' Rad said shortly. 'Maybe for the winter, maybe not. I don't know. I'll wait and see.'

'Yes, wait and see,' Pavel Grigorievich echoed him. 'Somewhere not too far from here then?'

'Not far,' Rad replied, no less briefly.

He had no wish at all to divulge where he was living.

'Got gas, then, have you? Central heating?' Pavel Grigorievich asked.

'It has heating,' Rad confirmed.

'With gas, why not stay the winter? That's the life.'

As they talked they had passed the House of Culture and the church, crossed the dam over the smooth snow-covered ponds, and turned on to a street leading up from the pond. The right side of the street was lined with crude timber framed houses of the Soviet era, with an attic second floor under sloping roofs, and an extension built on at the sides: porches, verandahs, pantries, kitchens. Their architectural illiteracy reminded Rad of earthbound wooden pterodactyls unable to free themselves from the force of gravity. The left side belonged to the new times: a straw-coloured brick wall surmounted by iron spears stretched like a rampart, and behind it a three-storeyed villa of the same brick and with turrets, venetian windows and a red tile roof rose, fortress-like, heavenwards. Closed circuit TV cameras looked down from the walls.

'You living in one a bit like that?' Pavel Grigorievich asked, pointing to the pale yellow house.

'No, not like that one.'

This was true. The house he was living in was one down from that: less land, no CCTV.

'But a bit like it,' Pavel Grigorievich persisted.

'Well, yes, a bit like it, you could say,' Rad agreed, moving the can to his other hand.

The street Pavel Grigorievich lived in was named in honour of that great proletarian writer who dreamed of a world with falcons but no grass snakes. They turned into it and Pavel Grigorievich, tapping Rad on the shoulder, raised his arm:

'That's home to me. The little blue one, see? The sun's still blazing in the attic window.'

Rad looked without any great enthusiasm to where his companion was pointing. Something akin to the other pterodactyls was now living out its last dismal days in the new era. Its blue walls could be glimpsed through the skeletal lattice of hibernating fruit trees. An attic window was indeed catching the sun and throwing its dazzling reflection right back at them.

'And over there, on the other side, towards the ravine,' Pavel Grigorievich gestured, 'that's where our big-shot Democrats live. The city mayor and his deputy. You can't really see it from here. When we go on a bit you'll see it better. It's a good life for our Democrats. I'm not up to it myself now, of course, but if anyone wanted to hang 'em I would give him the rope.'

Rad had no time to look properly in the direction Pavel Grigorievich was pointing or to think of an answer. As they were passing another pterodactyl, from under the gate, sliding its belly along the ground, a large brown dog with a docked stump where its tail should have been silently emerged and, once it was out, came bounding towards them with hoarse, furious barking. It was a cross between an Alsatian, a boxer, a Rottweiler, and God knows what else, a ferocious brute created by nature for the mindless protection of its master's property.

It was hurtling towards them with such an obvious intention of sinking its fangs unhesitatingly into what it considered an intruder on its territory that Rad, who had never been afraid of dogs, felt a suddenly twinge of terror in his stomach. He instinctively pulled the bag of loaves from his shoulder and brandished it, scaring the dog off. It leapt to one side, but only to start barking and immediately rush at Rad again. The can of paraffin was a hindrance. Rad let go of it and it fell with a heavy thud to the ground. The dog's snarling teeth, dripping glassy threads of saliva, missed Rad by a matter of centimetres. He collided with the can and it fell over on its side.

'What the hell is going on, Pavel Grigorievich!' Rad yelled. 'Call it off! It knows you!'

'Whoa!' Pavel Grigorievich shouted at the dog, for some reason addressing it like a horse. 'Whoa, do you hear me! Shake it off, Slava, fight it off, or it'll bite, it'll take off half your leg!'

From a courtyard on the other side of the street, flinging the gate open with a clang, as if he had been waiting for just this moment, a dishevelled man with a pitchfork charged out. Despite the cold, he was not only not wearing a hat, but his checked shirt was gaping open down to the navel. Under it, like a mock shirt front under a dinner jacket, a white vest peeped out, and from its V-neck luxuriant curls sprouted, only slightly less rampant than those on the man's head.

'Whose is that?' he roared. 'Is that the mute's dog attacking people again?'

'The mute's of course. Of course it is!' Pavel Grigorievich shrieked.

'I warned him! I told him to keep it on a chain! I told him what would happen next time!'

Continuing to fend the dog off with his bag of loaves, Rad noticed out of the corner of his eye that the man with the pitchfork at the ready was standing motionless nearby and seemed to be waiting for something.

The dog, its fangs dripping saliva, leapt again and this time did not miss. The jaws clamped on Rad's sleeve and, hanging on heavily, pressing against him with its front paws, it began shaking its head from side to side, trying to rip out the piece of sleeve it had in its teeth. Through its clamped jaws, like a merciless sentence on its victim, it uttered a ferocious, visceral growl. At this moment Rad was distracted by a joyful, tranquillizing satisfaction that his jacket had such thick sleeves. The tailors had not stinted on the synthetic insulation and the arms stuck out like the sleeves of a diver's suit. But for that stuffing, the hound would have sunk its fangs into his arm.

They were, however, only going to protect him for so long. It was a matter of time before the brute would rip a chunk out of the sleeve and hurl itself at him again. Guided by instinct, Rad violently plunged his fingers into its hate-filled brown eyes. The dog's jaws opened, releasing the sleeve, and it gave a plaintive yelp. Leaping to one side, it fell back on the ground, threw back its muzzle and emitted not a squeal but a wail, like a baby crying.

At just that moment, as the dog lay on the ground, the man with the pitchfork came to life, darted over and plunged the tines into its neck, throwing it over on its side.

Its howl must have been heard in heaven. The dog tried to get up, but the man pressed down on the pitchfork and the tines, with a grating and squelching sound, sank into its flesh and pinned it to the ground. Its shrill squeal was silenced as the pitchfork strangled it, and now the only sound coming from its throat was a wheezing gurgle. The dog's paws flailed the air, its head jerked, its body twitched, from its bared teeth a bright red trickle flowed on to the road, steaming and melting the snow.

'You shitbag!' the man gasped, his voice not unlike the gurgle of the dog, except that for the dog it was a death rattle and for the man only a reflection of his deadly exertion. 'I warned him! I said what would happen next time.'

'Enough! Stop it! Why are you doing that?' Rad yelled.

'It's nothing! Don't fret,' Pavel Grigorievich said with satisfaction. He picked the can up and kept it by his feet. 'That mute let it get right out of hand. It nearly savaged you, the brute. That'll teach him to keep his dog under control. You in one piece? It didn't get you to the bone?' he asked, taking a look at the white padding spilling out of Rad's sleeve.

"'Next time!" I warned him. "Keep it on a chain!"' the man gasped in tandem with the dying hound.

'Stop it!' Rad said, rushing at him and grabbing the pitchfork, but was rewarded with a blow to his ear which sent him reeling. He lacked the courage to intercede any more for the dog, sensing that the man would have squashed him like an annoying fly buzzing at a window pane. 'Well, fuck you!' Rad swore, turned and walked quickly back the way they had come, away from this place of execution of which he had been the unwitting cause.

'Slava!' Pavel Grigorievich called after him. 'The paraffin. Do I have to carry it myself?'

Rad gestured without turning round. Drag it home yourself, the gesture said.

'That's not good, Slava!' Pavel Grigorievich called again. 'You've brought it so far. It's only a little further.'

This time Rad did not even favour him with a gesture. He just wanted to get as far away as possible from where the dog had been slaughtered. To his shame, although he had tried to save it, he was secretly pleased things had worked out as they did. There was no telling how the brute would have behaved when it got back on its feet if it had not fallen victim to Curly-top's pitchfork. The terror he had felt in his stomach when the dog got out under the gate and rushed at him moved down now from his chest to his left leg. He could feel his calf trembling. He could not stop it, and dragged the leg behind him.

* * *

A few hours later Rad was sitting on a high swivel stool in front of the bar in the reception room of the villa with a martini in his hand and making conversation to a grey-eyed brunette charmer on the adjacent stool in blue jeans tightly stretched over round, slender buttocks. She was also wearing a light, burgundy-coloured woollen top over bare skin, with such a plunging neckline that the seductive curves of her breasts, raised by an invisible brassiere, peeked out at the light of day almost to the nipples. However, in the way in which she was looking at Rad there was also an innate seriousness which testified to intelligence. All evening she had been openly displaying her favourable disposition towards him. This put him on edge, but was agreeable. She belonged to the type he had always liked, for a night. It seemed unlikely she had been sent by those he was hiding from, but her type was also that type. If she was sharp-sighted, he thought, she would have seen that, despite his entirely respectable appearance, he was a loser.

She herself, judging by the fact that she was one of Polina's set, could safely be assumed to be a winner. Polina hung out only with winners, and could tell a loser from a mile off. She had a nose for those less than well-heeled and could not stand the smell, as she would have been unable to stand the smell of a down-and-out, had she ever chanced to find herself next to one. Rad was evidently an exception, a kind of well-scrubbed down-and-out, although it might only be that she had not yet got round to crossing him off her list. Or perhaps it was because her husband obviously had time for him. Or because, even though he was the caretaker of their place in the country, he was at least not an ordinary caretaker.

The raven-haired beauty had an art gallery. She was not just someone who arranged exhibitions in one: she owned it. She was the boss, the proprietor, the owner of the premises, a *biznesmensha*, or so, at least, she thought of herself.

'Artists, you know, are wholly incapable of evaluating their work objectively,' she told Rad. 'They suppose they have only to paint a landscape or a still life or an abstract composition and collectors will fall over themselves to buy it and shower them with dollars. The fact of the matter is that no one is going to buy their sad little painting in a hundred years: they couldn't lumber anyone with it for five kopecks. You have to tend artists like sheep. They would never find a lush pasture themselves, not in a lifetime. You spot one for them you think is just right, but they can't see it.'

'First you tend them, and then you fleece them,' Rad suggested.

'Oh, it's an open question who fleeces whom. Creative people are so greedy. They produce something for a ruble and want to sell it for ten thousand as a minimum. And how they pose as geniuses! You wouldn't believe it.'

'So you need to use the knout,' Rad interjected.

'Oh, come now! Why that? There's no need to belabour them: they're not cattle. They are geniuses, so they are child-like. You tend them like sheep, as I said. I didn't say cows. Stamp your foot at them or threaten them with a stick and they'll be off.'

'To lush pastures,' Rad again suggested.

'Oh, that's not always how it works out. Finding a really lush pasture, I mean. More often than not you have to settle for one that is …' – she searched for the word – 'I would say, rewarding.'

She had a way, when delivering her monologue, of stroking her nostril, and that was the only thing Rad found disagreeable. In every other respect he really liked her. Expressions like 'never in a hundred years' or 'lumber someone with' sounded charming coming from her, not vulgar in the slightest. She produced them like little gems.

'Perhaps you can tell me,' Rad said, taking another sip of his martini, 'what it takes to run an art gallery. Do you need a degree in art history?'

'The most important thing is to love art.' The beauty again stroked her nostril. 'And, of course, you need to understand it, to know what you're talking about. It's certainly desirable to have been educated in art history. I have.'

'Moscow State University?'

'Precisely.'

'Ah, then, we're birds of a feather,' Rad observed.

'Did you graduate in art history too?' the beauty exclaimed with the joy of someone who has encountered an accomplice in a mysterious, and profitable, business.

'Did I imply that?' Rad asked apologetically. 'No, I just meant we have the same alma mater. I studied Mechanics and Maths. I'm a mathematician.'

'Like Serge?' the beauty exclaimed with the same joyful tone of complicity.

'Like Serge,' Rad confirmed.

'Serge' was Sergey, the owner of the villa. A successful match for Polina, who had managed to entice him from his former family four years previously and now partook of the delights of the monied elite. He was the chief financial officer of a major company which even the 1998 default had only been able to sway slightly. It traded in steel and natural resources, and had a foot in the foodstuffs market.

Serge was also none other than the fellow student who had invited Rad to the get-together where establishing an opposition party to the communists was discussed. He had known and been on friendly terms with everyone there. Later Rad had seen some of those people in official television news programmes or other broadcasts. They had gone on to occupy high positions in the state. Surely he could pull some secret levers, press pedals hidden from outsiders, to free Rad from the noose around his neck? Rad asked him to help with something he could undoubtedly do with little trouble, namely, lend him the money he needed. All Serge did, however, was allow Rad to hide out at his dacha, which was only to his own advantage.

'Are you a finance officer somewhere too?' the young lady asked when he confirmed what he had in common with Serge.

Rad was looking at her quizzically. She evidently believed knowledge of higher mathematics was a sure-fire path to top management.

'No,' he told her, 'I'm not a chief finance officer, I'm …' He hesitated and, to his own surprise, heard himself say, 'I'm an invisible man.'

The beauty understood this major revelation in a fairly trivial manner.

'You mean, you're in intelligence, a spy?' she asked, evidently feeling she was now approaching something really mysterious.

Rad took his fit of excessive frankness in hand. The reason had, of course, been the martini, of which he had imbibed a fair amount; and the alarums and excursions of the morning with the bee, Pavel Grigorievich and the Hound of the Baskervilles which were evidently still jangling his nerves and demanding an outlet. He was also finding this dark-haired connoisseuse of the arts diabolically attractive and had been close to telling her about his real situation.

'Yes, I am Ensign Rybnikov, Japanese spy,' he said instead.

His companion, however, if she had ever read anything by Alexander Kuprin, had no recollection of that character.

'No, tell me the truth,' she said, disappointed.

'Yes, I really am. Well, no,' Rad had regained his poise. 'I am actually in the employ of Her Majesty's Secret Service. Lawrence of Arabia, and yours to command.'

His fair companion had never heard of the James Bond of the early twentieth century either.

'You're having me on,' she intuited. 'You don't want to compromise your cover. Quite right. Although I know a member of your profession who is far less secretive. I even know his name.'

'It won't be his real name,' Rad retorted with aplomb, playing along with his unexpected new image.

'You're quite wrong,' she responded. 'I know his whole family.'

'Then his whole family is not real,' Rad parried.

'They're as real as can be,' his companion persisted. 'My father and his have been friends for the past quarter of a century.'

'And you and my colleague used to make sandpies in the sandpit.'

'No, he's older than me, ten years older. He must be …' the beauty, swivelling round on her stool gave Rad an appraising look, 'about the same age as you. It's just that our family are friends with his.'

Rad was beginning to tire of this drift in their conversation. What did it matter to him who had been friends with whom and for how long?

'Right, what's his name then, this Max Otto von Stierlitz of yours?' He asked, unable to think of a way of bringing the subject to a close.

'Shan't tell!' she replied skittishly. 'You aren't saying so I'm not saying.'

'Let's have another martini,' Rad proposed, taking a bottle from the counter in front of him and unscrewing the cap. 'I can't imagine how the

Russian people lived through the years of totalitarianism without martini. I'm fairly certain the government collapsed because there was no vermouth in the USSR.'

'Oh, I happen to know that people who wanted to drink martini, or whisky or gin, had no trouble getting it.' His young lady readily moved her glass towards Rad. It was, however, still almost full. She was happy to drink, but was doing so in moderation. 'In the Beryozka foreign currency shops you could buy all those drinks. You only had to earn the right certificates.'

Rad topped up her glass and refilled his own.

'The problem, as I remember, was working in the right place to earn the certificates.'

'Oh, I don't know about that,' she said, taking her drink. 'I remember when I was very little we used to have the bar fully stocked with martini.'

'Boys and girls, girls and boys, ladies and gentlemen!' Polina shrieked from the far end of the living room, jumping up on to a black leather armchair. She was entirely bewitching: a wonderful, sinuous figure, a clear-cut, clear-skinned face with big, wide-open eyes and a radiant smile. Rad could see how his university friend would have been smitten, but just as obvious as her charm was the fact that everything about her was fake: fake delight, fake smile, fake sincerity. As he watched her, Rad was baffled. How could the CFO of a large trading company have been so blind to that?

'Ladies and gentlemen, ladies and gentlemen!' A crystal glass appeared in Polina's hand and she tapped a knife against it. 'As you know, we have with us this evening the famous poet and artist – she called out his name – a dazzling representative of postmodern art. He has just returned from the Venice Biennale where he received one of Italy's most prestigious awards, and here he is now with us! I want you all to welcome him!'

'Welcome! Hurray! Wow!' people called out, if rather halfheartedly.

'Again, again! Let's welcome our celebrated maître,' Polina demanded.

'Wow!' Rad's beauty squealed, making him wince.

'Bow-wow,' he mimicked her.

'No, it's only polite to give someone a welcome if you're asked to,' she responded.

'First he needs to earn his welcome,' Rad said.

'He earned it long ago. You probably just don't know,' she said, condescending to pardon him. 'He's one of our bestselling absurdists in the West.'

'I've managed to do something incredible!' Polina exclaimed, crouching down on the springy upholstery of the chair before propelling herself upwards. 'Usually, as everybody knows …' – she again gave the name of the maître – 'does not read his poetry in salons, but he has agreed to make an exception for us. When you are ready!' She applauded again and looked down at the shaven-headed, stubbly specimen standing morosely next to her chair in baggy canvas trousers a stevedore might have worn, and woollen blue, red and yellow checked shirt such as had been fashionable in the early 1990s, which was untucked.

Until she shouted, 'When you are ready,' the specimen had stood looking at the floor, but now with a slow movement full of concentrated dignity, he raised his head and looked morosely, but with the same concentrated dignity, round the room.

'I recite,' he confirmed.

Rad could not help but snort. 'We await being recited to,' he observed.

'Oh, don't interrupt!' the beauty said. She was perched on her stool, leaning in the direction of the maître and about to turn into one big ear.

The specimen in docker's trousers assumed a vacant expression.

A poem: 'Alexander Sergeyevich Pushkin', he announced.

Our Alexander Pushkin
was well known for loving fun
Always lugged around a shooter
Had a quite enormous gun.

He would shoot down with his shooter
Jackdaws, sparrows for the pot.
In the woods he killed a cuckoo
Being such a splendid shot.

Russians thought Danthès a loser
But he too was quite a shot
He considered Russians boozers
Till one put him on the spot.

Then Alexander Pushkin
Seeing Danthès with a mug
Drinking luke-warm Coca-Cola
Said 'You, sir, are quite a thug.'

Two men flashing their revolvers,
Came a horrid thunderclap.
(They were dashing those Decembrists
But their manners total crap.)

So Alexander Pushkin
Lies there bleeding in the snow
While Danthès flies out of Russia,
A malignant froggy crow.

I feel sorry now for Pushkin –
And what price his Nathalie?
Russians drink instead of vodka
Cola-Cola on a spree.

Our Alexander Pushkin
Never would forgive us that.
He would pistol whip the lot of us
He'd lay us all out flat.

So let those dogs of foreigners
Think Coca-Cola's fine.
In this world there's nothing sweeter than
Our own red Russian wine.

He was rewarded, when he finished, with applause which in Soviet times, Rad remembered, would have been described as 'tumultuous'. All around again shouted, 'Wow!'

'Wow! Wow! Wow!' his neighbour squealed, clapping her hands until they were sore.

'Bow-wow!' Rad barked again. 'In my humble opinion, that is total rubbish. Not to mention the fact that there were no revolvers or Coca-Cola in Pushkin's time.'

'Oh, you don't understand!' his lady companion said, turning to him despairingly while continuing to clap her hands raw. She was aglow with excitement. 'It's this modern trend: it's called Absurdism. Irony squared. Verging on self-parody.'

'Over the edge, if you ask me,' Rad observed. 'It's nothing more than a rip-off of the Oberiuts, only without the talent.'

'Which of the Oberiuts?' the lady asked pertly, but sounding hurt, as if Rad had blasphemed against something she held sacred.

'Oleynikov, of course. Although when Kharms and Vvedensky were writing verse it came out much the same.'

The beauty now eyed him, suspicious and puzzled.

'How do you know about the Oberiuts? You said you were a mathematician!'

'Is a mathematician not supposed to know about poetry?'

'Well, no. It just seems unusual,' she said, stroking her nostril. 'I'm sure Serge doesn't know the first thing about the Oberiuts.'

'I wouldn't vouch for that one way or the other.' Her way of fingering her nose was beginning to annoy him. 'Personally, I grew up in a family of scientists. Every six months we mounted an expedition to the Tretyakov Gallery, followed six months later by the Pushkin Museum. Once a year, without fail, we went to a recital at the Conservatoire or the Tchaikovsky Hall.'

'My God, how you have suffered!' the lady exclaimed.

'At all events, I can make up doggerel about Pushkin no worse than your Absurdist.'

'Are you sure? Well, go on, try!' the beauty said provocatively.

There was no going back.

'Right now?' Rad queried, trying to wriggle out of having to prove his point.

'Yes,' the beauty said. 'Right now.'

Rad took a gulp of martini, pushed the glass away and closed his eyes. 'Don't cock this up,' he enjoined himself.

After half a minute he opened his eyes.

'Right, here you are:
Alexander Pushkin
Though a top aristocrat
While his fancy friends were floating
Always voted Democrat.

'Is that all?' the beauty asked petulantly, stroking her nose.

'Yep!'

'Well, in the first place, that's only one stanza. You have to admit, it's a bit short.'

'But how long did I take?' Rad parried.

'Even so. And in the second place, you were imitating someone else's idea, just following in his footsteps, replacing drinking with voting.'

'And aren't all these Pushkin parodies just barking up the same tree?' Rad had expected a critical reception, but not that it would be so vehement. It was as if his instant stanza had been not just blasphemous but a desecration of the holy of holies.

'And anyway, what do voters and floating have to do with anything?' The beauty shrugged petulantly.

'At least as much as revolvers and Coca-Cola. Perhaps more, because what else are you going to get to rhyme with "Pushkin"?'

'They're completely beside the point.' The beauty's intonation made it clear she had no wish to continue on this subject. She swivelled in her chair to face the heir of the Oberiuts. 'I've missed all the rest because of you!' she reprimanded Rad, but the vehemence had gone and her enthusiasm was instantly rekindled.

While they had been fencing over his first poem, the heir of the Oberiuts had recited another, met with the same rapturous reception, and was into a third.

Rad too swivelled in his chair, stepped down, took his martini and wandered aimlessly round the perimeter of the room, away from the bar. She was dumb, this beauty, with her provocatively displayed titties and pert little butt. The seriousness in her eyes suggested intelligence, but it was a cleverness he could make no sense of. He concluded she was as thick as planks.

His erstwhile fellow student, formerly Sergey but now, through the efforts of Polina and her entourage, reincarnated as Serge, popped up next to Rad with the smile of the Mona Lisa on his lips.

'Not bored, I hope.'

'Forgive us the heir of the Oberiuts,' his da Vinci smile said. 'It's not my fault. For some reason Polina needs him.' He did in fact remind Rad of a mannish Mona Lisa.

'Actually, I've just composed an Oberiut poem myself,' Rad told him. 'Want to hear it?'

He whispered his creation in his patron's ear. Serge, having at first listened politely, when Rad finished, chortled with glee. He put an arm round Rad's shoulders and butted his forehead against his collarbone.

'Brilliant!' he pronounced, shaking with silent laughter and rocking his forehead against Rad's shoulder. '"His fancy friends were floating, but he voted Democrat." I like it!'

'Unfortunately, Pretty Woman over there didn't,' Rad remarked regretfully, nodding in the direction of his recent companion at the bar, when his friend had stopped monopolizing his shoulder.

'Jenny?' he asked, glancing over towards the bar.

'Why Jenny?' Rad asked, puzzled. The beauty was unambiguously Russian.

'Well, Zhenya, Yevgenia,' Serge elucidated. 'So she gets called Jenny. How are you getting on with her? I noticed you'd got her little heart going pit-a-pat.'

'No,' Rad said, taking another sip from his glass. 'I'll stay with the martini. She's into James Bond, Lawrence of Arabia or, at worst Ensign Rybnikov. She said she knows some spy.'

'Oh, she probably meant a guy called Tsekhovets,' Serge said, taking Rad's glass. He gave it a sniff and handed it back. 'What *mauvais ton*.

Respectable people drink gin, if not neat, then with juice, or tonic, of course.'

Serge fingered his glass and uttered some further praise of gin while Rad tried to remember where he had heard that name. Tsekhovets. Who did it remind him of? An unusual name, but he had known someone called that.

The apartment on Stoleshnikov Lane came back to him, Beefeater gin in liqueur glasses, Havana cigars and a face with a clownish nose.

'Would his first name be Dron, by any chance?' he asked. 'Dron Tsekhovets? Andronicus Tsekhovets?'

'No idea. I've never met the man. I only know his father, and not very well, unfortunately. Wish I knew him better. He's a big wheel. Not an oligarch, but what the Americans would call a tycoon. In fact not just any tycoon.' He named the company he headed. 'Ever heard of it?'

Rad certainly had. Given the existence in Russia of newspapers, radio and television, it would have been hard not to have heard of it, and if none of them had existed, he would probably still have heard of it.

'The father of the Tsekhovets I knew was a deputy minister in the days of the USSR,' Rad said.

Serge furrowed his brow, thinking back.

'That's right!' he said, jabbing a finger in Rad's chest. 'He was.' His eyes lit up. Rad's acquaintance with the tycoon's son had just dramatically raised his standing in his eyes. 'Well, that could be the answer to all your prayers. Can you imagine all the levers Tsekhovets Senior must be able to pull? Against that sort of godfather your enemies are minnows.'

Having declined to give Rad practical help, he was more than ready to offer advice.

'But how come everyone knows Dron is the Russian James Bond?' Rad enquired.

'Well, that's what Jenny says, and she probably knows. Over there ...' he waved a hand to one side in a gesture indicating the existence of certain foreign countries in which the Russian intelligence community might be thought to take an interest, 'presumably they haven't an inkling.'

'So where exactly is he, *over there*?' Rad asked.

'No idea,' Serge said. 'Jenny knows all about him. She's the one to ask. Anything you want to know about his daddy, just ask me. I know a lot about that!'

The heir of the Oberiuts finished reciting another of his deathless creations, and a mudslide of rapture engulfed the room.

'I'd better get back to Polina,' Serge said, slapping Rad on the shoulder.

'Of course,' he said.

He looked over towards the bar and met the gaze of Zhenya-Jenny. She was still sitting there, squealing 'Wow,' and looking over at him. Her eyes reflected a mixture of scorn and perplexity.

Keeping his eyes on her, Rad retraced his steps to the bar. His stool was still vacant and he climbed back on to it, abandoning his earlier resolution not to exchange another word with the lady. Well, why not? She really was a looker, seemed a bit smitten, and it was not as if he would have to share the rest of his life with her.

'Forgive me, Jenny,' he said, putting his hand on hers as she twisted the stem of her glass. 'I was wrong. The poems are dazzling.'

'You know my name?' she said unforgivingly, but without withdrawing her hand.

'That's what I went away for.'

She paused.

'And what you said about the poetry, were you just teasing?'

'We-ell,' Rad drawled, 'Let's just say I was winding you up.'

'But you liked them really?'

'Simply dazzling,' Rad repeated.

That smile of complicity in some secret and profitable enterprise reappeared on Jenny's lips.

'You appreciate them?'

'And how,' Rad said, taking full possession of her hand, removing it from the glass and raising it to his lips.

Zhenya-Jenny did not resist this encroachment.

'I hope not to find myself looking at the back of your head again,' she said, as he turned her hand palm uppermost and kissed a tender blue vein pulsing on her wrist.

'God forbid,' Rad said the first thing to come into his head.

He did feel a twinge of conscience. However dumb she might be, her pretensions were sincere and in pandering to them he was guilty of shameless self-interest. He decided to humour them in full measure, and more.

'I'm not forcing her and have no intention of doing so. She took the initiative, so she is only getting what she wants,' he placated his conscience, and ultimately that was true.

CHAPTER THREE

'Hi, Dron,' Rad typed, tapping with slow deliberation at the keyboard. 'The earth, it seems, really is round, and no matter which direction you go in you meet old friends. So, we meet again, if only in cyberspace.'

He wanted to write at top speed, breathlessly tapping away as fast as he could, but restrained himself, pondering each phrase. He was writing in Russian, but using Latin letters. Dron lived in America, and who could tell what software they had there. His computer might not be russified, and if he wrote in Cyrillic, Dron might receive a lot of gibberish instead of an email. 'Jenny' probably knew the answer to that, but she was sleeping. He would have to wake her up solely to ask that question, and had no wish to disclose quite how interested he was in her spy friend. It was bad enough that he had rifled through her handbag in search of her digital notebook. He would not have thought of looking there for Dron Tsekhovets's email address, but she had told him where it was herself, promising to let him have it later. If Jenny discovered he had dug it out without asking, who knows what suspicions might come into her head?

The thought of her notebook was like a splinter in his brain the whole time their exquisite gymnastics were pummelling the bed in his room, which until then had been wholly chaste. It had given him no peace, and afterwards kept him awake. He lay side by side with Jenny, who had surrendered her spirit to sleep no less wholeheartedly than she had surrendered her body to him, and he tried to persuade himself she must already be asleep. She must, she must … And if he could not get a wink of sleep, what was he supposed to do: lie there and wait for it to be day?

Rad started by trying to write the email in English, but after five lines deleted the text, and changed to Russian. His English was really not good enough to write the email the way it needed to be. That he could do only in Russian. Packaging it in Latin script was more complicated, but actually not all that difficult.

'It would be so interesting to hear how you have lived these past years,' Rad typed unhurriedly. 'I remember, when we met, it was fashionable to quote the Chinese proverb, "God forbid you live in years of change." Everybody was quoting it smugly, and laughing and saying, "Actually, it doesn't feel too bad!" Later we realised that was not a time of change, but only of a change of the stage scenery. The real changes were yet to come. I don't know about you, but I have experienced the truth of that proverb only too well. I'm not at all sure it is Chinese. Where would the Chinese get God from when they believe in Confucianism, which doesn't have a God?'

His fingers typed on and on, about the Chinese, the Americans, the Czechs and Balts, about everything imaginable, only omitting anything about himself. Well, almost anything. Just in passing, hinted at between the lines, here a sentence, there a clause, casually, by the by. No information overload, no off-putting neediness. It was less an email than a chat, cocktail gossip, the sort of thing you might have expected to hear in the salon of Anna Scherer, lady-in-waiting to Her Imperial Majesty.

Rad finished his email, read it through to correct the typos, and put it in the send folder. He dialled straight through to the service provider: in the middle of the night the lines were less busy, and it was cheaper. A click of the mouse and his email disappeared from the screen, zoomed along telephone cables, burst out as a beam of radiomagnetism into space, bounced off a satellite and whizzed back down to the other side of the world, arriving eight hours before it was sent and landing in the mailbox of someone he had last seen thirteen years previously.

The email sent, the splinter drawn, Rad instantly felt he had no longer the strength even to sit on a chair. His eyes were closing, his mind befogged, he was asleep where he sat. His feet describing circles on the floor, Rad made it back to bed, pulled off the tracksuit bottoms he had pulled on when he got up, tried to take off his shirt but found it too much bother. Unable to undo the buttons, he collapsed next to Jenny, pulled half the blanket off her, more or less covered himself and yielded to the embrace of sleep.

* * *

Rad was awakened by a knock at the door.

When he opened his eyes, he automatically looked at the clock opposite the window. It told him the time was nearly 10 o'clock. The light from the standard lamp was all but blotted out by the light of the new day, only the faint outline of a yellow oval still discernible on the ceiling.

The knock was repeated. Raven-haired Jenny blearily opened her eyes, looked sleepily at Rad and, confused by the sound, said, 'What the hell … ?'

before quickly rolling over from her back to her stomach, burying her face in the pillow, and lying still.

Lowering his feet to the icy floor, Rad realised to his annoyance that he had gone to sleep without taking off his shirt, which now looked as though it had been chewed. Out here he had to do his own laundry and ironing and, he now recalled, he did not have another ironed shirt to wear.

'Oh, shit!' he cursed, and called to whoever was knocking, 'Just coming!'

He opened the door to see the master of the house.

'Hi,' Serge said. 'You're not on the Internet are you? There are people needing to make calls on the outside line but it's constantly engaged. Or is something wrong at the substation?'

Rad, standing in front of his erstwhile fellow student in his underwear and a crumpled shirt, looked over to the table where the monitor screen was a dull grey, but a small oval window near the on-off button was glowing yellow. After sending his email, he had not only not taken his shirt off, but had also not got round to shutting down the computer or closing the Ethernet connection. The provider's server had evidently, on this occasion, decided not to offend the user by breaking the connection anyway.

Rad invited Serge in. The fact that Jenny had spent half the night in his room was obvious, and he saw no need to make a Punchinello's secret of the fact.

Serge came in, trying not to look at the white froth of the bed and the raven-haired head visible from under the blanket.

'Ah, did you not shut the computer down?' he asked, when finally able to move his gaze to the monitor.

'Profuse apologies,' Rad said, going over to the table. 'I claim extenuating circumstances.'

Serge emitted a throaty sound of complete understanding.

Rad sat down at the computer, moved the mouse, the monitor came to life. He clicked and, a few seconds later, the screen lit up to reveal the window of the mail program. At the bottom of the screen, among the tabs of other programs, was the Internet icon.

'You're weird!' Serge said, positioning himself behind Rad. 'What were you up to? Arousing yourself with porn sites?'

Rad did not reply. He clicked on the button to download mail and waited. The report window appeared, notifying him that mail was being transferred.

'You don't think you could wait to receive your mail?' Serge asked indignantly just above his head. 'People are waiting to use the phone!'

'Sure. Just a minute,' Rad replied.

He was staring intently at the mailbox window. So far everything was mass mailings, the first email, the second, the tenth ... but then the fourteenth or fifteenth was not. It was the first actual personal message he had received since he had been living here.

Rad clicked on the sender and the email appeared on the screen. It was written in Cyrillic and began, without the usual courtesies, 'Well, how about that!'

'Yes!' Rad responded, leaning back in his chair.

'Yes what?' Serge asked, disgruntled.

Rad took the message off the screen, replaced it with one of the mailings, and turned to look at Serge.

'An email from Dron!'

'Dron who?' he asked, evidently not remembering the name of the tycoon's son from last night's conversation.

'It's from Dron Tsekhovets,' Rad said, trying to contain his delight.

'Dron Tsekhovets? What Tsekhovets?' Then Serge remembered. 'Oh, you mean that one's son.'

'That one's son,' Rad confirmed. 'And incidentally, you have met him.'

During the night, as he was composing the email, he recalled that the three of them had been together when the opposition party was struggling to be born. He only could not remember whether his fellow student had stayed on, or had already left when he and Dron made their exit.

Serge, however, had no recollection of Dron at the gathering. He only marvelled at how their destinies had brought them together for a few hours in Moscow before again dispersing them.

'You don't say! That's amazing. The earth really is round!'

'Did you stay to the end or leave?' Rad asked.

'No, I'd had enough.' Serge's tone had a hint of condescension and *savoir faire*. 'It was so long-winded, and the metro closed at one. It wasn't like nowadays when you can flag down a car at two in the morning, or at four. I didn't have my own wheels then. But how about you? Did you stick it out to the end?'

'No, I didn't last the course,' Rad admitted. 'Actually, I left with Dron.'

'So you didn't get pulled in?'

'You mean the KGB turned up?' Rad responded disingenuously.

'Need you ask!' Serge exclaimed. 'What initiative ever happened without them sticking their noses in? They arrived, turned everything upside down: a search, witnesses, everybody who was still there got carted off in a police van to the station. There, of course, they were interrogated, statements taken, intimidated, but that was all. No kidney punches. In fact, they weren't beaten up at all. Not like today. They were humiliated, held until the following night, then just released. Why, didn't you know?'

'No, I didn't know that,' Rad said, entirely truthfully.

'It went no further than the police,' Serge continued, the note of condescension again discernible. 'Times had changed. It wasn't like the old days. They promised a lot of trouble, of course, the full array, but they didn't hassle anyone subsequently. In fact,' he recalled, 'later, in '95 or '96 it must have been, I got a phone call from a lieutenant colonel who needed to see me. Well, I pricked up my ears. In he came. It turned out he had been one of those doing the interrogating. What do you think he needed?'

'Tell me,' Rad responded.

'He wanted me to give him a job in our security section. "Note," he said, "in respect of yourself. We knew you had been there but didn't go calling you in and making difficulties."'

'Did you give him a job?' Rad asked intrigued.

'No, what use was he to me? He was nothing, a run-of-the-mill executive, a pawn. What did he have to offer? Finding a job was his problem.'

Emails had meanwhile continued to download, until the last message had migrated from the provider's server to Rad's computer. He clicked 'disconnect', the Internet icon went out, and the icons of his standard programs, as if relieved at the departure of this fly-by-night, gave each other a wink.

'All done. The line is free for someone else to use,' Rad said.

Now, however, the master of the house was in no hurry to leave.

'What has he written?' he asked.

'Who?' Rad asked, although perfectly well aware of the answer.

'You don't want me to see? You don't want to tell? A secret?' He patted Rad approvingly on the shoulder. 'Quite right too. Let it remain a commercial secret.' He made to leave, but stopped. 'Incidentally,' he again patted Rad on the shoulder, but this time to get him to look at him. With a nod in Jenny's direction, Serge lowered his voice to a whisper and said conspiratorially, 'Don't get too carried away. She's been spoiled rotten.' There was a confessional note in his voice. 'Once they get the taste for money, it's the end. They're hooked on it.'

Rad said nothing. He just wanted to get his teeth into Dron's email.

'Okay, I'll leave you in peace.' His silence had been understood. 'Only, find out what Jenny wants to do,' he said with a nod towards the bed. 'We'll be off in an hour or an hour and a half. Polina would like to party on and on, but I do have to put in an occasional appearance at work.'

'Will do,' Rad replied.

The door closed behind Serge and Rad immediately returned to the screen, found Dron's email in the list and clicked on it.

'Well, how about that!'

Rad looked to see when the reply had been sent: Dron had responded almost instantly. His own email had been sent in the early hours of the morning, which on the other side of the world was evening, and Dron had evidently been sitting at his computer. And here was confirmation. Dron wrote, 'I was about to shut down the computer when I thought I would check for email and, boom, there was yours!'

Dron's letter could not have been better. He wrote that he was always remembering Rad, regretted they had lost track of each other, and had talked a lot about him to his wife. There was more in that key, and at the end he suggested they should get together again, or at least write to each other, which he would look forward to. 'Tell me about yourself, your life, what you've been up to all these years,' he wrote. 'Perhaps we can work together on some projects.' He actually wrote that!

Rad stood up, paced round the room, clicked the lock button on the door handle, went away, came back and unlocked it. To say he was excited would have been an understatement: he was on top of the world. He would have liked a punch bag in the room to pummel mercilessly. He would have liked to be on the cinder track at the stadium and run 100 metres flat out. He would have liked to soar up into the air in a pole vault. And if he could have done all that right now, he would have set world records.

Right now was not, however, a possibility, so he fell forward full length to the floor, buffering the fall with his arms, and began doing press-ups. Twenty-one, thirty-three, forty-five, he counted. When he got past fifty, he heard his name.

'Radusik!' It was Jenny. 'Radusik!'

He had been awarded that pet name during the night.

Rad did one last press-up, jumped to his feet, went over to the bed and sat down.

'You're awake. Good morning, Jechka.'

The name had come to him that very moment.

Jenny grimaced with displeasure.

'Don't call me that. I don't like it.'

'You called me Radusik.'

'Oh, but Radusik is a sweet name, tender … loving,' she added after a caesura and in a tone of special intimacy. 'Do you know when everyone's planning to leave?'

'Yes, it's time to get up. They're leaving in an hour or so.'

He was keen to see her go. Ideally, he would have liked her out within the next five minutes. He wanted to be alone, alone with Dron's email.

Jenny, however, closed her eyes, rolled over and settled down to sleep some more.

'Great,' she said. 'I'll have a bit more sleep and, when they've all gone, I'll be waiting … Radusik,' she murmured.

* * *

Jenny demanded to be taken out for lunch in the town.

'I hate eating at home. Life is not given to us for staying within four walls. I want a hot meal, and I want it in a restaurant,' she decided. 'And we can visit the monastery at the same time. I haven't been there for a thousand years, not since school.'

'Are you thinking of becoming a nun?' Rad asked solemnly.

'Not likely. I can't imagine what it must be like, sitting within four walls with nothing but prayers.'

'Well why else would you want to go to a monastery?'

'Are you serious?' She looked at him with indignation. 'Contact with the holy places of history is very uplifting.'

'Did you make that up all by yourself?' Rad enquired, no longer able to conceal his irony.

'Oh, you're laughing at me!' Jenny exclaimed. 'I'm so naive. It's just too easy to fool me. I've suffered so much because of that – but I don't care.'

'Never say that you don't care or naughty boys will pull your hair,' Rad responded. He could not work out how to talk to her, what to talk about, or how, which was why he was stuck on this level of silliness. He found it unsatisfactory but could not move beyond it.

'Well I have never let naughty boys pull my hair,' Jenny said humourlessly. 'If they did I would pull theirs.'

'I'll bear that in mind,' Rad said.

They went through the house from floor to floor, room to room, from one building to another. Rad checked the locks on the windows, the taps in bathrooms, and cisterns in the toilets. He switched off lamps which had been left on, unplugged forgotten mobile phone chargers, tying up their flexes and handing them to Jenny to carry. As the houseowner had been home, this could have been regarded as his responsibility, but Rad felt overall security was his job and he could not go out before everything had been checked.

'Right, let's get our coats,' he said when the inspection was complete and the forgotten chargers had been piled on the hall table. 'To the monastery and a restaurant. The perfect combination.'

He had no desire at all to go to town. All he wanted was to sit down as soon as possible and reread Dron's email, take in all the nuances and write a reply. However, he could hardly just put Jenny out of the house, saying 'Go to your restaurant if that's what you want, but I'm perfectly happy with what's in the fridge.'

The courtyard was white with snow scarred by tyre tracks. Now, however, the only car remaining from the earlier herd was a modest, bright yellow Suzuki hatchback. It stood forlornly at the edge of the concrete apron Rad had cleared two days ago. Its snub nose was pressed up against the wall of the snow he had swept and it seemed bewildered to find itself alone after the recent babel of vehicles.

'Can you drive?' Jenny asked as they approached the car.

'So I'm told,' Rad said.

'Then you drive, please,' she said, pointing the fob at the car and pressing a button to unlock it. The Suzuki's security unit loyally squealed and turned on its sidelights, like a dog wagging its tail.

'When a lady is with a gentleman, it is really for the the man to drive. Otherwise it seems rather demeaning for both of them. Don't you agree?'

'I agree,' Rad said, opening the door on the driver's side, 'at least as far as driving a car is concerned.'

The car was a small miracle: as smooth as velvet to drive, responsive, with a quiet, sweetly running engine. Rad found it a delight.

'What a brilliant car!' he said, genuinely admiring.

Ever since he had been able to afford a car, he had driven only Russian-made Ladas. They had been the latest model, brand new, straight off the assembly line, but even so bore no comparison with this baby.

'Do you have a car?' Jenny asked.

'I had one,' he said briefly.

'What happened? Did you crash it?'

Rad paused.

'It got smashed up,' he said.

'You lent it to someone, and they ...?'

Rad paused again. He was hardly going to tell her about being on the wrong end of the Kalashnikovs with a moustached lady Armenian notary in attendance.

'I didn't lend it to anyone, but it got smashed up anyway,' he said finally.

'You aren't making sense,' Jenny scolded. He seemed to have a talent for making her resentful.

'Understand it whatever way you like. It isn't important,' Rad said.

That was little short of rude, but this time Jenny took no exception.

'I like the way you drive,' she said.

He took that to be polite conversation, not regarding his driving as a particular forte.

'I do my best,' he said.

'No, really,' she insisted. 'You drive with a kind of steadfastness and serenity.'

'I do my best,' Rad repeated.

The square in front of the monastery was deserted. The wind blowing the drifting snow across it was as insolent as those Poles in 1612 with their plans to bring Asiatic Muscovy into the brilliance of Enlightenment Europe. Only at the gate in the monastery wall did Rad and Jenny collide with a group of bearded men festooned with bags and rucksacks stuffed so full of books that they could not be zipped up. Corners and spines of bindings and fanned out pages protruded untidily. These, however, were not monks but some other category of people. Their clothes were as untidy as their baggage, and they marched loudly forward, not standing aside or paying attention to anybody around them. Rad and Jenny literally bumped into them. 'Yids ... Freemasons ... Democrats ... Russia ... by the balls ... string 'em up ...' For a few moments, Rad and Jenny were enveloped in a cloud of hot air.

After they had left them behind, Rad and Jenny walked in silence, as if needing to cool down after the heat they had been subjected to.

'You aren't Jewish, are you?' Jenny asked when they had walked on a little.

He looked at her in surprise. He had not expected that to matter to her.

'Only a Freemason,' he responded.

'No, I'm serious.'

'So am I,' he replied.

'You're clearly not a Jew,' Jennie concluded with satisfaction. 'That's all right.'

The way she said it left Rad feeling belittled.

'What are you talking about?' he asked.

'Oh, it just means I won't be marrying you.'

'Too right you won't,' Rad retorted. 'Did I give the impression I was asking you to?'

Jenny was looking at him, with a disconcerting intensity in her grey eyes.

'I don't need anyone to ask me. When I find the right person, I'll ask them.'

'So, what does it matter whether I'm Jewish or not?'

'Because I will only marry a Jew.'

Rad glanced at Jenny. This was quite some banter they were exchanging in the bastion of Russian Orthodoxy.

'Oh, you mean you're Jewish yourself?' he surmised.

'No, I'm not,' she said. 'Not even half-Jewish. I'm nothing. It's just that if a Jew was going to be unfaithful to you, he would make sure you never found out.'

'Is that what matters to you? You don't mind him being unfaithful, as long as you don't know about it?'

'Let's face it, all men are promiscuous.' The look in Jenny's eyes was alarmingly serious. 'And what you don't know, never happened. To top it all, Jews know how to make money. What's not to like?!'

'There are Russians who know how to make money too,' Rad said.

'But with Jews, it's guaranteed.'

Rad detected the same irascibility beginning to stir in him as had made itself felt yesterday as he sat listening to her raptures over the heir of the Oberiuts.

'I'm Russian,' he said. 'Russian. End of discussion.'

They had reached the monastery's central square. Inside the walls was as deserted as outside them. As they had been walking there they had set eyes on only a few people: an ungainly old woman in a large black shawl walking arm in arm with a patient, weary young woman who was helping her to reach her destination; a plump, elderly monk with a short leather jacket over his cassock, who was straining to hear what a layman was saying, a thin young man with a scrawny beard in a light coat which was clearly not keeping out the wind. Driven on by the cold, three seminarists were hastening somewhere, one after the other, each clutching a heavy book to their chests.

Jenny stopped in the middle of the square, turned to right and left, and began contemplating the architecture around her.

'I haven't been here for a long time,' she said at last.

'Yes, not since you were at school,' Rad reminded her.

'How did you know that?' she asked.

'The BBC broadcast it from London,' he averred.

'Oh, I mentioned it before,' Jenny recalled.

'Well, yes, you mentioned it, and then the BBC broadcast it.' Rad was still finding it easiest to talk claptrap with her.

A service was in progress at the Monastery of the Trinity and St Sergius, whose squat outlines and spare architecture, dating from the era of the Golden Horde's rule over Russia, was totally overwhelming. If outside the monastery had seemed deserted, inside the church was busy but not crowded. Rad and Jenny were able to move around freely to the droning of the priest and the recitative of the choir, breathing in the sweet smell of incense. They went round the whole of the building, and up to the casket with the relics of the monastery's founder who, more than six centuries earlier, had inspired the Grand Duke's militia to do battle with the army of the Golden Horde. They stood before it and, after a moment's reflection, Rad crossed himself. It was probably the first time he had done so since his pre-school days, when his grandmother still occasionally managed to take him to church. Out of the corner of his eye, Rad noticed Jenny imitate his movements.

'Have you been christened?' she asked, when they moved away from the shrine.

'Yes,' Rad said unwillingly. 'You too, I take it.'

'No. I haven't,' Jenny said. 'My father was a big figure in the Party.'

'Then why did you cross yourself?'

'You shouldn't peep,' she retorted.

Rad had the impression she was expecting him to ask more questions in order to keep the conversation going, but he made no further enquiries.

She returned to the topic when they were standing by the rotunda, erected on the spot where, according to legend, a spring miraculously appeared when the monastery was under siege some centuries later.

'Do you believe in that sort of thing?' Jenny asked.

Rad shrugged.

'If you don't believe it, you're accusing people of lying.'

'But it is difficult to believe?'

'I agree.' Rad nodded. To his surprise, he liked the way Jenny had developed his answer. He wanted to continue her line of thought. 'Faith needs to be based on knowledge,' he said. 'But, actually, knowledge also calls for faith. Does that seem paradoxical? It's not in the slightest. The people trapped in that siege saw the spring appear. They used it and it saved them. When the siege was over, the spring dried up. If you told them there was no spring there they would not believe you. They would have faith in their knowledge. We didn't see the spring, so we don't have their knowledge, which is why we have our doubts. The only way to dispel them is through faith. We should believe those people, our ancestors. If we believe, we gain knowledge. If we persist in doubt, we lose faith.'

'In other words, if you're to believe in God you need miracles. Is that what you're saying?' Jenny queried.

She had summarised what he said very precisely, even though he had not used the word 'miracle'.

'You need to be able to see a miracle, to recognise it.' He was suddenly possessed by an unrealised aspiration to stand as a professor, with a slate board behind him, and explain to an audience of many eyes the mystery of expressing the world mathematically. He soared heavenwards on its wings. 'Take mathematics, for example. I think there is good reason why many great minds who practised it came to believe in God. The Pythagoreans actually worshipped numbers. What, after all, is a number? Something that doesn't exist in reality, that people thought up because it was useful in everyday life. Five fingers, ten fingers, twenty fingers and toes. So as to keep a tally. But in fact, the whole world is encompassed by numbers. We can express everything that exists in numbers, if we just take the time to derive a formula. Is that not a miracle? Have you heard of the golden ratio?'

Jenny was listening to him with an expression of rapt interest.

'You are asking an art historian that? You won't get far in architecture and painting without the golden proportion. Shall I tell you who was the big expert on it? Leonardo da Vinci!'

The jibe was entirely without malice and Rad let it pass.

'In music too,' he said, picking up on her remark, 'the laws of harmony conform to the golden ratio. And what is it? Proportion, the ratio between values. And any ratio is a number. Where does that leave us? We find the Pythagoreans were right when they claimed that numbers were the foundation of everything. Tell me that isn't a miracle! Knowing about that miracle, I have no problem believing in the miracle of the spring.'

'But in the beginning was the word,' Jenny dropped on him.

Her affirmative tone was softened with an admixture of the interrogative.

For a moment Rad was in a quandary, unable to see how to reconcile the two concepts of number and word, at least without the opportunity for further reflection.

'Well, er ... that is more a metaphor,' he suggested.

'The word is a command and the number is its implementation,' Jenny informed him.

Rad looked at her in amazement. That was not at all bad. He began to feel remorse over his irritability as they were coming away from the monastery gate. Really, what did it matter that she was so concerned about her hypothetical husband's ethnicity? What concern of his were her quirks? Or her aesthetic predilections, come to that. So she liked what the heir of the Oberiuts produced. She was evidently not alone in that.

He quickly reined in his feelings. Whether she was dumb or intelligent was, ultimately, neither here nor there. What he needed from her he had already obtained, and he trusted she had obtained from him all that she had been expecting.

'Time for that restaurant, don't you think?' he said. 'We have had food for the soul and now it's time to feed the body.'

The restaurant was called the Russian Innyard, and Rad knew absolutely nothing about it except that it was the only one hereabouts. It was within a stone's throw of the square in front of the monastery. They had parked the Suzuki across the road from that. Every time he visited the town, Rad walked or rode past the restaurant in the bus, and its 'Russian Innyard' sign had become as much a part of the landscape here as the red-brick walls and domes of the monastery.

'Perfectly decent,' Jenny decided, sitting down at a table and looking around.

That was probably as much as one could say for it. 'Wonderful', 'sumptuous', 'original' were not epithets you could apply to a straightforward eatery with room for ten or so tables placed rather too close together. It was a modest facility for satisfying the biological need for food.

Rad ordered a seafood and cold cured sea trout salad for the starter, sterlet soup for the first course and sevruga for the second, as requested by Jenny. 'Let's declare a meat-free day!' she decided. The menu prices, despite the modest attainments of the establishment, were outrageous. Rad just wanted to shut his eyes and not look at them, but had to go ahead and order.

Then he had to pay for the meal. As he did so, he reflected bitterly that the money would have sufficed for three weeks of his hermit-like diet. He had not managed to keep enough US dollars out of the clutches of his erstwhile customers to graze in the lush meadows of expensive restaurants.

Dusk was already falling by the time they returned to Jenny's Suzuki, and twilight of a sort was about to descend on the relationship they had developed so rapidly yesterday on Serge's bar stools. Jenny was not yet aware of that.

He was again in the driving seat.

'Where are you going? We need to go straight ahead!' she protested when, before they reached the level crossing, he turned to the right.

The road to Moscow was indeed straight ahead, but to get back to Semkhoz they needed to divert to the right.

'What, are you going to abandon me here without driving back to the house?' Rad asked.

'You mean you actually are living here, at Serge's dacha?'

This had evidently only now become clear to her.

'I am indeed,' Rad confirmed. 'I told you, I'm the invisible man.'

'Really?' she asked incredulously. The light-hearted way she had understood his words yesterday had just been undermined. 'Well, who are you hiding from here, invisible man?'

'From life,' he said.

This was true, if imprecisely expressed.

She did not like that answer.

'Again, you're talking ... it's impossible to understand! One riddle after another.'

'That's the best you can expect from spies,' Rad said.

He saw she was feeling an intimation of twilight, but had yet to realise that the sun was almost set, the shadows had lengthened nearly to the horizon, and the air was heavy and becoming chilly.

They left the town and sped in a single minute through two kilometres of countryside which looked like a white canvas slashed by the dark line of the highway. The road looped through the village, the glass and concrete shop flashed past on the right, looking now in the twilight like an aquarium filled with yellow water. One more turn and Rad began to slow down. Beyond the former House of Culture, looming darkly behind the black skeletons of the park, where the road branched off up to the church on the hill, he drove on to the verge and stopped.

'Right,' he said, facing Jenny and thumping the steering wheel with both hands. 'Your turn. Straight on along the highway, not turning off to left or right till you come to the police checkpoint, left when you get there and keep to the main road. That will lead you to the Yaroslavl highway. Just keep straight on along that till you get to Moscow.'

Jenny looked at him from her seat and rubbed her nostril which, until then, she had only done while talking.

'So you really do live here?' she asked again.

Rad nodded.

'And you don't come to Moscow?'

'Actually, no.'

She paused again, pouting.

'I shan't be coming out all this way to see you,' she finally blurted.

'Fine,' said Rad.

The ensuing silence lasted long enough for the sun finally to sink beneath the horizon, the deepening darkness to spill over the firmament, and dusk to transition to night. Finally, Jenny said, 'Do you mean that?'

'Absolutely,' Rad said.

Perhaps that was not the whole truth. Maybe he would have liked their escapade to continue, within the bounds of possibility. Right now, however, all he really wanted was to get back and turn his computer on. He responded to her like a computer playing chess, selecting from all the possible moves the one which would most economically lead to the desired pre-programmed result.

'That's a shame,' Jenny said, moving her leg over to get into the driver's seat and obliging him to open his door and get out. 'Last night was splendid. And this morning. I really enjoyed it.'

Rad gave an inward sigh of relief. Her claims were on his organism and did not extend to the rest of his life. For her he had been no more than a piece of apparatus in the gym, and she had enjoyed a thoroughly satisfying workout. She could easily replace him.

'And so did I, Jechka' he said, already outside the car. He bent to kiss her goodbye but she turned away. Rad straightened up, stepped back, said, 'Safe journey!' and slammed the door.

Jenny took off the moment the door was closed, putting her foot down so fiercely on the accelerator that her well-mannered, velvety Suzuki almost leapt out of its skin. Before Rad had moved, however, she slammed on the brakes, opened the door and leaned out.

'You wanted me to give you Dron's e-mail address.'

Rad walked towards the car, shaking his head.

'I won't be needing it. Thanks!'

Jenny's face disappeared, the door was again slammed shut, the Suzuki again reared up, and there was a screech of tyres before he reached it.

Well, fine. What was done was done. He could hardly tell her why he no longer needed her to give him the address, Rad reassured himself as he walked briskly home along the verge. He did not like lying and had never been good at it. The lie he had had to tell her troubled him, the way a sore throat did when he had a cold. Nothing life-threatening, but it hurt.

CHAPTER FOUR

'I do need to warn you that this is the cheapest category,' the travel agent told him. She had a bird-like, chirruping voice which seemed to lull him, as if she were stroking his hair. Talking to her customer, she gazed into his eyes with such unfeigned friendliness that it seemed Rad must be the only person to whom she had ever wanted to sell a plane ticket.

'That's fine,' Rad confirmed. 'The cheapest is what I need.'

The agent tapped a number out on the telephone in front of her, dictated Rad's debit card number Rad into it, checked there was enough money to pay for the ticket, and dictated to her invisible contact the amount to be debited.

'All done. Your ticket is paid for,' she said, putting down the receiver. She took a device that looked like a rat trap from the shelf behind her, fitted the card into it, placed a multi-sheeted receipt on top and, with a crunch, ran a slider over it. 'This is for you,' she said, returning the card. She looked with satisfaction at the imprint left on the receipt and handed it to Rad. 'Sign in the top corner, if you would. The amount in rubles is shown lower left.'

Rad glanced at the amount and noted that it was what the agent had quoted over the telephone. Taking the signed receipt, she separated the sheets and returned the second copy to Rad.

'And your ticket. Don't forget that!' With special care, she gave Rad a slim blue booklet with a bright red stripe on the cover and AEROFLOT inscribed in large white letters on it. 'The most economical fare, as you requested. You cannot return the ticket ...'

'I'm not planning to,' Rad said studying its inner pages.

'You cannot change the date of departure or the date of the return flight,' she continued with an understanding smile in her chirpy voice. 'If you are late, miss the flight on departure or return you have no right of transfer to a later flight and the ticket becomes invalid.'

Rad looked up sharply.

'What?' he asked in astonishment. 'All sorts of things can happen. What if I suddenly fall ill? When you say the ticket becomes invalid, you mean I pay a penalty to replace it?'

'No,' the agent explained patiently. 'It becomes void, and no medical emergencies can be taken into account. You would need to buy a new ticket.'

'What do you mean?' Rad expostulated. He could not believe what he was hearing. 'If I don't fly, the seat will be free. You might be able to sell it to somebody else and I wouldn't even get part of the money? Is that it?'

'Those are the conditions,' the agent confirmed. 'I did warn you that this is the cheapest category.'

'But you never told me all that. It's an outrage!'

'I was assuming you were a seasoned traveller and would be aware that a cheaper tariff entails various restrictions, which you found acceptable.' Her voice remained soft and caressing.

'Well you shouldn't have assumed anything of the sort. You should have told me what you just said before you took my money!' Rad protested.

The agent said nothing, only continuing to gaze into his eyes with the same attitude of submissive friendliness which appeared to convey that, if he so wished, she would immediately surrender her body to him, right there on her desktop.

Rad emerged from the travel agency feeling he had well and truly been had for a sucker. In reality, though, even if he had known about all the restrictions, he would have had no option but to buy that category of ticket. The alternative fares were much higher, and the two weeks his ticket allowed should be more than enough for his purposes. What riled him, though, was that he had not made an informed choice; he had been taken for ride. He was upset. Free will matters, even if what you choose leads to the hangman's noose.

Out in the street, even though it was late December, the weather was warm: two degrees above zero. The snow was melting, slush was squelching underfoot, but the moment he came out on to the porch Rad pulled up the hood of his jacket and pulled it over his eyes, as if there was a raging frost and coming out bareheaded would mean instantly catching cold. He was afraid of encountering one of the villains. Of course, in a city with a population of fifteen million souls you should be able to hide better than a needle in a haystack, but there was always the chance two needles might meet in the centre. The centre of this particular haystack had a way of sucking in every stray needle like a magnet. There was nothing to stop two of them finding themselves in the same place at the same time. Randomness derives from probability.

The next item on his list was a visit to the clinic near the Sandunovsky Baths to get his last vaccination, against hepatitis A. Dron had listed what he needed in an email: hepatitis A, tetanus and diphtheria.

The travel agency was in Dmitrovsky Lane, between Bolshaya Dmitrovka and Petrovka. To get him to the clinic, he needed to go down to Petrovka, out on to Neglinnaya, pass the fortress-like Central Bank imprisoned behind its cast iron gates, and turn into Sandunovsky Lane. Instead, however, Rad avoided Neglinnaya and went up to Rozhdestvenka, where the Bank of Moscow stood on the corner. His Visa card was the property of the Bank of Moscow, which held his money.

He turned in to the bank to check how much was left on the card. An ATM obediently swallowed the card and a display lit up, listing the operations he could ask it to perform. Rad requested a mini-statement and, ten seconds later, was issued a length of paper with rows of numbers on it. While waiting for the ATM to regurgitate his electronic card, he glanced at the number which most mattered to him. After buying his air ticket, he had a balance of less than 400 US dollars. That particular ticket really was the only one he could afford.

On his way out of the bank Rad calculated that, if he restricted himself to a diet of buckwheat and fried eggs for the two weeks remaining before his departure, he could survive on just $50, which would leave almost $350 on his card. 'Just buy yourself a ticket and I'll cover the rest of your stay here,' Dron had written. It would not have been entirely accurate to say that Dron's suggestion of meeting halfway between America and Russia had filled Rad with delight. By agreeing, he had performed hara-kiri on his wallet, and the fact that he would be sponging off someone made him feel it would be his own guts he spilled out. For all that, when he read Dron's proposal, he punched one fist into the other hand and then slammed it down on the table so forcefully that the keyboard jumped in the air, the keys froze, and the computer began checking its hard disk. He could not have hoped for anything better than a personal meeting. 'I'm planning to take the wife to Thailand for two or three weeks in January,' Dron wrote. 'Why not join us? The country is magic, more like the Garden of Eden than a country. We'll be able to travel around a bit and talk heart to heart.'

'Oh, well,' Rad reflected, 'hara-kiri has probably just had a bad press.' He decided to draw a firm line at the point where his trip ended and the future followed it. On one side of the line was life as he now knew it, and beyond was the life which would follow. For now, that was a darkness, a void, an abyss, a blank sheet of paper. Either the Gordian knot would be sundered or ... He decided not to think about alternative futures.

The nurse he encountered in the clinic was not the one who had done the vaccinations last time. She had been the cold, trained, professional type. The ampoules in her hands had surrendered their brittle virginity as if resigned to their fate. He had not felt the injections, she had spoken not one superfluous word, completely the impassive automaton in a white coat.

Today's nurse was quite the opposite. He might have expected to find her sitting on the bench outside an apartment block. Her one priority seemed to be to gossip endlessly.

'What, going on holiday, are we? To a resort? Somewhere on the coast, I bet,' she rattled on as she filled out his vaccination certificate.

'No, it's not a holiday,' Rad told her reluctantly. 'I'm going on business.'

'Well, business is business, of course, but still it's summer there,' the nurse murmured dreamily.

Rad tensed instantly.

'How do you know where I'm going?'

'From your vaccinations,' she said just a little smugly. 'Somewhere in South-East Asia, eh?'

'Yes,' Rad conceded.

'Thailand by any chance?' the nurse asked archly.

'What makes you think I'm going to Thailand?' Rad asked.

'I had one patient getting his jabs,' she said, looking at Rad benignly. 'He was going on business too. A crocodile farm in Thailand he had. That's quite something for a Russian to be doing, don't you think? Doing something like that too, are we?'

Rad caught himself feeling he was watching a clown perform and could barely keep from laughing.

'No,' he said. 'The good Lord has not visited the running of a crocodile farm on me. I don't have my own company there. I'm just going for some negotiations.'

The nurse opened a glass cabinet, extracted an ampoule and syringe, and laid them out on the table in front of her.

'Oh, you businessmen have such a life! Flying and travelling and getting well paid for it. None of that for the likes of us. Stuck here we are without two kopecks to rub together. What sort of money do we earn working in a clinic? It's a joke.'

'Yes, we businessmen certainly do have an interesting life,' Rad agreed. 'And you're absolutely right: I'm flying to Thailand.'

He immediately regretted that. Why on earth was he telling her where he was going? God helps those who help themselves: why was she in such a hurry to find out where he was going? His mood soured.

'Let's get it over with,' he said, turning his back to her.

She was a terrible nurse. Although it was a subcutaneous injection, and only 1 cc, the needle felt like a splinter being driven in, and all the time she was pressing the plunger, she kept moving the syringe about.

'All done, and you hardly felt a thing' she prattled on, rubbing a piece of cotton wool over the injection site. 'You can go off now to Thailand with never a care in the world. If I had the opportunity I would cheerfully have a hundred vaccinations. Some chance, given what we get paid!'

It occurred to Rad there was really no way this nurse could be associated with *them*. That was sheer paranoia. She was trying to soft talk money out of him: that was the sole reason for her performance.

Without replying, he tucked his shirt into his trousers, buckled his belt, pulled out his wallet and extracted a fifty-ruble note.

'Thank you,' he said, handing over the money. 'I'm most grateful.'

'Really? And I'm most grateful to you,' the nurse said, taking the money with a giggle.

Her performance was over.

When he emerged from the clinic, Rad again raised the hood of his jacket and pulled it over his eyes, so that he seemed now to be peering out of a tent. He had just one more obligation, and that was to phone his mother from a public telephone. Then he could go, catch the train out to his secret lair, sink to the bottom of the river and lie there without surfacing for the two weeks remaining before his departure.

* * *

In late December, Serge asked him to buy a fir tree for the New Year, or perhaps go out into the forest and cut one down. 'We'll decorate it when we get there. Just make sure it's in place,' he instructed over the phone.

One option, then, was to go to the town and buy one at the New Year market, but that did not appeal. He had already been there to replenish the supply of his favourite bread, and had called his mother to still her anxieties, which meant she would not be expecting another call for a few days at least. Rad decided to find a tree of his own choosing in the forest.

By now a wintry blanket of snow covered the ground, but Serge had a supply of skis. Every time Rad went down to the basement, his eyes lingered on them: men's and women's, wooden skis and plastic, racing skis and mountain skis with boots which seemed to belong to a spacesuit. 'Serge' evidently frequented the resorts regularly enough to justify buying his own speed skis.

'*In the woods a tree was born, a little fir tree lean,*' he crooned, drawing a pattern on the pair of wooden skis he fancied with wax he had found down there, spreading it with a cork block. '*In winter and in summer it was just as green as green,*' he continued, lacing his boots, pulling down the gaiters, stamping on the spot to check they were comfortable. The children's song brought back memories of the unlamented Soviet era when everything had seemed settled once and for all. The sun would rise in the east and set in the west, just as reassuringly as the orderly routine morning activities at summer camp with the portrait of a little, curly-haired Lenin in the centre of a red star pinned to your chest. There would be a line-up of the Young Pioneers, their fiery, silky red neckerchiefs tied with that special Pioneer knot, their arms slanted in front of their foreheads in the Pioneer salute. It was all gone forever now, cast into the waters of Lethe, consigned to oblivion.

Rad wanted the branches of his tree properly protected, not stripped of their needles. In the basement he also found a length of sailcloth and some clothes line, which he disentangled, coiled, and put in a rucksack along with the sailcloth and a hand axe.

The sun's empyrean eye gleamed through the chilling cloud cover, blinding him after the semi-darkness of the house. Out towards the road, the trail left by earlier skiers was defined but not yet compacted, so his skiing was almost soundless. The trail was springy, a pleasure to follow, and Rad wished he had thought of going out skiing for pleasure before now. If he had not been on a mission today, he would have been glad to ski on and on.

Today, however, he did not want to go too far, in order not to have to drag the tree back a vast distance. On the other hand, fell a tree too close to the village and the sound of the axe would alert the locals. Rad knew from talk in the store that the forester lived nearby, and could be expected to react with alacrity.

Half a kilometre beyond the village, he turned off the trail, ploughing a furrow in virgin snow. Finding the right tree proved surprisingly difficult. Mature fir trees took all the light, leaving the saplings little chance to grow, and those that did defy their fate and strive heavenward were malformed and scrawny. It took him an hour and a half to discover one he deemed presentable.

Returning to the ski trail with his booty in its sailcloth shroud, Rad spotted another skier seventy metres ahead. He too had a tree, but its branches were only tied in with rope and, rather than carry it on his shoulder, he was dragging it along in the snow. Rad had no wish to catch up with this figure, even if he posed no threat, but the skier was progressing so slowly that he had little choice. When he was within thirty metres, he recognised the twisted silhouette of Pavel Grigorievich. Grigorievich's tree was almost twice the size of his, and enviably bushy. In his searching Rad had seen nothing comparable.

'Well met, Slava. You're a true Russian!' Grigorievich greeted him, nodding with approval at the tree on his shoulder. 'They expect us to go into town and choose from the rubbish they offer, and even pay good money for it! Why pay for water if you live by the stream?'

Despite the approbation, Rad felt as awkward as Adam, caught sinking his teeth into the forbidden fruit.

'Yes,' he said shamefacedly. 'It would seem odd to go into town to find a tree.'

'You're right, Slava, absolutely right!' Grigorievich agreed, wholeheartedly commending his fall from grace. 'Fat chance they're going to buy one for themselves in the market.'

'They?' Rad asked, although he had little doubt who was being referred to.

'Them. That lot, of course. Who d'you think I'm hauling this beauty back for? Me? My one's knee-high to a grasshopper, and what more do I need? I'm hauling this one back for our mayor, my dear neighbour, right? His nibs wouldn't lower himself to talk to the likes of me. No, it was his minions. All over me, they were, grinning like idiots. It's them ordered this beauty. "Good and bushy," they said. "Nice and straight." Not for the likes of him some half-bald apology from the market. Freshly cut, our Democrat wants it. Some Democrat! If anyone wants to hang him, I'll give them the rope.'

'Why so bloodthirsty, Pavel Grigorievich?' Rad laughed, remembering him saying those very words not long before.

'You'll see. Got it coming to 'em, they have,' came the vindictive response. 'It's the fat cats will weep the mouse's tears, them or, at the latest, their brats. God sees who eats our cheese.'

There they stood on a ski trail in the middle of a forest, two poachers with their illicit goods, conversing like waistcoated gentlemen who chanced to meet while promenading of a summer's day in the park. It was winter, however, and the frost was insinuating its way under Rad's jacket, causing his sweaty shirt to freeze and making him shiver.

'Well, Pavel Grigorievich,' he said. 'I have to be on my way. If you'll excuse me, I'll overtake you and go on ahead.'

He moved on to untrodden snow to get past, but Grigorievich stopped him.

'I'm thinking you'll perhaps give me a hand to get this brute back home. You're a young man. I see you ploughing ahead like a tank with that tree. You'll manage the two. I'm an old man. What strength do I have? This is doing me in. I need the money, that's the only reason I agreed, fool that I am. And now here I am dragging it along and holding in my hernia.'

Asking him to haul two trees was a cheek but, after a moment's reflection, Rad agreed. He was feeling guilty about declining to carry the old man's paraffin all the way home the last time they met.

'Well, tell me more. Did they offer you good money for it?' he asked, as he wedged Grigorievich's tree under his arm. He supposed he must be quite a sight, festooned with greenery like a sailor in 1917 festooned with machine-gun belts.

'Good money? Fat chance!' Grigorievich answered evasively. 'It's only themselves they pay well. They'd rather choke, even without a rope, than be generous to the likes of us.'

Rad moved off, but forging ahead with two trees was a lot more strenuous, and within five minutes he was so hot you could have lit a match off him. He was progressing no faster now than Grigorievich had been.

After 300 metres or so, the firebreak the ski trail followed came to a wide ravine covered in undergrowth. Where the downhill part ended, their trail met another snaking along the bottom. Rad stopped for a breather, laid the trees down on the snow and straightened up, flexing his shoulders and bending his back.

'It can't be that hard for a man like you, Slava!' Grigorievich exclaimed. 'You move like a tank.'

Rad looked at him and gave a wry grin. Grigorievich was no waistcoated dandy: more a crafty, smooth-tongued courtier.

'I do my best,' Rad said.

A figure in a green army jacket girded with a broad officer's belt emerged from the undergrowth on to the trail which ran along the ravine. Stamping the snow off his skis, he glided swiftly towards them, skiing, as they were themselves, without poles. Another leather strap ran over his right shoulder and, as he approached, could be seen to be attached to a rifle, visible through his legs as he advanced.

Grigorievich peered at him. 'Fuck!' he said. 'It's Misha the Forester.'

'Fuck!' Rad concurred.

'He's been waiting in ambush, the scumbag,' Grigorievich muttered with grudging admiration. 'Doesn't miss a trick. Stiff upper lip, Slava. You can guess what's coming.'

Rad could.

'But why the gun?' he asked. 'Is he trying to scare us?'

'Who knows?' said Grigorievich. 'Who knows?'

'Hey, Grigorievich!' the forester shouted as he approached. 'Up to your old tricks again, you sod! Think the law doesn't apply to you?'

'Sod yourself!' Grigorievich shouted right back at him. 'You should know better than talk to me like that!'

'Well enough I know how to talk to you!' the forester continued, not without a note of menace in his voice. 'And well you know you'll get no quarter from me!'

'Nasty bit of work!' Pavel Grigorievich muttered under his breath. 'We're up shit creek, Slava. Got the necessary paddle?'

'Hardly,' Rad replied equally sotto voce. 'I wasn't expecting to need money.'

'That's bad, Slava,' Grigorievich reflected.

The forester, an able-bodied man of around fifty, stopped three metres away from them. His broad peasant face registered no consciousness of right or wrong, but had written on it a steely determination to profit from the hours he had lurked in ambush.

'And who might this be with you?' he asked, indicating with a twitch of his eyebrows that he meant Rad.

'Oh, he's nothing to do with me, he's on his own,' said Grigorievich. 'Doesn't mean a thing we're skiing together. Perhaps I'm with him,' he suddenly added, giving Rad a wink.

Rad said nothing, leaving it to his acquaintance to do the talking.

'Well,' the forester said, 'much I care whether you're together or not. What are we going to do now? Take you to the police station to make a statement?'

'What statement? What are you on about?' Grigorievich was suddenly insinuating. 'Do you know who it is I cut this tree for? For the mayor himself. I'm on my way there right now.'

The forester's eyes became clouded under the strain of considering this complication.

'What, you're saying he asked you to get him a tree? Why didn't he ask me?'

'Ah, well, because I'm his neighbour, see? You're not.'

'His neighbour you may be, but I'm the effing forester!'

'Well, I can't answer for the mayor, of course.' A note of self-satisfaction was to be heard in his voice that he, rather than anyone else, should have been entrusted with such a sensitive assignment. 'He asked and asked me to do it, and who am I to turn down the mayor? He's at my house right now, waiting. We can go back if you like, you can see for yourself.'

'So you bought it for him at the market, did you?' the forester asked with heavy sarcasm.

'No, I grew it in my kitchen garden,' Grigorievich retorted, giving as good as he got. Rad, silently listening all this time to the conversation, was unable to suppress a chuckle. This stripped him of a kind of camouflage net which had apparently been keeping him from the forester's attention.

'And what about that tree, then. I suppose that's for the mayor too?' the forester shifted his gaze to Rad.

'Okay,' Rad said in a conciliatory tone. 'How much?'

'What do you mean, "How much?"' the forester returned to his sarcastic tone. 'Are you attempting to bribe a government official?'

'I'm proposing an amicable settlement.'

'And what if I don't agree?'

'Well, then we go to the police station and they take a statement,' Rad said. He was entirely confident that the forester had no interest in involving the police.

'Five hundred rubles off each of you,' he said.

'Off each of us?' Grigorievich gasped. 'You have to be joking! The tree isn't even for me. You go and ask the mayor to pay up. That's who you need to talk to.'

The gleam in the forester's eye faded. The gears in his brain were having trouble with this. They ground and crashed and sparked, and smoke seemed about to billow from his ears.

'Seven hundred and fifty from you,' the forester eventually declared, focusing his eyes as they unclouded on Rad. 'You were carrying the firs, so that means they're yours.'

'Think again,' Rad suggested. 'Don't push it!'

'You talking to me? Who d'you think you are? Who're you telling not to push it?' The forester grabbed the barrel of the rifle and pulled it forward to point at Rad. 'I'll soon show you. I'll fire straight in your belly and sow your guts in square clusters over the land. And Grigorievich will testify it was self-defence. Won't you?' he said, with a sideways glance.

Grigorievich responded with an obsequious giggle.

'Pay him, Slava,' he said. 'Go back to your house and get him the money. You don't need this. Why make trouble for yourself?' Without waiting for a reply, he prattled on with the same wheedling servility to the forester, 'He'll pay. Of course he will. He's a good lad. He knows what's what. Of course he will.'

This man was a courtier to the marrow of his bones.

'No, Pavel Grigorievich,' Rad said. 'I'm not paying for your mayor. You'll have to settle that yourself.'

'But Slava, Slava! You were carrying the trees like the forester says!' The crafty courtier manifested himself in all his cunning.

'From now on I'm carrying just mine,' Rad informed him.

'Well, there's no helping it. I'll have to bear the other one myself,' Grigorievich conceded.

There was no point in continuing the conversation. Rad lifted his tree in its canvas cocoon, slung it over his shoulder and started up the rise out of the ravine. The forester, he noticed out of the corner of his eye, had lowered the barrel of his rifle and was following behind.

'What, is this where you live?' the forester asked when Rad turned off the ski trail towards his house.

'Yes,' he answered shortly.

'I thought someone else owned this one.'

'But I live in it,' Rad had to elaborate.

'Oh, I get it.' The forester sounded relieved, as if having finally discovered the answer to a question that had been tormenting him for a long time. 'You're renting it, right?'

'Living in it,' Rad answered even more curtly.

He unlocked the gate and they went into the front yard. Rad left the forester on the porch, found the money, and went back out with a single 500-ruble note.

'What's this?' the forester said, taking the purple-sheened banknote depicting Peter the Great's statue in Arkhangelsk with two fingers, as if holding a dead mouse by the tail. 'Seven hundred and fifty, I said!'

'You'll have to get the rest off the mayor,' Rad said.

The forester's face muscles were working furiously. It seemed he had really believed he could rip Rad off for both trees.

'The cunts!' The forester screeched. 'They build all these houses here! Rent them out to God knows who! If it was up to me, I'd lock the lot of you in there in Moscow and set fire to the place like we did with the Frenchies in 1812! I wouldn't let you within a hundred kilometres of our forest!'

'Then who would you have to shake down for pilfering New Year trees?' Rad enquired with a grin.

'Think you can smirk at me? I'll show you!' The forester again pulled his rifle round. 'I'll show you cunts ... I'll put a cartridge in you ... You wait, the time will come! We'll hunt you down like hogs. We'll skin you shitty intellectuals! Rotten Freemasons the lot of you! A fine life you've given us. Didn't care for Soviet power, eh?'

'Are you sure you'd have got a bigger bribe under the Soviets?' Rad retorted. He had not meant to goad the forester but could not resist. After the eight hours he had recently spent looking down the barrels of two Kalashnikovs, the forester's rifle seemed about as scary as a child's pop-gun.

'Yes ... under the Soviets! I'd have put you in your place under the Soviets!' The forester's face, already flushed from the frost, became as red as an overripe tomato and looked as if at any moment it might squirt juice from every pore.

'Don't give me that! You'd have done nothing of the sort in the days of the USSR,' Rad said. 'Try telling your fairy tales about what it was like under the Soviet regime to little children. And stop waving that gun about or you'll be surprised what I'll do with it.'

He took a step in the direction of the forester, as if about to take the rifle off him. With a clattering of boots, the forester left the porch.

'We'll shoot you, just you wait! Slaughter the lot of you!' he vowed from down below, pushing his boots into the ski bindings. He opened the gate to make his exit, but turned to Rad and spat a juicy gobbet of phlegm in his direction. 'Like the Frenchies in 1812!' he yelled.

* * *

Rad was still conscious of the unpleasant aftertaste of the forester's threats two days later on New Year's Eve, which he celebrated alone, in front of a television set and with only an undecorated fir tree for company. Serge's promise to bring presents and fairy lights on the thirty-first had not been kept, so Rad scattered pieces of cotton wool over the tree's shaggy green paws to keep it from looking completely out of place in the room.

He sat in a chair with his feet on the coffee table, drinking martinis on the house and munching a slice of Borodino bread he had put in the toaster and then buttered. He saw the New Year in. What was on the television he neither saw nor heard. With the remote constantly hand, he hopped channels but there seemed nothing to choose between them, so he drank martinis and, when the bottle was finished, went over to the bar, took another, had his wicked way with that and retired to bed.

The master of the house appeared on New Year's Day, well into the afternoon, when a short, dreary afternoon was already yielding to dusk. He drove in to the courtyard in a cumbersome, glitzy BMW which, to a Russian eye, closely resembled a hippopotamus on wheels, accompanied by the equally glitzy carcases of a Mercedes 600 and Audi 300. These brought two of his colleagues and their wives, and that evening all the table talk was of cash transfers, marketing, accounts, budgets and kickbacks. There was name-dropping of companies and people, none of which Rad knew, or wished to know, anything about. The women, with peals of girlish laughter, primped their hairdos and freshened their lipstick with the aid of a mirror in their powder compacts, twittered on about dresses, the prices in boutiques and their holidays abroad, who had been where, what they had done, what they had bought. Rad felt like throwing up. He made an effort to join in the small talk both of the men and the women, and even did rather well with the latter, inserting a couple of apposite witticisms for which he was rewarded with an appreciative peck on the cheek from the lady of the house, confirming his status as a former classmate of her husband and friend of the family. 'Radchik,' she proclaimed, 'You're a poppet!' It was not long, however, before he was wilting. He was the odd one out here, which became more obvious with every remark he made, and was underlined by every word addressed to him, the proverbial round peg in a square hole.

A weighty bottle of Camus brandy graced the table. It had been produced with a flourish from a glossy box with a red ribbon embellished with a wax seal, and Rad decided, just as last night with the martinis, that the best partner for him in tonight's company would be this namesake of a writer and philosopher he admired. He moved the bottle closer and began a private tête-à-tête. He had, of course, little to contribute to the discourse, and limited himself to acquiescing as the philosopher's fortifying 40° wisdom was transferred to him gulp by gulp.

The moment arrived when Rad finally knew he was full to overflowing with existentialist wisdom.

'Ladies and gentlemen,' he exclaimed loudly, freezing the conversation at the table, 'you are talking twaddle. Total, unmitigated, irredeemable twaddle!' He had in fact not the slightest idea what they were now talking about, but was overflowing and felt an obligation, which would not be denied, to share his bounty with these other people. 'Marketing, budgets, kickbacks ... what does it all matter, ladies and gentlemen? Have you any idea what people think of you? Just a couple of days ago, a tribune of the Russian people told me without euphemisms, with no ifs or buts, that you are no more highly regarded than the Napoleonic army of 1812. The local people here would cheerfully lock you all up in Moscow, bar the gates and burn the city to the ground. They would cheerfully burn alive you and your progeny, all your family, and, if any of you escaped, they would take you hand and foot and throw you back into the flames! You are detested, ladies and gentlemen. You are doomed. Sentence has been passed. You have no idea how you are loathed, yet here you sit, like so many game birds, twittering on about money transfers and marketing, your credit cards and holidays on Lake Geneva. Wake up, for heaven's sake! Your lives are at stake!'

'Why do you keep saying "you"?' the colleague of Serge seated opposite Rad enquired. His demeanour was languid, but his eyes so sly that, when they focused on you, you instinctively felt for your wallet. This colleague had a way of pouting his lips when he spoke, as if intending to kiss the person he was talking to. 'Do you not include yourself as one of the French?'

The barb was well aimed, and Rad nodded.

'Oh, yes. They won't discriminate.'

'Well, then!' Mr Fox shrugged. 'Re-direct your invective at yourself.'

'At myself?' Rad expostulated, feeling right now an irresistible urge to expostulate. 'All the problems are with someone else, not with you. Is that what you're saying? Not with you who are so innocent, so good, so white and fluffy! When they drag you away to pluck your feathers, you'll soon see just how innocent you are!'

'There's really no need to be so personal.' Mr Fox's eyes narrowed and became even foxier, as if now he was going to openly help himself to that wallet.

'Listen, Rad. There's something I really want to tell you.' The speaker was Serge's other colleague, well into his forties and evidently the most senior at the table. He had a flabby, sensual face, masked by a fashionable stubble. Rad had noticed how deferential Serge was towards him, going out of his way to be attentive. 'You need to steer well clear of the dregs of society. That's all they are, dregs. Why should you care what they think? They live their lives, we live ours, and the two planes do not intersect. You and Serge,' with a sweep of his hand he bracketed Rad with his former fellow student, 'are mathematicians. You know the score. They view us as invaders and we view them as, well, not Frenchmen, anyway.' At this he became animated, and glanced around the table at the others. 'Am I not right?' he asked, revelling in his perspicacity, inviting his listeners to associate themselves with his insight. 'Not as Frenchmen, certainly.'

'They are cattle,' Mr Fox chimed in, pursing his lips in the direction of the speaker. 'Let us be open about this. Let us not beat about the bush. What have we in common with these cattle? The Russian people have always envied those at the top. That is how it has been and always will be. Why should we be afraid of them? Is there going to be another revolt, mindless and merciless? Let them try it! They will be the ones who end up impaled. No one is going to allow everything in Russia to be turned upside down again. We've had quite enough of that from them. An elite should be elite, with privilege cascading down from generation to generation, from father to son, from son to grandson. Elites need to be looked after, cossetted. Without an elite Russia has no future.'

Rad laughed scornfully.

'What, call yourselves an elite?' He waved his arms expansively. 'Some elite! A right bunch of aristos you are. You're weeds! Locusts! Munch-

munch-munch and you've gobbled everything up. We're in a quagmire now. Everything is just quicksands!'

His intimate discourse with the French philosopher had loosened the corset supporting his broken back, and now the pain broke out and raged in him like a Pacific typhoon, sweeping aside everything in its path.

Serge, who had been at the head of the table, materialised beside Rad. Continuing to rampage like a tornado, Rad suddenly felt hands under his armpits. Serge tried to pull him to his feet, lost his grip, and only succeeded in pulling him off his chair. Rad ended up on the floor.

'What the fuck!' he cursed, trying to get up with one hand on his abruptly vacated chair and the other on something soft.

'E-eek!' he heard a screech above his head and realised the something soft was a woman's thigh.

He sank back to the floor, took a look at the owner of the thigh and concluded it could only be Mr Fox's wife, especially given that she had been sitting next to him.

'Oops, sorry, madam!' Rad said, unhanding her. 'You're such a creep, Serge. You could see … why didn't you warn me!'

'Drunk out of his mind, the animal,' he heard Mr Fox exclaim.

'Weed!' Rad parried, trying with both hands to get a hold on the tabletop and rise to his feet. 'Locust!'

Now two people were hauling him up by the arms. Since Mr Fox was still seated opposite, the second person could only be Mr Stubble. He and Serge lifted Rad to his feet and dragged him away.

'That's enough! You're pissed out of your mind!' Serge whispered hotly in his ear.

Rad offered no resistance. The typhoon within was spent, the hurricane-force wind dropped, the thunderclouds parted, the tornado was over. He resisted only outside the door when he found they were leading him to the first floor stairs.

'Where are we going.' He dug his heels in and tried to turn in the direction of his room next to the kitchen. 'I go this way!'

'All we need now is the sound of you snoring in the next room!' Serge again hissed in his ear.

'You want me to sleep it off?' Rad asked, continuing his opposition to going upstairs.

'Yes, Rad. In the present circumstances that is essential,' Mr Stubble said firmly.

'I wasn't asking you,' Rad replied, nodding towards Serge.

Mr Stubble's answer was, however, also Serge's.

'I do, I do, I do!' Serge breathed hotly in his ear.

Rad gave a blissful, smug smile, his soul once more at peace, the storm having abated.

'Okay, let's go on up,' he acquiesced, allowing them to move him. 'I always wanted to live on your floor anyway.'

* * *

So ended the first day of the New Year. Rad could also remember going to sleep on a narrow couch raised at one end, and that he took his trousers off but, for some reason, not his jacket. Nothing else remained in his memory. When he woke it was already the second of January and he was freezing cold. A tartan blanket had fallen to the floor during the night. He was wearing a crumpled blazer and had a terrible hangover, but also a sense of having lived New Year's Day to the fullest. He had revelled in it, and that awareness rose and fluttered above him, like a banner flapping proudly in the wind.

Shivering with cold, he pulled on his trousers, went downstairs, got his outdoor clothes and, collecting the snow shovel from the pantry, went outside. In the courtyard a light, fine snow was drifting down from a uniformly overcast sky on to just one glossy carcase, Serge's BMW. He took this to mean the guests had not stayed overnight, and also that they had left very late, perhaps indeed in the small hours of the morning, and Serge had not felt like bothering with security and putting his car in the garage in the dark. When he had guests, Serge made a point of reassuring them by not putting his car in the garage, and if he was not leaving together with them, would drive it in only after they had all gone.

It was still quite early and the daylight was not yet strong enough to chase away the lingering twilight of dawn. Its languid lack of strength was remarkably in harmony with the hungover weakness suffusing his body. His indisposition seemed to proceed not from his person but from the world around him.

Catching himself having this thought, Rad sank the shovel into the fresh virgin snow, leaned on the handle and moved forwards, leaving a broad even path in the fluffy white snowfield.

The snow was not, actually, all that deep. Rad had cleared it on New Year's Eve and there was no need to clear the yard again today, but what more marvellous occupation could you imagine on a morning like this, with a head like his after the shenanigans of the night before? The rasping noise of the shovel as it scraped across the frozen concrete was as sweet to Rad's ear as a Mozart sonata.

The front door slammed as Rad, leaning over his shovel, was moving away from the house towards the fence. He stopped, leaned for a moment on the shovel, and turned round. On the porch, in a fur hat, dressed warmly and with a second snow shovel in his hands, stood Serge. He looked at Rad in silence, and Rad looked back, also in silence. He knew they would have to talk, but did not want to anticipate that by being the first to say hello, to appear to be accepting that he had made a fool of himself.

They stood there, looking at each other, for the best part of thirty seconds. Then the master of the house took hold of the haft of his shovel, raised it in the air and, still in silence, began slowly to come down the steps. At the bottom, he took a few steps in Rad's direction, lowered his shovel and cleared a snow-free swathe in the very middle of the snowfield, a part as yet untouched by Rad.

For ten minutes or so they clattered away, as if unaware of each other, although at times their paths actually crossed. A moment came when they were very close, only with their backs to each other. Each was aware of the movements of the other, and they turned simultaneously. Except that Serge straightened up purposefully a fraction of a second before Rad, obliging him to move quickly to catch up.

'I ought to punch you in the face, you Carbonaro!' Serge exploded, enveloping Rad in a gust of volcanic heat. 'You wrecked my get-together! I desperately needed that evening to be a success!'

'Come off it,' Rad said. 'You all work together, sit in the same office. Can't you talk to your colleagues there?'

'Don't pretend to be stupider than you are!' The volcano's crater spewed out another pillar of fire. 'Or do you really not understand? Seeing someone and talking to them is not at all the same thing.'

'Oh, come on. You'll find another opportunity to talk to your senior colleague,' Rad soldiered on, trying to ignore the volcanic heat coming his way. 'It's not the end of the world. You'll organise something else.'

The master of the house took this as if it was not the miscreant who had taken a punch in the face, but the offended party.

'Something else?' he shrieked. 'You think they'll come back for more of the same? Nobody will ever come back. They're sick of the sight of you!'

'*Never was a story of more woe,*' Rad commented. '*Sadder than the story of Juliet and her Romeo.*'

He regretted yesterday's upset and wished it had never happened. He would have preferred to be talking to Serge in quite a different tone. That is what he would have preferred, but this was what was happening. To keep him upright, his broken back needed the corset of insolence.

The quoting of Shakespeare evidently struck Serge as merely another affront.

'What have Romeo and Juliet got to do with anything? Because of you I'm no longer able to invite people here! Are you listening? Because of you!'

'And what?' Rad parried. 'Do you want me to hide in the basement, as if I'm not there, and wait until everyone has gone before I come out again?'

'Perhaps I do!' Serge responded. 'Don't forget whose house you're living in. I let you come to stay here, and I can perfectly well change my mind.'

Rad had been expecting this, and he was ready for it.

'Fine!' he said. 'I was going to ask you to free me from this dog's life anyway. You'll have to find someone else to be your unpaid security guard, because a week from now, no, eight days, you won't have sight or sound of me.'

The silence that followed was like a chasm opening in their conversation.

'Where are you going?' Serge asked after an eternity. The volcano was still bubbling, but there were no flames, no lava flow, only sulphurous fumes choking its fiery breath. 'Have you resolved your problem? Are you going back to Moscow?'

'No,' Rad said. 'Not to Moscow: to Thailand.'

'Where?' Serge said, as if sure he must have misheard. 'Thailand?'

'Thailand,' Rad confirmed.

'What, for good?'

'We'll have to wait and see. Maybe for good.'

Rad had had no intention of going as far as that. Of course, he could hardly have put off announcing his impending departure much longer, and there could not have been a more opportune moment than now, with the reappearance of the master of the house. Since, however, in the heat of battle he had vowed to depart, the logic of the situation seemed to demand a hint that he might never return.

'Well, well, well ...' Serge murmured, looking disconcerted. 'That's something you're free to decide.'

'Free to decide?' Rad queried. 'If you had agreed to stand up for me against those thugs as I asked, or given me a loan, I wouldn't be having to make a bolt for it now.'

'I did what I could,' Serge replied miffily. 'I'm not saying another word about that,' was the implication.

'Well, thank you anyway. I'm grateful for what you did,' Rad said.

Which was absolutely true.

'And what is taking you to Thailand, can you tell me?' Serge ventured.

'I'm going there to see Tsekhovets junior,' Rad revealed succinctly.

The utterance of this name had a magical effect on Serge, who seemed to bloom, his face breaking into an almost tender smile, as if here in the middle of his half-swept yard Tsekhovets senior himself had appeared to him.

'You managed to agree something with him?' his face continued to glow as he asked this new question.

'Yes,' Rad stated, confirming the obvious.

'So, what business is taking you to Thailand?'

'Oh, he's recruited me for his spy network,' Rad averred.

This floored Serge, who seemed from his ensuing silence to have fallen into a pit. Rad waited patiently for him to climb back out.

'Ah, yes, of course ...' his former classmate finally said. 'He's a spy, isn't he. But, I mean, you ... you're a civilian. You have nothing to do with that world ...' His uncertainty was palpable.

He clearly was more than half inclined to take Rad's assertion seriously, with only a shadow of doubt somewhere in the background. Anyone who had grown up in the Soviet Union could well believe anyone at all might belong to the secret police.

'What do you mean, a civilian? I am a lieutenant of the reserve.' Rad was enjoying his bluff, finding it fair compensation for the earlier part of their conversation. 'As, indeed, you are yourself. I seem to remember we first bumped into each other during officer's training at the University.'

'Ah, yes,' Serge recalled. 'I remember now. All the same ... Just like that?'

'Completely out of the blue,' Rad confirmed. 'All things are possible in Russia, if you know the right people.'

'Ah, string-pulling.' That explanation Serge found totally convincing. He had no further questions. 'Well, well, well ...' A note of liking was now clearly discernible in his voice. Rad was no longer just the person living in his house and acting as security. 'If you emigrate, all your problems will be solved. They won't reach you there.'

In the heavy air and half-light of a drawn-out morning, the front door banged again, interrupting their conversation. They turned to look in that direction. On the porch stood Polina, pulling around her a mink coat draped over her shoulders.

'Boys!' she exclaimed when she saw she had their attention, what way is that to behave! Scraping away with shovels at this hour of the morning! It grates on my ears. How is a poor woman supposed to get her beauty sleep? Serge!' She continued, addressing herself only to her husband. 'For goodness sake, you came out to stop him!'

Serge took hold of his shovel at the base, causing it to assume a horizontal position, and walked towards the porch.

'Guess what!' he called to her, ignoring her reprimand. 'Our Carbonaro is going abroad!'

'How so? Where to?' Polina exclaimed, glancing at Rad.

'To Thailand!' Serge shouted rather more loudly than necessary, in order to be sure he was heard both by Polina and by Rad, who was behind him.

'How lovely!' Polina exclaimed. She came down a few steps, as if reacting to a sudden gust of wind, but then stopped, not surrendering to its playfulness. 'But why? Are you going on holiday?'

Serge too had stopped half way.

'Yes,' he said, turning to Rad. 'Tell Polina why you are going to Thailand.'

'To sell banana fritters,' Rad said quietly, which was much closer to the truth than the explanation he had given Serge.

'To serve the Motherland!' her husband relayed, either mishearing Rad or, more probably, rephrasing for him.

'Go fuck yourself!' Rad counselled him.

'Go fuck yourself with all your questions!' Serge mistranslated for his wife.

There they stood, like people playing Chinese whispers, with Polina and Rad able to communicate only through her husband.

'Rad, did you really say I should go fuck myself?' Polina shouted over her husband's head. 'Have you turned completely feral here in your hermit's isolation?'

'Have you gone feral?' Serge relayed.

'Something like that,' Rad agreed.

'Yes he has, completely,' Serge confirmed to his wife.

'He might at least have phoned Jenny,' Polina commented from the porch.

'Well,' Serge looked at Rad. 'Did you hear? The decent thing would have been to phone Jenny.'

'What's she got to do with anything?' Rad asked.

'Well, absolutely! Who cares about her?' Serge demanded histrionically, addressing himself neither to Rad nor to his wife.

Without answering this evidently rhetorical question, Rad turned his back on both of them, bent over his shovel and rent the air with its rasping cacophony, deeming that the best way to cut the line on their Chinese whispers. A man at work is incommunicado.

'Rad! Rad!' As if to disprove this view, he heard Polina's voice over the sound of his shovelling.

He had no option but to stop scraping and turn to face her.

'Rad, come here!' she called from the porch. 'I can't come out there to you!' She raised a foot and shook it in the air to show she was wearing indoor shoes.

As he passed Serge, Rad instructed him, as if he were now the boss, 'Put the car in the garage so we can clear the area where you've parked it.'

'Yes, sir!' Pressing his hands to the seams of his trousers, Serge stood to attention.

'Comrade Lieutenant,' Rad corrected him as he walked past.

'Yes, sir, Comrade Lieutenant!' his former classmate barked, immediately adding, 'You're really into this, aren't you!'

'Rad, Rad!' Polina said when he reached the porch and stood there looking up at her. 'Look, tell me, really, why have you never phoned Jenny? She's been asking about you, and you haven't phoned once!'

'She's been asking?' Rad echoed. 'So what?'

'So what? Bizarre! You rogered the girl and that's it?'

Rad wanted to stun Polina, as he had her husband, with something like his spy story but now nothing came to mind.

'Why the hell would she need me?' he said.

'That's not for you to judge!' Polina retorted.

'Of course it is!'

'Oh, you really have gone feral, completely!' Polina, still enveloped in her fur coat, beginning shifting, almost dancing, from foot to foot. She might have seemed to be reacting to the cold, but Rad recognised this as a sign she was angry.

'Have you become completely desensitised? She's been asking me about you! And wondering why you haven't phoned!'

'Well now you can tell her, I've gone to Thailand, and that's why I haven't phoned.' Rad was irritated with himself. He had not hit the right note and everything was coming out too seriously. 'If she asks again, just tell her that. Okay?'

'Okay, okay!' Polina executed another of her dance steps. 'I get the picture. Only, no, I don't. Why are you going to Thailand if it's not for a holiday?'

Rad realised she knew nothing about Dron, only what had been relayed to her by Serge.

'I'm going there to save my skin,' he said. 'There's someone I have to meet, someone, incidentally, your Jenny knows. And that's enough, for God's sake!' he suddenly burst out. As suddenly as if he had been climbing a cliff face, and his foothold had broken away and, before he could clutch at anything, he too was hurtling down after it. 'I haven't phoned, I've gone feral ... for heaven's sake, don't you know why I've been stuck out here? Do you really not know?'

Polina said nothing. She stood up there looking frightened, no longer shifting about.

Rad turned on his heel and, dragging the shovel behind him like a clattering tail, went back to where he had been scraping before. Somewhere inside him a herd of cats was yowling and ripping him to shreds. He was ashamed of his lapse. It bore no comparison with yesterday's, but that exhibition had the excuse of his extended consorting with M. Camus. Today there was no excuse.

Serge, his shovel balanced, came loping easily towards him looking like a man on holiday.

'I'm just going to get the car keys to put the BMW in the garage, as instructed,' he said acidly as he passed.

'Up to you. Nothing to do with me,' Rad answered in a flat voice.

CHAPTER FIVE

At Sheremetievo, after passing through passport control and checking in one suitcase, Rad was left with a small bag over his shoulder. He sat some way from the boarding gate and pulled out the book he had brought to read on the journey. The people around were rushing from one duty-free shop to the next, a gaudily dressed crowd of tourists armed with the tickets they could now just buy in a travel agency without needing government permission, heading off to hang out on the beach, lie on the sand and subject their pallid winter bodies to the ultraviolet rays of the sun. There was electricity in the air. Rad sat stubbornly aloof from all that and read his book, although the light was poor.

The book he was reading was the 1990 reprint of Bunin's *Cursed Days*, typeset in the old, prerevolutionary orthography. A long time ago he had borrowed and read Dron's copy, but when he was packing he had looked through Serge's books at the dacha for something to read. He had pulled out one book after another, before stumbling upon this. He had weighed it in his hand, although it was as light as a feather, and decided this was the one.

'When you become utterly despondent at the sheer hopelessness, you catch yourself taking comfort in the redemptive thought that there will, nevertheless, come a time of reckoning and universal human anathematizing of these present days. You cannot exist without that hope. That is so, but what can you believe in now, when such an unutterably terrible truth about human beings has been revealed?' Rad read. He was surprised that he should have chosen this of all books to read on the plane. The days it was describing were quite unlike life in the present, but there was something in the text, or in himself, that made him find it as engrossing as a thriller. He gulped it down as if he had been parched with thirst and finally found water to quench it.

When boarding was announced, before joining the queue zigzagging in front of the entrance to the tunnel-like corridor, Rad pulled the peak of his hat right down to his nose and scrutinised those already in it from a distance. Of course, it seemed ridiculous to imagine that his crooks might have chosen to fly to the same destination and on the same plane as he had, but just because it seemed ridiculous was no guarantee that it would not happen. His former clients liked taking holidays and, from what they said, he had gathered they had done the rounds of the world's main holiday destinations, with the possible exception of Antarctica.

He saw no sign of former clients, however. A rowdy group of men in leather, with close-cropped heads on stocky, log-like necks, were elbowing people aside, in a great hurry to board first, but if they were gangsters, they were not his gangsters. There was no one he recognised among the couples, or among the families flying with children, although the faces of some of the fathers were well up to the standard of the thugs horsing their way through the boarding gate.

In the plane he found his was an aisle seat, which was what Rad preferred. He felt a prickle of satisfaction. It seemed like a good omen. That was idiotic, and yet it felt entirely real.

He sat down, fastened his seat belt, and plunged back into his book, emerging from it only when they were already airborne. The plane gained altitude and the stewards and stewardesses wheeled the drinks trolley along the aisle. They were dispensing J7 orange and apple juice, Moldovan red and dry white wine, and there seemed to be no demand for the bottled water.

'Mineral water,' he said, when the trolley paused by his seat. He was conscious that, with the variety of drinks on offer, asking for water must have struck the flight attendants as odd, especially for a man of his years. They were, however, inscrutable and it was the passenger sitting in front of him who reacted. Rad had been fitting his bag into the overhead locker at the same time as him, and had immediately noticed the man. Not only was he massive, there was something different about his face. It bore the expression of one who views the world with overweening contempt, as if he had looked under its skirt and found something thoroughly unsightly. It was a knowing expression. Rad was already sitting reading when he heard this individual exclaim, 'Watch it, will you! Nothing else is to go in there.' He made this announcement to the newcomer who would be sitting next to Rad, forbidding him to put his bag alongside his own.

'What are you on about?' the new arrival demanded indignantly. 'There's space in there. A bit tight, but it always is.' 'A bit tight is not good enough,' the big man said icily. 'I've got a laptop in there and it's the reason I'm on this flight. Do you think I'm going to let you squash it?'

Now, when Rad asked for mineral water, the big man turned round to stare at him like a perplexed entomologist, as if he were an insect which, instead of having six legs, was getting by with four, or perhaps even two. For himself he ordered wine and, in addition to the one free glass allowed, bought a bottle of red, French, no less, and on top of that a bottle of Cuban rum.

The flight attendants had moved on to the next row of seats, but the big man in front was still staring back at Rad. Eventually, Rad had had enough of it.

'Something bothering you?' he asked, taking a gulp of water from his plastic cup.

Inevitably, he was wondering whether this individual, whom he did not recognise but who seemed to know him, might have some connection with his former clients.

'I don't like people who don't drink,' he grunted.

'As is your right,' Rad said.

'You got a detox ampoule stitched in you?' the big man asked.

'Could be.' Rad felt no inclination to start a conversation.

He had probably chosen mineral water instinctively, feeling he ought to be completely clear-headed when he met Dron. He had a ten-hour flight ahead of him, but had no plans to open his heart to anyone, let alone someone taking an unexplained interest in him.

'You don't look the type,' was his fellow passenger's verdict after he had considered the matter.

This time Rad did not reply.

They sat for a while longer, eyeing each other in provocative silence, until what seemed like a shadow of weariness passed over the face of the big man and he turned away.

The exchange had left Rad with an unpleasant feeling. It was highly improbable the man knew who he was. In fact, if he had he would have been talking to him very differently, and yet something left him feeling jittery. Rad read his book. He ate the lunch served on a plastic tray with plastic dishes. This was an entirely passable piece of pork, with fancy pasta swimming in tomato sauce, but still he had a sinking feeling in his stomach.

When the big man had finished his meal, he got up and, swaying, headed for the toilet. He had finished the wine and was half way through the bottle of rum: his face and neck were brick red.

When he got back, the first thing he did, before sitting down, was to flip open the luggage locker, take out his bag and check the laptop was still there. After that, he put it back and squeezed his large body back into his seat.

The *Cursed Days* did not last forever, coming to an end about half an hour after the meal. Rad needed an alternative way to kill time. He regretfully slipped the book into the net pocket of the seat in front of him and stood up to follow the example of his fellow passenger. Evidently sliding the book into the net pocket caused the occupant of the seat in front some modicum of discomfort. When Rad stood up, the big man again turned round and glowered at him appraisingly with a look of righteous indignation.

'Watch it, will you!' he muttered irascibly. 'My nerves are on edge as it is. Just mind they don't snap!'

'Sorry,' Rad apologised, entirely sincerely.

The big man stared at him, as if weighing this response. He evidently decided that the unreserved nature of the apology was appropriate to the gravity of the offence against him.

'I don't trust non-drinkers,' he announced and turned back noisily to his initial position.

When Rad returned, he found a coloured customs declaration awaiting him. All around people, including those in his row, had armed themselves with ballpoint pens and were already doing battle with their English, printing letters in Latin script in the form's many boxes. As he was about to resume his seat, Rad noticed he was himself tempted to open the luggage locker and check his bag was still there. For a moment he had some sympathy with the agitation of the passenger in front of him who, when he glanced down, he noticed, was leafing with his massive fingers through his passport, looking for something. The pages were completely covered in overlapping multi-coloured entry and exit visa stamps.

* * *

As the wheels of the aircraft touched down safely on the concrete runway, the Russian passengers gave the captain a round of applause. The plane was still trundling towards the terminal building when everybody started unfastening their safety belts, standing up, opening the overhead lockers, pulling out bags and packing away their warm Moscow clothing in plastic shopping bags in readiness to disembark. The flight attendants rushed up and down the aisle insisting everyone must remain seated until the aircraft had come to a complete standstill. Their efforts were futile. The flight was over. The Russian passengers wanted out.

* * *

It was cool in the terminal, not too warm for a jacket, and the airport was the identical twin of hundreds of other airports. As Rad passed through passport control and customs, he all but forgot he had just been transported from the 56th parallel some 42 degrees closer to the equator. This only hit him when, wheeling his suitcase with his hand luggage perched on top, he stepped through automatic glass doors to the roadway outside. The air was so hot and humid it seemed to force him back inside, as if it was some unfamiliar, noticeably denser element. It was as if the barber had applied a hot damp compress to his face as a preliminary to shaving off a week's growth of beard. Rad halted, feeling a need to acclimatise to this new element before proceeding.

At just this moment his mobile phone rang, making him jump. He fumbled in his jacket pocket frantically, as if his destiny hinged on how quickly he retrieved it. Nevertheless, before pressing OK he glanced at the screen. It was not a Moscow caller and completely unfamiliar, evidently a wrong number.

'Hi there,' a voice greeted him. 'Everything okay?'

It was a man's voice, but no more familiar than the number. From the echo on the line Rad deduced this was a long-distance call bouncing off a satellite.

'I'm sorry,' Rad said, 'who are you calling? I think you must have a wrong number.'

There was a burst of laughter. The echo jumbled the signal from space and made it sound like coughing.

'I am calling you and nobody else!' the voice exclaimed. 'I gather you've landed!'

Rad realised this could only be Dron, and then immediately recognised his voice. They hadn't talked since Soviet times, but voices change little more than the epidermal ridges on a fingertip.

'Dron!' he exclaimed. 'This is great! Where are you?'

Rad had not been expecting to hear from him. Dron had written to say he was unable to meet him because he and his wife would be out in the sticks and only returning to Bangkok the day after he arrived. He had given the address of a hotel where a room had been booked for him, and Rad was mentally prepared to spend the day in a state of self-reliant weightlessness.

'Evidently in the same place as you,' Dron responded. 'As you've got your mobile switched on you're off the plane. Are you still at the airport?'

'Yes. I've just stepped outside. I'm by the exit.'

'Excellent.' Dron's cosmic voice resounded. 'Go back in and stay near the exit by the arrivals area.'

'Are you coming to meet me, then?' Rad asked.

'Sure am.'

'I thought you were out in the back of …'

'Change of plan,' Dron cut him off. 'Go back in and wait.'

It was only after some time that Rad noticed a woman who had stopped a few feet away was subjecting him to close scrutiny. He was awaiting Dron and his wife and had been paying no attention to anyone else, but her interest became so obvious that in the end he could not fail to notice it. She was the epitome of well groomed stylishness, wearing white slacks which stopped just short of her ankles, a long white blouse over them, and a knitted white hat with a broad brim at an angle. A smile played on her lips as she surveyed Rad, as if something was terribly amusing: either that his clothing was in outrageous disarray or that he was sporting a rainbow-hued mohican haircut. After a moment's anxiety, Rad regained full confidence that neither of these applied.

He looked away, but immediately looked back. She really did resemble Jenny. Not closely, perhaps, but there was a definite similarity with the expression in her eyes, the seriousness and undoubted intelligence. The mischief currently evident in them only made her expression the more serious and intelligent. She was older than Jenny, though, probably nearer his own age, and was certainly not Russian. An Englishwoman perhaps, or Dutch. Even, for all he knew, a Belgian?

The woman, meanwhile, was continuing to look at him and smile, but not in a way that suggested she found him ridiculous; more as if she knew him and thought he had a nerve not to recognise her. That, Rad suddenly concluded, was exactly what her smile was conveying.

'Nellie?' he asked hesitantly.

'I should think so too!' she responded, not in English or Dutch or Belgian but in purest Russian. 'He even remembers my name!'

How weird to have flown this far, to have landed in a completely exotic land, only for the first person he met to be not only a Russian, not only someone he knew, but someone he had known very well. Rad was hardly overjoyed. Irritated, more like. This was an acquaintance he could do without renewing, even in Russia, and most certainly not here when he was just about to meet Dron Tsekhovets.

'Well, well,' he said. 'It's been a long time.' He proffered the traditional cliché, not betraying irritation but not moving towards her either.

'Is that it?' Nellie ironised, also making no move. 'Is that all you can find to say after so many years?'

The smile, however, was still playing about her lips and, contradicting her words, she showed no sign of reproach. She seemed, instead, about to burst out laughing.

'Well, yes,' Rad mumbled. 'Delighted to see you, of course I am, only you'll have to excuse me, I'm waiting here for some friends.'

'Well, what do you know!' Nellie exclaimed. 'What an amazing coincidence! I'm waiting to meet someone too, in the very same place.'

Rad looked at her with a wild surmise, which rapidly solidified into certainty.

'What, are you married to Dron?' he asked.

'Well done! You finally got there!' Now Nellie did take a step in his direction, he took a step in hers, and she was the first to proffer her hand. It was rather broad, not petite, but her skin was amazingly soft, as if her sole occupation was pampering it. Shaking it took him back to that evening in the Conservatoire when he had sat, holding her hand in his. He did not remember her skin having been so soft back then.

'Why didn't Dron tell me in his emails that you were his wife?'

'Well, just because.' Nellie withdrew her hand. Her exultant smile faded a little now that she no longer knew something he did not, and Rad saw it replaced by that expression which had had the power back then to drive him wild: her awareness of herself as a chalice brimming with a priceless elixir. 'If you had known in advance, our little scene would have been much less piquant.'

'Yes, I must have been quite a sight,' Rad agreed, looking around. 'Where is he?'

Rad half expected to spot Dron nearby, splitting his sides at the spectacle he had arranged. Nellie read his mind.

'Oh, he's not here,' she said. 'There's someone else he has to see first. That's why we had to rush back. Someone is bringing him something. When it's handed over he'll be able to join us. We just have to wait here for now.'

'No problem.' Rad's diary was empty. 'Have you been married long?'

'Oh, a good one thousand years.' Nellie waved her hand and half-closed her eyes, as if she would have calculated how many years exactly, but the number was so vast that the task was beyond her. 'Although it was by no means immediately after you introduced us.'

Rad recalled how she had come to life at the Conservatoire the minute she started speaking to Dron, how skittish she had become, how her eyes had shone. They belonged to the same breed, and she had sniffed Dron out like a dog. Rad, on the other hand, was not in their class, as he had realised a considerable time later when their relations finally juddered to a halt.

'I never introduced you,' Rad protested.

'Oh yes you did,' Nellie said.

'What, did you slip him your phone number?'

'Would it matter?'

The audacity of this evasiveness simultaneously confirmed and denied his suspicions, but she was in any case absolutely right: it really did not matter how she and Dron subsequently met up in his absence. It was their own business, their private life. After a pause Nellie did, however, add,

'He looked me up at the Institute of Foreign Relations.'

And again, it really was none of his business whether that was what had happened or not.

'Do you have any children?' Rad asked. 'Dron didn't mention any.'

'No, we don't.' As always with childless women, her tone was defiant. 'And you?'

'A daughter,' Rad replied briefly. He too had little to boast about. Could he really say he had a daughter, when he had not seen her for almost two years? 'She's ten,' he added nevertheless.

'But am I right in thinking you no longer live together?' Nellie checked, instantly deducing the cause of his terseness.

'Correct,' Rad confirmed.

The thread sustaining their conversation had broken, and beads rattled and scattered over the floor. There was a pause. It was as if they had been counting off the beads of a rosary and suddenly had none left. They felt awkward, as if they had been baring themselves to each other, only to find that neither of them wanted that, and were now at a loss as to how to continue.

'Oh, where is he?' Nellie exclaimed, looking around.

'Dron?' Rad asked, as if she could have meant anyone else.

'Dron the Dread, the Bollockhead,' Nellie let slip.

He was taken aback, as if a cupboard door had swung open to reveal a skeleton. She had inadvertently given him a peep into the recesses of her relationship with Dron.

'That kind of language doesn't suit you,' Rad said.

It was very true. It seemed completely out of keeping with her appearance. The fresh, well groomed façade seemed to have been shaken by a tremor, its elegant lines distorted and now just a little vulgar.

'Oh, it wasn't meant,' Nellie said quickly. She laughed, once more the embodiment of fragrant elegance as if she had never said what Rad had heard. 'I can never resist a rhyme. They are so tempting.'

Rad decided to play along. 'I hope nobody has ever told you what your own name rhymes with,' he said archly.

Nellie's elegant appearance seemed almost able to transform vulgarity into wit, as if in a sufficiently expensive setting anything could be made to seem sophisticated. Rad recalled noting a similar phenomenon in the nonsense Jenny sometimes came out with, but could not recollect vulgarity in Nellie when, to his eyes, she had seemed little short of a reincarnation of Helen of Troy.

'Didn't you get names chanted at you when you were little?'

'Oh, yes. "Sad Rad is mad and bad".'

Nellie frowned, concentrating for a moment.

'That's fairly pathetic,' she remarked. 'Perhaps we can come up with something more original. Let's work on it. How about, "Rad the lad's a frightful cad"?'

Before Rad could respond, the man with the nose of a clown appeared out of nowhere, slapped him on the back, thrust a flat black bag into Nellie's hands, and gave him a bear hug. Rad did not even have time to get a proper look at him, only glimpsing Dron's hyperplasic nose which, however much the rest of him might have changed in the meantime, there was no mistaking.

'Rad, I'm glad to see you. Very, very glad, Rad!' Dron joshed, thumping him on the back.

'Hi, Dron, hello!' Rad thumped him reciprocally. 'What a joker, sending Nellie as your emissary!'

'Ah, caught you out, did I?' Dron exclaimed, taking a step backwards and glowing with self-satisfaction. 'And did you recognise my emissary?'

'I believe we had met in the distant past,' Rad parried.

'Indeed we did!' Nellie retorted.

'As the immortal Griboyedov wrote,' Rad said, '"*I thought to enter one room but found myself in quite another.*"'

'What do you mean by that?' Nellie protested. 'Weren't you glad to see me?'

'Yes, Rad, you'd better be careful how you fire off those literary allusions of yours,' Dron warned. 'They're heavy calibre, can do a lot of damage. Rad is a great expert on the classics.' His flattery, addressed to Nellie, was not without irony. 'Gosh, look! He's even been reading on the plane. I wonder what.' Dron deftly plucked the copy of *Cursed Days* from Rad's jacket pocket, glanced at the title and laughed. 'I don't believe it!' he said, handing the book back. 'In this day and age! Have you been reading that ever since you borrowed it back then?'

'Yes,' Rad replied, 'I'm still reading it.' He was recalling not only the book, but also how best to behave with Dron. 'Although this is not the copy I borrowed. I read that until it fell to pieces, although I've still got it at home. Sorry. I'll give it back when I have a chance.'

'Keep it,' Dron said, watching Rad put the Bunin back in his pocket. 'I'm not going to be re-reading it. Do you know when I first read *Cursed Days*? The Soviet Union was still intact, still monolithic. I must have been in ninth grade. My pa brought it home. It was one of those special editions for senior Soviet officials, to apprise themselves of the nature of the enemy. I remember the copies were individually numbered, and if you let one get into the wrong hands you could be expelled from the Party.'

'And I remember reading the whole of Nabokov in special editions,' Nellie contributed her mite.

'While I had no idea there even were any special editions,' Rad followed up with a deadpan expression, as if they were playing a game in which everybody had to say something.

'One-nil!' Nellie said appreciatively, clapping her hands as if they really were playing a game. 'One-nil to Rad, Dron.'

'Okay, Rad wins,' Dron announced, 'Prepare to be awarded a gold medal. Give me my bag back, will you?' he said, reaching out in Nellie's direction.

'I wasn't trying to hold on to it,' she said, passing it over.

For a moment the cupboard door swung open again and Rad glimpsed bleached bones.

'This bag keeps you in food and drink,' Dron retorted.

'You should add, "and keeps me in style".'

'And keeps you in considerable style,' Dron remarked.

The flat black bag Nellie had passed over seemed familiar. Rad had recently seen it, or something very like it, in someone else's possession.

'Well,' Rad said, trying to banish the untoward skeleton from his mind, 'shall we move?'

'We shall,' Dron confirmed, but stayed where he was, looked around, then beckoned someone over.

Rad looked to see who.

Displaying a set of sugar-white teeth in a broad smile, a round-faced Thai man of medium height with the coffee-coloured skin of someone of mixed race approached them, his short-sleeved blue shirt tucked into black trousers. When he saw Rad had turned to him, he placed his palms together and raised them to chest height in greeting, bowing as he walked. When he reached their group he repeated the gesture and bowed again, before holding out his right hand to be shaken.

'Tony,' Dron introduced him. 'Our Thai friend.'

'To-nee,' the Thai man repeated melodiously. 'How do you do?'

'Rad. How do you do?' Rad said in English, shaking the hand and looking in some puzzlement at Dron. Tony hardly seemed a Thai name.

Nellie understood his perplexity. 'That's quite normal for Thai people,' she told him. 'They use several names. When they are babies their real name is known only to their parents, so that evil spirits can't harm them.'

'How about that?' Dron commented.

The skeleton seemed so safely back in its cupboard that Rad was left wondering whether he had imagined it.

Tony, not understanding their Russian, looked from one to the other, his teeth still sparkling in a smile.

'How come he has such unnaturally white teeth?' Rad was wondering, but dismissed his interest as idle curiosity.

Nevertheless, as Tony's sleek black Toyota bore them on its Morocco leather seats along the expressway towards the city, it became clear that such dazzling teeth were not a genetic characteristic of Thai people. 'Laser tooth-whitening!' yelled the English-language hoardings lining the route, displaying smiling men and women with blindingly white teeth. Evidently teeth burnished to this extraordinary degree were a sign of prosperity, much as close-cropped hair now was for men in Russia.

'Is our driver a businessman?' Rad asked, leaning over to Dron in the front passenger seat and circumlocuitously avoiding mention of Tony by name.

Dron turned round to him with a grin.

'It's all show,' he said. 'There is no way he can really afford a car like this, or an apartment like the one he lives in. He goes to extremes to lead girls up the garden path. He's a complete sexual predator!'

'Don't speak about him like that,' Nellie reprimanded Dron from her seat in the back with Rad. 'You're being unfair. You don't know that.'

'Yes I do,' Dron replied with a chuckle. 'He's a sex fiend!'

'Well, in Thailand that doesn't seem to be regarded as such a terrible sin,' Nellie observed.

'Who is saying it is? No one.'

'So what does he do if he's not a businessman?' Rad interrupted their bickering. 'Where does he get the money to show off with?'

'He manages a fitness club in one of the hotels here,' Dron replied after a time. 'It's a top hotel, but he's only the manager. You would really think he was Mr Big but he makes around $12,000 a year. That's a lot for Thailand, of course, but you would think he was on $120,000 at least. He really turns their heads!'

'A fitness club manager,' Rad mused. 'He's a colleague.'

'Ah, yes!' Dron said. 'You wrote that you had some sports operation. A weight training gym, was it?'

'Exactly,' Rad confirmed.

'Well, we have lots to talk about later,' Dron said, turning back to face the traffic. 'A colleague of yours,' he told Tony in English, jabbing a thumb back towards Rad. 'He owns a fitness club.'

'Oh!' Tony cried happily, taking his eyes off the road for a moment and looking round at Rad. 'I will be so glad to share experiences with you.'

'You probably wouldn't enjoy sharing the experiences I've had,' Rad thought to himself, but aloud he said, 'It will be my pleasure.'

'A colleague! A colleague. That is so cool!' Tony exclaimed again, banging his hands on the steering wheel. There was something child-like about his emotion, at least in Rad's eyes.

'Dron and I are not brave enough to drive in countries like Thailand.' Nellie had detected Rad's lack of enthusiasm for sharing his experiences, but evidently also felt some explanation was needed for the appearance of Tony. 'As a rule when we go anywhere we rent a car, but in Thailand the traffic drives on the left. Have you noticed? And you never know how long you might have to wait for a taxi. It can be as long as in Moscow at the airport.'

Rad ignored what she had to say about taxis and Sheremetievo, and in any case had no objection at all to being driven by Tony.

'They drive on the left?' he asked.

For some reason he had not noticed. He had spotted that the steering wheel was on the right, but then Jenny's Suzuki in Moscow had been right-hand drive.

'Had you not noticed them driving on the left?' Dron asked, again half-turning to him.

'I see it now,' Rad said.

He had seen it before but not taken it in. The laser-whitening advertisements and road signs had been flying by like a mirror image of what he was used to, and oncoming cars rushed past on the right.

'Well, *mon cher*, we're not going make much of a spy out of you,' Dron opined.

'Just as well I have no ambitions along those lines, then,' Rad replied.

'What do you mean, you haven't?' Dron exclaimed, sounding dismayed.

'What gave you the idea I might?'

'Information received.'

His informant had evidently passed on his conversation with Serge when the two of them were clearing snow in the courtyard on the second day of the New Year. He had little doubt Dron's source must have been Jenny, who would have heard about it from Polina. Rad squirmed, as if he had accidentally taken a swig of vinegar. He felt as vulnerable in the presence of Dron and Nellie, as naked, as a newborn infant.

'Well, you can't believe everything informants tell you,' he ventured.

'We'll have to talk about this some other time,' Dron cut him off, and Rad found himself once more looking at the back of his neatly cropped head.

Nellie, having allowed Dron to take over the conversation, now sat looking silently out the window and made no attempt to revive it. A long succession of close-set, one- and two-storey concrete buildings with flat roofs, with wide, low windows set into featureless walls and deep terraces on the first floor, were strung along the roadside. There seemed to be a complete jumble of industrial and residential premises, shops and garages all mixed in together. Fruit sellers sat at bright, colourful stalls parked obliquely to the pavement; vendors of street food stood by two-wheeled carts with overloaded metal trays. Towards their roofs the concrete of the buildings seemed covered in oil stains, but these were evidently a kind of black mould. Scoring out the view of the buildings, endless trailing black cables and wires snaked above the roadside from one pillar to the next. Now and again a gap appeared between the buildings, and there an undeveloped green space was luxuriant with undergrowth and home to isolated, spreading deciduous trees. There were palm trees too, with felted trunks, but these seemed so natural they blended into the landscape.

'Is it cold in Russia now?' Tony suddenly enquired.

Rad stopped gazing at the passing scenery and looked at Tony, sensing from the tone of voice, clearly intended to be heard in the back of the car, that the question was addressed to him. Tony, half-turned to the rear, was driving with one eye on the road while simultaneously trying to bring Rad into the field of vision of the other.

'Ten degrees below zero,' Rad said.

'Ten degrees below zero?' Tony echoed. He glanced at his dashboard and again half turned to Rad. 'It is seventeen degrees above zero in my car now and not at all warm. Twenty-seven degrees colder! That must be terrible.'

Dron, Nellie, and Rad all laughed.

'No, that is not terrible cold,' Rad said.

'Not terrible? Then what cold in Russia is terrible?'

'When the air is thirty, or lower than thirty degrees below zero. In some places it even goes lower than forty degrees.'

'Oh!' Tony said, turning his back on Rad so abruptly it seemed as if the information had upset him. 'Lower than forty! That is unbelievable.'

'Do you understand him all right?' Nellie, still laughing, asked as she leaned towards Rad.

Tony's singsong English really was a problem. Rad had to strain to catch every word, and even to repeat them to himself to get the meaning. It taxed his brain, but he replied,

'No, it's fine. I understand everything, even what is unsaid.'

He was not too bothered about understanding everything in the conversation. What mattered much more was for him and Dron to understand each other.

Nellie's silvery laughter had been fading but now pealed out again.

'Even what is unsaid?' she queried. 'I don't think so. Do you know why he is asking you about the weather?'

'I expect he is just curious,' Rad replied rather unimaginatively.

'Of course he is, extremely curious,' she laughed. 'You're not going to guess in a hundred years why he asked.'

'He is trying to marry off his sister,' Dron interjected, turning to them. 'He has four, and suitable husbands had been found for all of them, but one has recently been widowed. Tony has his eye on a certain Swiss gentleman, but will need to get him back to Thailand. You, on the other hand, are already here.'

'He's determined to marry her to a foreigner,' Nellie said, quickly retaking the initiative. 'All the others have foreign husbands and are very nicely off, thank you. This fourth lady was married to a Thai, and see what that has led to.'

'She's absolutely delightful, twenty-six and a real beauty. You would fall for her instantly.' Dron was not going to let Nellie muscle in. He wanted to tell this story himself. 'Such an expressive face, wonderful cheekbones, lips. A real corker. We just met her when we were upcountry. Tony took us to meet his parents. She's a village schoolteacher. Perfect. How about it?'

'Sounds perfect,' Rad conceded, 'but in Russia we have thirty degrees of frost in the winter.'

'So what? She could get used to that. The top priority is for her to marry a foreigner.'

'No, Dron, thirty degrees of frost is a stumbling block,' Nellie said, although it was unclear whether she believed that or was just being awkward.

'And unfortunately, this prospective bridegroom is insolvent,' Rad continued.

'Yes. That really is a stumbling block,' Dron agreed. He was silent for a moment and then, without saying any more, turned his back on them.

'Incidentally, we are now in Bangkok,' Nellie said, looking past Rad's shoulder.

He turned to look in the same direction and found that the one- and two-storey buildings with occasional green spaces had all but disappeared. Their almost-limousine was speeding along a road in the city. These were still only the outskirts, and the spacious muti-lane highway was divided down the centre by a strip of green lawn; the pavements were wide and spacious and beyond them, separated off by concrete and lattice-like metal fences, were villas which gleamed as white as Tony's teeth and were set among green lawns; but already, immediately beside them, like a multi-tiered concrete jungle, thirty- and forty-storey skyscrapers were reaching skywards, jostling each other, the militant creations of a Southeast Asia rushing to sign up to Western-style civilization.

'Impressive,' Rad said, indicating these multiple testimonies to Babylonian aspirations.

'Isn't it,' Nellie agreed.

'This is a magnificent city,' Rad told Tony.

Tony responded instantly. He threw up his hands and banged them on the steering wheel.

'It is a terrible city! Like a giant squid! Traffic jams, you cannot get anywhere. Pollution! And so expensive!'

Dron, sitting next to him, hooted with laughter and exclaimed,

'Tony, Tony, you are a revolutionary! The Red Brigades! Death to Capitalism! War to the Palaces! Or at the very least, you are a Green.'

Tony was suddenly silent. He clearly did not care to be likened to a revolutionary, or even a Green.

'Am I wrong? Is it not true? I am right! It is so! I have a right to my opinion!' he responded, taking his eyes off the road and glancing at Dron.

'Actually,' Dron said in Russian to Rad and Nellie, 'it is not expensive at all. In fact, it is very cheap. Of course, it depends on how much income you have.'

'You can say that again,' Rad concurred.

The animation disappeared from Dron's face.

'Yes, well, we'll have to talk about that,' he commented after a moment, and Rad once more found himself faced with the back of his close-cropped head.

The streets meanwhile were becoming narrower and narrower, as were the pavements. The skyscrapers seemed to be squeezing the highway, trying to reduce it to a thread. Soon they were stuck in traffic at the intersections. Numerous mopeds were weaving forward through the jams closer to the crossroads. Girls sat demurely side-saddle on them, like aristocratic ladies on horseback in an eighteenth-century painting.

'Look! Why do they do that?' Rad asked. 'Isn't it dangerous?'

Tony hesitated, before observing, 'Thai girls are expected to behave modestly in public.'

Rad could see only the back of his neck, but thought it had flushed crimson.

'Don't ask improper questions,' Nellie said in Russian, 'or address them to me and Dron.'

'Absolutely,' Dron said, without turning round to them. 'Nellie and I are only too happy to answer improper questions, but our friend,' he avoided saying Tony's name, 'may be a sex fiend but he is oriental, a Buddhist.'

Then, slowing down, Tony spun the wheel, the Toyota swung into a courtyard, glided under a shady awning, and stopped by the glass doors of a back entrance.

'Welcome to Bangkok!' Dron said, turning to Rad. 'Your hotel.'

'My hotel?' Rad asked in surprise. 'Where are you staying?'

'We have a different one,' Nellie said.

'Oh.' Rad had assumed they would all be staying in the same place.

Dron reassured him. 'We're not far away. Thirty metres down the street, maybe only twenty-five.'

He opened the door on his side and put out his foot, as if signalling to the others to follow his example and get out.

Inside, behind the glass doors, a 'boy', a Thai man of twenty-six or twenty-seven, emerged from the darkness of the hotel lobby and, in a green uniform trimmed with gold braid and brass buttons, awaited them. As they opened the doors of the Toyota, he threw open the hotel door and stepped out on to the porch to welcome his guests.

CHAPTER SIX

This was his apartment. He had once lived in it. What had forced him to leave it, and even rent it out? Rad had no idea, but now it was time for him to come back and here he was. He walked through the apartment from the front door into the interior, and behind him, grumbling incessantly, followed its current occupant. 'Wot you doin' 'ere? Wot you want? We was gettin' along fine till you showed up,' the current tenant was mumbling.

He was the dishevelled individual who had charged out with a pitchfork and impaled the dog attacking Rad. He was wearing the same shabby checked shirt open to the navel as Rad had seen him in then, with the body hair sprouting in the V-neck of his white vest as luxuriant as that on his head. He clearly felt the apartment belonged to him, he was used to living in it, and not only found Rad's appearance unwelcome but seemed ready to challenge his right to the place.

The apartment was in a terrible state. The wallpaper was filthy and coming apart at the joins, the paint flaking off the ceiling, the parquet scuffed. The furniture was old, with peeling veneer, and there were stinking piles of rags everywhere, which evidently served this character, and whoever was sharing the place with him, as clothing.

Rad went into the furthest room, which had been his favourite. He had loved its spaciousness, its two large windows, and for the way the light filled it as a fresh breeze fills a well set sail. It was in an even worse condition than the rest of the apartment: the floorboards were rotten, the wallpaper torn off, and one window was crudely boarded up. The light from the remaining window was insufficient, and three-quarters of the room was immersed in a depressing twilight. The only furniture was a huge sprung mattress, on blocks of wood instead of a base. The floor around it was littered with rubbish: sunflower seed husks, scraps of wrapping paper, beer bottle caps, bits of string and pieces of stale food, and all of it covered in accumulations of dust and dirt. It was a dive, not a room.

'Could you not at least have swept the floor?' Rad asked the fellow as he contemplated this rubbish tip.

'No broom, is there!' the man replied.

'Could you not have used a brush?' Rad said, distinctly remembering that there was a brush.

'How the fuck am I supposed to know where the brush stays?' he dismissed that suggestion.

The brush was actually not fuck knows where but there, in plain sight, in the corner.

Rad took it and began sweeping the detritus into a heap. He could not bear the sight of these Augean stables, this dump. The geezer stood watching him brushing and muttered, 'Well, fuck knows where that came from, that brush of yours. It wasn't there. You knew where to look, that's why you found. it.'

Rad suddenly sensed someone else in the room. He stopped sweeping and looked towards the door. There stood Serge. His former fellow student was wearing a long, beautifully tailored cashmere coat. It was unbuttoned to reveal a white silk scarf flowing down in two streams to his knees.

'Carry on, carry on!' he instructed Rad. 'We need all this cleaned up. It's a disgrace, a complete pigsty.'

Rad did not rise to the bait and was in no hurry to resume his task. He stood there, looking at Serge and wondering what he was doing here. What made him think he could address Rad in such a lordly fashion in his own apartment?

'I said, carry on!' he ordered Rad testily. He beckoned the fellow in the checked shirt. 'And you, come here. I need a word with you.'

The fellow rushed to him obsequiously, slouched like an ape, his legs splayed and flailing his arms about. His face lit up with joy at the prospect of being able to serve Serge and his voice was an unctuous gurgle.

As Rad watched, he suddenly realised the apartment had not belonged to him for a long time, and that now the owner was Serge. That was why the dishevelled lout had been so offhand and ready to dispute ownership. Rad now had no such rights, but how had that come about?

They were already leaving the room, and Rad ran after them to tell them this was really his apartment. He, nobody else, was the owner, but the door closed behind them before he reached it and now there was no door, only bare wall. He was immured in what had been his favourite room and was now a pigsty. He was a prisoner, a Hercules doomed never to escape from the Augean stables. He could only go back to his labours and hope for some miraculous release.

In the distance he heard a ringing which signalled that release. Someone was ringing the doorbell and would release him from this incarceration and give back all that had been taken from him.

Rad woke up. He was asleep in a chair, with his arms folded and his head to one side. This had given him an extremely stiff neck. Raising his head, he groaned with pain.

The bell which had been assailing his eardrums stopped just as Rad realised it was the ringing of the phone on his bedside table.

He leapt out of his chair and rushed over.

'Are you ready?' he heard Nellie ask.

'What for?' Rad asked muggily, still half asleep and feeling he had just broken the wall down with his head and opened the door to answer the doorbell.

'For going out into the city, of course,' Nellie retorted.

Rad finally remembered where he was and what had happened. He was in Bangkok, in a hotel called Liberty Place, which was not altogether a hotel but a place where rooms were let for fairly long periods. A 'serviced apartment.' He was in his room and, while waiting for Dron and Nellie, he had fallen asleep. They had helped him fill out the form at reception, seen him to his room, given him an hour to settle in, and left him. Rad had unpacked his suitcase, shaved, taken a shower and changed into summer clothes, which took just over half an hour. Ready to meet them, he had sat down in the chair, folded his arms and surveyed the room. It was perfectly passable: a bed, bedside table, two chairs, a round table next to an armchair, and a mirror on the wall. Not five-star by any means, but it had air conditioning, and a fridge. Rad remembered thinking he might have time to take a stroll down the street before meeting up with Dron and Nellie, but had evidently not made it out of the armchair. Traversing forty-two degrees of latitude was clearly more demanding than taking the train from Moscow to St Petersburg.

'Where are you?' he asked, trying to remember where they had arranged to meet.

'Downstairs in the lobby, in your hotel, by reception, as agreed,' Nellie remarked.

'On my way,' he reported.

His room was on the fourth floor, so it would have been no disgrace to call the lift, but Rad decided to walk down. The outside of the stairs was the hotel's steel framework, and through openings he could see its inner courtyard to which, an hour ago, Tony's Toyota had brought them. A neighbouring plot on the far side of a concrete wall was wasteland piled with builder's rubble. In the middle of it an air compressor was roaring, and workers in orange overalls were scurrying around in the debris carrying snake-like black air ducts or breaking up slabs of concrete with pneumatic drills. They had evidently demolished one structure and were in the process of clearing the site to build a new one.

Nellie was sitting on a sumptuous L-shaped sofa in the lobby, alone. She was wearing the same knitted hat and white slacks, but had changed into a new blouse, also white, which, like the last one, fell freely to her hips. She remained the epitome of fresh, well-groomed prosperity. On a large round table in front of her, a plump, colour-printed newspaper lay open. Nellie was holding up the left-hand page. As he came towards the table, Rad read the title: *The Bangkok Post*. It was in English.

'Hello,' he said, stopping beside the table. 'Interesting reading?'

'Ah!' Nellie responded, quickly closing the paper. 'It's much like any other paper. There has to be somewhere to put all the advertising, and also to give the likes of us some idea about life in Thailand. There's been a murder, a body has been found, a suspect detained. Even that sort of thing goes on in Bangkok.'

'As everywhere else,' Rad commented.

'No, it's fairly unusual here,' Nellie replied seriously. 'Every time it's news: not like in Moscow.'

'How would you know what it's like in Moscow?' Rad felt obliged to defend his hometown.

'We follow what's happening, closely, and far from dispassionately.' Nellie rose from the sofa and, edging past the table, came towards him. 'Prepared to do your best to do your duty and defend the Motherland?'

'As a Young Pioneer of the Soviet Union,' Rad vowed, giving a response incomprehensible to anyone who had never worn the red neckerchief. 'But where's Dron? Is he outside?'

'You and I are on our own,' Nellie said. 'Dron has unforeseen matters to attend to.'

'What?' Rad was unable to hide his disappointment. He had been hoping to talk everything through with Dron without delay. 'Was it really that urgent?'

'How would I know?' Nellie raised and lowered her eyebrows. Rad remembered this way of feigning bafflement when faced with a question she would have preferred to avoid.

'But he will be joining us?' Rad asked hopefully.

'My company not enough for you?'

Rad had never been good at lying.

Nellie touched him on shoulder, propelling him towards the door.

'Come and enjoy a stroll with his deputy. Don't worry, big brother won't give up on you that easily. You're more likely to give up on him.'

That prospect was not to Rad's liking.

'Why would that be?' he queried.

'Oh, for heaven's sake!' Nellie exclaimed. 'Just because. Why because? Because because.'

Rad realised he was not going to get a coherent answer and had no choice but to accept whatever she proposed.

'Fine,' he said, 'let's go,' moving towards the door. He opened it for Nellie. 'Where to?'

Nellie said, as she passed him, 'You and Dron can go to Patpong later, without me.'

'Where's Patpong?' he asked, releasing the door and stepping out on to the porch behind her.

'The red light district, a place you can rent prostitutes.'

Rad had no answer to that. He was struggling to read this new, unfamiliar Nellie. Was she joking? Was she deadly serious? It was one thing to look innocent while calling her husband a bollockhead, but something else to talk insouciantly about despatching him to the fleshpots.

'Is that an obligatory part of the itinerary?' he eventually responded, in what he hoped was a suitably neutral fashion.

'No, only if you fancy it,' Nellie replied.

'Right. Well, thank you,' Rad said. 'I'll bear it in mind.'

They walked along a narrow street with a narrow little pavement and a narrow roadway that resembled a firebreak in a forest, only here the edge of the forest was high concrete walls with houses behind them. Overhead the black electric cables and wires snaked from pole to pole. Transformer stations were set in the middle of the pavement, obliging the two of them to step into the road periodically. Manhole covers wobbled under their feet. These were rectangular and concrete, with a circular opening at one end and a metal ring inserted for lifting them. Occasional cars passed, motorbikes puttered by with women sitting side-saddle on the pillion, and a three-wheeled covered scooter chugged along with a bench seat behind the driver on which an elderly European couple were sitting. The wife had a plump Siamese tomcat on her knee, and stroked it with knobbly, arthritic fingers. Near the houses, tailors were seated at hand- and foot-operated black and gold sewing machines which must have been a century old. Some were stitching away, while others were dozing as they waited for customers. It was so hot that under his clothes Rad's body was instantly enveloped in a sticky film of sweat. The humidity was potentiated by a smell in the windless air compounded of stagnant water in the sewers, rotting fruit and exhaust fumes.

'That's where we live,' Nellie said, pointing at a building they were passing. It had an awning the length of the façade and three doors giving on to the street: one for Coffee Max, one for Admiral Suites, and one for a 24-hour convenience store. The one bearing the legend 'Admiral Suites' was the least conspicuous. 'For People In The Know', it seemed to say.

'A "serviced apartment"?' Rad asked.

'A "serviced apartment",' Nellie confirmed.

'It's a good location. A café to the left and a convenience store to the right, open round the clock.'

'Yes, that's why we stay here,' Nellie said. 'It's a pity we couldn't get you a room. It's high season and incredibly difficult to rent a room just now. Half the population of the West spends the winter here. They stay two months or three, until February when the weather becomes unbelievably hot.'

'Half the West?' Rad queried.

'Well, the half of the West who can afford it,' Nellie went on. 'It's a Buddhist country, the people are friendly, the service is excellent, and everything is cheap. You'll see, everything is just incredibly cheap.'

Rad said nothing. If you've no meat in your soup, he thought, a small pearl might as well be the size of an ostrich egg.

'So, where are we going?' he asked.

'You and I are going to the Grand Palace,' Nellie told him, as if divulging a state secret. 'Do you want to know why it's called that?'

'Because it's something like the Kremlin for Russia?'

'Give or take,' Nellie said. 'Only the royal residence is elsewhere. This is just a source of revenue now. The tourists flock to it.'

'Like us.'

'Like us.'

'Excellent,' Rad said. 'No objections.'

'Of course you have no objections,' Nellie remarked, giving him a carnivorous smile. 'What choice do you have? I can take you anywhere I like.'

'Oh, you be a sly one,' Rad responded.

'You've only just noticed?'

Rad laughed.

'*Alas, before, my dear, my life was one of ease …*'

Nellie said nothing for a time, and when she did speak there was no hint of cut and thrust.

'What would you prefer?' she asked. 'We can take a taxi directly to the palace. Alternatively, we can walk to the metro, ride it for a few stations and then take a tuk-tuk. We don't want to take a tuk-tuk from here, it's too far. They're really only suitable for short trips.'

'What's a tuk-tuk?' Rad asked naively.

'Oh, of course, you don't know.' Nellie looked up and down the street. 'There's one.' She pointed at one of the converted scooters he had already noticed. It had its nose in to the curb and the driver was resting on his elbows in the passenger seat, with his feet on the back of the driver's seat. 'It's another kind of taxi, only without a meter. "Tuk-tuk" is really what they're called.'

'Let's take the metro, and then go by tuk-tuk,' Rad said. 'I'll see something of the city. In a taxi you don't know where you are or what's around you.'

'Good choice,' Nellie said approvingly. 'Until you've walked a city's streets you haven't seen it.'

While they were talking, they had passed the grandiose front drive of the Imperial Queen's Park Hotel, which rose skywards like a sheer cliff of sugared concrete in a sea of glittering glass. They turned into an alley as twisted as a crankshaft, walked past the back of the hotel, past a vast motorcycle park, and came out on to a wide street reverberating with the roar of traffic, in the middle of which a huge concrete trough was supported on great concrete legs.

'There's your metro,' Nellie said pointing to the trough. 'Although that's not what they call it here.'

'The subway?' Rad suggested, showing how cosmopolitan he was.

Nellie smiled.

'You're never going to guess.'

'The tube?' Rad recollected the name of the London underground.

'Just give up now, you're not going to guess. They call it the skytrain.'

'Well,' Rad conceded, 'as it's not on or under the ground but above it, skytrain is logical. Although metro would be more familiar.'

'Well, just call it the metro,' Nellie conceded.

The road they were walking along now was flooded not only with the lacquered bodywork of roaring cars and motorbikes, but was also very full of people. Carts with street food were parked in the middle of the pavement, their owners smiling broadly and gesturing invitingly. 'Hello-o. Nice food. Please!' Mixed in among the shops selling all manner of goods, their commercial jaws open the full width of their shopfronts, were massage parlours, tucked away and modestly peeping out at the light of day from the cool darkness of their open doors. Near the doors sat muscular Thai girls, their legs stretched out in front of them. 'Hello-o. Thai massage. Please,' their soft, melodious voices called, as they followed the progress of anyone who came near their bare feet.

Topping it all were the dogs lying all over the pavement, on their own, in twos, in threes. They were all the same colour, an opalescent ginger, intelligent-looking, with elongated muzzles like huskeys, only not so large.

Their eyes were so sad and disconsolate that, if you met their gaze, you just wanted to look away immediately. From time to time, they would get up, move from one place to another, and lie back down. When they stood up Rad could see they were suffering from some kind of skin disease: in their groins, on their bellies and thighs the fur was coming away, revealing bare skin which evidently itched constantly. These bald areas had been scratched until they bled, and were covered in scabs and sores.

When Rad and Nellie had once more walked round a group of dogs lying on the pavement, he to the left and she to the right, and came together again, Nellie slipped her arm into his.

'Let's stick together through thick and thin,' she said in the words of a patriotic song of their youth in the Young Communist League, immediately adding, 'Yuk, why are you so sweaty?'

'You, on the other hand, seem to move in your own air-conditioned microclimate.'

'Naturally,' Nellie said. 'Ladies never sweat.'

Rad felt awkward, both because she had taken his arm and because his arm was sweaty. Mainly, however, because she had taken his arm. She had no need to be supported by him, and he knew his Helen of Troy well enough to realise she did nothing without a reason. It signified the transgressing of an invisible but real boundary that lay between him and her as Dron's wife. It signalled a far greater degree of intimacy than there should be between them. What had Nellie in mind? Rad had no wish for anything more than a relationship appropriate with Dron's wife – no sighing over the past, no special confiding, no pretence of an undying mutual attraction to each other despite the passing of the years. She was Dron's wife and that was that.

'You need to instruct me,' he said, 'on where we are going, what we are seeing, and what this street is called.'

'The street is Sukhumvit Road,' Nellie responded promptly, her tone that of an obedient pupil, the cleverest in the class, who has been called out to the blackboard to give answers none of the others know. 'It is a proper road. You can see how broad it is, and it has a lot of traffic. It is very long. All the other streets, like the one we live on, are only side streets or "sois", as the Thais call them. They don't have names of their own, only the name of the road they lead off, and a number.'

'So what is our soi called?' Rad asked.

'Sukhumvit 22. Remember that, just in case. If you get on my tits, I may abandon you and you will have to find your way back on your own.'

'How can you even think of abandoning me?' Rad feigned disbelief.

'Only if you get on my tits.'

'Well you'd better not give me any reason to.'

'It's not me you have to worry about,' Nellie said after some hesitation. Rad noted with some satisfaction that he appeared to have won this round, at least.

The succession of buildings came to an end, and on their right was the park. It was an expanse of green lawns, asphalt paths with benches, occasional spreading trees and, in the distance, the starkness of a pond outlined by a ribbon of concrete, its curves suggesting a question mark without its full stop. A group of people in identical sports clothing of a white top and black shorts were engaged by the pond in what looked like ballet in slow motion. In unison their legs were slowly raised and bent, and then their arms.

'What park is that?' Rad asked. 'Is it open to the public?'

'Absolutely,' Nellie said. 'Although it's called a royal park. Imperial Queen's Park.'

Rad suddenly found himself feeling envious of the people dancing by the pond that ballet of a kind he had never seen before. He felt he wanted to join them, to know the meaning of what they were performing, and be able to animate the movements with that knowledge.

'Do you know,' he said to Nellie, 'I don't feel I'm in a faraway foreign country. I feel this is where I belong.'

'Of course you do,' Nellie replied briskly. 'We are an imperial people. Citizens of the former Soviet Union. For us Asian faces are part of our family. The whole world is our home. I'm speaking from experience. It doesn't matter where you travel, everywhere feels like home.'

The entrance to the metro appeared in front of them in the form of a stairway with a rounded, stepped roof and open sides. It was much as in Moscow, except that instead of directing you down into the ground, the stairs summoned you skywards. As was only to be expected of stairs leading to a skytrain.

'Are you ready to fly?' Nellie asked, pausing before the steps.

'Not entirely.' Rad had remembered that he was penniless. Dron had undertaken to cover all expenses during his stay when he invited him, but so far the promise had not been fulfilled. He needed to find an ATM and withdraw at least some modest amount from his debit card.

'Would I be right in thinking that flying through the heavens is not free of charge?'

'Correct,' Nellie confirmed and, showing insight, added, 'You don't have any local currency yet? It's called the Thai Baht.'

'Yes, I need to find an ATM,' Rad said. 'Do you know if there's one near here?'

'Of course.' Nellie's eyebrows appeared to be registering annoyance. 'But I'm not going to take you to it.' She beckoned Rad to ascend the stairs. 'My orders are to treat you as a kept man.'

That was a bit strong. Rather like a gulp of vinegar. In fact, however, all Nellie's words implied was that Dron, having made a promise, intended to keep it.

'Let's go,' Rad said, starting up the stairs.

The station was cool and spacious inside. Small shops were selling a variety of goods. The staff serving at the windows of the station's office wore dark uniforms which made them all but invisible. They were only there to give change, and tickets had to be bought from vending machines.

'Here's some money,' Nellie said, giving Rad a handful of coins. 'Learn to cope with this foreign technology. The cost of a ticket depends on how many zones you are travelling. At present we are at Phrom Phong station and we need to get to National Stadium.'

Rad studied the skytrain map, poring over the names beside the buttons while Nellie stood watching him with amusement. It was only when he inserted coins in the slot, pushed the correct button and the machine issued them two cards with a magnetic strip that she exclaimed approvingly,

'Wow! You know how to do it. Every time I come here I have to be told all over again.'

The turnstile swallowed the ticket and returned it on the far side of a narrow gateway.

When Rad had successfully negotiated the turnstile, Nellie instructed him, in the voice of a Moscow station announcer, 'Retain your ticket until the end of the journey,' before adding in her normal voice, 'You have to go through a turnstile to get out at the far end. If you can't cancel your ticket, you can't get out.'

Rad put his card into the breast pocket of his shirt.

'That's harsh.'

'Not as harsh as Stalin was with the people of Russia.'

Rad ignored the remark. It did not seem intended as a joke, but to be talking in earnest about the Ivan the Terrible of the twentieth century in these surroundings would be weird.

'Where do we go now?' he asked.

There was another staircase, taking them even closer to the heavens.

Delineated by the grey hatching of the sleepers, twin tracks, extrapolating to a point, tended through the heavens to infinity. In the sky opposite the platform, blocking it from its zenith to the ground, there hovered the face of a woman. Her purple eyelashes were enormous, like two great fans, and had the owner of the eyelashes been real she could surely have used them as wings and taken flight.

'Impressed?' Nellie asked, seeing where he was looking. 'That's the Emporium. It's a department store, a shopping centre. That's their advertisement.'

Rad could see now that the purple eyelashes were suspended from a building, and that the woman's forehead bore the legend, 'Emporium'.

'I am impressed,' he said. 'I didn't notice it from the street, but up here on the platform it hits you right between the eyes.'

'Advertising is the driver of commerce,' Nellie said, looking as if she had just made that up.

Far away in the sky, a train appeared on their track. The people around began clustering at the edge of the platform, for some reason forming tight little groups. Rad was about to occupy one of the empty spaces but Nellie drew him towards a cluster.

'What do you think that pattern is trying to tell us?' she asked, pointing to a line painted at the edge of the platform.

The line ran the length of the platform, zigzagging at regular intervals to the edge and then back again.

Rad guessed:

'It's indicating where the carriage doors will be?'

'Well done.'

This thoughtfulness for the passengers' convenience impressed him.

'There's something so European about that!' he exclaimed.

'No, actually it's very Siamese,' Nellie said.

'Siamese?' he queried.

'Yes. Siam was the old name for Thailand.'

'So Siamese cats are actually Thai?' Rad asked, recalling the elderly couple in their tuk-tuk.

'So it would seem,' Nellie agreed.

'It's still very European,' he persisted, after a moment's reflection.

'You're right. The Thais are drawn to Europe,' Nellie said, leaving to Rad speculate whether she had really understood his point or simply decided not to argue.

The train glided into the platform with the soundlessness of a Siamese cat on the prowl. The carriage windows were covered in advertising, and not so much as a shadow could be made out within. The doors, when the train stopped, lined up to within a centimetre opposite the space designated by the zigzag. They opened and cool air wafted out on to the platform, which was open to the heat from outside the station.

Inside, the windows seemed perfectly transparent, like one-way mirrors. The advertising only shaded them slightly, serving as a filter to moderate the brightness outside. Half the people in the carriage were European, and Rad looked around, straining his ears to detect whether anyone was speaking Russian. He heard Thai, English, German, what was probably Swedish or Norwegian, but no Russian.

'Do you think there are many Russians in Bangkok now?' he asked.

'A drop in the ocean,' she replied.

'Just you and me, then?'

'Well, we're not the only ones, of course.' There Nellie stood, indistinguishable from all the European faces around her, the very epitome of Westernness. 'But Russians usually head for the resorts. There's an island called Phuket, for instance, or they go to Pattaya. But even there you don't find many. Thailand is a destination for Westerners.'

Bangkok floated by outside the windows, a jumble of residential houses with red tiled roofs, countless hotels monotonously scraping the sky, multistorey car parks which looked like a hybrid of shelving units and honeycomb, and riotous islands of vegetation in between. The train stopped at stations, its doors discreetly opened and closed, the carriage emptied and filled up again. At Siam, a station testifying that the country's old name was not forgotten, Nellie and Rad changed to a different line, and National Stadium was the next station.

After they had negotiated the turnstiles and were going down the stairs to the street, Nellie took out her purse and gave Rad a banknote.

'Take this, please, to pay the driver. As I am with a gentleman, I'm not sure Thai people would consider it decent for me to pay.'

'Like a gigolo,' Rad thought wryly, taking the proffered money. He looked at the denomination of this colourful currency. One thousand baht. That would translate into twenty-five dollars or 750 rubles.

'Do I get to negotiate with the driver too?'

'You do,' Nellie said. 'You should never go over 200 baht, but I think from here to the Grand Palace should be about 100. A hundred and fifty at the outside.'

There was a sea of tuk-tuks by the station, strung out along the edge of the pavement like a swarm of dragonflies.

However, despite such a glaring lack of employment, the driver first in line, as indeed the second, the fifth and sixth, turned down Rad's request to take them to the Grand Palace. Only the seventh or eighth proved willing to negotiate. He was a grim-faced, wiry Thai with hard-bitten, sallow features and, as they talked, his eyes seemed to be probing Rad, as if they were not just discussing a fare but a transaction which might fundamentally alter his standard of living. Following Nellie's instructions, Rad started by offering the driver 100 baht, expecting him to respond with a demand for twice that amount. To his surprise, however, the driver accepted the suggestion without haggling.

'And you said 150!' Rad gloated in Russian, helping Nellie into the tuk-tuk.

'You saw how many of them were there looking for work?' Nellie replied.

'Well, why were they all refusing to take us?'

Nellie considered this for a moment

'They were probably waiting for some match at the stadium to end,' she suggested, rather lamely, he thought.

'If they were all waiting for something, why did this driver take us?'

'He's probably impatient,' Nellie replied instantly. 'Or perhaps he felt sorry for us.'

The tuk-tuk darted like a dragonfly through the stream of cars, switching from one lane to another almost at right angles, brazening its way forward at the traffic lights between cumbersome, beetle-like Nissans, Toyotas, and Opels towards the zebra crossings. A stream of warm air blew pleasantly over its passengers and Rad's shirt stopped clinging to his body. It was a very particular pleasure, riding along like this on a puttering 250 cc motorised horse-and-buggy, exposed from top to toe to what felt like an ocean breeze. In the age before the motor car, this must have been how it felt to sit in a cab, clattering over city cobblestones, drawn by a one-horsepower engine with clopping hooves.

The Grand Palace was surrounded by a white, crenellated wall, a Kremlin if ever there was one, except that these walls were not red, or as imposingly high as those in Moscow. Just like the Ivan the Great bell tower with its onion dome topped with a Russian Orthodox cross, like the domes of the Kremlin cathedrals, the multi-tiered spires of the palace buildings rose above the walls to the sky, the gilded peaks of innumerable stupas looking like space rockets, commemorative edifices erected to contain the ashes of Buddhist saints.

Rad came back to earth, gave his hand to help Nellie down, and took out his wallet. The thousand baht bill it contained looked forlorn in the midst of a gang of alien competitors. Rad separated it from them and handed it to the driver.

The driver noted the denomination, with a respectful but brisk movement put the note in one of the many pockets of his blue-grey jacket, and started extracting change out of another pocket. He pulled out one note, another, a third, delved into a second pocket and pulled out a whole bundle of notes, adding them to what he was already holding. He began counting, moving his lips as he concentrated. Nellie was standing some way off looking bored and indifferent, while at the same time managing with her body language to express impatience. 'How much longer is this driver of yours going to carry on thumbing through his money?' seemed to be the message.

'Can you hurry please?' Rad urged him.

The driver gave him a dark, unsmiling look.

'Yes, hurry,' he said, and went back to shuffling the notes in his hands. 'That everything,' he said, finally handing Rad a wad of money. 'Okay?'

Without answering, Rad began counting the change. Next to a one hundred was a twenty, after the twenty there was a fifty, then another hundred and a twenty. Rad lost count. Somehow, although this foreign money had the same denominations as Russian rubles and US dollars, the notes were worth a confusingly different amount.

'Okay?' the driver prompted him from his seat. 'Hurry?'

Rad finished counting the money, but was not sure he had got it right. He made it less than the driver should have returned.

'Just a minute,' he said, starting to count the money all over again.

The driver said something rapidly and irately in Thai.

'Rad!' Nellie called over. 'For heaven's sake, just let him go.'

'Go! Go!' Rad waved his hand at the driver.

The tuk-tuk, which all this time had been idly fluttering its dragonfly wings beneath the driver's seat, immediately gave them a shake, got in gear, and the tuk-tuk raced away.

Rad, still counting his change, went over to Nellie. Having finally arrived at a total, he found he had been absolutely right the first time. The driver had returned to him not 900 baht but 750.

'Damn!' he cursed.

'What, did he cheat you?' Nellie asked with a smile.

'He certainly did,' Rad said, upset. It would have been bad enough if it was his money, but to be cheated with someone else's was mortifying. 'And you said he was soft-hearted!'

'I was wrong. On the contrary, he was professional. He instantly recognised you as potentially a highly profitable customer.' Nellie again took his arm and led him along the fortress wall to the gate, where a restless crowd was waiting to go in.

'It would seem you haven't travelled the world all that much. Am I right?'

'Not all that much,' Rad admitted. *'Alas, before, my dear, my life was one of ease …'*

'From what I've heard, it hasn't actually been all that easy.' Nellie's tone was one of pointed irony. 'So he short-changed you. Too bad! But don't upset yourself over four dollars. A hundred and fifty baht isn't even four dollars!'

'You persuade me. I am upset no longer,' Rad said.

'Oh yes you are! You are, you are!' Nellie said, unconvinced. 'And you should really, really stop being upset. You're in Thailand, enjoy life. Relax!' She shook his arm. 'Go on, relax!'

A notice informed them that tickets were twenty baht for citizens of Thailand, and ten times as much for anyone else.

Rad handed the cashier the requisite 400 baht. It then transpired, however, that Nellie's bare feet, her pink toes peeping treacherously out from the cut-away front part of her sandals, were an insurmountable obstacle to entry. The rules were unambiguous that feet must under no circumstances be visible. She had to hire a pair of socks which, fortunately, were available conveniently nearby.

'Here's a brain-teaser for you,' Nellie said, sitting on the concrete verge of the porch next to the queue for the ticket office and pulling on her newly acquired black socks. 'Why can't you go in barefoot?'

'Is it disrespectful to go into sacred places with bare feet?' he wondered.

'That's what I'd like to know,' Nellie said. 'When you go into a Buddhist temple here, you're expected to leave your shoes at the entrance. Perhaps they just don't want me wandering about the palace giving everyone athlete's foot.'

'Or picking it up,' Rad suggested.

'Quite.' Nellie had finished pulling on the socks, put on her sandals and stood up. 'The only thing I don't understand is that the rule seems only to apply here. Explain that if you can.'

'I can't,' Rad confessed, raising his hands in surrender. 'I admit defeat. I am on my back. I meekly await execution.'

'Relax, relax!' Nellie said again. They were engulfed by the tourist crowd, its cameras snapping, its camcorders buzzing, and moved with it, over the broad palace road paved with great stone tiles, to the part of the palace to which the price of their ticket granted admittance, and the crowd around them generated a powerful field of emollient, aimless contemplativeness. 'Is this really so terrible?' he thought. A woman is talking nonsense. Nattering makes her happy. So go along with it, relax!'

'I am relaxing, relaxing,' Rad said. 'Just stop telling me to every sixty seconds.'

'Okay, I'll remind you on the hour,' Nellie replied imperturbably.

* * *

Rad was hungry, and the moment they emerged from the palace he decided to buy something from the kerbside vendors. Before his eyes he had the image, in the hallucinatory detail of a Flemish Old Master, of a lobster he had seen as he and Nellie were walking to the metro, its intimidating pincers like great tongs dangling down from one of the stands.

'Under no circumstances!' Nellie informed him, prohibiting any further thought of turning his gluttonous hallucination into reality. 'We will not be buying any street food. Do you want to avoid major unpleasantness?'

'Preferably.'

'Then resist!' Nellie said. 'Dron should be phoning shortly and we can go to a restaurant.'

Talk of the Devil … Before Nellie had finished speaking, the mobile in her handbag rang. She dug it out and held it to her ear. It was Dron the Dread.

'They'll be here in half an hour,' she told him, putting the phone away.

'With Tony?' Rad asked. He wanted Dron to be on his own.

'Presumably. He didn't say,' Nellie replied. She did not care one way or the other.

'Let's go for a walk while we're waiting,' she said. 'There's a wonderful park here, very English. We've agreed to meet there.'

It took only a few minutes to walk to it. A vast green expanse, the size of very many football pitches, extended out from the palace, and treetops rose towards the sky only around the perimeter. Groups of mostly elderly people sat picnicking at cotton or plastic tablecloths spread on the neatly mown grass. Young people who looked like students sat on folding chairs with books in their laps. Couples wandered about or lay on the grass, at risk of staining their clothes green.

Some two dozen people, mostly parents with young children, were kite flying. They were colourful kites, with long tails, and they were in the form of little dragons. They were evidently beautifully designed, and a small child had only to run a dozen steps for them to snake up into the air, then steadily climb and climb into the sky, and hang there like exclamation marks without their full stop. Some people tied helium-filled balloons to the dragons' heads, so their kites hovered in the sky like perfectly formed, if inverted, exclamation marks.

The kite seller wore a white T-shirt with the portraits of all four Beatles, and black, elasticated shorts that looked like satin. He had set up his pitch not far from the edge of the park near where the trees were growing, and his kites were laid in rows on the grass, dabbing its greenness with patches of red, yellow, purple and blue. In front of each kite, its round sides gleaming, stood a can of Pepsi or Coca-Cola with a length of twine wound round it, bridling the dragon's head. A short distance away, under the trees, the balloon seller stood next to a cart with bicycle wheels, a bunch of colourful balloons floating above his head and tethered to the cart handle.

'Want a go?' Nellie asked, with a nod in the kite seller's direction.

'Some other time,' Rad responded without enthusiasm.

'There may not be another time. We may not come back here.'

'Then I'll have to live without it.'

'Do you know what that is?' Nellie asked, pointing to a dazzling little white turreted house on a pillar nestling between the trees. It resembled the ornate homes of gnomes, elves and other imaginary little people as illustrated in fairy tales. It might have been a bird table but for its size, which was obviously disproportionate for any bird smaller than a griffin.

'I have no idea what that is,' Rad said.

'It's a spirit house,' Nellie announced. 'Remember we were talking in the car about the trick names Thai people use to stop spirits being able to harm people? Well, these are houses for those very spirits. You are supposed to have one by every home and every place you want to protect: a shop you own, a business, a farm, next to a pond or a park. You decorate it and put food in it. I ought to explain that all the land in Thailand belongs to spirits. Human beings are only allowed to use it. That means that only a Thai person can legally buy land here, not a foreigner. The spirits wouldn't stand for it. For example, there's nothing to stop a foreigner from buying an apartment in a residential block, but you can't buy an actual house, whether it's a skyscraper or a shack. The spirits forbid it.'

'How incredible,' Rad exclaimed. He found this kind of detail no less interesting than the palace itself.

Talking about this and that, mainly prompted by what they noticed around them, they crossed the park, walked along the shorter side, and crossed back the other way. Nellie's phone beeped to announce the arrival of a text message.

'Time to go,' she exclaimed. 'They've arrived and are waiting for us.'

They went back to where they had entered the park, and about thirty metres up the road spotted Tony's Toyota, snugly parked by the kerb, with three men beside it, all with their hands in their pockets, all in an attitude of waiting. They were Tony himself, Dron, and a tall, athletic man with vestigial dark hair closely cropped at the sides and a stark baldspot on top. He had the inspired, serious expression which almost invariably betokens an American.

'Good heavens,' Nellie said. 'Chris!'

'Who's Chris?' Rad asked. The appearance of this new face almost certainly meant further postponement of their conversation.

Dron saw Rad and Nellie, took his hands out of his pockets and waved his arms above his head.

'Chris is just Chris,' Nellie said. 'I had no idea he was here.'

'A friend of yours?'

'Perhaps.' Nellie was not looking at Rad or making any pretence of being interested in what he was saying. She had her eyes fixed on the trio by the Toyota, as if trying to work out something she needed to know and which was currently eluding her.

'An American?' Rad nevertheless persisted.

His insight into physiognomy acquitted itself.

'Yes,' Nellie replied curtly, after a pause.

They said no more until they reached the car, when the gift of speech was restored to her.

'Chris! What a surprise! I didn't even know you were here. Was it you didn't tell me, or Dron decided to surprise me? Which of you is responsible?'

She seemed to be entangling Chris in an outburst of greeting, like ivy entwining an arbour, using it to support its insidious fronds only, when it grew, to smother its host beneath a riot of luxuriance. Chris's face melted into a smile as he tried to extricate himself from the greenery rapidly entangling him. He gave answers, but compared with Nellie's torrent they seemed mere interjections and, in the end, he succumbed to her onslaught.

'I do beg your pardon,' was the best he could manage, his flattered smile giving way to one of embarrassment.

'A silly soppy yankee stuck a finger up his bum, he was looking for a dollar and a pack of chewing gum.' The words of a rhyme long buried in Rad's subconscious suddenly burst to the surface. As a result, when he came to shake Chris's hand, he experienced a momentary uneasiness.

'You're here on vacation, right?' Chris affirmed with open-hearted amiability as he vigorously shook hands.

'Yes, of course, on vacation.' Rad made no attempt to disabuse him.

Tony, radiating joyful goodwill, looked from one to the other, a beaming smile exhibiting his sparkling white teeth to great effect.

'The suggestion is,' Dron said, addressing himself to Nellie and Rad in English so that everyone could understand, 'that we should take a boat trip on the river before we go to eat.'

'Oh, but Rad and I are dying of hunger,' Nellie protested.

'No, Dron, if other people don't care for that let's go straight to a restaurant,' Chris hastened to intervene. The idea of a boat trip had evidently been his.

'Of course they like the idea!' Dron decided, firmly squashing this weak-kneed attempt at liberal consensus. 'Surely you would enjoy that?' he said, looking at Rad.

'Well, to tell the truth …' Rad began. He felt in no position to be too categorical. If their group was to be viewed in mathematical terms, he was a dependent variable in the equation. Even, very dependent.

'Surely you want to come too?' Dron added, switching his attention to Nellie without giving Rad an opportunity to finish.

'Why, yes, of course. Very much so. That's a lovely idea, Chris. A boat trip before dinner.' The speed with which Nellie executed this U-turn left no doubt that the American's whims should be humoured with a smile.

'Well then, that's settled!' Dron said. 'Tony, take us to the landing stage, will you?'

'At 200 miles per hour,' Tony responded with alacrity, opening the door on the driver's side and quickly returning to the cool microclimate of his Toyota.

Rad had supposed the boat would be along the lines of a comfortable Moscow waterbus, but the craft moored at the landing stage really was a boat. It was big, with nearly twenty rows of benches with backs, divided down the middle by a passageway. A synthetic blue awning was stretched overhead to keep the sun off, which Rad's head was almost touching as he walked along the aisle. There was no imperious captain's bridge, but a steering wheel at the front like that of a car, with a speedometer and oil pressure gauge on a dashboard, and that was it. Along the sides, obscuring the view, a length of transparent plastic shielded passengers from the spray. The only way to see the banks of the river was to stand up or look to the front, over the head of the helmsman.

The landing stages followed each other like bus stops, and within a few minutes the benches at the front had emptied and their whole party was able to move up behind the captain.

Rad now found himself on a bench next to Chris.

'Isn't this great?' Chris said. His expression even more inspired and his nostrils flaring as he breathed in the smell of the river. 'I just love being on water. How about you, Rad?'

'Of course,' Rad confirmed.

'How's life in Moscow, Rad?'

Rad grunted. That was a very good question.

'Difficult to give a short answer,' was what he said. 'Very mixed.'

'Yes, mixed, mixed,' Chris said, nodding knowledgeably. 'Moscow is all bright lights, just like New York, and the casinos are just like Las Vegas, but the investment climate still leaves something to be desired, don't you think?'

'The investment climate in Moscow is better than the weather now in Bangkok,' Dron said emphatically before Rad had time to answer. He had twisted round from the bench in front and, in order not to slip off, had to hold on to the back with both hands. 'What can Rad tell you about the investment climate? Well, Rad?' He glowered at him. 'Are you an expert on investing in the Russian economy?'

The required answer was clearly implicit in the question.

'No, Chris,' he said. 'I don't specialize in investment. I can't make head or tail of it.'

'Rad is my colleague,' Tony, who was sitting next to Dron, announced chirpily. Like Dron, he turned round, and now both of them were firmly holding on to the seat back. 'We are experts in running fitness clubs.'

'Oh, how interesting,' Chris replied politely.

Rad said no more. His eyes met Nellie's, in which he read the amused sympathy of a secret accomplice. The two hours they had spent alone seemed to have created a certain bond, barely perceptible but real enough.

Rad could not believe how quickly dusk fell. He thought he must be imagining it was getting dark, and it was only when the banks of the river began to fade away in the rapidly deepening twilight that he realised night was falling. But why so early?

Dron, Nellie, Tony, and even Chris, responded to his enquiry with the indulgent smiles of people who know about these things.

'Because it's winter, Rad!' Tony replied. 'It's winter!'

Of course! It was winter. He had forgotten that. It was the fourteenth parallel, but still in the northern hemisphere, so now was winter. Winter was firmly associated in his mind with frost and snow, and as it was hot here, he had assumed it was summer.

By the time they came to the last pier, they were the only people still in the boat. There were no more landing places for passengers, and further ahead they could see the superstructure of the port. Cranes hovered like huge spiders over its docks. It was the beginning of the estuary, and the river moved the banks apart with the ease of a champion weightlifter. The sea was not far away. Their helmsman refused to take them back. He did not sail in the dark: he was not equipped for it, Tony reported after talking to him.

'How can you run a business and not be properly equipped?' Chris asked in perplexity.

'Oh well, seems like that is how it is,' Tony answered, as if apologizing for his compatriot.

Nellie and Rad exchanged a glance of complicity. As Russians they were only too aware how a business could be run that inefficiently, and so, of course, was Dron.

As they alighted on to the pier, the teenager on duty informed them in brisk, rudimentary English that there were no more boats back. He had already taken off his green jacket with metal buttons, a uniform of sorts, thrown it over his shoulder and, clutching a large, half-empty bottle of Pepsi and a large packet of crisps, was waiting for his last passengers to vacate the landing stage.

'Can there be some mistake?' Chris asked him.

'No, no!' the boy replied emphatically, without troubling to smile. 'Nothing! Nothing!'

From the water, while they were on the boat, it had seemed it would be some time before darkness fell, but when they went ashore they could see that dusk had yielded to night. In fact, it was so dark they could not see the ground beneath their feet. There was not a single electric light ahead of them, only behind, on the poles of the landing stage they had left.

'Tony, do you know where are we?' Dron enquired.

'In Bangkok,' Tony said with an uneasy laugh.

All around were tumbledown slums, fences, waste ground, and not a light to be seen. A tree suddenly loomed up in front of them, bushes appeared, as if they had sprung up that moment, forcing a detour. Everybody trooped behind Tony, trying to stay close to each other, not saying a word. They walked in silence, the only sound that of their footsteps.

They first became aware they were approaching a street from its smell of rotting fruit and exhaust fumes. A spiky yellow beam of electric light blinded them as they moved past some obstruction; then there was another on a post, another in a window, light from the open door of a shop. Nobody said anything but they all, as one, Tony included, quickened their pace.

'Bangkok is really quite a safe city,' Dron said in the taxi they had all squeezed into.

It was a normal taxi, with a meter and a driver who did not haggle over the price, but only specified, before agreeing to take all five of them, that if the police stopped him, they would have to pay the fine. They could have avoided any risk of a fine by taking two tuk-tuks, only that would have meant splitting the group and Nellie had objected strongly to that. 'We stay together,' she repeated, firmly rebuffing all exhortation to the contrary and, for some reason, glancing towards Dron. It took them a good twenty minutes to flag down a taxi, with Dron periodically giving her quizzical looks which she appeared not to notice.

Now she was in the taxi, however, sandwiched in the back seat between Dron and Tony, she was emboldened to respond to her husband's remark.

'It didn't seem too safe,' she said, 'from what I read in today's *Bangkok Post*.'

'Oh, what was in the *Bangkok Post*?' Chris asked eagerly, turning in his seat. As the person with the longest legs, he had been awarded the front seat, next to the driver, where he was travelling in patrician comfort.

Nellie was silent.

'All sorts of things happen in Bangkok, you know,' she volunteered after a while.

'Well, what exactly? Don't keep us in suspense,' Dron demanded.

Nellie again took her time before answering.

'There can be times when it's really not reasonable to go off on safari,' she said cryptically.

This was completely opaque, but probably, just as Rad knew what she had in mind when mentioning the *Bangkok Post*, so Dron understood the reference to going on safari.

'Okay, Chris,' Dron said, 'let's just remain in ignorance. My wife likes riddles.'

'I'm wild about them,' she murmured.

'Yes, no, Bangkok really is quite a safe city,' Tony said, evidently feeling an obligation to defend the good name of his country's capital. 'I, for example, have never been to New York, but I have lived in London and Paris. I have lived in Amsterdam. I think Bangkok is more safe.'

'Oh!' Chris exclaimed, raising his index finger. Having turned, he continued unperturbed to travel backwards. 'New York is quite something. If someone approaches you on Park Avenue, if you're wise you'll turn out your pockets yourself and you give them all the cash you have on you.'

'What, on Park Avenue?' Nellie queried.

'Well, on Fifth Avenue, anyway.'

'Or perhaps on Broadway. Maybe on First,' Dron ironised, bringing the discussion to a close.

No policeman intercepted them on their way back to Tony's Toyota, which was parked at the landing stage from which their trip began. When they arrived, Chris paid the driver, resolutely fighting off Dron's equally determined attempt to do so.

'This trip is on the company,' he said, handing over the fare. He took the change and put it, together with a receipt, in his wallet. 'Lady and gentlemen, I strongly recommend travelling all expenses paid. It's highly profitable.'

After the cramped taxi, Tony's almost-limousine felt blissfully spacious.

'This is a very fine motor you have here, Tony,' Chris said. He was sitting in the back now next to Nellie, and Dron was again in front in the passenger seat. 'I feel I'm right back in the States.'

'For Americans, the whole world is America,' Tony said, quickly glancing back from the driving seat.

'I guess there's some truth in that,' Chris replied after a moment's thought. 'Not the whole truth, perhaps, but you have a point.'

The restaurant Tony drove them to was again on the river. It was located on a two-storey landing stage and, on the upper deck, beneath white reflector cones hung from decorative banners, dim lamps lit the area with a pleasing yellow glow. The tables were ranged along the railing and covered with long, deep blue tablecloths. The restaurant was unpretentious, but the view from this upper storey more than compensated for its ordinariness. In front of the black backdrop of night, a string of lights burned on the opposite shore, a bridge extended over dark water like a garland of light, and from the estuary a big steamer with two decks was a block of light floating like a rent in night's curtain, letting back in light from the hours of a day which was now beneath the horizon. Music was playing on the steamer, and the top deck was studded with dancing couples; the ship's wake reached their landing stage, and it slowly and cumbersomely wallowed like a huge animal.

'A corporate party,' Tony said, pointing towards the ship. 'Large companies often hire a boat for their staff. Or perhaps it is not a party,' he added immediately. 'Maybe it is a rich person celebrating something, a wedding, perhaps, or a birthday. But they must be very rich.'

'Never mind that,' Dron halted him. 'What matters is that this is a great location. You have excellent taste, Tony. Let's hope the food is as good.'

'Thai restaurants always feed you well,' Nellie said.

'You are right! You are right!' Tony nodded emphatically, pleased by her praise. 'Thai restaurants always feed you well.'

'Personally, I could just sit here and look at the river,' Chris announced, settling down in his chair. 'I can feel the view awakening the incurable romantic in me.'

Rad noticed that Dron and Nellie exchanged a quick and seemingly satisfied glance, but what it signified he had little interest in knowing. He could see this was not going to be the day for his heart to heart with Dron.

A waiter in a naval tunic brought a folder with the menu. Dron chose roast crab with curry; Nellie, fried rice with seafood; Tony, fried chicken with glass noodles; and Chris, who had just declared himself content merely to contemplate the river at night, ordered a double portion of sweet and sour fish. The Thai name of the fish was given in the Latin alphabet, but Tony was not able to translate it. Rad ordered last. After today's events, it seemed natural to take his lead from Nellie, and he ordered fried rice with seafood. Nellie clapped her hands:

'That makes two of us! Rad you have made a very wise choice. Dron, you are going to have such problems with that roast crab. You'll never work out how to deal with it.'

Dron raised his hands in front of him like claws.

'I shall simply tear it apart with these. Who needs cutlery?'

Now Tony clapped his hands:

'Completely right, Dron, completely right! That is definitely the good way to eat roast crab.'

Chris gave everybody his triumphant look:

'Wherever I am, I always prefer fish. Red, white, with sauce, without sauce. The main thing is for there not to be too many bones.'

'That depends on your luck,' Tony warned.

'Don't worry. I am always lucky,' Chris asserted.

They also ordered a few bottles of non-alcoholic beer and two bottles of Californian 'Chablis'. There was French Chablis on the list but Chris, as a patriotic American, insisted on the Californian wine. 'I can promise you, the French against the Californian is like Greek civilization against Roman.' Nobody felt this made the point he thought it did but, noticeably, nobody argued for the French wine.

The cutlery provided was a spoon and fork, with no knife. Tony drank only non-alcoholic beer, but the two bottles of wine proved insufficient for the four Westerners, who had to order a third and then a fourth. From time to time another steamer would sail up or down the river with music playing, again suggesting a tear in the curtain of night, and again causing their landing stage to sway. Coming back from the toilet, Rad stopped to look down into the water below. A lamp suspended over the railing cast a circle of light on the river, and the whole area it illuminated was teeming with fish. There were dozens, hundreds even, of big, strong, energetic fish cleaving the water in all directions with their shiny, scaly, torpedo-shaped bodies. The water appeared to be boiling. The restaurant probably fed them and, probably, one of their number was even fortunate enough to be being eaten at that moment by Chris.

Their meal lasted three hours and Dron settled the bill. Chris, despite his democratic affiliation to the Stars and Stripes, found Dron's intention of paying for everyone entirely acceptable.

Chris was staying in the same Soi 22 as the rest of them, at a hotel called the Jade Pavilion. It was a two minutes' walk from there to Dron and Nellie's Admiral Suites and two and a half from Rad's Liberty Place, so when Tony turned off Sukhumvit Road and stopped at the Jade Pavilion, Dron and Nellie decided the three of them would go on on foot. Tony had no objection: he had yet to drive back home.

Chris, with an inspired, triumphant expression, shook hands all round and, with a slightly rolling gait, strode towards the wide, imposing glass doors of his hotel. Rad finally found himself alone with Dron and Nellie but, even if Dron had taken it into his head to have their talk now, he would have had to decline. At the end of a long day and after a big meal at a restaurant, he was unlikely to be in the state of mind Rad needed.

When they arrived at Admiral Suites, however, Dron waved goodbye without more ado.

'Let's leave it till tomorrow. We'll sort everything out then. I've still got a few things to do today.'

'What else do you still have to do?' Nellie demanded, looking displeased.

This was purely for show, and Dron's response was brutally short and to the point.

'Shut it! As if you don't know!'

The first thing Rad did when he got to his room was turn on the air conditioner. It hummed and sent forth cool air. He stood under it for a time and then went to take a shower. When he emerged, he put on clean underwear and combed his hair, but it was only about 11.00 pm. In recent months he had never gone to bed that early and, to make matters worse, it was only 7.00 pm Moscow time. But if he did not go to bed, what else was there to do?

In the middle of the night he woke up feeling cold. The air conditioner seemed to see its job as being to recreate the conditions of a Russian winter for him. Half asleep, and swaying unsteadily, Rad dragged himself over to the control on the wall, turned it off, and collapsed back into bed.

Some time later, he was awakened by unbearable stuffiness. He could hardly breathe and was covered in sweat. He got up again, turned the air conditioner back on, it rustled obediently and again sent forth a wave of cool air. It would have been logical to turn the light on, reset the thermostat and choose a different mode of operation, but he was reluctant to banish sleep so completely. Without switching the light on, he groped in his bag for the winter jacket in which he had left Moscow, put on underpants and socks, and went back to bed, placing the winter jacket on top of the blankets. For a time, he was too hot, but he could hear the air conditioner humming away and knew he would soon be more comfortable. He did not notice that moment arriving but it evidently did, because he did not wake up again.

CHAPTER SEVEN

When Rad walked along to Coffee Max, Dron and Nellie were already there. The establishment, perhaps belonging to a mysteriously absent Max, consisted of quite a small room with two glass walls and divided into a front and back by a bar. In the corner where the glass walls met, a Panasonic computer with a full 19-inch screen was glowing on an office desk and at it, tapping away with her back to the front door, sat Nellie. Rad recognised her from behind, from the classic line of her upright posture which seemed to have been sketched by a designer, from the angle at which she held her head, and from the cut of her blouse which, although probably not individually tailored, was somehow completely her.

Rad saw Dron only when he was energetically waved to. Dron crossed and uncrossed his arms above his head. He was at the far end of the café, in the corner opposite to Nellie. He had slumped down until the back of his head was resting on the back of his chair and Rad had simply not noticed him.

Come here, come here, he gestured when he was sure Rad had seen him. He pulled himself upright in the chair and, as Rad negotiated his way between the tables, held out his arms in greeting.

This extravagant gesture suited him. It was commensurate with his nose, and the moment Rad thought about that, he again felt awkward about looking straight at his face. That would have been more predictable yesterday, the first day of meeting again after so many years. His egregious nose seemed to express the very essence of the man, parading his innermost nature for all to see with a frankness nobody would have chosen.

'I was beginning to think you wouldn't make it this side of doomsday,' Dron exclaimed when Rad got to the table. He lowered his hands and pointed to a chair opposite. 'As we used to say in the far-off days of our youth, take a pew.'

Rad pulled the chair out, sat down and glanced at his watch. One and a half minutes past nine.

'We said nine, didn't we?' he said in surprise.

'Quite so, quite so,' Dron conceded, 'but Nellie couldn't wait any longer.'

'I just saw her. She's sitting at the computer.'

'Quite so. She got so tired of waiting she's gone to check her e-mail.'

Rad was aware that Dron was pulling his leg and that, in all probability, he and Nellie had got here just a minute or two before him, but he didn't risk answering in the same tone.

'Well, good, while she's replying I'd like to outline to you in a couple of words …' he began, deciding to strike while the iron was hot.

A look of reproach appeared on Dron's face.

'Do stop it! There's no need to be in such a hurry. We need to sit down together and talk everything through thoroughly, unhurriedly. There's time enough. When's your return ticket for? Not another fifteen days.'

'Fourteen now,' Rad reminded him.

'Fourteen days,' Dron corrected himself. 'That's still plenty. Don't get in a frazzle. Loosen your tie, unbutton your collar, unwind now you're here. Relax, as we say in America.'

Rad recalled Nellie saying just that yesterday, only without the metaphors: 'You're in Thailand, relax,' she had said as they went into the palace.

'Don't forget, Siam is a land created for letting go of worries,' Dron continued in the tones of a news commentator. 'The Americans discovered that during the Vietnam War. They brought their soldiers here to recuperate from jungle warfare.'

'Yes,' Rad said, 'and turned Thailand into an international brothel in the process.'

Dron frowned.

'Stop it! Stop it! Anyway, not all of Thailand, only the bit around Pattaya. And is it all down to the Americans? The Thais, or rather the Thai women, see sex as a perfectly ordinary way to earn a living. You can make a livelihood working as a wife, which is preferable, but you can also do it by working as a comfort girl. It's not that big a deal. Do you want to go to Pattaya?'

'I don't know,' Rad responded. 'I hadn't thought about it.'

'We'll do it,' Dron promised, as if Rad had said yes. 'We'll drive down there and have a good time.'

'Where's that you're planning to have a good time?' came Nellie's voice from above them.

She had soundlessly approached their table from the flank.

'We're talking about taking a trip to Pattaya,' Dron said without a flicker of embarrassment. 'I was giving Rad a quick briefing on the local priestesses of love.'

'Good morning, Rad,' Nellie said glancing at him briefly. She sat down, made herself comfortable and looked at Dron with an expression of irony. 'Eighty percent of your priestesses of love are HIV-positive. Did you remember to enlighten your friend about that?'

Dron chuckled.

'No, I hadn't got round to that. By the way, I'm not convinced that figure is accurate. Eighty percent seems high. Clear exaggeration.'

'Well, seventy-nine then. That's still too many.'

Dron put his hands back in his pockets and slid down in his chair again.

'No, it's an exaggeration. It must be. They're professionals, so they're bound to be using condoms. And anyway, everybody knows prostitutes develop immunity to the virus. And do you really think they're all registered with doctors? Of course not. That eighty per cent will be among those the statisticians managed to pin down in their surveys. I don't imagine the gathering of medical statistics is all that great in Thailand.'

When he had finished, Nellie said, 'They use condoms! If you offer a Thai prostitute more money to do it without a condom, she'll agree without blinking. It's the Thai mentality.'

'How can you be so sure?' Dron asked from his position of inferiority. 'Are you talking from experience?'

'Of course I am,' Nellie said bluntly.

'Re-eally?' said Dron. 'What unexpected details. You live with your wife God knows how many years, and look what you suddenly find out!' he said with a sly grin to Rad. 'So what should I do now?' He turned back to Nellie. 'Send you for a medical examination?'

'You'd do better to go for one yourself,' she retorted with equal bluntness.

Rad felt he was a voyeur witnessing a double striptease. He had already encountered the skeleton in their cupboard, although without being introduced, and was now being treated to a tour of their sexual indiscretions, which he really did not want.

He sat there, very unsure how to behave or what to say. A waitress came to the rescue, appearing at their table, notepad and newly sharpened pencil in hand.

'Are you ready to order?' she asked in English.

Breakfast could be Continental or American. Continental breakfast comprised fruit juice, toast with butter and jam, ham or cheese, and a croissant. American breakfast differed only in the addition of an egg, which could be boiled, fried, scrambled or made into an omelette. This was a European establishment.

Dron ordered American, Nellie Continental, and Rad sided with Dron. The American breakfast was more expensive, but since Dron had ordered it, he felt so could he. Russian breakfasts are, after all, substantial.

Dron said as much when the waitress had gone, leaning back in his chair and patting his stomach:

'A Russian needs to recharge his batteries properly in the morning.'

'Who are you calling a Russian? Yourself?' Nellie asked deprecatingly.

'Yes, I am a Russian and nobody but a Russian,' Dron said complacently, as if failing to notice her tone. 'Just living in the USA doesn't mean I've stopped being Russian. I'm more Russian than Russian Russians.'

'Blessed are the believers,' Nellie commented tartly.

'You don't need the Internet?' Dron asked Rad when they had paid the bill and were heading, with Rad last in line, for the door.

'Check your e-mail, send it? It's free here for customers, but you only get fifteen minutes.'

'No, I don't need anything,' Rad said.

'Sure?'

'Very sure,' Rad confirmed.

They went outside and paused on the porch.

'What?' Nellie asked, glancing at Dron.

'I'm just wondering,' he said looking out at the road,' whether we should go to Chris or let him come to us. No,' he said, clapping his hands together. 'Let's go back to ours. Chris can come to us. Coming back?' he asked, putting an arm round Rad's shoulders. 'We're taking it easy, eh? Do as we please. Come and see the life we live.'

'Sure,' Rad agreed. He could see the long-awaited conversation would take place when and if Dron so decided.

Max's café shared a common awning with Admiral Suites. Rad took a few steps in the wake of Dron and Nellie and entered their hotel through its discreetly inconspicuous door. It was dark inside, the walls, furniture and reception desk all in dark browns, all very worthy and ponderous, all emphatically solid, the whole place emanating conservative respectability. The manageress, sitting at reception, gave Dron and Nellie a familial smile and subjected Rad to a look as if mentally photographing him for purposes of future identification. The boy standing beside the reception counter in a black tunic was a wizened, elderly Thai with the figure of a teenager. He flung open the door for them with such zeal that Rad felt his hand itching to pull a banknote from his wallet to give him a tip. He refrained from doing so only because Dron and Nellie accepted this service as impersonally as if it had been rendered by a robot.

The spirit of conservative respectability ruled no less on the floor to which the lift conveyed them. The thick pile of the carpet in the long, windowless corridor was the deep red of a certain kind of China tea, and the dark brown doors of the rooms, gleaming with a silky matt varnish, reflected back the same shade. Even the air in the twilight of the corridor seemed to have taken on a velvety tinge of dark brown varnish. Rad supposed this was the atmosphere of rigorous primness which was obtained in Great Britain in the reign of Queen Victoria.

'Oh, no. You ain't seen nothing yet,' Dron said. 'This is but a faint echo. The Regency Park, not far from here, is where you find the spirit of the Victorian age in all its glory. They have a restaurant there. We should go to drink in the atmosphere.'

'It is really lovely there,' Nellie continued. 'We stayed a couple of times. Wonderful memories!'

They stopped outside a door. Dron took a plastic card out of his pocket, a kind of magnetized key, swiped it through the door mechanism, a click, a green light, Dron pressed the door handle and the door opened.

'Dear guests, please enter,' he exclaimed, standing aside.

'Are you calling me a guest?' Nellie demanded.

'What are we but visitors in this world,' Dron said like a world-weary sage.

'Maybe so, but in this room I am not a guest,' Nellie said, as if there was an important distinction here which was not to be blurred.

'You are not a guest,' Dron confirmed in the same tone of worldly weariness.

'Go on in, guest,' Nellie said to Rad.

He entered. The hallway was unusually spacious for a hotel. So was the bathroom, which was like an operating theatre: its door was open, and Dron and Nellie had left the lights on. The dimensions of the hallway and bathroom together suggested that the room itself was unlikely to be small.

Rad took a few steps further in and confirmed that, if you took out the furniture, fifteen couples could waltz in it comfortably without risk of bumping into each other. Even with the furniture in place, the room did not seem cramped, notwithstanding the fact that the double bed in the middle appeared to have been designed for a cyclopean couple. There were two similarly cyclops-friendly armchairs, a cyclopean television on a stand, with a cyclopean music centre on its lower shelf. At the opposite wall were a large round white marble table and two kitchen chairs, and the entire rear wall and part of the wall adjacent to the table were given over to a kitchenette with glass-fronted shelves, little cupboards, a sink with a kitchen table next to it, a refrigerator and an electric cooker with a chromium-plated extractor hood above it. Behind the glass front he could see crockery on the shelves, and on the kitchen table an electric kettle shaped like a samovar stood sentinel, its white flex snaking back to the wall socket.

'This is a home from home,' Rad exclaimed.

'Exactly,' Dron said. 'That's why we're here. What says "home" to a Russian? A kitchen and a stove. Anything else is icing on the cake. Where does a Russian talk freely? In the kitchen.'

Rad thought back to the aftermath of their conspiratorial meeting, when they had gone back to his home at Stoleshnikov Lane.

'Well, as I remember, we didn't have that historic chin-wag at your place in the kitchen.'

'And as I remember, we weren't exactly smoking cut-price Prima cigarettes,' Dron remarked, removing an imaginary cigar from his lips. He puckered his lips and breathed out slowly, re-enacting the ritual of exhaling. 'You can hardly smoke Havana cigars in the kitchen.'

'So what right do you have to call yourself a Russian?' Nellie asked, in the tone of voice Rad had heard her use when asking just that question in Coffee Max.

Dron appeared not to have heard.

'Nellie doesn't cook anything in this kitchen herself,' he continued, 'but she keeps me supplied with glasses of tea. How could a Russian survive without tea?'

They had evidently been bickering like this for the past millennium. It seemed to be a war of attrition.

'Do you drink your tea hot, living in America?' Rad hastened to interpose himself. He really had no wish to occupy a ringside seat while they slugged away at each other endlessly. 'I though in America people drank their tea cold.'

'People in America drink everything. The only thing they don't drink is methylated spirits. That's one habit they don't have.' Dron liked his image, and chuckled, pleased with himself. 'How could a Russian not drink hot tea? We certainly do, in large quantities.'

Rad did not have time to field the next blow, because Nellie got in first. It was, however, not only not belligerent, but quite well mannered, if barbed.

'Shall I put the kettle on now, Russian person?' she asked.

'Yes, yes, do,' Dron encouraged her. 'Take a pew,' he said, addressing himself to Rad and waving towards an armchair. Both, however, were piled high with clothing and such items as a hair dryer, a toilet bag with shaving requisites, a personal stereo with headphones, and bags containing cosmetics. When Dron noticed, he gestured instead towards a kitchen chair by the table. 'No, better sit there. Place is a mess.'

Nellie, filling the kettle at the sink, took this personally.

'Well, perhaps it's wiser not to invite guests when the place hasn't been tidied up,' she said, turning to look in their direction.

'Good heavens Nellie, I'm not a guest,' Rad protested, not sitting down but instead walking over to the picture window, which extended from one wall to the other and took in half the sky. 'I'm not a guest, I'm a living greeting from the Motherland.'

Dron liked that.

'Do you hear?' he asked Nellie. 'Rad is not a guest. Let alone an uninvited one,' he added after a moment.

'Then there's absolutely nothing to complain about,' she ground on inexorably. She turned off the tap, put the kettle on its base and switched it on. 'Disorder is the natural state of things. Chaos is life and orderliness is death.'

'Not bad,' Dron said approvingly. 'Not bad at all. I may even agree.'

He was being conciliatory with her today. Not putting her down, allowing her to make little digs and, when he started bullying her, immediately back-pedalling. Nellie was behaving in the same way. It was as if today they needed each other's support, and were not allowing themselves to overstep a certain mark.

Having invited Rad to take a pew, Dron sat down on one of the kitchen chairs himself, but almost immediately got up again and followed Rad over to the window.

'Admiring the view?' he asked.

The view was virtually the same as from Rad's room at Liberty Place, only the vantage point was higher and a bit to the left. The main difference was the extent of the panorama, as Rad remarked.

'Yes, great view,' Dron agreed. 'I like to stand here in the morning and look out at the city. Real urban landscape, grabs you by the balls. Splendid city.'

'Splendid,' Rad confirmed. 'If only it didn't smell so bad.'

'Ah, yes, the smell, well ...' Dron concurred. 'That grabs you by the balls too. You have to get used to it. It's just the way Bangkok is.'

'For a Westerner with money, though, life here is very agreeable,' Nellie chimed in. 'If you want to avoid the smells, just breathe the filtered air from your air conditioner and don't go outside. You could perfectly well manage your investments without ever leaving this room, for instance. Profit and loss. Profit and loss. Dron!' she demanded her husband's attention. 'Show Rad the workspaces.'

'Well, yes, indeed, take a look at this.' Dron took Rad by the arm and steered him back into the room. 'Absolutely true, you could just sit here and never go out, except into cyberspace. Get your meals brought up from the restaurant.'

He stopped in front of the nearer of two doorways in the wall, the one by the television. Rad had already noticed them: they were narrower than usual and had no doors, but what was in there he had no idea. The light was not on, and the doorways did indeed look like an invitation to a spacewalk.

Dron went in, fumbled about for a moment and, with the click of switch, the darkness was flooded with light.

'Come on in,' he invited Rad.

Rad went in. It was not exactly a room. At no more than three or three and a half square metres it was, at best, a study; more exactly, as Nellie had defined it, it was a workspace. The matt brown desk top gleamed prestigiously, and in front of it was a businesslike black leather swivel chair. The entire wall behind the desk and to the right of it was occupied by a rack divided into compartments for books, folders, diskettes and CDs, and anything else that might be required to keep a computer workstation supplied with everything needed to manage your investments.

An open Sony laptop stood on the table. The screen was not lit and there were no computer or compact disks in any of the compartments or on the desk, but it was clear from the folding plasma screen's bolt upright deportment that this was a warhorse which had been in the thick of the fray until its master departed for breakfast, and was ready to rush back into the melee the moment its rider gave it a nudge. Behind the computer was the flat black bag of heavy duty polyester which Rad recognised from the airport. It had evidently contained the laptop which was now raring to go.

'That's brilliant!' Rad said. 'So you sit here,' he nodded toward the laptop, 'and grow your investments.'

Dron spread his fingers in the air in a gesture indicating approximation.

'Not exactly. That's the wife's rather exaggerated idea. Everything is a bit more complicated.'

'But your trusty comrade adjutant is at the ready I see,' Rad said.

'He certainly is,' Dron agreed.

Rad went back out to the main room.

'Is it the same in the other one?' he asked, pointing to the second dark portal.

'Exactly the same,' Dron confirmed. 'I sit in here, Nellie sits in there, and no one can tell who has made money and who has lost it.'

'Actually, Coffee Max suits me better,' Nellie interjected, rattling the tea things. 'Send an email, get a reply. Besides, I'm not allowed anywhere near that laptop,' she said, as if passing the ball to Rad.

'Although that is the comrade who keeps you in food and drink,' Rad said, taking the pass.

'Indeed it is,' Nellie replied, taking the ball back.

'What makes you think it's the computer does that?' Dron demanded, as if he had caught Rad spying on their bedroom through the keyhole.

'I'm just repeating what you said yesterday,' Rad exclaimed, taken aback by the reaction.

'I said that?' Now it was Dron's turn to be surprised.

'You did, you did,' Nellie proclaimed as witness for the defence. 'You just didn't say how well it keeps me.'

'I think you may find he did,' Rad said in his best lawyer-speak. 'I believe you may find he said it "keeps you in considerable style."'

Rad felt the laughter with which Dron and Nellie greeted this sally was forced, as if they had inadvertently let him stray on to ground to which he should not have have been admitted.

'Kettle's boiled,' Nellie announced from the table. 'Who wants what kind of tea?'

'Let's come over and choose,' Dron said, turning off the light in his 'workspace'. 'Nellie has as many different varieties as there are drugs in a pharmacy. Let's see what we fancy.'

No sooner were they sat round the table than Dron's mobile rang. There had been time only to pour boiling water over the teabags in the cups and wait for them to infuse, but not yet to take a sip. Dron stood up, pulled out the mobile and pressed the answer key.

'Hello!' he said in English, and his face flushed with pleasure as he heard the voice of his caller. 'Good morning, good morning!'

'Chris?' Nellie asked in a low voice.

Dron nodded.

'Have you had breakfast?' he enquired. Chris said something and Dron nodded again, but now the nod was addressed to his invisible caller. 'Okay. Fine. We're ready too. Right away. Come on down.' He took the phone from his ear, pressed the key to end the call, and looked first at Nellie then at Rad. 'Chris is already on his way out of the hotel.'

'And?' Nellie enquired.

'I would like to leave him with the best possible impression of our meeting,' Dron replied, as though her short 'and?' had had more behind it than a simple enquiry about their plans. 'Let's get back down. Good luck to our tea. We can have some somewhere else if we want. No objection?' he asked, looking at Rad.

Rad shrugged and stood up.

'No objection,' he said.

He really did not mind what they did, whether it was sitting drinking tea, going on an excursion, or anything else. His one preoccupation was not to miss the moment when Dron would be in the right mood to hear him out.

* * *

'He looks to me to be a terrible sensualist,' Chris said, pointing at a large photographic portrait of Thompson hanging in the hall just before they came out. 'A lascivious, lecherous old man. You can tell just from the look of him.'

'There is something of that about him,' Dron concurred with a chuckle. 'It comes through in that other photograph particularly,' he said, indicating a photo in which Jim Thompson, a white-haired American gentleman who looked as if he might smell of brandy and a good quality *eau de cologne*, was sitting in a boat with a net. 'He looks like he spent his time passing life through a dragnet.'

'You know where he was coming from?' Nellie asked.

'I know just where he was coming from,' Dron confirmed rather smugly.

'Really?' Chris gazed at him in mock horror, which was perhaps not entirely mock. 'No, to live solely for pleasure, without a sense of inner dynamism, would be deadly, unbelievably boring.'

'Well, he was also trading in silk,' Rad ventured.

'That was immediately after the war, when he first moved here, as I understand,' Chris persisted. 'But then he became rich and rested on his laurels and lived just for the moment. That would be a dull way to live.'

'So then he added spice to it by looking all over Thailand for old houses and brought them back to his estate,' Nellie said, although it was not clear whether she was standing up for Jim Thompson or following Chris in condemning him.

'Well, for that we owe him a big thank-you,' Dron said, clasping his hands behind his back and making a deep bow to nowhere in particular, but presumably to the spirit of the former US spy, infiltrated into Thailand during the Second World War, who returned after leaving the service to become rich, occupy himself with buying up old houses in the countryside throughout Thailand, and thereby laid the foundations of the future museum of traditional Thai architecture.

'Well, of course, that is very true, so, "Thank you,"' Chris agreed solemnly. 'He spiced up his life and, as a result, we have the opportunity today to enjoy this wonderful collection of examples of Thai architecture.'

That was rather grandly expressed, and Rad expected Dron to puncture the pomposity, but he did not. Rad could see he was tempted to, but resisted the temptation.

'It looks to me as if he just liked Thai women,' Nellie remarked, pointing to a photo of Thompson, beginning to show his age, with a sturdy young Thai lady beside him with whom, according to the caption, he lived the last years of his life and who was considered to be his wife. 'Look how he's cuddling her.'

Dron, Rad and Chris all gave an involuntary smile.

'Well, what's wrong with that?' Chris said magnanimously.

'She seems to like it,' Dron noticed.

'She does,' Rad agreed.

'Aha! And you just wish you were in his place.' There was disdain in Nellie's voice.

Rad and Chris watched to see how Dron would get out of that, as, given that Nellie was his wife, he was obliged to. He succeeded, with the virtuosity of a tightrope walker.

'Come now, my dear,' he said. 'The place by my side is already occupied by you.'

Their guide, a frail, middle-aged Thai with dazzling, laser-whitened large teeth, now stood with a friendly smile at the door leading back to the entrance hall with its large box for the museum's overshoes. His smile indicated that the tour was over and it was time to clear the museum in readiness for the next tourist group.

'Well, lady and gentlemen,' Dron said to all of them, while looking at Chris. 'Have we had our fill of impressions? Shall we go?'

'Sure, let's go,' Chris nodded, and was the first to head for the door.

The light outside, after the shade in the house, was painfully bright and, as they came out, everyone stood for a moment, blinking and shielding their eyes as they accustomed themselves to the blinding noonday sun. When the pupils of their eyes finally adjusted, they found themselves once more in the short street of old Thai houses re-erected by the American ex-spy in the heart of Bangkok.

'I wonder,' Chris asked Dron, 'how my compatriot was able to own an estate here when, as you explained, a non-Thai has no right to own land?'

'That is indeed the case,' Dron said, spreading his arms in a gesture of regret. 'Maybe he became a Buddhist and took Thai citizenship, but that is only a guess.'

'Would you like to invest in property here, Chris?' Nellie asked.

Chris circled his hand vaguely in the air.

'I'm just interested to know how it would be done.'

'How to get round the law, you mean?'

Chris did not care for that wording.

'No, I mean how one comes to a compromise with the law.'

Rad grunted.

'What?' Chris asked, giving him a wary look.

'I expect he paid a bribe and the problem went away,' Rad surmised.

Not yet knowing the word for a bribe in English, Rad used the euphemism 'money in an envelope', but everybody, including Chris, understood what he meant.

'You think so?' he said.

'Unlikely,' Dron said. 'This is not Russia.' He was standing beside Rad and, as he said that, patted him sympathetically on the shoulder. 'It's more probable,' he said, again addressing Chris, 'that the deeds were in the name of an indigenous Thai. His wife, I imagine,' he said, alluding to the young lady in the photograph. 'There's a whole industry here in Thailand, making out documents in the name of a Thai, while the real owner is someone else. The official owner is paid a commission and, after that, doesn't interfere. A lot of people make a living that way.'

'That I can believe. That rings true,' Chris said, pleased.

'Are you seriously interested?' Nellie asked again.

Dron intervened.

'Don't go on at him,' he told her in Russian. 'Chris, just let that remain your business secret,' he added in English.

'Sure, sure,' Chris said, still looking pleased.

'Well, shall we go and have lunch?' Nellie said, changing the subject and gesturing in the direction of an open-air restaurant at the beginning of this artificial village street. It was by the side of a small pond framed by concrete banks, which made it look like a swimming pool.

'Lunch! Lunch!' Dron said, loudly supporting her.

Chris looked at his wristwatch.

'Why, yes, it's past noon. Just the right time.'

Rad couldn't help following Chris's glance, or trying to guess what his watch must have cost. He couldn't see the manufacturer, but judging by the fact that the case and bracelet were made of rose gold, he supposed it must be worth a fortune.

'How about you?' Nellie thought it only decent to bring Rad in on the communal decision.

After his substantial breakfast, Rad's stomach was not calling out for as much as a poppy seed, but given everybody else's enthusiasm it would have been impolitic to demur.

'I'm with the collective,' he said in Russian.

Dron laughed again and slapped him on the shoulder.

'Always with the collective! I was sure you must be a Jew,' he said, also in Russian, 'and only passing for someone from the Central Russian upland. Going along with the collective every time!'

Chris was looking on with envious curiosity.

'What are you being so cheerful about?' he asked Dron. 'Are you telling jokes? Can you translate?'

'Oh,' Nellie said, beating Dron to it. 'It's not worth translating. Just crude Russian humour.'

The restaurant was full to capacity of tourists who had completed their visit to the Jim Thompson House, but Dron's party was lucky: a table had just been vacated by the edge of the pond. Large, purposeful fish were parting thick strands of pond weed in the clear, greenish water. A boy working on the other side of the pool was busy with a transparent plastic hose. He pulled one end out of the water onto the lawn, wedged it between two stones, and began hauling the rest out onto the bank.

'What do you think he's doing with that hose?' Nellie, who was observing him, wondered.

'Earning his living,' Dron muttered, manifestly uninterested, after glancing briefly in his direction.

A spirit house was peeping out through the leaves of a tree with multiple trunks, which was growing at the far end of lawn. The house was painted a vivid brown, yellow and red, the three-dimensional embodiment of a picture-book dwelling for gnomes, elves, or trolls.

Nellie opened the menu the waitress had brought, but closed it and again broke the silence:

'I remember I wanted to be photographed the last time I was here next to that spirit house, but it didn't happen.'

'Well, make up for it now,' Dron said, not looking up from the menu.

Nellie reached for the top of the menu Rad was holding and bent it down, commanding his attention.

'Could you help me make up for it?'

Dron, his nose still in the menu, pulled a digital camera out of his pocket.

'Equipment for making up for lost time,' he said, passing Rad the camera. 'Know how to use it?'

'Life is the best teacher,' Rad said, getting up from the table.

He and Nellie left the restaurant and, when they were far enough away, she said,

'For heaven's sake, stop being so edgy. And stop worrying.'

'What do you mean?' Rad asked. 'Do I seem on edge?'

'Are you not? It seems to me you are, just because you haven't had a chance to talk properly to Dron. He's flying out tonight. Chris, I mean. Once he's gone you'll be able to talk. Don't worry.'

Rad mentally thanked her. The information was welcome.

'Who is Chris anyway?' Rad asked. 'What's he doing here?'

'Do you really need to know?' Nellie said. 'That's Dron's business. A few days ago they took out someone who got too curious. You understand what I mean by that?'

'Of course.'

'So don't stick anything that might get whacked in where it's not wanted.'

'Or I might share the fate of the man who owned this estate?'

In 1967, the American ex-spy travelled for some reason to Malaysia and disappeared. What business took him there, what was behind the trip, remained a mystery. There were witnesses who saw him run over by a truck and his body loaded into it, but no trace of either the truck or Thompson's body was ever found.

'Guard that tongue of yours,' Nellie responded.

They skirted the pond and stopped just short of the spirit house.

'Let me show you how to operate it,' Nellie said, trying to take the camera from him.

He did not let her.

'Is your name Life?'

'What do you mean?' Nellie asked, puzzled.

'I told Dron I would let life teach me how to use it.'

Nellie laughed, and for the first time since he had known her she was laughing lightheartedly, freely, without innuendo. It was the laugh of someone having fun.

'This is a new side of you,' she said. 'Something I didn't know.'

'I have the impression I don't know you even now,' Rad said.

Nellie took her time over answering.

'I suppose not. I have the same impression about you,' she said eventually.

'Time for the photograph,' Rad decided. 'Where do you want to stand: next to the spirit house, behind it, some distance away? Don't worry, I'll work out how to press the button.'

He knew how to take photographs with a digital camera. Actually operating this highly technical achievement of human ingenuity was straightforward. If you'd used one once, you could do so again.

When they got back to the table they found that, in order to save time, Dron had ordered for them: Phad Thai, the same as for himself and Chris.

'It's a fry-up of rice noodles with prawns and other forms of marine life,' he told Rad, using his hands to represent a pile of food. 'It's not spicy, and even a bit sweet. Usually a hit with Westerners.'

'You count me as a Westerner?' Rad asked with a laugh.

'Absolutely,' Dron threw up his hands. 'From the point of view of Thailand, you're a Westerner.'

'I'd have thought that from the point of view of Thailand I was a Northerner,' Rad said. 'Like an Eskimo for us.'

'If that's what you prefer, consider yourself an Eskimo,' Dron said graciously.

They did not have to wait long before their order arrived. Nine out of ten of the restaurant's customers were Westerners, and their favourite dish was no doubt prepared in advance in prodigious quantities.

'Delicious!' Chris pronounced after they had been eating for a time.

Rad found Nellie looking at him. 'Go on, say how good it is. It's the least you can do,' he read it in her eyes.

'Delicious,' Rad echoed, nodding judiciously. 'Very nice.'

The boy working the hose appeared on the bank by the restaurant. He pulled it out and stretched it along the pond's cement surround. Then he worked on it, lifting part, moving forward and lowering it, then lifting the next section, moving forward and again lowering it. The hose snaked round the pond, coiling and uncoiling, coiling and uncoiling, as if it were crawling, moving its body along by contracting its muscles like an endless, transparent serpent.

'What on earth is he doing with that hose?' Nellie asked, putting down her spoon and fork and looking across at the boy.

The question was addressed to no one in particular and, after they had all looked across, they returned to their Phad Thai, assuming someone else would answer her question.

'Dron!' Nellie persisted. 'What do you think he's doing?'

'Does it matter to you?' Dron gave her a quick glance, while continuing to eat his lunch. 'He's pulling a hose about, watering the plants. Think of the heat. The transpiration must be amazing, and it isn't going to rain until March.'

Dron's answer evoked a smile from Rad.

'Why would he be manipulating a water hose that way?' he asked. 'This hose is not for watering plants.'

'Well, what's it for?' Nellie asked, switching her attention to him. 'What else do you use a hose for?'

Rad had no idea. He cudgelled his brains.

'It's a hose for oxygenation,' he announced, not without a note of self-congratulation in his voice. 'It's for oxygenating the pond so the fish don't suffocate.'

'Of course, that's it, oxygenation,' Chris latched on. 'I was thinking that, but wasn't sure. That was an excellent question, Nellie. And you, Rad, have an excellent analytical mind.'

'You're too kind, Chris,' Rad and Nellie said at the same time.

'But actually, I really wasn't asking a scientific question,' Nellie went on. 'I was wondering why he is here messing about with a hose and not at school? It is, after all, term time.'

On this occasion, Dron decided to answer without further prodding from Nellie.

'It's probably because his family needs the money,' he mumbled with his mouth full.

'His family is short of money so the boy gets deprived of an education?'

'The family comes first in Thailand, you know that.'

'But that is a terrible way to treat a child. It isn't fair.'

'Oh, Nellie, just leave it to the Thais.' Chris looked across at her with the smile of an adult talking down to a child who has said something totally absurd but perfectly excusable. 'This is a different country, not like the US, not like Russia. We mustn't overlook that. The attitude towards education is quite different here. Their values are different. They're happy with life the way it is and have no great hankering for education. Most of them, at least.'

Dron put down his fork and raised the index finger of his left hand.

'And it is just as well that that goes for a large part of the local population, that they are not hankering after education. If they had a high level of education, I'm afraid, life here would be a lot more expensive, along the lines of Japan. And Westerners would have to find somewhere else to take their holidays.'

'No doubt about that,' Chris concurred.

'Well, I don't like it at all,' Nellie said after a pause, continuing to watch the boy. She turned to Rad. 'What have you got to say about it?'

Dron headed Rad off before he had time to answer:

'Look, just pack it in, will you, Nellie? It's a complete waste of time getting so worked up about this. You'd think you'd joined the Social Democrats. That lad of yours has absolutely no desire to go to school. If you tried herding him there with a big stick he wouldn't go.'

The boy, meanwhile, had dragged the coils of the hose to the middle of the pond and was very close to their table. He cast the end of the hose, weighted with a grinding wheel, into the water and, with a glug, it sank to the depths. The boy straightened up, rubbed the dirt off his hands, and looked quickly over towards the restaurant, as if wanting to check that his audience there had appreciated how efficiently he had dealt with everything. He turned, made his way briskly back along the edge, scrambled out at the end of the pond and disappeared into the bushes. A short time later, the surface of the pond at the point where he had dropped the end of the hose began to bubble.

'Rad!' Chris exclaimed and, leaving his food, threw up his hands and clapped. 'Your theory is confirmed in practice. You don't happen to be a specialist in stocks?'

'Rad is a specialist in fitness,' Dron replied on his behalf, and from the way he said it, it was clear there was to be no disagreement or offer of further clarification. A specialist in fitness he was, and no more.

In the light of this, Rad instead replied to Chris with an obscure gesture, the precise meaning of which he himself would have been hard pressed to explain.

'A specialist in fitness?' Chris exclaimed in amazement, as if seeing Rad in a new light. 'Oh, yes, Tony said yesterday you were colleagues. You know, from looking at you I never would have thought that.'

'Indeed. Rad likes to pretend not to be what he really is,' Dron said with a wink to Rad.

Apparently this was to be regarded as a joke, which left Rad feeling he had little choice but to play along.

'Actually, Chris,' he confided earnestly, 'I am an alien from outer space. I am really green all over, with antennae on the top of my head and eyes like binoculars. My homeland is one of the planets of Alpha Centauri.'

Nellie was shaking with stifled laughter.

'And which planet exactly would that be?' she asked, pulling out a handkerchief from her handbag and dabbing her eyes.

'After so many years, I can no longer remember,' Rad confessed, crestfallen, forcing a laugh now from Dron and Chris.

'You know, Rad,' Chris said, 'you have a feature untypical of Russians. Well, of course, I don't have that many Russian friends, but they don't seem very good at laughing at themselves: they take everything very seriously.'

'That's interesting. I had the same impression about Americans.'

'No, Americans love to laugh at themselves. Although, of course, Americans are very varied.'

'So are Russians,' Rad held out. 'It must just be the kind of Russians you've met.'

'What a useful exchange of views.' Nellie seemed on the verge of laughing again, but was evidently restrained by the anxiety, widespread among women, that her mascara might run. 'None of you know what other people are really like.'

For dessert they ordered ice cream with fruit syrup. When the waitress placed a wide glass bowl full of different coloured scoops in the middle of the table there were exclamations of horror, but within ten minutes all that remained of the refrigerated mountain was a whitish, rainbow-coloured puddle at the bottom of the bowl.

'One thing we Americans really love is ice cream,' Chris said regretfully, abruptly putting his teaspoon back on the plate in front of him. 'There's no denying it.'

'Russians eat it without love,' Rad said, also regretfully, echoing Chris. 'We just gorge ourselves. It's a peculiarity of Russians.'

'A fine impression you're giving Chris of Russians.' Judging by her tone of voice, Nellie's reproach was serious.

'Oh, it's all just a joke!' Chris raised his hands, as if to pacify Nellie. 'I've already got the measure of Rad. He's a joker.'

As yesterday, it was Dron who picked up the bill. Lunch for four came to 800 baht, a little over twenty bucks, less than you would pay in Moscow for a meal like that for one person.

If the artificial street in the museum, strewn with reddish crushed gravel, had an air of rustic calm and wholesomeness, the real Bangkok street, the minute they passed through the gate out of the estate, assailed their ears with the noisy puttering of swarms of tuk-tuks bring new visitors and taking away those whose visit to the Jim Thompson House was over. It subjected them to a wave of oppressive heat from the asphalt and concrete underfoot, and again breathed over them that smell compounded of exhaust fumes and rotting food. A pack of stray dogs, lying on the other side of the street, suddenly got up, trotted lazily to another location five metres away, and flopped down again, their tongues lolling out of the side of their mouths.

'Right, on to the Temple of the Reclining Buddha?' Dron asked Chris.

'As that is your recommendation, then, of course,' Chris said.

They had evidently already been considering this and were now just confirming the decision.

'I certainly do recommend it. I certainly do!' Dron said. He turned to Rad, his eyes gleaming with anticipation of a special pleasure, the nostrils of his egregious nose flaring. 'This is a monastery near the Grand Palace where you went yesterday with Nellie. It has a temple where the Buddha is not in the usual sitting posture, but lying down. Let's go and see it and also take in a massage. Thai massage is miraculous, wonderful! It's indescribably relaxing, and it's right there, in the monastery. What do you think? Does that sound good?'

Of course it did. What choice did he have?

'I'm with the collective, rest assured,' he said in Russian.

Dron chuckled, but this time didn't extend the metaphor.

'It's indescribably relaxing,' he said in English. 'Indescribably.'

* * *

Surrounded by a massive white wall, from the outside the monastery resembled yesterday's Grand Palace. Just as there, stupas stretched their space rocket-shaped roofs from behind the walls towards the deep ultramarine of the sky.

Outside the gates stood a dozen young women, dressed in hill-tribe costume and with posies of yellow flowers in their hands. When Rad and Nellie, Chris and Dron had settled up with their respective tuk-tuk drivers and moved towards the gates, the girls, their eyes sparkling with joy and twittering in greeting, came rushing towards them, holding out the bouquets. It reminded Rad of a scene he had watched many times during his childhood and adolescence on television, when Young Pioneers rushed to greet the leaders of the Communist Party at their congresses, or on the Lenin Mausoleum during the parades. Only now, the role of the Party leaders had been usurped by four Westerners.

The enthusiasm of the girls was so natural and infectious, their smiles and chatter so touching, that Chris and Rad instinctively reached out to the flowers, although they really had no need of bouquets and would only have to drag them around with them afterwards.

'Don't take the flowers! Don't touch the bouquets,' Dron and Nellie rushed to warn them.

Rad and Chris quickly pulled their hands back from the flowers.

'Are they contaminated?' Chris asked anxiously.

Nellie gave a quick smile.

'No, no,' Dron said more seriously. 'You won't catch anything off them, Chris, not at all.'

'It's just a form of begging,' Nellie said. 'Officially begging is banned, and even severely punished. They won't say a word about you giving a donation. They will make a pretence of selling you the flowers, and you make a pretence of buying them, and if you then choose not to take the bouquet after buying it, that is entirely up to you.'

Dron set an example by taking out his wallet and sorting through the banknotes in it.

'Of course, you are under no obligation to buy them, but how can you refuse in front of a monastery?' He took one note from the wad in his wallet and gave it to the girl standing in front of him. 'Twenty baht will be enough. For them that is the equivalent of twenty dollars.'

'What do you mean, twenty dollars? Nellie scoffed. 'It's fifty cents at the current exchange rate.'

'Twenty dollars, twenty dollars,' Dron repeated. 'Psychologically speaking, I mean.'

Rad and Chris followed his lead, took out their wallets and donated the requisite amount to the girls nearest them.

'Thank you,' Dron said to the girls, who were still swarming around them in an expectant semicircle. They stopped smiling, stopped chattering, and streamed back to their post by the gates.

'So there we are,' Dron said to Chris. 'Nobody has broken the law but the money has been transferred. In Russia we say, "The wolves are fed and the sheep intact."'

Chris nodded.

'Yes, Dron, I understand, but this kind of double standard is terribly damaging for a society.'

Dron laughed.

'Don't draw comparisons with American society, Chris.'

Chris looked at Rad.

'Are things as complicated as this in Russia, too?'

Now it was Rad's turn to smile.

'No, Chris, in Russia we don't have any subtleties like this. People just beg, without trying to put a good face on it.'

While they were talking, they had come through the monastery gates. Unlike the palace yesterday, entrance was free. They could regard their 20 baht donation to the girls with the flowers as the entrance fee.

There were only slightly fewer people milling around in the monastery than there had been at the palace, and the direction in which the crowd was moving reliably indicated which temple held its main attraction, the Reclining Buddha. The side paths were dotted with shaven-headed monks in orange and yellow robes. Along the sides of the paths, thirteen- to fifteen-year-old boys were busy tending the bushes and flower borders, pruning dead branches with secateurs, hoeing weeds, watering the soil with hoses and planting out seedlings.

'It's interesting that we don't see any of the monks working, only boys,' Rad remarked. His comment was rhetorical, but he was vouchsafed an explanation.

'That's because they are still allowed to,' Dron said. 'The boys are novices, not yet ordained. A monk is not allowed to do work, at the most he can act as an organizer, otherwise he is expected to meditate, pray and give teaching. They have no right to possessions, not even a change of clothing. All his property he carries with him, along with a bowl for alms. What he is given is what he lives on. A monk is, in effect, a beggar.'

'But I thought begging was forbidden!' Chris exclaimed in perplexity.

'The point is that they don't beg,' Nellie replied instead of Dron. 'You yourself choose to give them what they need, food or money.'

'And buildings, factories and steamships,' Dron added with a chuckle. 'Some monks are very rich, although their property is not registered in their name. It is not legally their property.'

'Nothing out of the ordinary, then.' There was disappointment in Chris's voice. 'Having property registered through nominees sounds close to fraud.'

'Who can say?' Dron did not go along with that. 'My understanding is that the majority of them are in fact very poor.'

'The majority always are very poor,' Rad allowed himself to say sententiously.

His remark fell flat, as if he had just said something tactless that they all felt was best ignored.

The inside of the temple was like an aircraft hangar, only instead of an Ilyushin or a Boeing, its high, echoing expanse was taken up by a gigantic golden effigy of the Buddha, lying on his right side and with a hand propping up his head. The statue was forty or fifty metres long, and the people by his feet at the far side of the temple seemed toy-like.

The sheer scale of the figure did make quite an impression.

They walked round it and came back to the Buddha's head.

'Do you know why he is lying on his right side?' Chris suddenly asked.

'No. Why?' Dron answered on behalf of all of them.

'Because after his Enlightenment he no longer needed to sleep; he only rested and meditated. But if you lie on your left side, you feel your heart beating and that is distracting, so he always lay on his right side.'

'Chris, you're amazing!' Nellie exclaimed delightedly. 'How do you know that?'

'Yes, Chris, how do you know it?' Dron asked admiringly. 'I've never heard that before.'

Chris, looking pleased with himself, shrugged.

'I studied Buddhism a little when I was a student. I found it interesting, but later decided this was knowledge I couldn't use and forgot all about it.'

'No, you didn't forget it all!' Nellie again exclaimed, as if defending him from himself. 'You've remembered that.'

'Well, yes, I guess I have remembered some of it,' Chris agreed, a little complacently.

They came out of the temple, put their shoes back on and went down the steps. At the foot of the stairs a very old Thai lady with a face like a ridged hose was sitting on a folding seat selling lotus flowers, a set of three incense sticks and a candle, and what looked like notebooks with loose yellow leaves. On a plywood dais beside her, two identical Buddha figures twenty or twenty-five centimetres high were sitting in the lotus posture. They seemed much aged, with their gilding peeling off like a stubble and ruffled by a breeze which threatened to completely deprive them of their golden covering. In front of the Buddhas was a platform with an iron container full of loose, dry sand, out of which there rose a sparse forest of candles with flickering flames and smouldering joss sticks.

Dron was about to conduct their group past the old woman, but Chris suddenly stopped beside her.

'Dron!' he called. 'Do you mind if I light a candle? To pay my respects. Buddhism is not a religion, it is a teaching, and the Buddha is not a god, so if I light a candle to him I don't automatically become an apostate of Christianity.'

Dron came back and shook his head reassuringly.

'No, you're right,' he said, his tone entirely serious, very understanding and sympathetic. 'The Buddha is not God and I should have invited you to honour him. I do apologize. Thank you, Chris, for correcting me.' He reached for his wallet. 'And we can gild the Buddha at the same time.'

'Gild the Buddha?' Chris asked in surprise. 'What's that?'

'There.' Dron pointed to the old lady with her yellow notebooks. 'What do you suppose that is? It's gold. Absolutely pure gold leaf. You take a piece, put it on an auspicious place and press it firmly. You crease it with your nail to make it stick.'

'Ah,' Rad thought, 'so that's what the stubble is. It's not a layer that's peeling off but one that hasn't been firmly enough applied.' And the Buddhas, in all probability, were not ancient. They might have come from the workshop only yesterday.

'So what's an "auspicious place"?' he asked Dron.

Dron was already busy, standing in front of the old lady, pointing to what he needed, so it was Nellie who replied.

'It just means you put the gold leaf on whichever part of you is ailing. If the problem is with your head, you fix it on the head; if it's your hand, you put it on a hand, if your heart you put it near the heart.'

'No, no!' Chris said, seeing that Dron was buying four sets of joss sticks and candles. 'I have to pay for myself.'

'Of course,' Dron immediately agreed. 'But for you, may I?' he asked Rad.

'Yes, of course,' Rad replied.

He had had no intention of offering a candle, let alone gilding the effigies, but when Dron asked, he automatically agreed.

The old lady handed Dron three sets of sticks and candles, tore a sheet out of her notebook and, as she passed it over, explained something, jabbing a finger at it. Dron nodded agreement and, to an outsider, it might have seemed he really had understood what she said to him. He was a good actor.

'Here you are,' Dron said, giving Rad and Nellie their sets. Holding out the sheet in front of him, he tried to prise up the edge of the foil. The gold had been rolled on to a sheet of plain paper. It was divided into several segments, and came off the paper in rectangular strips three centimetres long and a centimetre and a half wide. 'Some for you, and some for you!' He peeled the segments off the paper and laid them in Rad's and Nellie's hands.

Chris beat them to it. While they were still sharing out the gold, he had lit his candle and the incense sticks and stuck them in the sand in front of one of the Buddhas. His zealous insistence on paying for his own incense sticks was in marked contrast to his willingness not to burden himself with needless expense in restaurants; and, unlike the taxi fare, he had no prospect of getting a receipt from the old lady for his purchases, so his offerings to the Buddha were not going to be on the firm.

'How do you do this?' Chris asked, opening his hand to reveal a strip of gold leaf. You evidently didn't have to buy a whole sheet at a time. 'Get the gold to stick, I mean.'

'Just a moment,' Dron said. 'I'll get my hands free and be with you.' He lit his candle, placed it in the sand, and lit the joss sticks from it one after the other.

Rad and Nellie followed his lead.

His hands now free, Dron took its last remaining gold strip from the two-thirds empty sheet of paper, put it on his middle finger and, after a moment's thought, placed it on the Buddha's chest, just above his left nipple. He then energetically began rubbing his fingernail over it as if determined to ram it inside.

'Always a good idea to look after the heart,' he said to Chris. 'Good idea?' he asked Rad. 'You don't mind if I put it on the heart?' he enquired of Nellie.

'That depends on your motivation,' Nellie replied tartly.

'I didn't make a wish,' Dron assured her.

He took his hand away. The middle and one end of the strip were fixed so perfectly that the joint between it and the layer of gold beneath was invisible, but the other end, tirelessly springing back up, just would not lie down, and the gold bristles covering the Buddha had one more bristle added to their number.

'Now I see,' Chris said.

He chose the other Buddha for his gilding, and his movements as he put the gold leaf on the Buddha's brow just above the bridge of his nose and set about pressing it down with his nail were so definite and firm that no one could be in any doubt that he knew what he was doing.

'How interesting!' Nellie said when Chris straightened up. His strip was welded to the Buddha without a trace. 'But why on the forehead, may I ask?'

'It's a secret, a secret,' Dron leapt to his defence.

'Well, even if it is a secret, it's not one that really has to be kept,' Chris said. 'It's the Third Eye. I want to be all-seeing. But really all-seeing. I want to be able to see what's going on ten metres under the ground.'

'Well then, I ...' Nellie did not finish her sentence. She looked at Dron, glanced at Chris and Rad, stepped over to the dais and quickly put her gold leaf, one scrap and then another, on the Buddha's belly. She pressed it with her fingertips, then scored it with a nail and, disregarding the end sticking up, stepped back.

Rad found himself infected by the sudden seriousness of the atmosphere. He had been going to slap his gold on anywhere, most likely on the feet where there was almost no gold and the grey-black cast iron of the effigy was most obvious, but now he felt there should be meaning in his gilding of the Buddha. Leaning towards the platform, he wondered for a moment where best to apply it.

He put one scrap of gold on the solar plexus of one Buddha and then on that of the other. He had three scraps, so one Buddha got two.

'How interesting!' Dron said, parodying Nellie. 'But what does it mean?'

'If we may ask,' Chris added with a smile.

'It's a secret,' Rad said.

He remembered reading somewhere that the spirit resides in the region of the solar plexus. He supposed that the malaise afflicting him merited being called spiritual.

'Fair enough,' Dron concluded. 'A secret is a secret. But don't forget,' he added, wagging a finger at him, 'nothing is secret that shall not be made manifest.'

'That all depends on you,' Rad retorted.

'Ah!' It took a moment for Rad's comment to sink in. 'Patience, patience! Let's go now for a massage.' He looked across to Chris. 'Are you ready for a real Thai massage?'

'Ready!' Chris replied with a bravura that suggested he was mentally straightening his shoulders.

'Then let us go forward!' Dron exclaimed, pointing towards two squat, unprepossessing white pavilions nearby. Rad was reminded of the innumerable statues of Lenin pointing towards a radiant future which had so graced the Soviet era, now ignominiously consigned to oblivion.

CHAPTER EIGHT

Thai massage differed from conventional massage in that what was kneaded was not the muscles but the ligaments and joints. Slowly, thoroughly pressing down, not relenting for a long time, starting with the toes and gradually working up higher and higher, rolling the patient over from their back to their belly, from one side to the other, the masseuse sometimes pressed so hard that the pain almost stopped the patient from breathing.

The massage couches were large and wide and could easily have accommodated two at a time, and the masseuse as she worked did not stand alongside but sat with her feet tucked under her, moving up the couch as she worked her way up the body. Up on the ceiling the blades of several fans rotated, driving currents of fresh air through the massage room, and from the entrance, where coarse sackcloth bags were being steamed, came the aroma of the herbs they contained. When the massage reached the abdomen, the masseuse got down from the couch and shuffled in her flip-flops over to the entrance, collected one of the bags and brought it, and with it a hot blast of herbal fragrance, to the couch. She climbed up again, placed the bag on the sacrum and, leaning her full weight on the bag, began kneading the pelvis.

You could choose an accelerated massage, which lasted half an hour; a standard, which took an hour; and a full massage, which took two hours. Dron dictatorially ordered a full massage for everyone. If the day up to the massage had already been flowing as leisurely as a lowland river, when Rad lay down on the couch, time stood still and became eternity.

Even eternity, however, proved finite. One after the other they got up, removed the uniform baggy green pantaloons issued for the duration of the massage, got dressed in a nook behind a screen and, when they had paid, came back to the outside world one after the other. Despite signs that dusk was falling, it was as warm and steamy outside as in a Russian bathhouse, but the obtrusive, composite smell of the streets was attenuated by the expanses of the monastery, and their nostrils were in no hurry to despatch the tang of the air in the massage room to memory. Rad noticed Chris, Dron and Nellie all looking blissed out.

'Wonderful!' 'I feel reborn.' 'It was unimaginably relaxing.' They all exchanged their impressions.

'Well? How was that? Excellent, eh?' Dron interrogated Rad.

'And how!' he felt obliged to enthuse.

The exchange of impressions was cut short, however, when it suddenly became apparent that Chris's plane would be taking off two hours earlier than Dron had supposed. Instead of the meal at Regency Park with which Dron had been planning to crown the day, Chris would need to leave for the airport in the very near future. They would have to rush back to the hotel, grab Chris's luggage, and rush to the airport. The pace of the day changed abruptly from the flowing of a lowland river to the racing of highland rapids. Although, for Rad at least, it threatened soon to spill out once more into lowland sluggishness.

Not far from the monastery gates they found a rank of 'taxi-metres', normal, metred taxis, and within half an hour, after languishing just a couple of times in traffic jams, were back in Soi 22 outside Chris's hotel. Chris went to his room to get himself ready, and the three of them waited for him down in the lobby. There was a bar there and, to pass the time, they ordered coffee, cakes, and a shot of brandy to add to the coffee. It was when they had done so, taken a sip, and were leaning back in the chairs savouring the taste, that Dron invited Rad to dip back into the lethargic river they had left behind at the massage pavilion.

'Could you spend this evening looking after yourself?' he asked. 'I need to take Chris to the airport. Nellie will come with me, but why should you have to? You've only just arrived from the airport yourself.'

To be left on his own, knowing no one within a radius of 8,000 kilometres and with nothing to do, was a less than exciting prospect, but he had little choice.

'Sure, no problem. I'll look after myself,' Rad said.

'You don't mind?' Dron asked, taking another gulp of coffee.

'If I do, I manfully won't let it show.'

Chris came back down twenty minutes later, by which time they had finished the coffee and were sitting waiting for him. The bellboy, a young man in his mid-twenties, was wearing a red uniform which made him look like a nineteenth-century lancer in the dragoons. The moment Chris emerged from the lifts the boy was at his side, taking the handle of his suitcase and respectfully rolling it along. Chris stopped at the reception to hand in his key and the boy stood a short distance off, with the same alert and respectful expression on his face.

The taxi ordered for Chris was waiting at the door.

'All the best, Chris,' Rad said, extending a hand when the suitcase had been stowed in the boot, the boy had appreciatively received his tip, the doorman had received his, and Chris had taken his seat next to the driver. 'It was a pleasure meeting you. I enjoyed our time together.'

'Oh, you're not coming with us?' It was only now Chris realised Rad was being detached from the group. He shook the hand Rad proffered and said, 'Yes, I enjoyed spending time with you too. Good luck. Who knows, we may meet again.'

'You will, don't worry, you will,' Dron said confidently, standing by the open back door waiting for Chris to be seated. Nellie was already inside. 'Chris is just flying home to discuss a few things but he'll be back in a week's time. Isn't that right, Chris?'

Chris avoided a direct answer.

'We've got things to discuss,' he said. It was unclear whether he meant he had things to discuss with colleagues in America, or that he would be discussing his return privately with Dron.

'See you tomorrow, Rad,' Nellie called from the interior of the car.

'Yes, see you tomorrow,' Dron said, getting in.

The car doors slammed in succession, the taxi turned smoothly and drove down the ramp to the road. It turned left and surged away with all its many horsepower.

Rad stood alone at the hotel entrance. The doorman, who had been keeping his distance, approached and asked in his sing-song Thai English,

'May I be of assistance to you, sir?'

'No,' Rad replied, 'I don't think you can,' and moved on.

* * *

'Patpong?' the receptionist at the front desk repeated. 'You like direction go to Patpong?' He evidently found Rad's Russian English as difficult to follow as Rad found his Thai English.

'Patpong, yes. How go Patpong?' Rad repeated as simply as he could.

If the receptionist had been a woman he would probably have been embarrassed to ask, but as it was a man it was marginally less embarrassing.

'Patpong, ah, Patpong!' the receptionist, now sure he had understood correctly, nodded with satisfaction. 'You need to walk skytrain station, travel Silom station, then go Sala Daeng. There crowd. Where crowd go, you go.'

Conveying this information, the receptionist was as inscrutable as an ATM dispensing cash. The card was valid, the PIN correct, the sum requested within the limits, so here's your cash.'

'To Sala Daeng, change at Silom,' Rad repeated. 'Thank you.'

'You are welcome. Glad to be of service,' the receptionist recited with a professional smile.

At first, after everyone had departed for the airport, Rad could think of nothing better to do than return to his room at Liberty Place. It was a four-minute walk, the lift took a further minute, making a total of five. He went in, closed the door and wondered what to do next. First he turned on the air conditioner and stood for a minute or so in the stream of cool air. Next he went to the bathroom. After a shower he changed into clean clothes, but then the question of what to do returned with a maddening smirk. It was already dark outside, but the whole evening stretched before him. Of course, he should eat. Go down, find a little restaurant, but what a prospect! To sit alone at his table, killing time, order another cup of coffee, then another, and eventually have to get up, pay the bill, and leave.

The word Patpong, a place name Nellie had mentioned, came into his mind, like the beam from a lighthouse lighting up the darkness surrounding a ship at sea in the night. 'The red light district.' Had she been translating the name from Thai or just describing the area? Rad quickly put on his shoes, shoved his passport, wallet and a comb into his pockets, turned off the air conditioner and left his room. A visit to the red light district had a certain logic to it. A monastery during the day and the fleshpots in the evening: there was a pleasing symmetry there. He went down in the lift, walked over to reception and asked, 'Tell me please how to go to Patpong.'

By now he was an old hand at reaching the skytrain, and made his way through the maze of sois and courtyards like a seasoned expat. He effortlessly bought a ticket from the machine, inserted it in the slot of the turnstile, passed through and collected it on the other side. He went confidently up to the platform and took his place at the correct spot by the zigzag line where the carriage doors would open.

When he reached Sala Daeng most of the passengers got out, and Rad duly followed the crowd in accordance with the receptionist's instructions.

Carried along, he passed through the turnstile, descended the stairs and found himself in a street lit as bright as day. In this open space the crowd ceased to be a crowd and he seemed just to be in a busy street, but there was a clearly discernible current in the flow of people.

The street along which they flowed passed a crossroads and they again became a crowd, the like of which put the crowd at the station in the shade. Both sides of the pavement were packed with stalls, and the flow squeezed through a narrow space between them, compressed to the point where it resembled a landslide. Rad was part of it, and his elbow touched someone to his left, his shoulder collided with someone on his right. People pushed against him from behind and he pushed against people in front of him. The faces were mostly European, young, old, and in-between, all ages, men, women, neither of the sexes predominant. He noticed African faces, Indian, Japanese, but only very occasionally, Thai. Nearly all the Thais were manning the stalls which seemed to be selling everything that might conceivably appeal to the tourist heart: clothing, underwear, souvenirs, crockery, kitchen utensils, electronic gizmos, cameras, watches, toys of every description, spirit houses and effigies of the Buddha. Rad was particularly struck by the ironmongery on offer: in among the door handles, hooks and latches, furniture fittings and locks, moulded metal ashtrays and blanks for keys were dully gleaming rows of lead, aluminium, plastic and brass knuckledusters, to fit over two fingers, three, or a whole fist; spiky steel mitts with straps like watch straps and sharp-pointed flick knives as streamlined as sharks, with short blades the length of two joints of a little finger; and other knives which were the length of a dagger with sleek grooves down their blades to channel blood. So far, however, apart from this hardware, there was not a hint of sleaze.

That district came to an end and ahead was another crossroads, as he could tell from a narrow gap in the row of stalls. The crowd, however, did not head into the gap but turned right into a channel formed by stalls. Rad looked up and saw on a corner lamp post, under the Thai inscription, 'Patpong 2' in English. The crowd had brought him to his destination.

He had taken hardly a dozen steps along Patpong before a male voice to one side whispered in his ear, 'Sexy girls. Please.'

The voice was soft and gentle, the words not said but murmured, as if a caressing zephyr had formed them from the air.

Rad looked round and his eyes met those of a small Thai man with an engaging smile.

'Sexy girls,' he repeated just as softly and gently, took his arm and drew him out of the stream.

Rad looked to see where he was being taken.

In the phalanx of stalls between the shopfronts and the roadway was another gap, which this time led not to a road but to a doorway draped with a heavy, rubbery looking black curtain. Another Thai, standing beside it, caught his eye and immediately took hold of the curtain and drew it aside. After turning on to Patpong, the street lights had become noticeably dimmer, so the light pouring from the interior seemed as bright as day. Inside, right in front of the entrance, a dozen and a half girls in lacy white panties and bras, positioned like chesspieces on a high stage, were dancing to soft, melodious music. Or rather, they were undulating like leaves on a tree playing in the breeze, drawing attention to themselves. Involuntarily, his eyes ran hungrily over bodies almost as primordially naked as Eve's.

'Very young, very nice girls,' his Thai guide intoned, caressing him with his gaze and continuing gently to draw him towards the open gate of the Garden of Eden.

Rad shook his arm free and the guide immediately released him. The Thai at the door let the curtain fall back and the gate was closed. A moment later he found his friendly guide had dematerialised, swallowed up by the ground like a serpent of temptation with the ability to move through space, appear and disappear.

Rad slipped back into the stream feeling stunned. Peeping through a chink in a wall has consequences. Even if the scene spied on reveals no secret, the chink itself endows the scene with an enticing aura of mystery. It was as if behind that heavy curtain was an absorbing computer game into which, unlike the games on a screen, you could enter and become a participant, even if the voice of intuition warned that the price for taking part might prove unaffordable.

What was on the counters of the stalls no longer interested him, no matter what they were displaying. He was searching now for the next gap in the row of stalls, and was soon rewarded. A new tempter appeared, only this time did not take his hand but barred his way.

'Please, sir,' he drawled caressingly, nodding almost unnoticeably towards some stalls by a row of houses.

Rad paused to look in the direction indicated. The entrance to this house of sin was, like the last one, hung with the same heavy, rubbery material, only this time it was louvred. The slats were swaying clumsily near the floor, evidently because of a draught caused by the difference in temperature outside in the street and within the premises. Here too a Thai stood at the entrance and, as soon as Rad turned, raised a slat to reveal a triangular vision of a steamy sensual paradise. The only difference was that here the stage was not directly opposite the entrance but to one side. From outside only the edge of it was visible, with one dancing girl and half of another. They were in exactly the same tight lacy white panties and brassieres as the last, which seemed to be a kind of uniform, and in exactly the same way they were moving their legs on the spot in time to the music.

'Please, sir. Please, sir,' the tout again cajoled him.

Rad did not like the way his path was being blocked, as if to forcibly divert him into this establishment, and said abruptly, 'Go away!'

The pimp instantly stepped aside and disappeared into thin air. The Thai at the door robotically cut off the triangular vision of Sodom and Gomorrah.

The touts now came in shoals. Outside some establishments the role of tout and doorkeeper were combined and, identifying a potential client, the man merely drew back the edge of the curtain and gestured invitingly. Failing in his efforts at enticement, he would again hide this latest sunny, triangular vision of Eden from the general public.

Rad's sense of arousal was urging him to yield to the fleetingly revealed blandishments of these corners of paradise. At times he was tempted just to dive through one of the curtains, and a couple of times even allowed himself to walk over to one, but he had only to feel the hand of a tout or doorman in the small of his back, purposefully propelling him forwards, to react against it.

He had just decided to continue to the end of the street and then give up on Patpong, when a voice came to him out of the general hubbub. It was calling his name. Rad ignored it. It must just be coincidence. The voice, judging by the soft, protracted way it was singing out 'Ra-ad', must belong to a Thai. Perhaps 'rad' was a demand, a request, a suggestion of some kind in Thai, and someone was just uttering it more loudly than usual. Nobody here could be calling his name.

But then he heard it again, louder than the first time, more distinctly but, most significantly, with the intonation not of a demand, or a request, or a suggestion but of somebody calling his name.

Rad looked in the direction of the voice. An arm raised above his head, a small, round-faced Thai man was looking his way from the market stalls past which crowds were streaming in the opposite direction. He had the coffee-coloured skin of a mulatto and, catching Rad's eye, smiled, placed his palms together and raised them to his chest, bowing. When his smile revealed dazzlingly white teeth Rad at last recognised Tony from yesterday, the owner of the almost-limousine.

Rad was not just pleased to see him, he was overjoyed.

'Tony!' he shouted, rushing towards him, wending his way through the crowd like a particle in Brownian motion. Tony stood waiting for him, his palms still placed together as if in prayer, and separated them only when Rad was at his side.

'That is so amazing!' Tony said, shaking Rad's hand and flashing him a smile as dazzling as that of any black man. 'I am standing here and suddenly whom do I see? Are you alone here?'

'Yes,' Rad confirmed. 'As you are yourself, if I'm not mistaken.'

'Not at all,' Tony said. 'I am here with one of your fellow countrymen.'

He pointed to a Russian nearby. Rad found his compatriot was a big man, massive, even, built like a brick wall and with an expression on his face which suggested he knew so much about the seamy side of the world that he had only contempt for it. An instant later Rad recognised him too. He was the man who had been sitting in front of him on the plane from Moscow. His compatriot, looking at Rad, seemed also to be trying to remember where he had seen him.

'I've seen you before,' he informed Rad, in Russian, in lieu of a greeting.

'I expect it was in the same place where I saw you,' Rad said, also in Russian.

The man narrowed his eyes, as if taking the measure of Rad.

'He is a friend of Dron also,' Tony said, joining in their dialogue, in English, with a beatific smile and indicating Rad. 'Dron asked me to bring Michael to see Patpong,' he added, now to Rad. 'We are walking here and suddenly we see you!'

'A friend of Dron?' his companion repeated in Russian, still sizing him up. 'Was it you he was telling me about yesterday?'

'Quite likely,' Rad replied. 'Although unfortunately he made no mention to me of you.'

'He would have had his reasons,' his compatriot replied unfazed. At least he now had a name, presumably Mikhail. 'But where have we met?'

Rad was tempted to torment Mikhail a bit longer but somehow the occasion was not right.

'We saw each other on the plane,' he said. 'You were sitting in the row in front of me, so my seat was behind yours.'

Mikhail looked him up and down again, and the expression of contempt softened to one of indulgence. Evidently what he had seen and heard fell within certain required parameters.

'You didn't drink,' he said, wagging a finger at Rad. 'No detox ampoule in you, but you didn't drink.'

'What a failing in the light of Russian tradition.' Rad meant to hold his sarcasm in check, but did not manage.

Mikhail did not take offence. On the contrary, he seemed to appreciate Rad's sarcasm.

'What a joker!' he exclaimed. 'What a joker: you wouldn't drink, but here you are the next day, like greased lightning, in Patpong.'

'Here I am,' Rad agreed.

'That's a good start,' Mikhail conceded, holding out his hand. 'Tony calls me Michael, but most people call me Mike. I like that.'

'How about Misha?' Rad enquired as he shook his hand.

'Mike,' Mikhail repeated. 'Or Michael. What's your name then, if it's not a secret?'

'Just call me what Tony calls me. I'm Rad,' Rad finally introduced himself.

'Rad?' Mike repeated. 'How about that! Never heard that name before.'

'Radislav in full,' Rad elaborated.

'You a Pole or what?' Mike asked. 'It's them have all these names ending in -slav.'

Rad shook his head. 'Not as far as I know. At least I haven't heard anyone in the family talk about Polish connections. It's just an old Slavic name.'

'You sure it's in the Church calendar?' Mike growled, sounding as if he was expecting to unearth something questionable about Rad.

'Probably not.'

'Thought not,' Mike said, as if he had succeeded. He turned to Tony and asked in English, 'How about it? Shall we bring him along?'

This resumption of English restored Tony, who had shown signs of wilting, back to his default state of euphoria.

'Rad! Do you agree? Will you join us? Please agree!'

It was the best option on offer, even if Rad might have preferred to be without the company of Mike, who was, unfortunately, the person extending the invitation.

'Better to be in bad company than none,' he said, turning round an adage he had learned at school, without knowing at the time it was attributed to George Washington.

'Oh, Rad, what do you mean?' Tony said, seemingly concerned that they might really be considered bad company.

Mike, however, saw the joke.

'That's the Russian way,' he declared. 'That's my kind of language!' He looked pleased and approvingly held out his hand to Rad again.

Rad had no option but to shake it again. He had a feeling that this handshake was sealing some unspoken mutual obligation they both understood and would have to honour unconditionally.

'Rad, Mike and I are just out for a little walk.' The look of concern on Tony's face gave way to a crafty smile, which seemed to restore his self-confidence. 'Just to wherever our feet take us.'

'And they will take us to wherever our desires want us to be taken,' Mike elaborated. 'The main thing, as a classic of the Soviet cinema tells us, is to make sure our desires are matched by our opportunities.'

'What does "Soviet" mean?' Tony asked.

'What sort of question is that?' Mike asked scandalised. 'Soviet means Soviet, what else?'

'Yes, Tony, there once was a country called the Soviet Union,' Rad explained. 'Until 1991. It was the same as Russia. Well, not quite, but near enough.'

'Ah, Russia!' Tony exclaimed. 'Yes, yes, I remember. They used to say "Soviet Russia". So what happened in 1991? Why did they stop calling it Soviet?'

Rad and Mike looked at each other in some perplexity.

'Tony, do you mean you really don't know?' Mike enquired.

Tony hesitated. He was obviously doing his best to remember what had happened in 1991 in a country far away to the north.

'Do you, Mike, know which year our King ascended the throne?' he countered.

'How on earth would I know that?' Mike asked.

'So, in just the same way I do not know what happened in your country in 1991,' Tony explained with a flush of satisfaction.

'We had a revolution in 1991, Tony,' Rad said, 'and the Soviet Union ceased to exist.'

Tony's face lit up with the joy of recollected general knowledge.

'Oh, yes, of course, I heard about that. So it was in 1991. A long time ago. I was still studying at university.'

They were back in the stream of visitors, but going in the opposite direction, back to where Rad had come from, only now that did not matter. Now that he had company everything felt different. In company, he too was just out for a little walk, an activity which needed no purpose or meaning beyond itself.

'Well, how about that?' Mike, reverting to Russian, pointed out to Rad the stall selling knuckledusters and knives. 'Is that really allowed here?' Without waiting for an answer, he asked Tony in English, 'What's this? Isn't this kind of stuff banned in Thailand? It's weapons, for heaven's sake.' Tony did not understand the question.

'Banned? Weapons? No, of course it is not banned.'

'You mean I can just go up and buy it?'

'Of course.'

Mike glanced over to Rad and made a screwing gesture by the side of his head.

'But it's dangerous just to sell it like that,' he said, turning back to Tony. 'It's incitement to commit a crime.'

Tony finally understood what he was talking about.

'No, it is not dangerous,' he said casually. 'If you do not sell it openly it will be sold on the black market. The people who need it will buy it.'

'But so openly? Pay your money, find a dark spot, and solve your financial problems!' Mike could not believe it. 'It's pandering to the criminal instincts in people. If I buy it I'm going to take it and use it. Is using it allowed?'

Tony laughed.

'No, it is not allowed to use it. Of course not!'

'Why's that?'

'Because if you want to buy it that is up to you, but if you use it you will answer for it. It is your responsibility. If you use it, you will be punished. Thailand is a free country. Freedom means having choice. If you choose to commit a crime, go ahead, but we have the death penalty in Thailand.'

'The death penalty is a good thing,' Mike said with particular feeling. 'Only how can you say you have a free country? You have a monarchy.'

Tony's round, gentle face, hardened. It looked as if, were you to punch it, it would be like hitting a rock.

'Monarchy is a form of rule,' he said. 'Buddhism makes a person free. Buddhism is freedom itself.'

'Tony, you are a philosopher,' Rad said before Mike could get another word in with, possibly, a negative reaction to what Tony was saying. 'I hadn't expected that.'

The rock that Tony's face had become softened.

'All Thai people are philosophers. Buddhism is a philosophy.'

The stream had washed them up at one of the heavy black curtains over the entrance to Sodom and Gomorrah, and the guardian at the gate invitingly opened a triangular window into the blinding electric light. The three men instinctively glanced inside, slowed down, but did not move any closer, so a moment later, the gate was again closed.

'Well, mate,' Mike said, laying his massive paw on Rad's shoulder, 'What do you say we get some girls? Are you up for it?'

He had not asked the question in Russian, which indicated it was intended also to be understood by Tony.

'What about you?' Rad hedged.

'One is so minded,' Mike answered, removing his hand from Rad's shoulder. 'To come to Bangkok and not eat forbidden fruit? What do you take me for, pal?'

'Michael never stops,' Tony said with a smile. 'He is the real Russian bear people write about.'

'Unlike me?' Rad felt a twinge of jealousy at failing to be included in Tony's admiration.

'You, Rad,' Tony hesitated in some confusion, 'you are Russian, but you are not a bear.'

'What am I then?' Rad pressed him.

Tony considered him for a moment.

'You,' he said, 'are a mustang.'

The comparison was unexpected.

'We don't have mustangs in Russia,' Rad said. 'You're mixing us up with North America.'

'No,' Tony said. 'No mixing up.'

'A Russian mustang, eh?' Mike savoured the words. 'That sounds pretty good. So, how about girls? Are you in?'

'Join us, Rad,' Tony said, touching his arm and giving a friendly grin. 'You need a local guide. Without a local guide you might not know the right way to behave.'

'In other words, land in shit,' Mike interpreted.

Rad hesitated, unable to decide which path to take. In his mind, like a prohibitive fiery sword, was Nellie's assertion that morning in Coffee Max that eighty per cent of Thai sex workers were infected with HIV. On the other hand, the sight of the Garden of Eden with its Thai beauties in their innocent white lace encouraged him to discount that statistic, extrapolating it to a negligibly small quantity. The temptation was very strong.

'How much does it cost?' he asked, feebly attempting to remain in the ranks of the virtuous.

'Only money,' Mike retorted instantly.

'I'm a bit short of money just at the moment,' he said, teetering on the brink of a fall from grace.

'I can tell you how to save money, Rad,' Tony interjected with his helpful smile. 'That is what I am here for. For example, we can eat now in an ordinary restaurant. If you go to one with girls it is much more expensive.'

'Let's go for an ordinary restaurant,' Mike agreed. 'What do you think, Rad? Or are you full already?'

'I could eat a cow,' Rad admitted, mentally observing his relief that the visit to an establishment with girls was being postponed. He would have said he could eat an ox, but did not know the English for 'ox', so settled for a cow. Tony laughed. He knew nothing of Rad's linguistic difficulty and was impressed by the metaphor of the cow.

'Chicken, though. I recommend chicken,' he said. 'In Thailand we cook chicken very beautifully. Let us leave our cows to give milk.'

The ambient light had meanwhile increased almost to daytime levels. They had emerged back on to the road from which Rad's Patpong researches had begun.

Tony darted into the space between two stalls which led to the crossroads and Rad and Mike followed. The well-lit street which opened up before them was a perfectly ordinary Bangkok road, an uncluttered expanse of highway with cars, motorbikes and tuk-tuks flying by, evening pavements with hardly anyone on them, unencumbered by market stalls, and studded with concrete posts bearing electric cables. It looked like the setting for a computer game in which they had just progressed from one level to another. They seemed now to be in a different world, wholly unlike the one they had just left. To complete the similarity, all that was needed was for a monster, conjured up by the scary imagination of a computer designer, to fly round the corner and scorch them to cinders with its fiery breath.

No dragon eventuated, however, they crossed the road, and two minutes later were sitting in a quiet, respectable-looking restaurant, poring over the menu. This had been brought to their table by a pretty, boyish waitress, as thin as a bamboo cane, almost before they had time to take their seats.

Within five minutes their meal was on the table and Rad and Mike were drinking a toast in American brandy.

'I thought you didn't drink!' Mike exclaimed when Rad agreed to join him.

'Only when I don't feel like it.'

'Spoken like a true Russian,' Mike declared, clearly warming to him. 'Definitely a Russian mustang!' He had been going to order 300 ml but, having now found a drinking companion, ordered a bottle. 'We'll manage that?' he asked. 'We certainly will,' Rad replied heartily, feeling that before they returned to Patpong it might be as well to introduce a certain distance between mind and reality.

Their frisky waitress re-appeared at the table, scrutinised it for a moment for any sign of disorder – an unneeded plate, perhaps – and, finding no irregularity, spun on her heel and departed equally swiftly. Mike stared lustfully after her. She was very pretty.

'Tell me, Tony, can I come to an arrangement with her?' he asked pointedly.

'Oh, no. She has different work,' Tony pronounced with only partly concealed satisfaction. 'She will not do that for money. She may consent, but only if you court her properly and she likes you. Of course, she will assume that you are intending to marry her. Thai girls consider a man they sleep with as already their potential husband.'

'Can you believe that!' Mike shook his head in total perplexity, his eyes still staring in the direction in which the waitress had disappeared, as if she had announced her engagement to him.

Tony shrugged. He was unrelenting.

'Then, alas, you have no chance. A Thai girl needs to know you will do anything for her. Are you married, Michael?'

'What's that got to do with anything?' Mike responded defensively. The brandy about to be poured down his throat was halted half way to his lips.

'Oh, just asking,' Tony replied casually. 'I am single, and for the present that is how I intend to remain.'

Rad recalled Tony's four sisters, three of them married to foreigners and one married to a Thai and recently widowed.

'It's very cold in Russia, Tony,' he said. 'For five months of the year it is winter, thirty degrees below freezing, and summer lasts only three months.'

Tony seemed dumbstruck by Rad's ability to read his mind. Dron and Nellie had imparted the information about his ambitions for his sister in Russian, so he was unaware of just how well informed Rad was.

'Why are you telling me about Russia?' he queried.

'Oh, just thought you might be interested,' Rad said casually. 'In Russia we say that a trouble shared is a trouble halved.'

The puzzlement disappeared from Tony's face.

'Yes, Dron mentioned you have troubles in Russia,' he nodded.

'Troubles?' Mike glanced at Rad. 'In Russia everybody has troubles. Show me a Russian who doesn't have troubles!'

Tony put down his spoon and tapped a finger on his chest. 'We make our own troubles,' he said. 'I do not like troubles. I avoid them.'

Mike finally imbibed his long delayed brandy.

'Tell me your secret, Tony,' he said, 'What do you do for women? Do you go to brothels?'

'There are no brothels in Thailand,' Tony replied with a note of pride in his voice. 'In Thailand no one can be forced to sleep with another person for money.'

'But people do?'

'If they choose to. Since you ask,' the note of pride became even more pronounced, 'I have never in my life paid to sleep with anyone.'

His next glass of brandy again halted on its journey to Mike's lips.

'How do you manage that, if every girl will only sleep with someone she expects to marry her?'

Tony sighed.

'I have to pretend, even though that is a sin. My misconduct will probably have a bad effect on my next life.' He smiled wickedly. 'But then, what makes you think I only sleep with Thai girls?'

Discussing this topic was not making him blush in the slightest. In fact, he seemed to enjoy revealing these confidences. Perhaps the presence of Nellie had inhibited him in the car yesterday.

'So where do you find these girls who are not Thai?' Mike enquired with evident interest.

'Oh,' Tony said with the same crafty smile, 'I work in the fitness club of a big hotel. There are almost no Thai people there.'

Mike's hand was brought back into play and the brandy completed its journey

'Tony,' he said when he recovered from the fiery liquor, 'you are a very wicked man. I understand now how you come to be working for Dron.'

'Yes,' Tony responded inscrutably, 'Dron is my friend.' It was difficult to tell whether he was boasting about it or merely stating a fact.

* * *

When forty minutes later they got up from the table, Rad was floating. It was that agreeable state when you are certainly not sober, but neither would you say you were drunk. Everything is slightly unsteady, and the objects around you are slightly out of focus, as if you were under water. And as if you really are under water, your arms move slowly, you move your legs slowly forwards, your eyes focus slowly, and you think slowly too, with a time delay, as if your thoughts too have to overcome the resistance of the water. Not a drop of the bottle of American brandy was left and, although Mike drank more, Rad had not drunk much less. He thought back to the last time he had been thoroughly hammered, last winter when the ground was covered with snow and it was New Year's Eve, an age ago. But then, overcoming the resistance of the surrounding water, his mind sharply enquired what age ago he was talking about. It had been only a very short time ago. He remembered that now, in spite of his short-sleeved shirt, it was not summer but winter, that he had spent New Year's Eve in Russia but was now in Thailand, forty-two degrees closer to the equator. He had also got respectably drunk at Polina's autumn party. It was ridiculous to think that, if he had not got slewed at the bar sipping James Bond's favourite drink, he would probably never have come back into contact with Dron.

The recollection of James Bond, despite the slowness of his thinking, inevitably drew memories of Jenny in its wake and Rad, not for the first time, felt thoroughly ashamed of himself. He had treated her abominably. Of course he had not been looking for a relationship – how could he have been? – and yet he felt there was no excusing his behaviour.

His memory did not retain the moment when they crossed the frontier with the rubbery black curtain hanging from the door lintel and passed from the street into the womb of the brightly lit Garden of Eden. Rad found he was already inside, seated at a massive round table between Tony and Mike. In front of each of them was a cardboard beer mat and, moving like a shadow, an ethereal waiter they could not see but whose presence could be inferred from the white apron he was wearing, was setting tall, half-litre glasses of beer on them, non-alcoholic in the case of Tony. In connection with this unremarkable fact, Rad and Mike were mocking him mercilessly, hoping thereby to distract attention from their own shameful lack of *savoir faire* in this unfamiliar environment. Tony was fully aware of the situation and did not react to their pinpricks, only smiling and chuckling in response.

'Look around, friends, look around,' he urged them after a while. 'If you do not like the girls here we can go to some other place.'

'Are there better girls some other place?' Mike enquired.

'It is a matter of taste,' Tony responded sagely.

'And that stuff, you know, that ping-pong thing, do they do that here?' was Mike's next question.

'What ping-pong?' Rad heard his interested voice enquire. 'Have they got table tennis here instead of billiards?'

This time it was the turn of Tony and Mike to scoff.

'They fire ping-pong balls with their fanny,' Tony finally explained. 'More accurate than any ping-pong bat. Maybe straight at your head.'

'So do they do that here?' Mike repeated his question.

'No, not here,' Tony finally answered. 'Not everywhere. We would need to look specially. For the ping-pong show you have to buy tickets. They have actresses, not just girls. But we can try, walk around, find out where they have it.'

'Yeah, I fancy that,' said Mike, dipping his upper lip in the foaming glass and looking avidly at the apple orchard blossoming on the platform, swaying as if the music from the loudspeakers was a gentle breeze.

'Be interesting, of course,' Rad chimed in, his hand imitating Mike's action as he raised the beer glass to his lips, and the expression on his face was probably no better than Mike's as he looked across at the apple blossom.

'We'll just get this beer down us and go,' said Mike.

But they went nowhere. They found that the tables around them, almost all of which had been empty when they came in, were now occupied. The girls on the stage came down one after another from the stage into the hall, and the apple blossom began to thin out rapidly. Mike became alarmed.

'Hey look at that! They're making off with all the best chicks!' The exclamation came out in Russian, and also in Russian, he asked Rad, 'You chosen yours?'

The question obliged Rad to admit to himself that he had. Until asked, he hadn't realised it, but yes, he had chosen, in the sense of, if he had been going to choose anyone, then it would have been this one.

Mike, of course, had chosen his.

'Tony, how is this done? Fix it, will you?' Mike commanded. The glint in his eyes when he looked across at Rad was that of a successful predator. 'Who gives a fuck!' he burst out in Russian, completely unaware of the fact.

With a wave of his hand, Tony beckoned the bar manager and said a few words in Thai, pointing towards the platform. For half a minute they sat in silent anticipation, before apple blossom showered down on them, if not on their heads, then in the sense that girls settled on the chairs next to them. 'For Christ's sake, what am I thinking of!' Rad wondered as a cold wave of common sense broke over him. Setting out for Patpong, his firm intention had been only to glimpse this life, to inhale something of the smell of it, but beer after cognac had seen its black operation through to completion. Sound sense, having fleetingly appeared, immediately disappeared again and now, prompted by Tony and in accordance with the imperious expectations of 'his' girl, the table was soon completely covered in food. In part, admittedly, because Mike was similarly providing for his lady. He tried to make polite conversation, asked her something and immediately forgot her answer, and told her a bit about himself. He was Russian businessman, owner of a sports club, a respected member of his community. Mike, in his account of himself, was also an entrepreneur involved in special projects, perhaps not quite a member of the elite but certainly belonging to the cream of society. The denizens of paradise could barely express themselves in English, evidently knowing only such words as were essential to earning their living. Tony, watching Rad and Mike with a benevolent and encouraging expression over his denatured beer, assured them they could talk uninhibitedly to each other in English because connected English speech would be well beyond the ladies' ability to understand. 'These are village girls without higher education,' he said with a laugh. 'Just like in a club in Moscow,' Mike remarked condescendingly to Rad. 'The only difference is that here it's not all under the counter: you get to see exactly what you're paying for.' Rad mumbled his agreement. The idea again visited him that he had not intended to let things go this far and should stop while there was still time, but this prudent thought vanished as abruptly as it had appeared.

How long had they been sitting there? It was impossible to tell. Time dissolved like a sugar lump in hot tea. It did not stand still, it dissolved without trace. The girls ate their meal, washed it down with mango juice, twittered to each other in Thai, and from time to time exchanged a few words, with some English thrown in, with Tony, but paid no particular attention to Rad and Mike. 'They're getting us going, the minxes,' Mike suggested. He put an arm round the shoulders of his girl, and placed his big, shovel-like hand on her stomach. 'No, no, no,' she twittered, adroitly wriggling out of his clutches. 'Don't do. I not yours.' 'You haven't agreed terms with her yet,' Tony explained. 'Until then you don't have any rights. Maybe you just want to buy her a meal.' He went on to explain that 1,000 baht for the night would be enough, but 200 baht was payable to the bar for effecting the introduction. The bar had no rooms of its own, but if the girl agreed you could take her to a hotel. 'What, can she still not agree?' Mike broke in in astonishment. 'Well, only if she finds you very disgusting,' Tony replied. He continued his instruction: you could take her back to your own hotel if you wished, or another one which was closer. They always had rooms for a one-night stay. That would be about another 1,000 baht.

A thousand to the girl for the night, a thousand for the room, two hundred for the bar, and on top of that he had to pay for the meal she had just eaten. Rad realised he was in deep doo-doo. He had next to nothing left of the Thai money Nellie had given him when he arrived. Barely enough to pay for the meal even. 'Tony, can I pay in dollars?' he asked. 'Not according to the bill, of course,' Tony replied, 'but they will not refuse it, only they will calculate at a poor exchange rate. The girl will take dollars, of course, no problem.'

'I'll pay for the food,' Rad decided mentally, 'and that's the end of it.'

An hour later, however, he was sitting in a tuk-tuk, proceeding like a speeding bullet down a deserted night-time street in Bangkok, fresh air blowing in his face and a girl sitting beside him with his arm round her waist. She covered her throat with her hand, evidently suffering from weak tonsils. Mike and Tony had dissolved into the seething cauldron of Patpong which, despite the lateness of the hour, was bubbling away and seemed likely to continue to do so until morning. He supposed Tony would be driving home in his big car, and Mike must have rented a room, as he intended, in a hotel near Patpong. 'Cor, I wouldn't have said no to that chick in the restaurant! She was pretty. I wouldn't have minded a bit of that.' Such were his parting words to Rad. 'She has different work,' Rad said, primly repeating Tony's words, and again thinking that all this had to stop right now, only he could now no longer stop himself.

He could not find a single Thai banknote in his wallet to settle with the tuk-tuk driver. Remembering what Tony had said, Rad handed the driver ten dollars. When they got into the tuk-tuk they had agreed 200 baht which meant that, at the official exchange rate, he should get 180 back. The driver pulled some notes out of his pocket, handed them to Rad and drove off. When Rad counted them he found they amounted to a modest fifty baht, but there was now no one to complain to. The girl, while he was paying the driver and then counting his change, stood demurely at a distance, her expression one of tolerant boredom, as if to say, 'What's it got to do with me?'

She was far from ugly, had a sweet face, and was not old, although not as young as she had looked on the stage. Her straight, black hair was shoulder length, curled at the ends, and held back at the sides of her head by three large, yellow metal clasps with a plastic mother-of-pearl trim. In slacks under a long blouse which covered her hips, she seemed to have short legs, but Rad knew from watching her on the stage that her legs, although not long, really were not short; they were entirely proportionate, and anyway, he had never fancied girls with long legs.

'Let's go,' Rad said, putting his hand on her hip and drawing her with him towards the glass door of Liberty Place.

The duty receptionist, as they passed on the way to the lift, glanced at Rad to make sure he knew him, glanced at the girl, and looked away without further interest.

Rad swiped his room key card through the reader, the lock clicked, and the lift was at their service. In the lift he pressed the button for his floor and slipped his hand under the girl's blouse, pushing up the cup of her bra and taking her liberated breast in his hand. He felt an access of lust and would gladly have taken possession of the treasure he had brought back from Patpong there and then in the lift. He felt like a mariner in the age of discovery, who for months had been out at sea alone with his animal lusts.

When he took her breast in his hand, the girl placed both her hands on his hips, pressed herself against him and laid her head on his chest. 'Darling,' she said. 'Lover.' Her name was Lana, or so she had introduced herself, but this was doubtless only the European shell in which she hid to elude the wrath of the spirits and keep her real self safe for their protection.

The lift stopped, the inner doors opened, Rad let go of her breast. Lana moved her head away, he moved his hand away from under her blouse, and opened the outer door. The corridor was empty. A lone fluorescent light shone near the ceiling. Behind the doors of the other rooms the silence was absolute, as if there was not a soul in any of them and they two were the only guests on the entire floor.

Rad swiped his key card and opened the door, to be met by a rush of stiflingly hot air containing zero per cent oxygen. He went in, turned on the light, went over and quickly turned on the air conditioning. He did not hear Lana coming in and, turning, found her still standing meekly at the door, unable to enter until invited.

He found that touching.

'Come in,' he said, inviting her.

She stepped in and pushed the door closed behind her back. It swung back smoothly and the lock closed with a metallic click. With the same meek expression, Lana glanced quickly round the room and moved across to the armchair, the hem of her loose blouse brushing Rad as she passed. She sat down, crossed her legs firmly at the ankles, and placed a little white handbag of folded yarn on her knees. Without knowing who she was and why she was here, he might seem to have been visited in the night by the soul of innocence, and certainly not by a priestess at the altar of sin.

Rad found he did not know what to do next. Now they were together, he could not help feeling that, with a woman you have bought, everything should be quite different from how it was with one who had chosen to go to bed with you. This was his first time with a woman who did it for money. Until now, he had been as amateur as Tony. Of course, women had taken money from him, extorted it, on occasion stolen it, but going to bed with one in return for a fee was something new. Rad had butterflies in his stomach, as if he were about to undergo some initiation rite.

'Do you want to take a shower?' he asked. The desire for instant rutting which had possessed him in the lift was replaced by a desire to delay the inevitable for as long as possible. Was he scared?

Lana looked up puzzled, as if wondering why a shower should be necessary.

'I think …' she began slowly, choosing the English words.

'Take a shower,' he said.

It was an order, and she obediently got up and went to the bathroom. She took her white handbag with her.

While she was splashing in there, he sat dully in her chair. He saw it as hers. The tireless air conditioner blew a jet of cool air from the wall opposite. He had set the thermostat to 'cold', and the climate in the room was now suitable for human habitation.

Lana came out carrying her clothes, a towel round her hips, and a pleased smile on her face at a job well done. She put her clothes and handbag on a chair and advanced on Rad.

'Enjoy!' she cooed, leaning over and caressing his face first with one breast then the other.

Her breasts were of modest size, but beautifully rounded, two mounds, pert, firm, and with large, amazingly erect brown nipples.

For a moment Rad caught the nipple rubbed on his face with his lips, but immediately released it. He put his hands on the armrests of the chair and began to stand up, obliging Lana herself to straighten up and back away.

'I now in shower too,' he said, dispensing with the verb.

The bathroom was hot and stuffy. The soap was on the edge of the bath, covered with a grey cap of foam which had not had time to settle. Lana had washed herself thoroughly.

Rad paused for a moment, wondering whether he ought not to take his clothes off in the room, but decided to undress right where he was. He did not want to leave the ID and wallet in his trouser pockets unattended. Lana, he recalled, had taken her handbag with her into the bathroom. He wondered what she had in it. Not jewellery, presumably.

He stood under the shower for twenty minutes or so, although to freshen up two minutes would have been plenty. He stood there, lashed by the hot jets, in the hope they would wash away the chill. He could feel the sweat pouring out of him as if he was in a steam room. His woozy head cleared, the objects around him ceased to sway and became only too distinct, but the chill was not being washed away.

He turned the water off only when the bathroom was so steamed up that he could no longer see the far wall and the ceiling had begun to rain condensation.

After drying, before emerging from the bathroom, Rad surprised himself by putting his clothes back on, as if the lady in the next room was waiting to engage with him in higher mathematics. He wiped the misted mirror with a damp towel, looked at his blurred reflection and combed his hair. Thus attired, buttoned up and with his hair neatly combed, he opened the door and went back into the room.

He went back in, expecting to find it refreshingly cool, but it was again at the oven-like temperature they had encountered half an hour before. The counterpane had been removed from the bed and Lana, covered with a sheet, was lying there with her black hair streaming over the pillow. On the table by the head of the bed was a long, fiery red flat box, presumably containing condoms.

'*O-diya!*' Lana exclaimed in dismay at the sight of him fully dressed.

Without replying (and what reply could he give to this incomprehensible exclamation?), Rad looked across to the air conditioner's control panel. It was turned off. Not turned up, turned off.

'What on earth?!' Now it was his turn to be perplexed.

Lana, following his gaze, understood.

'Too cold!' The smile on her face was apologetic but confident. She had no doubt she was within her rights in turning the air conditioner off. She was not Rad's slave, she was temporarily his employee, only it was not her hands she worked with.

'My throat,' she said, bringing her hand out from beneath the sheets and pointing to her neck.

'Too delicate.'

'*O-diya!*' Rad exclaimed, deciding this must be a Thai word expressing surprise.

'Why?' Lana now asked in turn.

'Because this is more like a crematorium than a bedroom,' he was tempted to reply, but did not.

A delicate throat! In this heat she was afraid of the cold! Might her delicate throat not be caused by the heat?

Rad looked silently at the prostitute lying in his bed and tried to think how best to tell her to get up, get dressed, and get out. He had identified the cause of his misgivings as they had entered the room. It was nothing to do with initiation rites, or at least, not only with that, just as the condoms on the bedside table were only part of the story. Much more to the point was that what he could pay her for sating his lust was far less than the 1,000 baht agreed.

Still unsure how to tell her that her services were no longer required, he retreated from the bed and turned the air conditioner back on, after which the best he could manage was to say,

'If it is too cold for you, get up.'

'What?!' she screeched, throwing back the sheet and jumping out of bed. 'What?!'

As was only to be expected, she was stark naked, and Rad's eyes were riveted by her black pubic hair, which was shaved in the form of an arrow pointing down between her legs.

'What?' she again demanded. 'Why?'

She was incensed. She was insulted. All the obedient readiness to serve and delight, which had been evident in her every movement and the intonations of her voice, had vanished. She was a fury, a witch, an angry snake baring venomous fangs.

Rad was completely at a loss. He had had no experience with ladies of this profession. He should simply have taken his wallet and, without a word, given her money, but instead, trying to avert his eyes from the black arrow piercing her pubis, snarled, as if looking for a fight,

'Why? Because I change my mind.'

Most likely this was beyond her competence in English, even without his Russian accent. He should not have tried to explain himself.

'You must! You must!' the snake swaying combatively in front of him hissed.

He must what? Sleep with her since she was in his bedroom?

More probably, Lana meant that, whether or not he slept with her, he should pay up, but by now they were completely at cross-purposes.

'You must!'

'No.'

He could not imagine what she needed in her bag. Still shrieking, only now in Thai, she rushed over, unzipped it and, a moment later, had a long shiny object covering the fingers of her right hand. That it was a knuckleduster Rad realised just too late.

It was not a lady-like blow. The impact was enough to blind him for a moment. The sparks that fell from his eyes into the encircling gloom would have sufficed to set Rome ablaze. He clutched his head as everything circled and lurched. He thought he was about to collapse.

He felt something wet and sticky under his fingers. His eyes began to see light again, which rapidly grew brighter, and as it did so he saw the outline of Lana making for the door. He next realised that she was making off with his wallet: the unpleasant sensation his thigh recalled feeling while he was in darkness had been Lana's hand pulling it out of his pocket. It contained all his cash and his debit card.

'Halt!' Rad yelled as he rushed after her, suddenly recollecting the command from his training at the university's military department.

Everything that happened after that was etched in his memory as one big, blazing fireball of embarrassment.

Lana had jumped out into the corridor, but he leapt out after her, grabbed her by the hair and pulled her up short. She screeched in pain, tried to turn round, and fell to the floor, dragging him after her. In her haste to get out of the room, she had not dressed, only seized her clothes. He, on the other hand, was entirely presentable. A naked prostitute and a fully dressed man: what would people make of that? Rad pondered this as, still restraining Lana, he got to his feet.

The urgent need to ponder it arose from the fact that he had an audience: the other hotel guests on his floor were now in the corridor. Five, six, seven respectable-looking people were staring in bewilderment and horror. 'Disgraceful!' 'What's going on?' 'How awful!' 'Good God!' 'Hey, come and take a look at this!' From one of the rooms an irate male voice could be heard calling reception:

'Phone the police, please! Right away! People are being killed up here!'

Lana meanwhile was screaming something in Thai, but all he remembered of it afterwards was frequent repetition of the word 'farang'.

In front of all these witnesses, Rad plunged his bloodstained hand into Lana's gaping handbag, felt around and retrieved his wallet.

'All is okay!' he said, waving the wallet at his fellow guests, who were keeping their distance. 'Do not phone police. There is no cause.'

Lana, spattered with his blood and with the tools of her trade very publicly displayed, showed no sign of quietening down.

'Shut up!' Rad barked at her. 'I pay you! I pay! Be more calm! I pay you! Do not worry!'

Whatever she thought he was saying, she did at least stop freaking out.

Still conscious of the independent witnesses, Rad opened his wallet and leafed through the notes inside it. He owed her 25 dollars, perhaps a bit more; thirty would have been more than enough and he had a twenty and a ten, but he pulled out two twenties. After all that had happened it seemed best to err on the side of generosity.

'Here!' he said, handing Lana the money.

She snatched it from his hand, glanced at the denominations and, to Rad's great surprise, her face lit up with gratitude.

'Thank you!' she said, blowing him a kiss, before adding, 'darling!'

Several of the witnesses were heard to giggle.

'Want to put your clothes back on?' he asked, nodding towards the open door of his room.

'No-no. No,' she said quickly, probably not understanding what he had said so much as reacting to the suggestion she should go back into his room. She pushed her feet into her shoes, which had come off when she fell, and made hurriedly for the door to the stairs, evidently planning to get dressed there.

'Sorry!' Rad said, turning to his fellow guests, who were still gawping. He shrugged. 'I beg your pardon!'

No one responded.

'Sorry,' he repeated and went back to his room.

'You have blood running down your cheek,' he heard a concerned female voice behind him.

Now, however, he did not respond and, without looking back, firmly shut the door behind him.

CHAPTER NINE

Rad was wakened by the telephone ringing. He sleepily fumbled about on the bedside table, found the phone, fell back and put the receiver to his ear.

'Hello,' he croaked.

'Are you asleep?' he heard Dron enquire.

'Not now,' he said, still with his eyes closed.

'Were you perhaps thinking of getting up?' Dron said, and something in his tone put Rad on the alert.

'Probably,' he said. 'What's the time?'

'Morning,' replied Dron. 'Greet the dawn!'

Rad would have expected him to answer such a specific question by telling him what time it was. It was hardly a state secret, and the fact that he avoided answering was a clear indication that this conversation held some deeper significance.

Rad opened his eyes, threw off the blanket, put his feet on the floor and sat bolt upright.

'What's wrong?' he asked.

'You're asking me?' Dron responded instantly, like a fencer taking a lunge.

'Well, you ask me,' Rad said cautiously.

Silence from Dron's end of the line.

'What on earth have you done to get yourself evicted?' he asked.

'Evicted? Me?' Rad exclaimed.

'Yes, you,' Dron confirmed.

Now it was Rad's turn to be silent. He would have liked to believe Dron was joking, but the events of last night did not allow that luxury. Only, why was it Dron passing him the information?

'I can't help wondering,' Rad said, 'why this information is coming from you?'

'Because I'm the person who booked the room for you. I booked it, so I carry the can. "Kindly get your protégé out of our hotel."'

'What, did they phone you?' Rad asked.

'Me it was they phoned,' Dron informed him. 'So what the hell did you do?'

Rad moved the receiver away and exhaled noisily. What a great start to the day.

'It's a long story,' he said, bringing the phone back to his ear. 'What time do I need to be out by?'

'Check-out time is noon, so you've got till then.'

Rad felt like a schoolboy in first grade who has done something naughty. He has never faced punishment for doing something wrong before and has no ready-made defence reaction as he faces the yawning chasm of impending retribution for his sins.

'Oh,' he said unconfidently, 'well, perhaps I should shave, take a shower, and we can meet.'

'Half an hour from now in Coffee Max,' Dron instructed.

Rad heard the pips of the dialling tone as the connection was broken.

He put the receiver down slowly. Next to the telephone lay the bright red pack of condoms. He picked it up and turned it over, but this material reminder of the night before evoked no emotion beyond a sense of ironic admiration for the warning traffic-light red colour of the packaging.

He threw them back on the table and got off the bed. Coffee Max, then, in half an hour.

When he stepped out of the lift and walked past reception there were three people behind the counter: yesterday's receptionist, the girl who was taking over from him who, Rad recalled, had been on duty when he arrived, and the hotel manageress, a robust, middle-aged Thai woman in spectacles, with business-like cropped hair and wearing a dark business suit rather too tight for her solidly built body. Yesterday's receptionist, noticing Rad, murmured a few words in Thai, and the duty receptionist and manageress turned to look at him. The manageress, indeed, skewered him with her gaze. None of them responded to his 'Good morning.'

Dron was waiting for him. He sat in a corner at the furthest back table, sipping fruit juice from a tall, heavy glass. Grapefruit juice, judging by the colour. He was alone.

'Morning,' Rad volunteered. He tried to appear relaxed and cheerful. The worst was behind him and all that remained was to clear up the mess. 'Where's Nellie? On the Internet?' He looked back towards the computer by the entrance, but in front of the monitor, staring motionlessly at the screen, was an elderly gentleman, perhaps Japanese, with a colourful cravat tucked into his shirt.

'Nellie is back at the hotel,' Dron said, 'drinking her favourite fruit tea. I decided not to embarrass you in front of her. Was that a mistake?'

'Very fair. You're a brick.' Rad pulled out a chair and sat down opposite Dron. 'Yesterday, you see, I took a prostitute …'

'What!' Dron exclaimed, bursting with laughter and hurriedly putting his fruit juice back down on the table. 'You old dog! So what then? You turned the place into Sodom and Gomorrah?'

Rad nodded.

'Something like that. What did they tell you?'

'By way of explanation? Nothing.' Dron brought his laughter under control, picked the juice up again and took a sip. 'They only said that the other guests staying there did not wish to have you in a neighbouring room and that, for the sake of the hotel's reputation, they were obliged to withdraw their hospitality. They said it was fortunate that people on your floor had not insisted on involving the police.'

Rad shuddered. The only good thing about yesterday's incident was that the police had not been called.

'I was stupid. I invited her back, and when we got to the room …'

As briefly as possible, avoiding unnecessary detail, he told Dron what had transpired between him and the lady, and how she came to be out in the corridor in her birthday suit. Dron listened avidly, chuckling at the spicier moments in the tale.

'My dear fellow,' he said when Rad had finished, 'Your story has a positively biblical dimension to it.'

'How so?' Rad queried.

'Well,' said Dron, 'it's the Tower of Babel all over again. The reason God created the confusion of languages was so that people couldn't come to terms between themselves.'

'Ah,' Rad sighed with relief. 'In that sense. No, the Tower of Babel is spot on. I thought you were coming back to Sodom and Gomorrah.'

'We'll get to Sodom and Gomorrah soon enough, you can rest assured,' Dron promised, laughing again. 'Look, you'd better order breakfast,' he added, pointing behind Rad's shoulder with his chin. 'What's it this morning: Continental or American?'

Rad looked round to find the waitress behind him, waiting.

He asked for two glasses of juice and a coffee. Right now he really was not up to anything else.

'I gather you also hit the bottle last night,' Dron remarked after the waitress departed.

'I did,' Rad confirmed. 'With a friend of yours.'

'What friend of mine?'

'With Mike. At least, that's what he asked me to call him.'

The instant Dron heard the name of his 'friend', his expression changed. His face now looked like a plaster death mask.

'How come you know him?' he asked expressionlessly.

Rad saw immediately that not only had his acquaintance with Mike not been part of Dron's plans, but that it was bad news. If he had known that, he would have kept quiet, but how was he to know?

'We met somewhere,' he said as uninformatively as possible.

'How?'

'Tony introduced us,' Rad said, trying to remain uninformative.

Dron subjected him to the inquisitorial stare of a tax inspector. Then his expression began to soften, he slapped his forehead, and became again the Dron Rad was familiar with.

'Ah, picked up your lady in Patpong, did you?'

'Yes,' Rad confirmed.

'And what were you doing there? Who told you about Patpong?'

'Nellie, forgive me, was my informant.' Rad spread his arms apologetically.

'And there, by chance, you ran into Tony.'

'There I ran into Tony.' Rad was not surprised he guessed that. It would have been stranger if he had not.

'You're a randy old dog,' Dron said, taking another sip from his glass. 'A randy old dog. No other way of putting it.'

The air behind Rad's back stirred and a moment later the waitress was at the table with a full tray: two glasses of grapefruit juice for him and, for Dron, his omelette, ham, toast and jam.

Rad took a glass of juice and, in a single draught, all but drained it.

Dron sat looking at Rad without touching his breakfast, or even picking up his cutlery.

'So, how did you get on with Mike? What did you find to talk about?'

'We talked only about girls,' Rad assured him.

'You don't say …' Dron remarked rather too emphatically, as if he had just caught him out lying.

'Only that,' Rad assured him.

Dron, continuing to look at Rad searchingly, felt on the table for his knife and fork, picked them up and, without looking down, began blindly cutting himself a piece of the omelette.

'Forget Mike, okay? You've never seen him, didn't talk to him or hang out with him in Patpong. Not yesterday, or the day before, or ever. You imagined it.'

Rad nodded.

'As you will.'

He took his glass and finished what was left of the juice. Dron finally looked down at his breakfast, speared a piece of omelette and despatched it to his mouth.

'One oddity, though, before I finally forget everything,' Rad said. Yesterday's encounter could not be so instantly deleted from his memory. 'Mike and I flew here on the same plane. His seat was immediately in front of mine.'

'How about that!' Dron mumbled with his mouth full. 'Out of 250 pax … Why do you mention it?'

'No reason. None at all. It's just a surprising coincidence. Given that there were 250 seats on the plane …' At this point he could have stopped, but decided to gild his coincidence a bit more. 'He had a laptop in a bag. He was really jumpy about it, wouldn't let the man in the next seat put anything near it in the overhead locker.'

'A laptop?' Dron repeated, but only after a pause, during which he cut a new piece of his omelette and put it in his mouth. 'So, what if he had. It's behind you. Forget it!'

He was looking down at his plate but, when he finished, he looked up, their eyes met, and Rad felt that now it was his face that was turning into an expressionless death mask. He had seen an open laptop on the desk in Dron's workspace at Admiral Suites, the flat black bag at the back of the shelving, the bag Dron had appeared with at the airport after making him and Nellie wait while he met someone, and that was the selfsame bag Mike had had on the plane. Other people's secrets were the last thing he needed right now, to land himself in some business that had people flying halfway round the globe!

'Dron, I've forgotten,' he said. 'All of it. Believe me.'

'I'll try,' Dron replied grimly.

The penny had dropped for Dron too. He had understood that Rad had made the connection between the laptop in the plane and the one in his workspace. The question was, what consequences would that shared realization now have?

The next ten minutes of their breakfast passed in silence. Dron ate his omelette, supplementing it with small pieces of meat cut from his gleaming bacon rasher, then set about the toast, spreading it with jam and biting off a quarter of a slice at a time with his yellowed but powerful teeth. Rad drank his second glass of juice, now in a more leisurely fashion. When the waitress brought the coffee, Rad's black, Dron's white, Dron said, as he poured the cream into his cup and stirred it.

'So, what are we going to do? You need to sling your hook from Liberty Place. No two ways about that.'

The life had come back into his voice, and to Rad's ears the tone of semi-malicious glee was like a healing balm.

'What are we going to do?' he hastened to take up Dron's invitation to resume their earlier conversation. 'We finish breakfast, I take my case and leave it with you while we look for a new place for me to stay?'

'Hold your horses!' The liveliness in Dron's voice could not conceal the moralizing. 'Your suitcase, no problem. We're not going to have you carting it off to the left luggage at the railway station. But as for finding a new place for you to stay … There is nowhere. Every hotel is crammed, taken, booked out right through to March when the hot season begins. This is high season! I had to stand on my head to get you into Liberty Place, and that was booking in advance. If you had just turned up, you would have been staying in one hotel for a day, then having to move to another for another day. You'd have been running around every day just looking for a place to live. Not a holiday, more a bed of nails.'

Rad was disconcerted. He had not expected any problem.

'Well, I didn't come here for a holiday …'

'You didn't? Well I did. Who gets to look for a place for you to stay? Me!' It was hard to tell if Dron was seriously tearing him off a strip or just acting the part. 'Or were you thinking of staying at the Oriental Hotel?'

'I'm really not fussy,' Rad said modestly, trying to maintain his air of insouciance.

'You're not fussy! Have you any idea what a room there would cost?!'

'How could I?' Rad parried the question with one of his own.

'Don't even think about it,' Dron laughed. He raised his coffee cup and leaned forward as if to clink glasses. 'There is another option,' he said, preparing to take a sip. 'A bit more interesting, too. What do you think of this?'

He and Nellie had been planning a trip to the north, to the mountains. They had been intending to go later, after giving Rad an opportunity to drink in what Bangkok had to offer, but since he now had no roof over his head, Dron suggested they leave immediately, today. The train to Chiang Mai, the capital of the north, left in early evening and there should be no great problem about changing their tickets, except that they would probably have to go second class. What could be a problem was finding a hotel. They had booked for a later date, which meant they would have nowhere to lay their heads, but Chiang Mai was not Bangkok. If they were prepared not to stay right in the centre but on the outskirts, and in a less luxurious hotel, they would be bound to find something. That was not going to be a problem. In the meantime, Tony could get to work with his contacts in Bangkok, and by the time they came back Rad would have somewhere to stay.

'In Thailand, as in any other Asian country, everything is based on patriarchal relations,' Dron concluded his announcement and returned to his coffee. 'It's good to have a hundred rubles in the bank, but better still to have a hundred friends to draw on. With friends and relations, you can get anything, the moon out of the sky if need be. Capitalism is fine, but scratch a little and you'll get something straight out of the *Mahabharata*.'

'Or replace the *Mahabharata* with the *The Tale of Bygone Years*,' Rad remarked.

'And?' Dron looked puzzled

'And you get Russia.'

'Ah!' Dron liked that. 'Of course. No two ways about it.' He finished his coffee, put the cup firmly back on its saucer and pushed it to one side. 'So, what do you think of my proposal?'

Rad had nothing against it. Why not go to see the north? If Dron had proposed going to see the south, he would have had nothing against that either. What he was eager to do was finally to have the talk that was the reason for his having come here.

'Dron, that's a great suggestion,' he said, draining his cup in turn. 'But when can we talk business? Chris has left now.'

Dron threw up his hands to stop him.

'Wait, wait! This is too soon. Right now we have to be thinking about getting packed … Wait some more!' He moved his chair back and got up. 'You go and get ready too. Settle up with the hotel and bring your things round. Here …' He pulled out his wallet, took out a wad of thousand-baht notes, counted out a few and gave them to Rad. 'You must be running a bit low, eh?' He evidently thought it appropriate to accompany this with a knowing wink. 'Get the old circulation going again, eh?'

Taking the money, Rad felt humiliated. He could not bring himself to thank him. Instead he asked, although it was not a top priority at that moment, 'Hey, do you by any chance know what "Odiya" means in Thai?'

'"Odiya"?' Dron repeated. 'Never heard it, but we'll soon find out. Hang on.' They had just arrived at the bar to pay the bill and Dron, before requesting the barman to call the waitress, asked him, 'What do you think "Odiya" means?'

'I'm sorry, what was that again?' The barman had evidently not recognised a word in his own language because of the foreign pronunciation.

'Repeat the way you said it,' Dron said, turning to Rad.

Rad cursed to himself. He really did not need all this.

'O-odeeya!' he said, meticulously imitating his prostitute's intonation.

'O-odeeya!' the barman exclaimed, recognizing the word from the way Rad pronounced it. '"How unpleasant!", something like that. "What a bad situation", "How disgusting!" It is the English expression, "Oh, dear!"'

'Satisfied?' Dron asked

Rad was more than satisfied, but the lady whose reactions yesterday were causing him so much trouble today had used another Thai word which had lodged in his memory.

'What is a "farang"?' He asked the barman.

'Oh, even I can tell you that,' Dron butted in. 'A "farang" is a white person, someone who is not Thai, a foreigner. Anything else you want to know?'

'No, that's it.' Those were the only words in Rad's Thai vocabulary.

As they were going towards the door, the elderly Japanese gentleman with the cravat, who all this time had been on the Internet, was just getting up from the computer.

'So disgrace!' he exclaimed in English to Rad and Dron, throwing up his hands in despair. 'So disgrace! Invest money so uncompetent!'

They noticed tears flowing down his cheeks. Perhaps he was not really speaking to Rad and Dron but to himself, or even to nobody, to fate, to the heavens. He had evidently been following the progress of his shares.

'Poor man,' Rad muttered.

Dron was having none of it.

'Life is a gamble,' he declared as he opened the glass door into the street and held it for Rad. 'One person wins, another loses. If you don't feel up to it, don't gamble. That way you won't lose. But you won't win either!' he added, wagging his finger like a schoolmaster.

* * *

The train was standing at the platform ready for boarding but the doors of the carriages were still closed. From the roof to the wheels, they gleamed like a glossy photograph, and as Dron's party advanced towards them they were enveloped by humidity: evidently the train had been washed immediately before being put into service. Opposite one of the carriages in the middle of the train the conductors were being given their orders. Without exception, they were men in khaki-brown uniforms rather like boiler suits and stood like a line of soldiers while their chief, in a similar uniform, viewing them with the imperious gaze of an overseer, barked his instructions as if issuing commands before battle. The conductors' faces, their jaws firmly clamped shut, radiated zeal to serve and awareness of their responsibilities.

'See that? That's how Russia needs to be governed!' Dron commented. 'That's the only thing Russia understands. It's part of Asia, eh?' he said, referring back to his and Rad's morning conversation in Coffee Max.

'Yes,' Rad agreed.

Nellie was dressed in 1920s style for the journey, in a striped trouser suit of fine linen with a silky sheen, in a small, close-fitting straw cloche hat reminiscent of the twenties of the century in which they were born and had as yet lived the greater part of their lives. She was walking a little apart in order not to get in the way of their wheeled suitcases and seemed not to be listening to their occasional remarks, but at this she straightened up and veered towards them.

'Oh, Rad, are you going along with that?' she asked. 'Are you really agreeing with Dron?'

Rad felt even less inclined to debate the subject with her than with Dron.

'Let's wait and see how they actually perform in the job,' he said evasively, nodding towards the parade of conductors. 'Whether their talking-to has any practical effect.'

At this moment the conductors were evidently ordered to fall out. Their line-up, which a minute before was rock-like, straight as a taut string, came to life, lost its rigour and collapsed. The conductors milled about and their Brownian motion resolved into two groups which step by step moved further apart, one towards the back of the train and the other towards the front.

'Thais treasure their jobs the way a dog treasures the favour of its owner,' Dron remarked as they hastened to their carriages. 'Sometimes, when you see them working so diligently, you imagine they have a tail and you can see it wagging with delight.'

'Well, one category of humanity which doesn't have tails is Russians,' Nellie said heatedly.

'Russians don't,' Dron readily conceded.

'What do you think?' Nellie asked Rad.

'No, that's true. Russians don't have a tail,' Rad responded. 'Although, actually,' he corrected himself, 'perhaps they do. Only not a dog's tail.'

'What kind then?' Dron enquired pointedly.

'A devil's tail?' Nellie inferred.

'Something like that, 'Rad said. 'Although I decline to take the responsibility of making that assertion.'

Dron snorted, amused.

'Come on, no pussyfooting! If they do, then it's absolutely the Devil's tail. A long, curly tail with a tassle on the end. It wags its owner and performs the functions of a brain.'

'Dron, you're a russophobe!' Nellie exclaimed indignantly.

'Nothing of the sort!' Dron objected. 'I'm a sincere, top-quality russophile, but like any true russophile, I love my people with my eyes open and have no inclination to trust them blindly.'

'That's the ideology of Russian aristocracy,' Nellie declared, as if pronouncing a verdict.

'I'm happy to take that as a compliment,' Dron said.

They arrived at their carriage. The conductor, in eager anticipation of his passengers, was standing beside it. The door was open, revealing steps which led inside. Barely glancing at their tickets, he seized both suitcases and ran with them at the steps. Dron's suitcase was as big as a good-sized trunk and it was simply unrealistic to try to take both up at the same time. After performing a comical dance on the first of the steps the conductor had to abandon his attempt to carry both in by sheer willpower. He put Rad's suitcase down on the platform, grabbed Dron's with both hands, and mounted a second assault. This was successful. Rad lifted his suitcase to follow him but the conductor, now abandoning Dron's case, swooped down and seized it out of his hands. 'No-no,' he said horrified, carrying it off. 'No-no!'

After dragging the two suitcases to their seats, the conductor accepted tips from Rad and Dron and, without a word of thanks, immediately ran back to his post by the door.

'What have you got to say now?' Nellie asked Dron triumphantly.

'Ye-es,' Dron admitted shamefaced. 'Not really your typical Thai.'

'Looks like not all Thais have doggy tails,' Nellie continued, rubbing in her victory.

'Okay, okay,' Dron conceded. He was reluctant to admit defeat. 'But he'll perform his duties with religious fervour. Wait and see!'

Their seats were not far from the entrance. The carriage was like a Russian second-class carriage, except that the passageway was not to one side but down the middle, and there were compartments to both sides of it. The floor of the compartments was raised about twenty centimetres above the level of the passageway, and although the compartments were not partitioned off from it, the fact that they were raised created the illusion of a separate space. Each had wide, upholstered seats facing each other corresponding to their tickets, but there was no sign of a second, upper bunk, which made it look as though they would be spending the night sitting up.

That was Rad's immediate question, delivered with an expression of mock dismay as he took in his surroundings. Dron and Nellie laughed at such ignorance.

'No, really,' Dron said. 'How could you even think such a thing? Do you suppose we are not white people and could be expected to sit upright all night? Everything opens up and moves apart. Don't worry, second class is certainly not first class, but you surely don't imagine I would let my wife travel with the plebs?'

'Or yourself,' Nellie remarked a little huffily.

'Perfectly true,' Dron agreed. 'I wouldn't travel cattle class myself.'

The compartment occupied by Dron and Nellie was directly opposite Rad's, so when he had stowed his suitcase under the seat, Rad moved over to sit with them. There would have been little room for two if he had tried to sit with Dron, so he sat next to Nellie.

'Oh, what on earth have you done to yourself?' Nellie exclaimed, clasping his head in both hands and inclining it towards herself. 'You've got a wound!'

Close up, the lock of hair which masked the bump on his head and the coating of dried blood where Lana's knuckleduster had impacted was not thick enough to conceal it on close inspection.

Rad removed Nellie's hands from his head.

'It isn't a wound,' he said. 'It's the consequences of one.'

'And what was the cause of the consequences?' Nellie asked in the tone of an investigator interrogating a suspect.

'The usual, I accidentally tripped,' Rad responded in character like a real suspect avoiding self-incrimination. He recalled a Chekhov character suspected of derailing a train: *'We make sinkers for our fishing lines out of the nuts. We don't unscrew all of them, of course. We leave some. We're not idiots!'*

Nellie looked with impotent irritation at Dron:

'What about you? What do you know? What happened?'

Dron was again shaking with laughter.

'We really need you to get to the bottom of it, don't we! Nothing happened. You can see for yourself, the man's sitting there alive and well. He fell over. He's told you. Stop going on at him.'

Nellie paused for a moment.

'You've got some secrets, haven't you?' she said. 'Is that why you left me in the room?'

Dron shrugged.

'You said you wanted to stay.'

'But you didn't try to persuade me to come with you.'

'True,' Dron agreed.

Nellie was silent, then looked again at Rad's head.

'Is that why we changed the tickets and are leaving Bangkok?'

'Keep your guesswork to yourself,' Dron said. He did not raise or modulate his voice. On the contrary, it seemed to be colourless, blank, and from Nellie's changed expression Rad could see that she would be keeping her guesswork to herself. 'Why don't you show us the photos you've had back?' Dron said, putting some colour back into his voice.

At just this moment, the other passenger in Rad's compartment appeared, obliging him to leave Dron and Nellie to their concerns. His fellow passenger was neatly dressed, in a jacket and tie despite the heat, a young, managerial-looking man who spoke English with the rapidity of machine-gun fire. He had two bags, one of which was large, but carried both to his seat without the conductor's assistance. He and Rad checked to see who had which place. Rad had the upper bunk, which did not worry him in the slightest, but the young man insisted he should make him a present of the lower one, repeating, 'You are senior, you are senior.' His teeth gleamed laser-white, just like Tony's. His friends were in a different carriage, so he asked Rad to look after his luggage while he went to enjoy some time with them.

The carriage, meanwhile, had filled up. The conductor, calling out something in Thai, frantically ran down the aisle into the interior, evidently checking for anyone seeing someone off or fare-dodgers, before running back and disappearing behind the door at the end of the carriage. There was a moment of silence, and the train moved off.

'Toot-toot!' Dron said to Rad from his compartment.

Nellie wordlessly showed him the pack of photos she was holding.

The train, gathering speed, emerged from the twilight of the station, the platform was left behind, and he blinked at the pale lilac light of departing day. Rad was more interested in the accelerating succession of live scenes outside the window than in scenes of life transfixed by the click of a Japanese digital camera's shutter.

'Shall we enjoy the scenery for a bit?' he suggested.

'Do you think there's anything to enjoy?' Dron queried.

He had a point. As its smart glass and concrete façade faced the roads and sois, the city had its backside to the railway. Wretched shanties which looked to be made of cardboard stood almost next to the track, peering through weak-sighted windows at the world outside. Some of these miniature windows were lit, revealing impoverished interiors. In the wide-open doors, wrinkled old women sat on folding chairs, with their arms on their knees, their hands with swollen veins dangling wearily between their legs. Washing was drying on the branches of trees. A young woman in an apron smeared with blood and slime was gutting a fish with a huge black knife. A man was chopping wood with a long-handled axe. Pots and frying pans were piled on open fires in hearths composed of pieces of concrete slab, and beside them women were turning something over in the pans with fish slices and knives, or stirring something in the pots. A boy and girl aged six or seven pursued a chicken fleeing from them, fell upon it in the dirt, and the two of them carried it back to an old man with a meat cleaver waiting for it beside a chopping block black with blood. In a tiny bike repair workshop, with its doors thrown open and littered with the skeletons of bicycles and motorbikes, a man stripped to the waist was squatting in front of an upended bicycle, tightening its spokes. Beyond the cardboard-looking workshop Rad could see a dusty road covered in loose chippings. A barefoot ten-year-old, in trousers which did not reach to his ankles, with a shaven head and stripped to the waist, was single-mindedly rolling the rim of a bicycle wheel down the road, directing it with a rigid piece of steel wire.

In a blinding flash, Rad found himself back as a ten- or eleven-year-old in a courtyard on the outskirts of Moscow, chasing an old bicycle wheel in exactly the same way. He recalled the name of the piece of heavy steel wire, specially bent at the end so as to fit into the rim of the wheel and slow it down. It was called the *pravilka*.

The next instant he was imagining himself as one of the inhabitants of this backside of the city; someone who would open their eyes here in the morning, and in the evening, falling asleep, close them in this same place. Day after day, year after year, for a lifetime. It jolted him like an electric shock.

He would not want to live that way. It would be more like living a bad dream than a life.

Rad turned away from the window and looked across at Dron and Nellie. They too had moved to the side of the carriage, and the backs of their heads told him they were engaged in the same occupation as he had been. Nellie was clutching the pack of photographs on her knee.

Rad got up, stepped down into the aisle and back up into their compartment. Nellie turned round.

'Well,' she asked, 'seen enough of the scenery?'

'Yes,' he said sitting down next to her. 'I'm ready for the photos.'

Dron too turned away from the window with obvious relief.

'What makes photographs better than life,' he said, 'is that they make life artistic.'

'Especially colour photographs,' Nellie added.

'I had colour photography in mind,' Dron said. 'Kodak and Co. varnish reality.'

'But Tony's village really is lovely,' Nellie remarked, baffling Rad.

'His village really is lovely,' Dron agreed, no less puzzlingly.

What they were talking about, he understood when Nellie began showing the pictures. They were snaps she had taken during their trip to visit Tony's family. His parents' house from the front, from the side, from the verandah. A splendid meal on the verandah, the table being a rug spread on the floor, decorated with a vase of carefully selected, exotic flowers. On mats around it, Tony's mother and father, Tony's uncle, the uncle's wife, Tony's nephews and nieces, the wives and husbands of the nephews and nieces, Tony himself, Dron, and next to him Tony's widowed sister.

'Look, isn't she lovely?' Dron said, snatching a close-up photograph of Tony's sister out of Nellie's hands. He first admired the picture himself, then turned it so Rad could see. 'Look at those cheekbones, her lips, the slant of her eyes. Really lovely!'

'Have you fallen for her?' Nellie asked.

'A bit,' Dron said with a chuckle, passing the photo to Rad.

Tony's sister was very pretty, and very young.

'Is she really twenty-six?' Rad exclaimed, surprising himself by suddenly remembering her age.

'I told you, Thais look younger than their years,' Dron reminded him.

'Your tickets, please,' a shrill Thai voice speaking English and coming from the passageway intruded on their conversation. It was a team of three inspectors in an opalescent grey, entirely military-looking uniform, and it seemed clear that, if anything was amiss, they would take no prisoners. Dron had the tickets. He showed them, and the team, satisfied, proceeded to the next compartment.

A minute after the inspectors, a girl in a light brown cheese-cutter cap and blouse with epaulettes looked into their compartment. She was from the restaurant, and taking orders for dinner. In contrast to the inspectors, she was friendliness itself. The smile on her face gave the impression of having appeared on it at the moment of her birth and never having left.

'There,' Dron said, addressing himself to Nellie and simultaneously to Rad when the waitress had gone. 'Did you see that tail? Really curly, really fluffy!'

'Would you prefer her to have been offensive instead, like in Russia?' Nellie asked.

'I certainly didn't notice the inspectors having any tails,' Rad said, aligning himself with Nellie's party.

'They're just good at hiding it,' Dron said, wriggling out.

The waitress reappeared with rectangular plastic containers before they had finished looking at all the photos. 'Here's dinner,' she announced, placing the containers on one of the seats in Rad's empty compartment. She asked them to be patient for a moment longer, bent down and, with a clatter, pulled out from beneath the floor of Rad's compartment a table which was almost identical to the non-movable tables which stick out in a Russian compartment, only this one was not square but long, and extended almost the width of the compartment. She deftly attached one edge to a metal flange at the window, snapped a support out from the underside of the table, and fitted it into a hole on the floor which Rad had not noticed. She went through the same procedure in Dron and Nellie's compartment, and then three lidded plastic boxes were taken from their container and placed on the table. 'Enjoy!' She swept up the other containers and moved on. The whole time, the smile never left her face.

While they were eating dinner it became completely dark outside and the lights came on in the carriage. The air conditioner efficiently sent a wave of cold air down the passageway, perhaps, indeed, cooler than they might have wished.

The waitress returned, collected the empty plastic trays and set Dron and Nellie's table for tea and coffee. The glasses really were glass, and the solid teaspoons were cupro-nickel. 'Enjoy,' she said again, pouring boiling water into the glasses from a large electric kettle with a graduated transparent side.

Rad felt a shiver of anticipation as the moment of the long-awaited conversation inexorably approached. Today was the day. Perhaps in five minutes' time, perhaps in an hour. Nothing could stop it. A train journey was the perfect setting.

Rad and Dron, finishing their coffee, moved to the table in the empty compartment and Nellie, recognizing that she was going to be spending the evening on her own, had taken a book from her bag to commune with an ethereal companion mass produced for the purpose by the renowned American publisher, Random House.

'Right, as I see it …' Dron had just said, inviting Rad to tell his story, when the young, managerial type whose bags were stowed under one of the seats in Rad's compartment popped up like a jack-in-the-box in the passageway. He still had his jacket buttoned, the top button of his shirt was still fastened, and he had not loosened his tie, as if even on the train he was obliged to continue performing his important managerial duties.

'I am back. Thank you for taking care my things,' he said, giving Rad the unreservedly respectful smile of a younger person addressing his senior. 'I hope I have not been absent too long?'

Rad did not have it in him to reply with the courtesy the occasion called for. What a moment to turn up!

'Actually, you're welcome to stay a bit longer with your friends,' he growled. 'I'm not going anywhere.'

'Oh, no-no. That would be awkward. I've already said goodnight to them.'

Then, quite unexpectedly, Dron seized the initiative.

'Sit down, do sit down, friend.' He was suddenly, most uncharacteristically, all aglow. He indicated the seat next to him. 'Or would you prefer to sit by the window?'

Rad's fellow passenger did not prefer to sit by the window: the seat next to Dron suited him admirably. He would just like, though, to get a book out of his bag.

'Oh, well let me move all the same. That will be more convenient for you.' Dron got up and moved to the seat next to Rad. 'Perhaps you need to eat,' he asked, watching Rad's fellow passenger pulling his bag from under the seat. 'Actually, we've already eaten, but perhaps you want to get out some of your own supplies? Do bring them out, don't be shy.'

He said this with such sympathetic concern for all his neighbour's foreseeable problems, with such manifest liking for him, that it would have been impossible not to respond with a similar degree of liking and openness.

Dron and Rad were informed that their neighbour had already eaten with his friends. Within five minutes they also knew that he really was a manager, in a trading company which specialised in the wholesale purchasing and selling of fibreglass fabrics; that the company had Japanese owners; that he often had to travel to Japan; and that, in addition to English, he was fluent in Japanese.

'Oh, my God!' Dron exclaimed, dreamily half-closing his eyes. 'At your age, I too so wanted to learn Japanese. Alas, the opportunity didn't present itself.'

'Why do you think it is too late?' Bobby asked.

His name was Bobby. 'And your name in Thai?' Rad asked with some interest when his neighbour introduced himself. 'Oh, for my English-speaking friends I am just Bobby,' he said.

'Oh, Bobby, I'm not as young as you,' Dron said in an envious tone in response to his suggestion that it was not too late for him to learn Japanese. 'Nothing is quite so easy nowadays.'

'How old are you?' Bobby asked straightforwardly.

'We are thirty-five,' Dron said, indicating himself and Rad.

Rad was actually thirty-six, but he let it pass.

'Well, I'm only slightly younger!' Bobby announced triumphantly.

It turned out he was already thirty, and soon to be thirty-one.

'I told you,' Dron said to Rad. 'Thai people look younger than their years.'

'No, it is Europeans who look older than theirs,' Bobby quipped.

Their conversation flowed and glided and leapt like a mountain stream gathering speed, seemingly by itself, following its natural course, impelled by their shared interest in each other. Bobby said he was going to Chiang Mai to see his parents, or rather, not actually to Chiang Mai but to his parents' home which was about eight kilometres outside. It was his mother's birthday and he was taking her presents; he had three days leave from his job; his mother had wanted him to become a monk when he was little, because that brought merit to the whole family, but he had declined and now wanted his mother to forgive him; he sent his parents 250 dollars every month, and they were using the money to buy paddy fields because that was a secure investment and it could be looked on as his future pension.

Rad gazed at Dron with admiration. How adroitly he got the conversation going under its own momentum, and persuaded Bobby to reveal so much about himself. It was an exceptional talent.

Bobby talked and talked. He told the story of his life, and the book he had taken out of his case lay unopened on his lap. Rad's own conversation with Dron was clearly on the back burner.

Rad looked across at Nellie. She was sitting, leaning back in her seat, communing with her Random House friend. He got up and went to the toilet. There were two WCs, opposite each other. Inside, everything was gleaming with cleanliness. A thick, broad roll of paper towels hung from the wall, and beside the toilet was a toilet roll of immaculate two-ply toilet paper. The liquid soap dispenser over the sink was filled to capacity and, close by the capacious toilet seat of sparkling white plastic, in a nickel-plated holder, hung a rubber hose with a shiny nickel-plated nozzle, allowing you to use the toilet as a bidet.

When he returned to his seat, the conductor had just gone into Dron and Nellie's compartment. Without a word, with rapid, automatic movements, the man slightly raised the table, extracted the support from the hole in the floor, folded it back, lifted the table off the flange on the wall and, stepping down into the passageway, slipped it back under the compartment floor. He moved back up into the compartment, and now the object of his silent, automatic actions was the upper bunk, so sleek that, if you did not know, you would never guess it was pressed against the carriage wall. Something clicked beneath his hands, the bunk came away from the wall, turned through 180 degrees, crashed down and was supported by heavy metal brackets ready to take the weight of a human body.

'Very neat!' Rad remarked to Nellie in Russian.

'Yes, I'm never quite quick enough to work out how they do that,' Nellie replied.

The conductor stepped back down into the passageway, and again bent and pulled a ladder from the same dark recess. He extended it to twice its length, placed it vertically up to the top bunk, there was a short metallic clink and the ladder was fixed to the bunk's protective guard rail.

'Thank you so much!' Nellie said in English.

The conductor said nothing. He was already in Rad's compartment, where Dron and Bobby were sitting and Bobby was writing something for Dron on a piece of paper.

The conductor grunted something at him in Thai and, grasping the edge of the table, prepared to dismantle it. Bobby spoke to him and, from his gestures, it was clear he was asking the conductor to leave them alone, promising to do everything himself. The conductor obstinately shook his head and sang out something in rapid, irate Thai.

Bobby took the paper he was writing off the table.

'He says,' Bobby explained in English, 'that he has his job to do, and he is absolutely right. I was wrong to try to stop him.'

The conductor had already removed the table from the metal flange beneath the window.

'We should let him do his job,' Dron agreed.

Bobby wrote a few words, balancing the paper on his knee, and handed it to Dron.

'This is, in addition to the business card, my address in Bangkok,' he said.

'Are they trying to get us to go to bed already?' Rad asked Bobby.

'Yes, it's past eight o'clock. It's time. We should lie down,' Bobby said.

'In Thailand people go to bed earlier in the winter,' Dron said in Russian. 'That's not something you've yet had an opportunity to observe. Anyway, see how dark it is, and electricity is not cheap.'

'By the way, we arrive in Chiang Mai a few minutes after seven in the morning,' Nellie called across. 'So it's really not such a bad idea to go to bed now.'

The conductor had lowered the upper bunk and was now taking the ladder out from beneath the compartment floor.

'In any case, what is there to do on the train other than sleep?' Dron added.

He translated his words into English for Bobby.

'Oh, personally I get enough sleep on the train to last me for a week,' he said.

He still had not loosened his tie or undone the top button of his shirt. His only concession had been to take off his jacket.

Half an hour later Rad, having drawn the synthetic grey-blue curtain which hung from hooks dangling down from the top shelf, lay in his bottom bunk, covered with a large gauffered sheet issued by the conductor as a blanket, trying to sleep. Despite the previous night's sleep deprivation, he was not the least bit tired: rather, he was on edge. He had been in Thailand for three days now, and had not even made a start on the one thing he had come here to resolve!

CHAPTER TEN

The air was fresh, chilly even. None of the three of them were prepared for that. They had not put on anything warm and now, off the train, exclaimed in surprise. 'The mountains,' Bobby enlightened them with the knowledgeable air of a local.

The square in front of the railway station was extensive and deserted, and had the feel of wasteland. Only in one or two places was it enlivened by truck-like vehicles painted the colour of fire engines, with low, enclosed bodies, along the sides of which a continuous window extended like a slit. Around each of these beetle-like vehicles, like bees bearding at the hive entrance, small groups of people clustered.

'Taxis,' Bobby said, indicating them.

In fact, people mostly did not stay there for long. They went to one 'taxi', stood there for a time crowding round it, and then went on to another. Some, however, stayed, tossed their bags into the body of the truck, which did not have a tailgate, and climbed inside up some steps.

'What's that all about? Is the driver deciding who he'll take and who he won't?' Rad asked, recalling the situation at railway stations in Russia.

'No, what right would he have to do that?' Bobby looked at Rad with such surprise that he was clearly not sure the question could be serious. 'He will drive where the first passenger wants to go, and can only take others if they are going the same way.'

All four of them went to the nearest taxi, Bobby exchanged a few words with the driver, who was standing nearby, and changing back to English, gestured to them to climb in.

'Please get in! That is lucky. He is going in your direction.'

'After you,' Dron said to Nellie, pointing to the steps.

Inside were benches on both sides, each seating five or six people, and a gap between them all the way up to the driver's cab. Three passengers were already seated, with their suitcases in the aisle and cardboard boxes wrapped in sticky tape piled on top of each other. The only seat for Nellie was in the middle of a bench, and Dron and Rad, after placing their cases in the aisle, had to perch on the very end of the benches.

Bobby was standing outside and looking pleased that everything had worked out so well. He gave them a thumbs up.

'Nice meeting you, everybody! Good luck! I will find another taxi now which is going in my direction.'

'Nice meeting you, Bobby, thank you for everything! Good luck to you too, goodbye!' Rad and Nellie called to him, waving.

'I'll phone you, Bobby!' Dron shouted, in place of a farewell.

The driver, standing outside and looking up the aisle, seemed disappointed he could not fit in a couple more passengers, but there was clearly no space.

Their taxi took off so fast that Rad and Dron had to clutch at the bench they were sitting on in order not to fall out.

'It's called a *song-thaew*, a bench-taxi,' Dron said, as the vehicle speeded up and then drove smoothly along.

'A two-bench taxi more like,' Rad observed, unaware that he had just added two more words to his Thai vocabulary. That bent for precision seemed virtually all that remained of the profession he had had to abandon.

'No, it's a bench-taxi,' Dron insisted. 'That's its official name: a bench-taxi.'

'Really, Thais are such well-intentioned people,' Nellie said to no one in particular. 'Take Bobby. He is simply delightful. A pleasure to know.'

'You think so?' Dron queried. 'He smells money, does Bobby. Money. That's why he's a delight to know.'

'What would make him think that?' Rad asked, feeling he ought to join in the discussion.

Instead of Dron, however, Nellie answered.

'What makes us think anything? We think it because we want to believe it.'

Dron did not lodge an appeal against that.

Their taxi flew along the deserted morning roads, braking on the bends and then taking off again. The breeze rushing through the window slits did not allow them to forget the nearness of the mountains. Nellie huddled up, clutching her shoulders.

To the left of the road, looking down on rows of buildings which seemed stunted by comparison as they drowned in all the greenery, an impressive building drew itself upwards, like a gigantic white sail in the ocean of the sky. On its roof a sign proclaimed in large letters: Sheraton. There were mountains of earth and rubble strewn around it, the windows of the upper storeys were not yet glazed, but the brand name already hovered in the sky, staking its claim. The taxi flew up on to a bridge across the river and, when it reached the other end, turned right, raced on another hundred metres and, braking sharply, came to a standstill.

'River Ping Palace,' the driver turned and shouted through the window between his cab and the body of the songthaew. River Ping Palace was the hotel they had been able to book instead of the one awaiting them a few days hence.

Rad and Dron barely had time to jump to the ground before the driver was there, pushing them away so he could unload their luggage for them. The aisle now clear, Nellie got up and moved to the step. Rad, well brought up as a child, instinctively offered her a helping hand.

'Much obliged,' Nellie said, stepping down and withdrawing her hand.

Dron, paying the driver, gave Rad an ironical smile,

'You're quite a gentleman!'

'I am,' Rad concurred.

'Young ladies like that,' Nellie rejoined, as if defending him.

The songthaew departed, leaving them in front of a wide double gate with a wooden arch ornately inscribed with the hotel's name in English. Through the gates they could see a spacious courtyard covered with grey gravel, and the corner of a wooden house with a stairway leading to the first floor. It resembled the houses they had seen at the Jim Thompson museum.

'Are you frozen?' Dron asked. 'Let's go!'

He and Rad took the suitcases and, with Nellie between them, proceeded through the gates.

On the left side of the courtyard a robust, silvery Toyota 4x4 was parked under a soft, sloping canopy of reeds; to the right, peeping out of luxuriant vegetation, a functional single-storey building stretched deep into the property. Judging by the smells emanating from it, this was the kitchen.

Noisily hauling their wheeled cases over the gravel, they crossed the yard and stopped by the corner of the house. There was no one around. Between the house and the utility building there were trees with multiple trunks, and birds sang in their intermingling crowns. A path of square concrete slabs cut diagonally through this thicket; a slender black ridged hose ran along it. The end of the hose had been left on the ground under the trees and water babbled from it as if from a spring. Her bare feet slapping noisily on the concrete slabs, a girl of about thirteen suddenly jumped out from the thicket. She was wearing long shorts and a baggy sweater too big for her, which made it look like a dress. She stopped for a moment, stared at them in amazement, and rushed back without a word.

Dron gave Rad and then Nellie a triumphant look.

'There!' he exclaimed. 'I said it was a country hotel!'

Back in Bangkok, when he finally managed to book a place for them to stay, he had put down the phone and said, 'We are going to be staying at a hotel in the sticks. Not five-star, not four-star, not any-star. A hotel in the sticks!'

'Yes, it certainly is in the sticks,' Nellie responded, in a tone which might equally have been registering satisfaction or irony, as she looked around the yard, her gaze lingering on the reed awning which served as a car port.

'Well, Rad and I think it fits the bill nicely, don't we, Rad?' Dron retorted, with a jibe at the circumstances behind their abrupt change of plan.

Rad shrugged,

'Just as long as the toilet isn't outside.'

'Oh, do you think it might be?' The disbelief in Nellie's voice was mixed with a readiness to contemplate that possibility.

'No chance,' Dron said. 'Even if it's out in the sticks, it's still a hotel, and Thai hotels allow for the possibility of foreigners staying at them. You couldn't expect a foreigner to put up with an outside toilet. They'll even have a shower in the room. I guarantee it.'

Rapid footsteps were heard on the concrete path and, out of the thicket, appeared a Thai lady of about their age, or a little older if they allowed for Thais looking younger. Her smile displayed teeth of the same laser-whiteness as those of Tony and Bobby.

'Oh, you've already arrived! So early!' she pattered away in fluent English. 'So you came on that early train? I thought you would be flying. Why would I think that?'

'I have no idea why you would think that,' Dron said drily.

'Yes, I wonder why I thought you would be flying!' She burst out in tinkling laughter. She seemed to radiate such energy you should be able to plug a lamp into her and it would light up. 'Call me Esther,' she said, holding out her hand to Dron. 'I am the owner of this hotel. I am happy to welcome you. I am happy to welcome you,' she said to Rad. Her handshake was as energetic as everything else about her. 'I am happy to welcome you,' she said, not overlooking Nellie.

A moment later, the connection between her boisterous welcome and their early appearance became evident: their rooms were not ready.

'Come with me, have a cup of coffee after your long journey, it will be my treat. She took Dron by the arm and firmly pulled him along the concrete path into the thicket. Her instinct was unerring: she had immediately identified him as the shaft horse and Rad and Nellie as the trace-horses. 'Let's drink some coffee, breathe some fresh air, get to know each other better, and by then everything will be ready.'

'She's a real Amazon, isn't she?' Nellie said in Russian as they followed her and Dron down the path.

'An Amazon!' Rad agreed unhesitatingly.

The path through the thicket was not as long as it seemed. After a couple of dozen steps the undergrowth ended and the path led out to a spacious area paved with ceramic tiles. To the right was the restaurant's verandah with a row of tables, and to the left, decorated with intricate wooden carving, was a gazebo with a massive table and benches. Immediately beyond the paved area was the river they had just driven over, and steps led down a metre and a half to where the muddy river was lapping. The opposite riverbank, some eighty metres away, was primal and pristine and rose heavenward in separate tiers of grass, bushes and trees. Only near the bridge, where the sail-like Sheraton Hotel hovered, had the greenery been ripped out by the roots. Like a scalp, the ground was revealed in all its unsightly dusty-brown nakedness, and on its bare skin, despite the early hour of morning, the metal joints of a bright orange excavator were clattering, bending and unbending, its long, articulated neck plunging into the water and rising back out. The bank was evidently being turned into an embankment. The view from the paved area, if you could ignore the clattering orange brontosaur, was stunning: the kind of view for which even an outside toilet could have been forgiven.

'Are you sure?' was Nellie's response when Rad shared this thought with her. 'And even the mosquitoes?'

There really was an oversupply of mosquitoes, which had periodically to be flapped away. Rad had despatched a couple already by clapping his hands.

'Every silver lining has a cloud,' he generalised.

Esther took them to the verandah, sat them at a table, and went over to the bar counter, where another girl was gazing at them as if they were visitors from outer space.

It struck Rad that they really were from another world. The girl behind the bar was about fourteen, if, of course, his European eye was getting it right this time. She had pure, delicate features, and an expression he could only describe as extraordinarily graceful. As Esther approached, the girl immediately looked to her, ready to be instructed. She seemed to be standing to attention, determined not to miss a single word her employer uttered. As soon as she heard what Esther had to say, she moved like clockwork around her space, unscrewing the top of one jar, then of another, wielding a small spoon like a sickle, tugging the handles of the coffee machine, pressing one button then another, getting herself enveloped in steam, and there in front of Esther on the counter were two chunky porcelain mugs of lazily steaming coffee.

'Please! It's my treat!' Esther said, placing the mugs on the table with a beaming, laser-white smile. 'The third one is just on its way. My barmaid works miracles.'

'She's a fine girl,' Dron responded, glancing towards the bar.

'Incidentally,' Esther said, leaning toward them and lowering her voice slightly, 'she is not a girl.'

'What do you mean, she's not a girl?' 'What was that?' ' What is she then?' the three of them exclaimed at once. 'A boy?' Dron said, lowering his voice like Esther.

'Yes,' Esther said. 'But he prefers being a girl. And he does make a beautiful girl, don't you think?'

'He certainly does,' Nellie confirmed.

'So he ... she ...' Rad was flummoxed. He could not think what gender to use in relation to a boy-barmaid. 'Is he physically still a boy, or wholly a girl?'

Esther and Dron smirked condescendingly.

'No, no,' Esther said. 'Physically she is a boy. Perhaps later she will choose to have the operation. I don't know.'

'Let me explain,' Dron said in Russian. 'This is Thailand. It is a country where a woman has an easier life. A woman in Thailand will never go hungry, but it can be tougher for a man. If a boy's family notice that he is a bit effeminate, they just raise him as a girl. They talk to him as a girl, they dress him as a girl. Only in poor families, of course.'

'Well, knock me down with a feather duster!' Rad said, stunned.

'Have you never heard of that before? Nellie asked in surprise.

'Never!'

'Well, consider yourself enlightened now,' Dron concluded.

The boy-barmaid came from behind the bar, her high heels clacking on the tiles, and brought the third mug of coffee to their table.

'Your coffee,' she said in a singsong voice, pushing her boyish treble to the top of its range and blushing crimson, the very epitome of an acutely self-conscious young lady.

'Oh, thank you.' 'Yes, thank you.' 'Thank you very much,' the three of them responded simultaneously, trying their hardest not to stare.

'Good girl,' Esther said approvingly, matching her words to the barmaid's clothing.

She clattered back behind the bar, and was immediately replaced by the girl in a sweater who had been the first to spot them. She was clutching a pile of linen.

Judging from the tone of her voice when she spoke to Esther, there was something she had not understood.

Esther's laser smile disappeared. From the way she silenced the girl, it was instantly clear that she was the employer, the boss. Fair, probably; strict, definitely.

Esther sent the girl on her way and, in an instant, her smile came out again.

'Forgive me, I will have to leave you. Enjoy your coffee. My lovely girl makes excellent coffee.'

She went off after the girl in the sweater, and Nellie glanced anxiously at Dron:

'Do you think something is wrong?'

'Who cares?' Dron replied lazily, sipping from his mug. 'It's their problem. Pay money and everything will be just fine.'

Rad took a sip also. The coffee was strong and pleasingly fragrant. The proportion of sugar was just right to take the edge off the bitterness without neutralizing it. It really had been brewed by an expert.

For the next five minutes they savoured their coffee, looking at the river, at the quiet stirring of the leaves in the trees growing near the house, and at the sunlight dappling the trees on the opposite shore. Waving away the tiresome mosquitoes, they exchanged a few words among themselves, before again looking at the river, the leaves, and the excavator dredging away, dipping its head in the water, scraping its bucket along the riverbed, and lifting it back out full of mud. Water gushed from its drainage slots, but while the excavator was conveying the mud to the heap on the riverbank, the torrent slowed to a trickle and then stopped altogether.

Esther reappeared with a smile that could have lit a dozen light bulbs.

'One double room is ready, a suite on the second floor. Please feel free to go up when you are ready.'

Dron and Nellie finished their coffee and stood up. Dron pulled out the handle on his suitcase and prepared to move off, but then returned it to the upright.

'Wait for me here. Don't go anywhere,' he said to Rad. 'I'll take the case up and come back. While Nellie is unpacking, taking a shower and whatever, we'll talk.'

'I'll be here,' Rad said, instantly coming over hot and cold.

Dron was back in no more than a couple of minutes. He quickly crossed the tiled area between the house and restaurant, pulled back a chair opposite, sat down and moved it back closer to the table.

'Right then, let's hear it. Tell me all that happened to you over there.'

* * *

So, unexpectedly, trying to suppress the shivers which periodically ran through him from the morning chill of the mountains, but reluctant to be distracted by opening his suitcase to take out something warm, Rad finally got to tell his story. Dron listened without interrupting, only asking occasionally for clarification of some point, and looking at him so intently that Rad suddenly began to find himself focusing once more on that clownish red nose. Since they had met at the airport, this was only the second time he had had that problem. The first was in the morning of his second day in Thailand, in Max's cafe. He had found himself trying not to look Dron in the face, as if he would be able to read in Rad's eyes what was bothering him. Dron seemed not just to be listening to his voice, but scenting his story with that nose, as if the words had not just meaning but an aroma which indicated their real essence much more than their literal sense did.

'Yes. Quite a story. No two ways about that,' Dron said when Rad finished his tale. 'But look, I thought that sort of thing only went on in the nineties under Yeltsin. It sounds just too brazen for it to be going on now, in 2004. That Armenian notary sitting out in the corridor!'

Rad had not expected Dron to believe what had happened immediately. The scepticism came as no surprise.

'How long have you been living outside Russia?' he asked.

'O-oh!' Dron drawled, 'it's been a while, but I go back there regularly.'

'I draw your attention, sir, to the fact that you said "there"!'

'There?' Dron repeated, and for a moment stared at Rad blankly before the penny dropped. 'Ah, "there"!' he exclaimed. 'Oh, yes, of course. Still, what can you do? Apologies. Yes, "there", you're quite right. But I know what is going on. Everything. I have access to all the information.'

'Nobody has all the information.'

'To the things that matter.'

'Perhaps my little incident was one that didn't,' Rad said.

Dron pondered this in silence before nodding.

'I take your point. End of discussion. Can you tell me more?'

'At your service.'

'At my service … at my service …' Dron repeated, as if assessing the implications of the words. 'Then tell me how you managed to get yourself into such a tangle? I'm not asking how it came about that you, a mathematician, came to be involved in bodybuilding. That just happened, right?'

'It did,' Rad confirmed. Dron was plainly being disingenuous, saying he would not ask, and then going right ahead and asking, as if just to make conversation, as if he was not that interested. Rad saw an opening to reply with military brevity, the more so as there was precious little to add.

Dron pretended he really had not been prying and it was Rad who had interrupted him in the middle of what he was saying, not letting him finish the question.

'Yes, so how did you manage to get into such a tangle?' he said again. 'You must have had to work at it. Did you really not have anyone to turn to for backup?'

'No. Who could I have turned to?'

'So you didn't have a team watching your back? People you owed, people who owed you?'

'What team?' Rad asked in surprise. 'A small personal business. I carried it all on my own shoulders. I did everything.'

'Ah!' Dron's eyebrows shot up knowingly. 'You were a loner, the sole warrior on the battlefield. That makes things a lot clearer.'

'It makes what clearer?'

'It makes it clear why this happened to you. No man is an island. You can't do anything on your own in business, big or small. Without a team you get nowhere. Without a team you'll only …' Dron stopped, searching for the right word. 'Well, anyway, it doesn't matter.' He did not expand. 'You must be in a team, that's the point. If you're in a team, the moment things start going wrong, they're right there minding your back for you. Whether you're right, whether you're not doesn't matter. If you're one of the gang, by definition you're in the right.'

'The law of the pack?' Rad shook his head. He was still finding looking at Dron awkward. When he looked at him he saw his nose, and Dron seemed to know it. 'No, I can't hunt with a pack, that's not for me. Savage someone else just because he doesn't belong … I can't do that sort of thing!'

'Well, but what if it's you who are being savaged? How are you going to defend yourself?'

'I can't do it!' Rad said, shaking his head again. 'I just can't.'

'And because you can't do it, you are in this tangle …' Dron countered.

'Listen to me, will you? Listen to me!' Rad was losing it. He felt he was in the electric chair. 'I don't need anyone to tell me how to live my life. It's not my life that's the problem right now. My problem is its antithesis.'

He took his mug with what was left of the coffee. His hand was shaking as he put the mug to his lips and swallowed a mouthful of the coarse, semi-caked grounds, which made him retch.

Dron was looking at him from the other side of the table with the serene detachment of a sage.

'So, how would you like to see the matter put to rights?'

Rad spat the grounds back into the mug, took a handkerchief from his back pocket and wiped his lips.

'How? I just want them off my back. I want them to forget about me, and for me to be able to forget about them.'

'So, the choice seems to be either to beat their brains out, or hand them $100,000,' Dron summarised.

'Is there a third option?' Rad asked.

'The third option is for them to forget about you all by themselves. To forget you and never remember you again. Is that a credible alternative?'

Rad shoved his handkerchief back in his pocket.

'Some chance of that! Like they're going to just forget me. They'd lose face if they backed off.'

'So that alternative we can exclude,' Dron said. '*Quod erat demonstrandum*. That leaves the other two options: beat their brains out, or hand over $100,000.'

He paused, awaiting Rad's response, but none came. Rad had said all he had to say: it was time for Dron to do the talking.

Dron said nothing for a long time, and neither did Rad. It was eventually Dron who broke the silence.

'Had you considered just getting out of the country?'

Rad did now respond.

'Well, how could that work? What country would take me? Who needs me? Illegal immigration? Wash dishes for a pittance in a restaurant, sleep in a hostel?'

Dron resumed his earlier expression of the serene, detached sage.

'So we can rule that out. Which brings us back to beating their brains out or handing them $100,000.'

With that he was silent again, but his silence had the force of an invitation to Rad to decide which of the only two available options he preferred.

Rad forced himself to look Dron in the eye.

'Dron, I don't mind. The main thing is to get a result. Whatever is best. Whatever is easiest.'

'Nothing is easiest,' Dron said. 'I hope you realise I'm going to have to ask my dad, and before I can do that I need a proposal to put to him. He's hardly going to just decide to take $100,000 out of the kitty, or divert the intelligence services to sort out your problems for you. What's in it for him?'

Rad had been expecting something like this.

'The fact that it's you making the request?' he suggested.

'I need to have a reason to make the request. I've already told you' – a flicker of irritation troubled the serenity of the sage – 'I can only ask on behalf of a member of our team. If you're not in the team, I can't ask on your behalf.'

Rad had unthinkingly taken up the mug of coffee grounds again and was moving it towards his mouth, but stopped as the porcelain touched his lips.

'Can you not just say I'm one of the team?' he asked.

'I could say that, but why would he believe me?' Dron shook his head emphatically, as if vividly imagining the possible outcome of such an unwise move. 'You have to be genuinely part of the team. Then we can move forward.'

Part of Rad was beginning to see the direction Dron was moving in, but another, much greater part of him, did not want to.

'Well, what about your own network?' he asked. 'Or rather, your connections?'

'What connections?' Dron asked in apparent surprise.

'Well …' Rad stumbled. 'From what I've heard, you work for a certain organization which is not without influence in Russia.'

'Forget that!' Dron interrupted him. 'Forget that gossip. Women talk all sorts of nonsense. I'm a businessman. I represent certain interests of our family business to the outside world. That's all there is to it. Do I make myself clear?'

This was the second time he had come down so hard on Rad. The first had been yesterday, when he discovered Rad knew Mike. There were similarities between the situations. Now, though, Rad felt he had nothing to lose.

'Look, just lend me $100,000,' Rad said. 'It's a lot, I know that, and I won't be able to repay it in just a month or two. Perhaps not in a year. But as soon as I do get back on my feet, you'll get it back. I'll flog my guts out but I'll get it back to you. You know me well enough to believe that.'

'What do I know about you?' Dron asked, mitigating his words with a self-deprecating smile. 'I know the Rad of yesteryear, but since then the times have changed everyone out of all recognition. In some people the only thing that has remained constant is their external appearance. Do you not agree?'

'Are you saying you don't believe I'll give the money back?'

Dron waved a hand in the air.

'Let's just assume I don't have it.'

Dron's refusal was disconcertingly direct. Their conversation had driven abruptly into a brick wall. He felt he had smashed his face against a windscreen at high speed. He wasn't dead, but the pain was scarcely believable.

Esther materialised out of thin air, like a spark of electricity, a guardian angel appearing at just the right moment. In her hands was a key ring with a fluffy charm with a Thai face on it attached to a long serrated key.

'Now your room is ready too,' she said triumphantly, handing Rad the key. 'You can move in any time. Enjoy your holiday.'

'Thank you very much,' Rad replied mechanically, taking the key.

Giving him a smile, Esther turned her attention to Dron.

'Breakfast is on the house. When would you like it? Now, later?'

'Shall we give it half an hour?' Dron asked Rad. 'Take a shower, freshen up? In half an hour's time,' he said to Esther, without waiting for Rad's agreement. He got up and invited Rad to do the same. 'Let's take a break from our discussion. We can come back to it later, tomorrow, or the day after. There's no hurry. Think about what I said.'

For some reason, as Rad got up, he looked over to see how the excavator was doing. It had tucked its articulated neck in to its massive body and was conveying the sludge dredged from the riverbed over to the bank. An abundance of filthy yellow water streamed from its bucket.

CHAPTER ELEVEN

The day was blazing hot. A merciless pagan sun god bleached the sky the colour of faded jeans, the heat no less in Chiang Mai than in Bangkok. Their bodies were covered in a film of sweat, as if they were steaming themselves in a sauna. Only a pleasant coolness rising from the soles of their feet suggested the possibility of compromise with the world around them: the entire monastery area was paved with tiles polished to a mirror-like smoothness. Shoes had to be left at the entrance, so only the width of a sock or stocking separated their feet from the stone floor.

The monastery was built on top of a mountain. An area reclaimed from the forest was packed with temples, stupas, commemorative columns, statues of hideously snarling dragon-like spirits, reminding mortals of the realms of the underworld. On a long marble pedestal shaped like a sarcophagus stood the sculpture of a white elephant carrying the Buddha's ashes to his secret burial place. Afterwards the elephant never had to work again, but grazed carefree in a fertile valley for decades before its own time came. All this was recorded on a massive blue plaque in a brown frame at its feet. Everything was decorated with gold leaf, the stupas, the sculptures, the columns and roofs of temples. The gold gleamed and the entire monastery appeared to be a chip off the sun, placed by a higher will on the highest point of one mountain in the grey-blue ridge overlooking the city. Along the walls of a temple were several dozen bronze bells, half the height of a person, with long, easily grasped round clappers. Each of the monastery's many visitors found it necessary to toll at least one or two of the bells. Dron and Nellie tolled five or six, but Rad was suddenly moved to go from one bell to another, bend down and take the clapper, toll the bell and move on to the next. So doing, he made his way right round the temple, ringing them all and losing track when the count was over forty.

'Does that have some kind of significance for you?' Nellie asked when he got back to them.

'It means you will quite certainly come back here,' Dron said before Rad had time to reply.

'Is that the belief?' Rad asked, without answering Nellie.

Dron snorted, and Nellie, who had understood everything without needing his answer, burst into peals of silvery laughter.

'I wouldn't put it past you,' Dron concluded.

It was their second day in Chiang Mai. Yesterday, as soon as they had settled in, they went for a stroll through the city, into souvenir shops, asking the price of all sorts of knick-knacks but buying nothing. They visited a ruined palace complex with what in the past had been the city's biggest stupa, rode in a tuk-tuk, had lunch in a neat, totally European restaurant serving European food, and found themselves on the opposite side of town from the one where they were staying. They walked through the deserted halls of the National Museum, which in Russian would have been described as a local history museum, and saw flint stone-age tools excavated in the area, then spent a long time trying to get a taxi back to the city centre. Nellie suddenly announced she wanted to play golf and that they should go and find a golf club. Dron promised her they would, but when they finally got into a songthaew, he asked the driver to take them to the city centre, where he went in search of a hairdresser who could provide another service as specific as Thai massage: cleaning out the ears. This took around forty minutes, after which it seemed a good idea to have something to eat again. On this occasion they went to a mainstream Thai establishment, eating their way through a mountain of brown fried rice, and when they came back out Nellie thought it was too late to go to a golf club. 'That's good,' Dron said approvingly. 'Don't you get enough of that delight back home? If there's no business interest, chasing golf balls round a course is enough to make you die of boredom.' They rounded off the evening with a visit to the night market. Whole blocks had been transformed into a vast market place. The crowds flowed past the stalls like one compacted mass, and it seemed as if the whole city had turned out, only the local people were on one side of the stalls and the tourists on the other.

The idea that they should visit the monastery on the mountain had come from Esther at breakfast time. As the previous day, it had been cool at that hour, but by the time they had driven up the winding road to the car park in a songthaew, then climbed on foot to the monastery up a broad set of stairs bounded on each side by a balustrade in the form of an infinitely long dragon, it was hot. The blue of the sky had faded and the tongues of the stray dogs, lying flat out on the concrete steps, were hanging out like neckties.

Dron's mobile phone rang while they were standing on the monastery's viewing platform looking down on the city. The mountain was perhaps

400 metres high, and below the platform palms and other tropical trees had their branches bristling upwards like brooms; the city lay spread out before them in the valley like a three-dimensional topographic map.

'Who needs me now?' Dron muttered as he took the phone from his pocket. 'Oh, Chris! Hello!' he said a moment later.

Listening to Chris, Dron moved away from Rad and Nellie and the balustrade which curved round the observation platform, deeper into the monastery, away from the crowd into a more open space. Nellie looked after him anxiously.

'Interesting,' she said. 'I wonder what this is leading to?'

Rad was the only person the remark could have been addressed to, so he responded, 'What do you mean?'

Nellie looked at him.

'Perhaps our life is only how somebody is imagining us?' she said after a pause.

Her eyes were unseeing, as if turned in on herself. Rad was not at all sure she could see him at that moment.

'That sounds like an idea you might have expressed at a seminar on Marxism-Leninism back then,' he commented.

'Back then I wasn't yet thinking about things like that,' Nellie said, the focus coming back into her eye, and now he knew she was seeing him again. 'Young minds are agile but foolish, don't you think?'

'*Out of the mouths of babes comes truth*,' Rad stonewalled with a proverb.

'I'm not talking about babes,' Nellie said earnestly.

Dron came briskly back, snapping his phone shut and putting it in his pocket.

'I need to return to Bangkok,' he said. 'Today.'

'What's the hurry?' Nellie asked, but without any great suggestion of surprise in her voice, as if the disruption of their trip had always been on the cards, and it was just a pity it had happened so soon. 'Why? Is Chris flying back?'

Dron nodded.

'Exactly.'

'Get him to fly here.'

'That would have been neat,' Dron agreed. 'Only he had no idea we were here, the ticket is in his pocket, and he's virtually on his way to the airport.'

'He could fly here from Bangkok.'

Dron nodded again: 'That would be good, certainly. But what if we suddenly need to get all of them together. Would I summon them all up here?'

'Who is "all of them"?' Nellie asked.

Dron suddenly looked hard at Rad.

'Rad knows,' he said.

The reference to Mike was blatant. What was less obvious was why Dron had made it.

'Lord love us, Dron, how could I know that?' he said, leaving Nellie in the dark. 'And if I ever did know anything, I've forgotten it.'

Dron looked satisfied. Perhaps the only reason he had mentioned Mike was to test Rad's promise in Coffee Max.

'I'm not asking you to fly back with me,' Dron said to both of them, but addressing Nellie. 'Stay here and keep the room for me. I imagine I'll be back in a day's time. I'll check out his proposals and be straight back.'

'Is it a good sign that Chris has come back so soon?' Nellie asked.

Dron gestured vaguely, before saying, 'It's not bad.'

Their shoes were waiting for them at the exit exactly where they had left them. On each landing of the steps with the endless dragon handrails, children brightly dressed in clean clothes were hanging about. They were playing tag, or 'guess which hand', and seemed completely engrossed in their games, but as soon as anyone resembling a tourist approached, they came running to them and all at the same time loudly offered to be photographed: 'Snap! Snap!! Flash!' But no sooner was a lens focused on them than they all turned their backs and, looking up at the person aspiring to be photographed with them, confidently called out, 'Ten baht! Ten baht!'

Upon receiving their advance, they turned in unison to the lens, with joyful grins stretching from ear to ear. One group of children for some reason particularly moved Nellie. Only Rad had a sufficiently small note, which he gave to the oldest girl in the group, which none of the other children seemed to mind. Through the agency of Dron and Sony Corporation, Nellie's descent from the monastery was recorded for posterity.

'Why didn't you get your photograph taken?' Nellie asked Rad reproachfully when they moved on.

'He can't stand small children,' Dron replied gravely on his behalf.

'Really?' Nellie asked Rad in surprise.

'No, it's actually that I can't stand seeing my own ugly mug among children's sweet faces,' Rad blurted out the first thing that came into his head, possibly at the bidding of his subconscious.

'I think you have a very nice face,' Nellie said after a pause. 'I think you would look splendid surrounded by children.'

'He's just not sure the children's faces would look good enough next to his own,' Dron elaborated with the same gravity.

Nellie looked at him then at Rad.

'I think you're both just playing the fool,' she said uncertainly.

'That's all we're born for,' came Dron's riposte.

Rad was reflecting that Dron's imminent departure would defer their conversation for at least another two days.

'To tell the truth, Dron, I would be happier not playing the fool,' he said.

Dron did not react.

They reached the end of the steps and went down to the large asphalted area in front of it. Souvenir shops to the right of the steps had their doors thrown invitingly open, several tourist buses were clustered near the slope leading out of the square, and songthaews were arriving and departing with great regularity. Fifty metres to the left of the steps was a restaurant, and from the open windows of its kitchen came the smell of food, barely detectable but sufficient to get their mouths watering. Their intention, when they arrived at the monastery, had been to lunch in this subtly seductive restaurant, but the plan now needed revision.

'Let's go straight back down, find out what flights there are, buy the ticket and have lunch after that,' Dron proposed. Nobody raised any objection.

Five minutes later, a songthaew was bearing them down the mountain, the road now unwinding, and a breeze blew in through the window slots. After the heat within the stone confines of the monastery, the marked coolness blowing over their bodies was bliss.

* * *

Check-in for Thai International Airlines Flight TG117 from Chiang Mai to Bangkok at 19.50 had closed, and indeed boarding was already in progress. Dron was saved by his lack of luggage. 'Only this,' he said, waving an overnight bag at the girl behind the counter, which he could easily carry on as hand luggage. She hesitated, but then punched his ticket, noted something down in her papers, and handed over his boarding pass. 'Only be quick, very quick,' she urged, pointing him in the direction of the metal detector and boarding gate.

'Okay, see you soon. I'll phone.' Dron hugged Nellie with one arm, stamped a hasty kiss on her lips, and extended a hand to Rad. 'So long!'

'Say hello to Chris from me,' Nellie said.

'Of course, absolutely.'

'Safe journey,' Rad said.

Dron withdrew his hand and wagged a finger at Rad.

'I'm entrusting my wife to your care. Don't seduce her! Understand?'

'Dro-on!' Rad spread his arms reproachfully, at a loss for an answer.

There was no reaction from Nellie. She only repeated, 'Say hello to Chris,' as if Dron had not already promised to do so.

'Hurry along please!' the girl called to Dron from the counter.

Holding the bag to stop it flopping on his hip, Dron disappeared into the depths of the airport's labyrinths, and Rad and Nellie were alone.

He immediately felt ill at ease, thanks to Dron's parting instruction. What a rum character: he grudged him a loan of $100,000 but trusted him with his wife.

'Shall we move?' he asked Nellie.

Even saying that took an effort. It seemed that no matter what he said, it would sound forced.

'Yes, of course,' Nellie replied with a shrug, avoiding his eye.

She, too, was feeling uncomfortable, and doubtless for the same reason.

But there was work to be done. They needed to find a tuk-tuk, negotiate with the driver, then race through the darkness to their hotel, sitting side by side. It all helped to dispel the awkwardness, so that by the time they were back at the familiar double gate, it had almost gone.

'I want to take a shower,' Nellie declared as they were tramping across the gravel to the hotel.

That implied before supper. Or rather, before dinner, because mere supper had disappeared from her and Dron's vocabulary.

They agreed to meet in half an hour at the gazebo by the steps down to the river, and parted.

Half an hour later, Rad was there, but Nellie appeared only twenty minutes after that.

'I hope I'm not late?' she asked, with an expression that indicated she knew perfectly well she was late, but wanted him to consider her as punctual as a queen.

'Well, if you are, what's it matter?' Rad said with an ironic display of insouciant magnanimity.

He was engulfed again by the awkwardness he felt at the airport, and hastened to demonstrate to Nellie, as she had just demonstrated her feminine wish to be appreciated, that he was not a suitable candidate before whom she should be revealing it quite so nakedly.

They went to dine at an open-air restaurant near the hotel, which the three of them had identified the day before as a suitable venue if they got back late and did not feel like going out. The restaurant was a spacious wooden platform on the bank of the river. Oil lamps burned on wooden poles around the perimeter to ward off mosquitoes. Another couple of lamps, smaller, were brought by the waiter as soon as they were seated. He set them down on the table and, after asking permission, lit them. From the river came the splash of water, the occasional croaking of frogs. A pathway of moonlight lay over it. Taken together with the aromatic smoke rising from the burning wick of the oil lamps, the atmosphere was distinctly romantic.

But Nellie had either decided to adhere strictly to his implied recommendation not to see him as a man, or her demonstration of femininity had been without any ulterior motive. At all events, the only evidence she vouchsafed of carnal cravings at dinner was her hearty appetite. Not even the bottle of dry French wine they got through caused that to slip.

It was after ten when they returned to the hotel. Rad accompanied Nellie to the foot of the stairs to her first-floor room and stopped there.

'Good night. See you tomorrow?' he said with the rising intonation of a question, supposing that to put it in the affirmative might seem flat-footed.

'Yes, good night. See you tomorrow,' Nellie replied, with a clear implication that it was a relief she would finally be alone. Rad felt a twinge of regret that he had not asked the waiter to serve them a bit more promptly.

He headed towards his own room, but changed his mind and went back to the stairs and up to the first floor. There was a balcony at the head of the stairs, with a sofa, armchairs, a glass-topped coffee table and, in a small bookcase by the wall which he had noticed that morning, several dozen books and some magazines in English. Since he had nothing to do in his room and did not yet feel like sleeping, he turned on the terrace light, opened the cupboard, and met the new day browsing through a novel published in Canada, penned by an earlier appreciative guest of the hotel who had presented it as a gift to future guests.

* * *

The next day a trip to the mountains had already been booked, and when Rad, after a shave and a quick shower, took himself to the verandah restaurant, Nellie was already there. She was sitting at a table by the railing, facing the entrance and eating her breakfast. The sun, which had barely detached itself from the horizon, was behind her and lit up her hair, so that she appeared to be endowed with a golden halo. Hearing approaching footsteps, she looked up.

'Hello!' she said, beating him to it. 'I see you slept soundly.'

'Good morning,' he said, approaching. 'And I see you are ready to eat the moment you take your head off the pillow.'

Nellie laughed, pleased.

'A healthy appetite is a sign of good health.'

Rad pulled out a chair and sat down opposite her, facing the rising sun. Its rays, low in the sky, slipped over the surface of the water without infusing it with light: it was a dark brown, brackish colour and had the stillness of a swamp. A fine mist hovered above it, and the sunlight, reflected in its transparent haze, filled the air with a barely detectable but perceptible golden radiance. Fog blurred the outlines of the Sheraton beyond the bend in the river, and the sail floating in the sky looked markedly bigger than it actually was. The orange bulk of the excavator on the other bank was immobile. Its articulated neck ending in the sledgehammer bucket was broken in the middle and resting heavily on the ground in front of its tracks, as if it were too weary to keep it aloft and was resting in this position to recover its strength before resuming its heavy labour.

The barmaid appeared at the table. She began listing all that was on offer, but her English was such that Rad understood only the words 'boiled eggs'. 'Give me the same, please,' he said, pointing to the plate in front of Nellie.

'Do you not have any wishes of your own?' Nellie asked, looking over at him.

'My only desire is to follow in the wake of your own choices,' Rad replied unthinkingly. He had no sooner said it than he recognised the possibility of his words being wildly misinterpreted. Nellie, he could immediately see from her eyes, had registered the ambiguity.

'Really?' she said after a pause.

Yesterday's awkwardness at the airport, which had seemed quite forgotten, proved only to have been lurking in some deep place ready to leap back out at any moment, like now.

'Were we going to be collected from here?' he asked a little later, although perfectly aware of what had been agreed at the travel agency and in no need of reminding.

'Collected?' Nellie echoed.

'Ah, yes. We are being collected,' he said as if, in the course of asking the question, he had recollected the arrangement.

They were finishing their coffee when the excavator on the other bank belched abundant fumes of black smoke, juddered, raised its bucket off the ground, swung it from one side to the other, and moved forward towards the edge of the bank. It lowered its neck into the river, scraped the bucket along the bottom, and raised from the water its first helping of river mud of the day. Nellie, following Rad's gaze, turned in her chair and for a while also watched the resurrected orange brontosaur.

'It's a blot on the landscape, and yet it animates the overall picture wonderfully, doesn't it?' she said, turning back to Rad. That was amazingly precise. She had expressed exactly what Rad was feeling but had not put into words.

'You a bit clever, or wot?' he exclaimed.

'I may not be completely witless,' she admitted.

The car came for them about ten minutes later. It was a cherry-coloured Toyota minibus, perhaps not very new, but very well looked after. The ride was soft and springy, the brakes responsive and powerful, and the steering obedient. Rad could feel all that physically the moment they set off. He suddenly remembered Jenny's yellow Suzuki hatchback in which, after they had spent the night in bed together, he had driven her to Sergiev Posad. The memory was so clear that he unexpectedly felt a longing for her. He remembered her hands on his shoulders, her round little buttocks in his hands, her habit of stroking her nostril while she was talking. It was all so incredibly vivid that he almost asked after her. How was she? What was she writing to Nellie in her emails? He made the effort not to.

There were two people in the Toyota: one young and one old Thai. The young man was very young, twenty or twenty-two, or was he? The elderly one was more than elderly, almost an old man, but both were wearing suits and ties, except that the older man's jacket was a bit worn, out of shape and sagging. Both had gleaming, laser-white teeth, although those of the older man might just have been false teeth. The older man was the driver and acting as the guide. The younger was evidently there as his assistant, or for work experience.

'We have three more places to visit to pick up other members of our group,' the elderly man said, turning the steering wheel at the same time as turning back to talk to them. His English was fluent but, perhaps because of dentures, so indistinct that Rad could pick out only isolated words and had to ask Nellie to translate. 'I will tell you later about our route and what we are going to see, when our whole group is together. In the meantime, admire the views of our wonderful city, which was established on the territory of the ancient kingdom of One Million Rice Fields about 700 years ago. I hope you can understand my English?' their guide and driver said, exposing the entire expanse of his magnificent teeth and, as luck would have it, addressing the question specifically to Rad.

Nellie hastened to reassure him.

'We understand, we understand,' after which she placed her hand over Rad's, which was lying on his knee. 'I'll carry on being your translator. I like that.'

When she came to the end of this announcement, her hand remained on his. Yesterday's awkwardness was ruptured as easily as a spider's gossamer web, leaving no trace behind. It was now, instead, replaced by a clarity whose content must inevitably be given form. All that remained to be decided was what that form was to be. The absence of Dron seemed to dictate it almost as inexorably as the rising and setting of the sun.

Rad tried to defend himself from himself by conjuring the image of Jenny, who had just so palpably reminded him of herself. But in vain: the image of Jenny was defunct. Like a burned out straw fire, only pitiful remnants of ash remained to smoulder into nothingness. His displacement did not work, and instead it occurred to him how similar they were, Jenny and Nellie. Not so much in their faces, as in their manner, their type; their ways, their speech, the expression in their eyes. Even, in fact, in their neat, rounded butts.

He had a feeling that, if Nellie did not take her hand away very, very soon, the next weight on his hand might be that of her bum.

Rad took her hand and, with considerable reluctance, placed it in her lap. While he was doing so, Nellie was looking at him wryly.

'Scared?' she asked when her hand was in her lap. 'What are you afraid of?'

'Let's not do this, Nellie,' Rad said gently.

She raised her eyebrows in seeming amazement.

'Who said anything about doing anything? I would like to act as your interpreter. Did I suggest anything else?'

The Toyota turned off the road into a side street and stopped outside the high, spacious porch of a hotel, a great concrete slab as white as snow and riddled with rows of windows. The older Thai turned to Rad and Nellie and said, 'Literally one minute.' He opened the door and jumped out. The younger man also turned, gave them a big smile, but said nothing.

'Do you want me to translate what he said?' Nellie asked.

'Won't be a minute?' Rad volunteered.

'Oh, can you really do without me?'

'Only with simple phrases.'

'So I'm not fired?'

'But no salary,' Rad specified.

'Oh, he needs me! He needs me!' Nellie exclaimed, clapping her hands.

The hotel's glass door opened. The driver emerged and, behind him, two Thai girls animatedly twittering between themselves. They were definitely Thai, but at the same time there was something in the structure of their faces that was not. It was not their features, but in their bone structure.

The driver rolled back the door of the minibus and the girls, still twittering, lowered their heads, came inside, said hello briefly, not in the usual expansive Thai manner, and took their seats behind Rad and Nellie.

They were still twittering, and it became evident they were twittering in English. It had none of the usual Thai singsong, but was authentic, clear English, and despite the speed at which they were firing words at each other, Rad could by and large understand what they were saying.

The driver climbed in, pulled the door to behind him, turned the ignition key and the Toyota was on its way.

Nellie leaned towards Rad:

'Do you know what they are?'

Rad shrugged,

'How could I?'

'Mixed race. They're the children of Thai women who have married Westerners. They've come to their historic homeland as tourists to get back to their roots.'

'What makes you think that?' Rad queried.

'We'll check,' Nellie said and, without more ado, turned back in the seat and, changing instantly from Russian to English, said loudly,

'Hello, my dears! Let's enjoy the tour together. My name is Nellie and my friend's name is Rad. How about you?'

The girls told her their names.

'We are from Russia,' Nellie next announced, which, by and large, was true. 'Where are you from?'

They were from Canada.

'Are you studying there, or is that where you live?'

The girls, interrupting each other, unhesitatingly told her they were studying there, but that they also lived there, indeed, they had been born there, and Thailand was where their mothers were from and they just loved coming here and travelling around the country.

'Well?' Nellie said, turning back and settling herself on the seat beside Rad. 'Did you hear that? Who didn't believe me?'

'Nice work!' Rad said. 'I am overcome with admiration.'

'I'm the wife of a spy,' she commented casually.

'So he is in fact a spy?' Rad asked, although, after his conversation with Dron the day he arrived in Chiang Mai, that was no longer of practical importance.

Nellie subjected him to a long, highly meaningful gaze, although what the meaning was Rad had no way of telling.

'As if I would know,' she said eventually.

'What? You're saying you don't know if he works in intelligence or not?' Rad exclaimed in surprise.

'Yes. I do not know,' Nellie said.

'How could a wife not know?'

This time, Nellie just shrugged.

'Or is it something you're not allowed to know?'

'I expect that's it,' Nellie agreed.

Rad had again the feeling that he was rummaging about in the remotest, most junk-filled rooms of their relationship. The chaos was mind-boggling, and through the chink of a slightly open cupboard door, the skeleton's bones he could see had been bleached by time.

The Toyota stopped at its next hotel. The driver again jumped out and, leaning forward, raced up the steps and disappeared into the entrance. This hotel too was concrete and more concrete: man-made caves piled one on top of another and riddled with glass.

'It's wonderful that we're not in something like that,' Nellie said, looking out the window with Rad. 'How does it compare with our country hotel with breakfast by the river?'

Rad agreed.

'You're right.'

'Dron has an animal ability to sniff out the absolute best. In everything. In anything you can think of. Whether it's choosing beer …'

'Or which country to live in,' Rad finished the sentence for her.

Nellie's silvery laughter rang out again.

'It's an animal sense of scent, completely feral. I'm more used to it now, but it still amazes me. It's feral.'

'Just what a real spy needs,' Rad concluded.

'Oh, is that really something to joke about?' Nellie made a gesture as if brushing away an annoying fly. 'Is he a spy? Is he not a spy? That's got nothing to do with it. It's something he was born with, like the colour of his eyes, or the shape of his ears.'

'Or of his nose,' Rad was tempted to add, but recognised that would be a joke too far.

'Look, tell me about your life in America,' he said a little later. 'I can't even begin to imagine it.'

'What our life there is like?' She paused. 'Well, perhaps I will … But first you tell me whether you've managed to have your talk about whatever it was.'

Now it was Rad's turn to hesitate.

'You really don't want to know.' One thing Rad did not want was to discuss his story with Nellie. Dron could tell her the details if he wanted, but Rad had no wish to rake over it all with her. To weep on a woman's shoulder? That would be too much humiliation. 'If it comes to the crunch, could you influence his decision-making?'

'Unlikely,' Nellie responded immediately. 'In fact, just plain no,' she added.

'Then it's pointless for me to burden you,' Rad said. 'In any case, he and I haven't finished talking about it. It's ongoing.'

'Oh,' Nellie said knowledgeably, 'Dron can string people along. That's another of his talents. He's a past master at stringing people along. He'll take you for a ride, you can be sure.'

The driver returned from the hotel unaccompanied. What he said to his young companion in the cab was in Thai, but needed no translation. His customers had ratted on him.

At the third hotel just one person was picked up, an elderly, neurasthenic-looking Japanese man with a digital camera round his neck. He seemed half-drugged, his movements slow, his reactions slow, his speech slurred. His exhausted appearance came from deep bracket-shaped wrinkles on his cheeks, the melancholy in his eyes, and even the wispy black moustache on his upper lip which was intended, apparently, to give a certain machismo to his features but which only enhanced the appearance of nervous exhaustion.

'What a weird character,' Nellie remarked quietly, leaning towards Rad. 'He's scary.'

'Nonsense,' Rad said, but involuntarily glanced across at the Japanese, who was sitting in a single seat in their row. 'What is there for you to be afraid of?'

'He's stoned out of his mind,' Nellie said.

'Or nuts,' Rad agreed.

'You don't think he's a terrorist?'

Rad could not help smiling.

'Some target we are for terrorists. He's not a terrorist, that I'm sure of.'

The driver looked back. There were ten seats in his Toyota and five passengers. His eye took in the empty seats and he pursed his lips ruefully. Business was disappointing. Rad empathised.

He was, however, a stoic, or rather, a real Buddhist. The regretful expression was immediately replaced by a smile and, turning his head, looking at one moment at the road ahead and the next back at his passengers, he began his singsong commentary.

'So, the first stop on our itinerary today will be a visit to a typical hilltribe village. We will reach it in one hour, travelling in this wonderful vehicle manufactured in the country of one of the members of our group.' He gave the Japanese man a grateful smile, but the unexpected compliment caught him off guard and he blinked rapidly, as if dazzled. He leaned forward in his seat as if about to answer but, after blinking for some time longer, fell back and covered his eyes with his hand, as if the compliment had not only dazzled but hurt them. 'So, when we leave the minibus, we will go on foot for about forty minutes to the village,' their driver and now their guide continued, still turning his head back and forth. 'The second highlight of our trip will be an elephant ride. You do not need to do this if you are worried about riding on elephants. It is optional. Our third stop will be a visit to a village with traditional weaving where you can buy fabrics created by expert Thai weavers. Our fourth highlight will be a visit to a waterfall, and our fifth will be white water rafting down a mountain river.'

'How about that!' Nellie exclaimed, interrupting her translation for Rad. 'I didn't understand the bit about rafting when we are at the travel agency. If I fall in, will you save me?'

'Do you think Dron would approve?' was the best Rad could think to say.

'That's the deal, is it?' Nellie queried in an undecipherable tone of voice. 'Only if Dron would approve?'

Something latent broke through in her words, a dark, icy chasm yawned in front of him, and Rad had a strong sense of having strayed into territory where he had no business to be.

'And at the midpoint of our programme, we have lunch in an upcountry restaurant,' the driver continued, finishing his introduction. To his surprise, Rad found he knew all the words and had understood.

'They're not going to let us die of hunger,' he said, to let Nellie know there was no need to translate.

She nodded.

'That's lucky,' she said, but in a way that suggested there was more to be said. Rad waited, and a little later Nellie did continue.

'Do you know, Dron once left me to die? Do you want to hear about it?' Rad was silent, not knowing what to say. She did not wait, and brought the topic to an end. 'I may tell you about it another time.'

They said nothing for the rest of the journey. The city was left behind, vehicles, both oncoming and driving in their direction, became few and far between, the road narrowed to single-lane, and to both sides there were rice fields, 'paddy fields', Rad remembered they were called, separated by raised green borders. Some had been harvested, others were flooded. In those which were flooded, here and there isolated figures were bent double, displaying their backsides to the sky, their trousers rolled up to their knees, at work in the water. Then the road, at first barely perceptibly, but then unmistakably, began to climb. The rice fields were replaced by wooded slopes and, first on one side then on the other, these had been cleared of trees and turned into meadows in which small herds of cows were grazing. The cattle were dusty brown, stocky, muscular, had unusually long snouts, straight, fork-like horns that pointed forwards, tight, small udders, and it was only after puzzling over this for a long time that Rad worked out they were water buffaloes.

An hour later, the Toyota stopped on an extensive asphalted area with a lone Honda saloon parked to one side. Their driver-guide turned and smilingly gestured to them.

'Please disembark! We have arrived.'

His young helper also turned, gave everyone a smile, but still said nothing. He seemed not to have uttered a word the whole way.

During the hour's drive, the sun had climbed from the horizon to a height where it was beginning to beat down, and they needed to shed some of their clothing. Nellie stripped off her sweater and was now in just a cream-coloured top with short sleeves. It looked very simple, but was beautifully cut, as were her white linen slacks which reached to halfway down her calves. There was a refinement of line about both which made their simplicity seem the height of sophistication. The next part of their trip, the guide announced, would be on foot.

A path in front of them headed sharply downhill. Their guide walked ahead, constantly looking back, and his assistant brought up the rear. After five minutes the trail brought them to a rift in the ground overgrown with bushes, along the stony bottom of which a voluble stream was flowing, sometimes hidden by undergrowth, sometimes revealing the nakedness of quicksilver water sparkling in the sun. The rift was spanned by a narrow bamboo bridge with wire handrails: two people would be hard pressed to pass on it. Rad stepped on to the bridge behind the guide and the Japanese man. It was like a living thing, responding to every movement of every person crossing it, swaying simultaneously in all directions: up and down, from side to side, and seemed bent on throwing off all those walking on it, like a recalcitrant horse trying to rid itself of an incompetent rider.

'Let me go in front, so you can watch over me,' Nellie said.

Rad moved aside and they moved on.

The Japanese man stopped in the middle of the bridge, blocking the way. The wire handrail was supplemented at this point by additional poles and, leaning on one of these, his camera dangling vertically from his neck, he was looking down. Or rather, he was looking down at the stream seething ten metres below their feet, then at their guide who had gone on ahead, then at Rad and Nellie who were approaching. It was impossible to pass him and, when she reached him, Nellie was obliged to stop too.

'Is anything wrong?' she asked? 'Are you all right?'

'It is terrifying, is it not?' he said, instead of replying. 'Is it not?'

'Not in the slightest,' Nellie said with intrepid casualness. 'I am with my friend,' she added, indicating Rad.

'I would like to tell you my story,' he said, ignoring her remark. 'You see, after the death of my wife I feel all the time like I am on this bridge.'

The words of reproach Rad was about to address to him for holding everybody up remained unspoken.

'She died six months ago, a little less, but that "less" is only three days and need not be counted,' the Japanese said. He was addressing himself only to Nellie, as if unaware of Rad's presence. 'I loved her very much. I loved her as a Japanese man should love his wife. I loved her as Japanese men now have forgotten how to love: sternly, but faithfully. I gave her all the money I earned. I travelled with her to Europe. We went to Paris, Venice, Barcelona. We went to America, not only the North, but also to South America, Brazil, Argentina. I took her even to Russia when that country was still called the USSR. There is a river, the Yenisey. We sailed down it almost to the Arctic Ocean.'

Nellie gave Rad a glance which said, 'The Yenisey, how about that!'

The Thai-Canadian girls and the young assistant arrived behind them. 'What's up? Why are we standing here?' they asked. 'Why have we stopped?' It was the voice of the young Thai, who had finally spoken.

'We need to move on,' Rad said, touching Nellie on the shoulder. 'Tell him to move.'

'We need to move on,' Nellie repeated to the Japanese.

'But I want to finish telling you my story,' he persisted. The yearning in his eyes was unbearable. 'I would like to know your opinion, as a woman.'

'You can finish your story as we walk on,' Nellie said reassuringly.

The Japanese gave her a meaningful look. 'I will hold you to your promise,' said his yearning eyes. He turned and continued across the bridge to the edge of the ravine, where their guide was waiting for them with an expression of anxious puzzlement.

'Don't leave me alone with him,' Nellie whispered in Rad's ear before starting after the Japanese.

Stepping off the bridge, barely waiting for Nellie to set foot on the ground, the Japanese immediately latched onto her again.

'When my wife died,' he said, as if his story had not been interrupted, 'I found that all her life she had kept a diary.'

'Like Sei Shōnagon,' Nellie said, showing off her knowledge of the Japanese classic.

The Japanese, not having expected a response from her, was disorientated for a moment, before gesticulating to indicate his disagreement.

'No, she was not Sei Shōnagon. She kept a diary in order to write in it about her lovers. She recorded how she met someone and, most importantly, how she made love with them. In great detail. Every orgasm.

She had fifty-three lovers, and compared every one of them with me. Only three of them were better, and I can take some comfort from that, but it is a poor consolation. What do you think?'

Rad could see that Nellie was furiously searching for an appropriate response to that question, but it turned out to be purely rhetorical.

'Several times she wrote that she wanted to kill me,' he continued, 'in order to be free. She even considered the best ways to do it, but decided not to because, after all, only three of them had been better, and besides, she was afraid she might be left without a source of income. And here I am now, alive, and she is not, but I cannot consider this real living. I am hooked on tranquillisers, and what kind of life is it if you are dependent on such drugs? I had a job in a good company but now I have no work. I lost my job and have no choice now but to travel round the world while my money lasts. But I cannot imagine what will happen when it runs out. I am thinking now that we are about to ride elephants. Do you think it is dangerous to ride on elephants?'

Nellie looked helplessly at Rad: how should she reply? But before Rad had time to give her any guidance, the Japanese was off again.

'I suppose that, in my position, the more dangerous, the better. My wife led what was in reality a very dangerous life. I sometimes think she had the right idea. We are all cheating each other in one way or another, so why not think big? One should cheat on a grand scale. What do you think? She got pleasure out of life by deceiving me; I was deceived, believing she was faithful to me, and also was happy. We both took pleasure, in deceiving and in being deceived. People cannot help cheating each other. Cheating makes the world go round, cheating and violence. They go hand in hand. Invariably. Think! She wanted to kill me. Was that because I was somehow standing in her way? Nothing of the sort! She wanted to kill me because deceiving another person is to exert a kind of power over them. She wanted her power over me to be unlimited, and unlimited power over another person is power over their life. Cheating, if it is totally unaccountable, invariably turns into violence.

The bridge had long been left behind, the trail was now steadily uphill, but the Japanese continued uninterruptedly to expose to Nellie the secrets of his true relationship with his wife. Nellie was buckling under the weight of his revelations but continued steadfastly listening, and only the glances she occasionally exchanged with Rad made it clear they were getting her down. It was time to come to her rescue.

Rad, who had been trailing half a pace behind Nellie and the Japanese, pushed his way in between them, propelling Nellie forward and, looking the Japanese straight in his yearning eyes, said, 'Listen, friend, do you not think you are taking up too much of my girlfriend's time? I would like to have some of her time too, but you are getting all of it. I do not like that.'

The expression which appeared on the anaemic face of the now silent Japanese was one of obsequious agreement. He seemed to have been expecting a similar intervention and was only surprised it had been so long in coming.

'Forgive me, forgive me,' he muttered. 'I did not mean. It just happened. I am not making any claims on your girlfriend, of course not.'

He fell back behind them, and Rad and Nellie found themselves at the head of the group with only their guide still showing the way, his back covered with a tight-fitting jacket.

'Perhaps you were a bit,' Nellie paused, choosing her words, 'hard on him? His wife has died …'

'She has, and she left quite a diary,' Rad said.

'Well, precisely. What a story …' Nellie sounded guilty.

Rad stopped.

'Do you have any stories like that you want to tell?'

Nellie stopped too.

'Do you really want to know? I'll tell you. You asked for it.'

Rad said nothing. He had by no means been trying to elicit revelations from her to rival those of the Japanese. He did not really want to hear her stories.

Without waiting for a reply, Nellie moved on up the track and he followed.

'But why did he decide to turn to me rather than you?' Nellie asked a little later.

'Because you're a woman. What would his interest be in telling all that to a man? Talking to a woman about it is as if he is taking revenge for what has happened.'

'A kind of proxy revenge?'

'Probably.'

'But perhaps he really did need advice of some kind from me.'

Rad grinned.

'Well, go back and give him some.'

'Oh, no way!' Nellie exclaimed in horror. 'He's addicted to tranquillisers. Didn't you hear?' Then, for some reason lowering her voice to a whisper, she added, 'That's why he's so weird.'

'Yes. If he's on tranquillisers, that explains it,' Rad agreed.

'I don't take tranquillisers,' she said, rather defensively, after a pause. 'But you know, I would like to tell you things too.'

Rad fell silent again. If it looked as if he was going to be hanged, that did not mean he had to make the rope with his own hands.

The village which was their main destination appeared quite unexpectedly. They went down into another hollow, up another rise, then into a grove of widely spaced deciduous trees with dense, spreading crowns which provided dense shade, and suddenly, between the trunks, they spotted something manifestly man-made, then something else. The village was in a wood, and through the trees one house could not be seen from the next.

There were, in any case, only one or two buildings in the village. A thatched awning on rickety supports had a long table fixed in the ground in the middle of it. Another shelter was in the form of a round gazebo, only without railings. There were two reed huts, one larger, the other smaller, and, near the smaller one, a reed kiosk with the kind of wares you might find at a service station. A little distance on was a double row of stalls and, on the edge of a ravine, a toilet with two cubicles. The toilet, unlike the other buildings, was concrete, stood out like a sore thumb, and looked like a newcomer from a world foreign and hostile to everything surrounding it. Here and there mottled brown hens strutted around in search of food, and two dogs were lying in the shade with their tongues hanging out.

'You are welcome to go in,' the guide said, indicating the closed door of a hut to Rad and Nellie, having guessed they were discussing whether that was allowed.

Rad pushed the door. It was not locked and easily opened inwards. There was little light inside, and it would have been very dark if the daylight had not seeped through gaps between the reeds composing the walls. There was surprisingly little inside: no furniture, unless you counted a kind of chest or large box by one of the walls, which was covered with a piece of dark material. There were also several large earthenware pots by the door, but that was all. On the earthen floor in the middle of the hut, its embers glowing, a fire with two half-charred logs sticking out of it was smouldering. An iron cauldron with a ladle stood on a round metal tripod over the fire, and inside it some porridgy brew was bubbling in an unhurried sort of way.

One after another, the three of them came back out. After the squalor of the hut, the world outside, open to sunlight and with the pillar-like tree trunks seeming to support a rustling green roof above their heads, seemed truly to be a temple.

'Why do the people who live there agree to let outsiders into their house?' Rad asked the guide.

He hesitated for a moment.

'We pay them,' he said. 'You might like to buy a souvenir,' he added, gesturing towards the row of stalls.

With the skill of a professional magician, the guide then vanished into thin air. Left on their own, Rad and Nellie walked slowly over to the stalls, their thatched roof a vivid yellow against the green foliage of the trees.

They had taken only a few steps when they were forced to a standstill. They seemed suddenly to have become entangled in children. There were only four of them, three boys and one girl, each one younger than the last. The oldest was at most four years old and the youngest barely two. They did not try to take Rad and Nellie's hands, or cling to their clothing, but somehow managed to get artfully between their legs, twining round them like vines and making it impossible to move on. Looking upwards with their trusting brown eyes, they tried to catch Rad and Nellie's eye and, as soon as they succeeded, began to babble, 'Snap! Flash.' Even the dribbling lips of the two-year-old repeated after her seniors, 'Sna … Sna …!'

'There's no escape. We need a photo,' Nellie said.

'These little children are working?' Rad said, more affirmatively than interrogatively.

'Yes, of course,' Nellie replied. 'Here, take this,' she said, pulling out of her handbag the Sony Dron had left.

Rad took the camera, stepped back a few steps, turned it on and began moving it about to get the image on its small screen just right. Nellie, surrounded by little children, dazzled him with her smile and raised an arm with the hand gracefully turned outwards, every inch *la belle Hélène*, conscious of her own worth and helping herself unstintingly to life's pleasures. The children at her feet were truly life's little flowers, whose sole purpose was to adorn her.

Rad was about to press the shutter button and capture the scene when Nellie abruptly lowered her hand, the smile disappeared from her face, and *la belle Hélène* with it.

'Fuck!' she exclaimed, looking to one side.

Rad followed her gaze to the Japanese who, evidently long-sighted, was holding his camera as far as he could from his eye and inspecting on its screen the image he had just captured. His exhausted, yearning features were now aglow in a smile of ecstasy.

Nellie rummaged in her purse, found a 10-baht note and gave it to the eldest of the children.

'Wait, what are you doing? I haven't taken the picture yet,' Rad said in surprise.

Nellie, looking over, nodded in the direction of the Japanese.

'No, but somebody else has! He's photographed me, the bastard!'

'So what?' Rad asked, looking over at the Japanese man again. The man put his hands to his heart and, with the same blissful smile, bowed to Nellie. 'Leave him to it. Why are you so upset?'

Nellie looked daggers at Rad. She no longer had the children around her. With the same magical professionalism as the guide, having earned their money, they had disappeared somewhere in the village and, no longer garlanded with them, Helen of Troy's halo was extinguished.

'You want him to wank over my image? Is that what you want? What other use does he have for me.'

Rad felt his blood would boil, such inner heat seared him. He felt dizzy, in a sweat, his temples throbbing. She had just promised herself to him. Straight out, openly. She had not just promised, she had obliged him to intimacy. Not by saying 'wank'. That, he knew by now, was entirely in her style. It was how she had said it that imposed the obligation. She regarded him as hers, a man she had a right to complain to that he had allowed another male to encroach on her person, and it did not matter two hoots whether the offence had been real or imagined. It implied they were already one flesh, and he was responsible for protecting her femininity.

He went over to Nellie and handed her Dron's redundant Sony.

'Right, do you want me to take his camera? Smash it? Make him delete the image? What is your desire?'

Sarcasm proved the right approach. The indignation in her eyes flickered and, like a snail quickly withdrawing back into its house, retreated and was replaced by equanimity.

'Well,' she said, taking the camera, 'forget it. Let him live. But then you just must give me a souvenir to remember this place by. So that I have pleasant associations.'

'Easy,' Rad said. 'Are sapphires cheap in Thailand?'

For a village with only two houses, the stalls were crowded with six vendors, three on one side and three on the other. People evidently came here from other places to trade. A girl of about thirteen was selling shawls, scarves, and home-sewn shirts of Thai silk. An ancient, wrinkled old lady, her skin like a piece of tree bark, offered a variety of items carved from wood, from kitchen utensils to a serrated frog with a special pestle which, if drawn slowly over its back, caused it to emit a sound remarkably like a frog croaking. Two plump middle-aged woman were standing in front of bits of jewellery made of silver and semi-precious stones, which were laid out on heavy material. Another girl had trays of fruit and homemade sweets, and another old lady, not as old as the one selling the wood carvings, had an army of dolls of both sexes with brightly painted faces and dressed in colourful folk costumes.

There was no sign of sapphires or emeralds, but an abundance of jade.

'Choose, madame,' Rad said, making a sweeping gesture which encompassed the entire market, when they had proceeded along both counters. The prices were not just low, but under the radar.

'I have already chosen. Have you not noticed?' Nellie said.

'The bracelet?' Rad asked.

When they were walking along the stalls they stopped at the jewellery, and she had spent most time turning over an elegant silver bracelet finely chased with a local design, but had put it back without saying anything.

'Amazing. You noticed!' There was more than approval in Nellie's voice: she was very pleased. 'There, now I'll have something to remember today by,' she said as she slipped the bracelet on and waited while Rad paid for it.

Rad made no response. It was as if he had not heard.

As they were leaving the village, a new tourist group was coming up the path towards them. This, however, was not a group of five: it had twice as many people as theirs. Rad intercepted their driver-guide's look as he surveyed them. His eyes were filled with envy to see a business competitor twice as successful as he was.

On the approach to the bridge they met yet another group, but with only one more customer than theirs. This time their guide was perceptibly relieved: he was still behind, but only slightly.

No sooner had the Toyota moved off than the Japanese made another attempt to talk to Nellie. She and Rad were on the seat behind him, and he turned round, affecting not to notice Rad. He gazed at Nellie with that anaemic, yearning look in his eyes and said,

'Now we have elephant riding. Are you not afraid?'

'With my friend beside me,' Nellie said, defiantly laying her head on Rad's shoulder, 'I am afraid of nothing.'

The Japanese sat for a long time yet with his head turned back, evidently trying but failing to come up with an answer. Sitting with his head twisted backwards was uncomfortable and, saying no more, he turned away.

* * *

The elephants, their legs like wrinkled pillars, were stepping from one foot to the other. They were crowded round a large tree with multiple trunks, beside which, at a height appropriate to the elephants' size, was a wooden platform at the top of a steep ladder.

The elephants swung their trunks from side to side. Their necks were weighed down with long chains in several strands, with one end attached to their right leg. It hung down on either side of their head almost to the knee, perhaps to restrict head movements. The mahouts sat, with their legs bent at the knee, on the back of the elephant's head just behind its ears and, if one raised its head too high, would probably slide off. Two-seater wooden howdahs were fixed with ropes to the elephants' backs and bedded on a thick, multi-layered mat of sackcloth. Rad approached one elephant from the side and tried to reach up to the seat, but was not tall enough.

'Rad, what are you doing!' Nellie squealed. 'Get back! It might step ...' She did not finish the sentence.

Rad obediently got back. And indeed, what had possessed him to try to measure how high the seat was from the ground? As if it was not only too obvious.

'This way, please,' the mahout invited them from his position, pointing to the howdah and making the elephant press its immense body against the platform. The platform creaked and the crown of the tree rustled. It had been erected there for a reason: but for the tree, the platform would not have withstood the pressure from the elephants' massive bodies for long.

'This way, this way!' their guide relayed the message, gesturing invitingly.

'This way, please, since with me by your side you are afraid of nothing,' Rad said, taking Nellie by the arm and leading her to the ladder.

As soon as they reached the platform, they sensed how immeasurably stronger an elephant was than a human. The elephant, restrained by its mahout, was rubbing against the platform, moving away from it and bearing down on it again, and the platform heaved under their feet like the deck of a ship.

'Rad, I'm scared!' Nellie exclaimed.

'With me by your side?' Rad reminded her.

She gave him a charged look and moved to the edge of the platform. Supporting her, Rad helped Nellie get a foot on the sackcloth matting, she bent over, grabbed the back of the seat, pushed off with the foot still on the platform, hovered over the seat, found her balance and sat down.

'Phew!' she exclaimed. 'Let's see how you get on.'

'Easy!' Rad replied.

But just as he was pushing off from the platform, the mahout stopped restraining the elephant, and it started moving, its back rippled as if a great wave was sweeping over it. Rad was tossed up and down and, if Nellie had not grabbed him by the shirt and pulled him towards her, he might well have fallen to the ground.

'There, I saved you,' Nellie said smugly when he landed rather heavily in the seat beside her.

'Much indebted, milady,' he said in some relief.

The mahout, a lad with broad cheekbones, wearing jeans and a swamp-coloured T-shirt, had a blue kerchief tied like a turban on his head. He looked round to make sure everything was in order, a condescending smile playing on his lips, and then they were again looking at the back of his head. Under his direction, the elephant, its chain jangling, was already following its route and, with every step it took, a great wave swept over its back, rocking the howdah as if they were sitting in a boat. The only inconvenience was that they could not dangle their legs down and their knees were pulled up awkwardly to their chins.

'Have you had an elephant ride before?' Rad asked.

'No. Imagine that!' Nellie said. 'Somehow I just never have, although this must be the fifth or sixth time I've been in Thailand.'

'Have you travelled the world?'

'Yes.' The shortness of her reply was evidently significant.

'You've been to Africa?' he asked impetuously.

Nellie made a strange noise, as if she had been expecting to laugh but had, instead, giggled nervously.

'That's where he left me to die,' she said after a pause. 'I told you. Remember?'

Rad's answering grunt signified that, yes, he did remember.

'He literally left me to die,' Nellie said heatedly. 'Literally. We were on a safari. He'd decided that was what he wanted. Well, why not? It sounded great. Only we had a completely terrible hotel. Not even a hotel, something more like a hunting lodge, a kind of shelter for people they'd brought for the stalking. The nearest village was a hundred kilometres away. No roads, no communication, but the helicopter would be back for us in two days' time. I got stung by a scorpion. Literally – a scorpion! The local people told me what it was. My leg was swollen. It turned blue. I lost the feeling in it!'

'Serious!' Rad said.

'Well, now listen closely, so you know who you're dealing with. You may find it helpful.'

'I'm all ears,' Rad assured her, eager for her to continue.

Nellie again gave that odd, strangled half-laugh, half-giggle.

'I would have croaked if I hadn't saved myself. But he just went off hunting. There was a wounded lion that needed to be finished off. The license was burning a hole in his pocket. "What scorpion?" he said. "The nonsense these people come out with! You'll be fine." And off he went. The only medical supplies the people down at reception had were aspirin and iodine. They brought me that and said, 'Don't worry, people don't always die.' Of course, that was maybe just the way they spoke English, but to be told not to worry in that situation! Then they brought me a cup of complimentary tea. "This is the only other thing we can offer you." Very touching. What do you think I did with their tea?'

'Drank it?' Rad hazarded a guess.

'I drank it,' Nellie confirmed. 'And actually, it helped a lot. It really cleared my head. Dron had this knife, like a scalpel. I took it, seared it over a cigarette lighter and made an incision. There was something black in there, like a sting. I dug it out. There was a lot of bleeding, of course, but I didn't try to stop it. On the contrary, I pressed my leg to make it bleed more. The iodine came in useful then. So did the aspirin. Do you want to see the scar?' She pulled up her left trouser leg, exposing the calf, and pointed. 'There, do you see?'

A small scar, a couple of centimetres long, had healed unevenly. It stood out, pink and pale on her smooth, depilated skin. Nothing special about it, until you knew its history.

'What did Dron have to say?' Rad asked.

Nellie lowered the trouser leg.

'We'll come to Dron in a minute,' she said. 'I bandaged my leg, took the aspirin, and lay down. Then those people from reception were knocking at the door. "Are you still alive?" Just like that. When they saw I was, they started making small talk. "You're lucky it was only a scorpion. We have poisonous snakes here too. See that tree with the branches coming in the window? They sometimes crawl up it to the first floor." At that I'd had enough. How I yelled at them! So, what do you think? Ten minutes later I hear a strimmer buzzing. I look out the window and find them cutting the grass round the tree. So snakes couldn't hide in it, or slither up to the trunk. That was decent of them, don't you think? They were at least showing concern.'

'Undoubtedly,' Rad agreed.

'Anyway, then I fell asleep. When I woke I found the swelling was beginning to go down. By evening I had the feeling back in my leg and knew I would live. Dron arrived back. They hadn't found the lion and he was tired and grumpy. I told him how I was and what had happened. His response? "I was sure you'd survive." Those men with the strimmer had shown more concern!'

She stopped, and Rad was tempted to ask why she went on living with him, but held his tongue.

'Look,' he said to break the silence. 'How interesting! The mahout always lets his elephant stop to feed, and only then makes him go on.'

Their whole group was now on the elephants. The Thai-Canadian girls were sitting together, the Japanese had in with him a Taiwanese from another group which arrived at the same time as theirs. A whole column of elephants, with Rad and Nellie at their head, was proceeding along the road, which was stone hard from their trampling. Their elephant reached a steep, wooded hill about 200 metres from the platform and turned on to a path along the foot of it. The rocky cliff face looming over the path was forbidding, but trees, bushes and grass grew on every patch capable of sustaining life, and sometimes concealed the underlying rock so effectively that it disappeared completely. These were places where the elephant chose to stop. It reached its trunk up to the greenery, ripped off a whole quantity, and despatched it into its mouth. The mahout let the elephant pause where it wished, to detour, and even raise its front legs up the rock a little to reach the leaves it wanted. He allowed it to fill its mouth, and only then touched its ear with his goad, a small stick with a sharp hook at the end. At his touch, the elephant obediently moved on.

'Give someone enough freedom to fill their belly and you can demand what you will,' was Nellie's response, but she said it in such an absent manner that it was clear she had not yet returned from the past to the present. 'You are probably wondering why I go on living with him,' she said after a short pause. It was as if she had read his mind.

'That's entirely ...' he began, but Nellie interrupted.

'I'll tell you. You let yourself in for this when you asked me what our life is like in America. You asked, so now here is the answer.' Nellie took a deep breath, as if preparing to dive. 'I have nowhere else to go, Rad, absolutely nowhere. Would you believe it? Do you remember who my father was?'

Rad had no option but to play along. He said, 'I remember he was the Soviet ambassador to somewhere in Latin America, but don't remember which country.'

'That isn't important,' Nellie interrupted. 'He was an ambassador, Extraordinary and Plenipotentiary. Not bad, eh? But that was during the Soviet era, and when the government changed he was thrown out. In 1992 he was recalled and put on the reserves' bench. As we saw later, he just needed to mark time for three years or so while everything settled down and he would have been back in harness. Instead he started making a fuss, phoning here, phoning there, having a word with this one and that one. I remember they did offer him an opening: here's a small jewellery factory, privatise it and live off that. He got on his high horse: I'm a diplomat, not a factory manager! He wasn't adaptable enough to realise they wouldn't throw him another bone. That was the end. After that nobody talked to him any more. He would phone, and somebody's secretary would say the boss was in a meeting, not in the office right now, couldn't talk. He had a heart attack, a stroke, and then it was the Vagankovskoye Cemetery. Where did that leave me? I'm not a businesswoman. I'm just not cut out for it.'

Rad hesitated to ask her what now seemed the obvious question. After she had shared such intimacies with him, he felt he had little choice but to complete his invasion of their privacy.

'Why don't you have children? If you had a child your life would be transformed.'

'Thank you so much. Did it take you a very long time to think of that?' Nellie's voice was heavy with sarcasm. 'Shall I go into the grisly details?'

'No, that's entirely up to you,' Rad said, beating a retreat.

But she had decided to tell him everything, and not just at that moment either.

'I can't have children with Dron. He's sterile. Orchitis. Have you heard of it? Inflammation of the testicles. Flu can have complications. It isn't his fault. If anything it's mine for not having dragged him to see a doctor. We were young, just married, and for both of us it was our first trip outside the USSR. Can you imagine it? He can fuck anyone now and nobody will get pregnant!'

The skeleton, so many times glimpsed but whose existence had not seemed proven beyond doubt, had fallen out of the cupboard with a crash.

Rad had no idea what to say. Whatever he said could only be inappropriate, and to say nothing was not an option.

'Well, but surely,' he mumbled, 'there must be many ways to get round that problem.'

'Really?' Nellie exclaimed. 'Many ways? Kindly enumerate!'

Rad felt a growing desire to give back as good as he got. The sarcasm was uncalled for. After all, he had not asked to be introduced to their skeleton.

'Well, you could, for example, adopt,' he did nevertheless say in as conciliatory a tone as possible.

'I can have children and you are suggesting I should adopt?' Nellie exclaimed in the same accusatory tone.

Rad decided to give her both barrels.

'Well, put out for some negro,' he said.

She seemed to choke. 'Why a negro?'

'If you're going to have a child by someone other than your husband, you might as well make it clear to everyone. Since you can't get away from him because you're scared, scared of being poor, scared of being penniless, scared of not being able to travel the world!'

'How crude you are!' Nellie said, trying to move away from him, except that there was nowhere for her to move to. They were sitting hip to hip, shoulder to shoulder, squashed up against each other. Was it this titillating touching of each other that had prompted her to such openness? 'How crude you are!' she repeated, further irritated because she could not move away. 'What gives you the right to be so rude to me?'

Rad was already ashamed of his intemperateness. He took Nellie's hand. 'I'm sorry,' he said. 'Don't be angry. I was wrong. Forgive me.'

What happened next, he was not expecting. Nellie turned, leaned over to him, and nestled her forehead against his cheek.

'Rad!' she said with a groan. 'Rad, save me. You promised you would. Keep your promise. Please, Rad!'

He sat immobile, afraid of doing something that might offend Nellie again. The wave sweeping over the elephant's back rocked their boat, again, and a third time, and still he could not bring himself to move.

'What are you asking, Nell?' he finally ventured. 'How can I save you. Who would that leave to save me? Right now I'm in a predicament ... I'm a beggar, Nellie. Less than a beggar. I'm in no position to save anyone.'

For a short while they rode on. Nellie did not take her head away from him, but then she did, and when she next looked at Rad there was no trace of the plea she had just breathed in his ear.

'You're pinning your hopes on Dron?' she said. 'Dron won't come to your rescue. Have I not convinced you? Or if he does, it will be at a price you really won't want to pay. I gather you need money.'

An instant later, Rad was cursing himself for a fool. He hadn't meant to, but he did it: he spilled the beans.

'A hundred thousand, Nell. Of your yankee friends. Bucks, greenbacks, cabbage leaf. My roof collapsed on me. Do you speak that language? My roof's roof flipped and he came down on me. I'm on the run. Like some revolutionary. But how long can you stay underground for?'

'Ooh là là!' Nellie exclaimed. 'Ooh là là! That's really tough. Poor you!'

Rad was raging against his own stupidity.

'For God's sake!' he exclaimed, 'let's just do without the funny stuff! Cut it out! I said nothing, I told you nothing, you heard nothing. End of story!'

The elephant, stopping for another of its feeding breaks, tried stretching to reach some leaves it particularly fancied. It had long since turned away from the mountain and was walking through a valley, slowly making its way back to the platform. The valley was full of rises, as if a piece of paper had been crumpled and and then flattened out, only not very carefully. The tree whose leaves the elephant was minded to sample was growing on one such hillock. The tip of its trunk was open and ready to curl round the object of its desire, but no matter how the elephant strained upwards, it could not reach the leaves. It lowered its trunk, moved its weight to its back legs and, in a sudden movement, reared up and placed its front feet on the slope. The seat tipped back; Rad and Nellie, clutching the armrests for dear life, fell back along with it, their legs in the air. It seemed that the next moment they would lose their grip. Nellie screamed.

The mahout, keeping his place on the neck with difficulty, yelled at the elephant, swung and sank the hook of his goad into it. The elephant abandoned the leaves, which it had just managed to grasp with its trunk, itself responded with angry trumpeting, but lowered its feet and abandoned any further attempt. It moved on along its designated route. When the mahout stuck his goad into it, Rad had a glimpse of raw flesh. The elephant had a bloody wound behind its ear. Its obedience was born of pain.

'Oh, I was so frightened,' Nellie said with a nervous laugh.

Rad was reminded of the Japanese.

'It's no shame to be frightened in a situation like that. The Japanese, though, was scared even before he started.'

Nellie again emitted that strangled half-laugh that had been such a feature of their conversations today.

'And were you scared yesterday?' she asked.

'What? When?' Rad asked.

'Yesterday evening. Why didn't you try to follow me into my room? You didn't even make the attempt. That was hurtful.'

Rad again raged inwardly, but this time it was an impotent rage. She was a hard cookie, was Nellie, a very hard cookie!

'Surely not?' he exclaimed. 'I offended you? Excuse me, I knocked on your door but you didn't open it.'

'You knocked?' In Nellie's tone surprise was tempered by doubt. 'When?'

'Last night. And you didn't let me in.'

Nellie continued to look at him in the same conflicted manner.

'Did you really knock?'

'And how! You must have been in the shower.'

Slowly, as if surfacing from a depth comparable with the Mariana Trench, Nellie's lips parted in a derisive smile.

'You liar!' she said. 'You ought to be ashamed of yourself.'

As he got off the elephant onto the platform and then helped Nellie, Rad found he was feeling relieved. Riding an elephant had proved monotonous, and half an hour instead of a full hour would have been plenty. His relief was, however, only partly to do with the ride. Now it was over, there was a prospect that all mention of their mutual disclosures during their *tête-à-tête* would also be over.

For the rest of the day, Rad tried to ensure that he and Nellie found themselves alone together as little as possible. At lunch in a roadside restaurant with long tables for six, he contrived to have their guide sit between them and the guide talked happily to Nellie all through the meal. For a time she translated odd sentences for Rad, but constantly bending down to the table and raising her voice was awkward and she eventually gave up. Rad was only too pleased for the rest of lunch to be left to his own devices.

On the way to the waterfall, and after they got there, Rad managed to keep the Taiwanese, who had partnered the Japanese man on the elephant ride, between himself and Nellie. His group, after the elephant ride, seemed to have become attached to theirs. Wherever Rad's group went they were there too, only travelling in their own minibus. The Taiwanese had interesting things to say. The Japanese man had told him his story, and Rad had little difficulty getting the Taiwanese to share his impressions. As a Chinaman, the Taiwanese could not resist a dig at a denizen of the land of the rising sun.

'The Japanese are a nation of depressives,' he mused, standing near the waterfall and admiring the crystal cascade as it roared down the cliff. 'We once breathed life into them with our culture. Their perception of it was refracted through their own innate mentality and they became an inordinately aggressive nation. For now that aggression has been suppressed, which always leads to depression.'

The Taiwanese was a psychologist, and analysing the nature and logic of phenomena was his profession. He devoted himself to this with all the zeal characteristic of psychologists, and Nellie followed and questioned him no less devotedly, leaving Rad once more in peace.

For the rafting, he and Nellie again found themselves side by side, perched on a low bamboo seat, but it was impossible to do more than exchange occasional remarks. A gentle stream became a rushing river and developed into rapids. Their long, narrow bamboo raft was seized by the current, water gushed over it, breaking in waves over their legs and drenching the seat. Neither Rad nor Nellie thought, when the wave drenched them for the first time, to raise themselves, and the water flooded almost to their waists. Their Thai raftsman stood at the bow, pressing a long bamboo pole down to the riverbed, steering the raft in the right direction and pushing it away from the banks. Approaching one particularly turbulent rapid, he lifted a second pole lying at his feet and invited Rad to help him from the stern. With the rapid behind them, the raftsman gestured to Rad that he could sit back down, but Rad stayed with his pole at the stern until journey's end.

Only the decorated ends of thatched roofs in the villages along their route peeped over the top of the steep banks. Every village had two or three engines, obviously pumps, clattering away. They had hoses hanging down into the river, evidently taking water for irrigation. In shallower spots, children stood shivering in the river, splashing and playing. Older, pubescent girls had let down their hair and were dipping it in the water, cupping it in their hands, squeezing it, dipping and squeezing it again. They gave the tourists a grave, condescending look, as if what they themselves were doing was a necessary part of the world's business, and was more than could be said for floating down the river on a raft.

Their guide and his young assistant met the rafts when they rounded a sharp bend, at a place where the river was peaceful and quiet. The surface was so placid that, if they had not known its true character, they might have taken it for a lowland stream. Their passports, cameras and watches, which they had handed over for safekeeping, were returned to their proper place in pockets and bags and on wrists, and their guide, with the smile of a man looking forward at last to a rest, pointed to a tortuous path leading up the steep riverbank.

'This way, please! Your bus is waiting.'

The sun had set, the air was a heavy mauve, and day was fading before their eyes, peacefully surrendering to night its power over half the Earth. Just as soon as the minibus set off, darkness rushed at the windows, leaving nothing for the eye to see beyond them. The world contracted to the confines of the Toyota which, with the litheness of a tiger, hurled its iron body in pursuit of the flash of light it cast ahead of itself. All that was outside disappeared, annihilated. Only the Toyota was real.

Nellie turned from the darkness outside towards Rad and said,

'That was splendid. A wonderful day.'

'Great,' Rad said. 'Great,' with the same grave condescension as the teenage girls kneading their hair in the river.

The city street lights came upon them with the suddenness of a predator pouncing on its prey. The prey, its engine humming, surrendered without demur, like a submissive rabbit, to its fate. It flung itself into the jaws of the city and passed rapidly into its brightly lit digestive tract, satisfied to serve the predator as its next meal. Rad was startled by the associations coming into his mind.

The Toyota's return route mirrored the morning route. First back to his hotel was the Japanese. As he left, he bowed individually to each fellow passenger, saving Nellie till last.

'We had a most remarkable talk,' he said, his haggard face full of guile. 'With you beside me I was afraid of nothing.' At the door he paused, turned around, and added, 'You have something of my wife about you. I saw her in you.'

When the Toyota arrived back at the hotel of the Thai-Canadian girls, there was a sudden animated discussion in Thai with the elderly guide's young assistant. The gist of their conversation became evident when they got up to leave and the young assistant giggled and exchanged a few words with the guide. He laughed, waved him on his way, and the young man gratefully placed his hands in front of him, bowed quickly to his senior, then opened the door on his side and jumped down after the girls.

'Young people!' the guide exclaimed to Rad and Nellie, before driving on. There was in his knowing, forgiving smile also a hint of satisfaction which he could hardly contain.

'Wicked old pimp,' Nellie grunted in Russian to Rad as the minibus picked up speed.

'What makes you think that?' Rad asked.

'Back there in the village I saw him nudging the young chap, as if to say, "Get in there!" It was very obvious. Perhaps that's his son. Would he really mind if one of the girls took him to Canada? Years ago it was her mother emigrated there, and now perhaps one of them will take the boy back with her. Everyone here seems just to want to get out of this paradise and head for the hell of the capitalist West.'

Rad thought back to how the driver's young assistant had been behaving during the tour. He really hadn't seemed to be an assistant or an apprentice. Nellie might be right.

'Is that what you're living in over there,' he asked. 'A hell?'

'Well, it's certainly no paradise.'

'And what about here? Do you really believe this is a paradise?'

'Don't be tiresome,' Nellie said, ending the conversation.

* * *

The wooden gates of the River Ping Palace were wide open, as if it were daytime, but in the hotel itself not a single light was on and the garden seemed irrevocably immersed in night. Only through the leaves of the thicket between the house and the kitchen building lamps shone tremulously from the square by the restaurant. The evening, however, seemed to stretch ahead of them endlessly. They had yet to have dinner somewhere, and before that, Rad needed a shower and a change of clothes.

This thought annoyed him. He had nothing to change into. His trousers had dried out on the way back, but judging by the water stains on the legs, they must look much the same at the back. He could hardly go out looking like that. The only other trousers he had were shorts, but he could not wear those. Other than in seaside resorts, people in Thailand evidently found shorts offensive.

He had no option but to ask Nellie whether Dron, when he departed, had left behind any spare trousers. Nellie's silvery laugh rang out once more.

'Oh, you poor dear,' she said. 'You haven't got any trousers. Well, come along, we'd better find you some.'

As he stepped into the room Nellie shared with Dron, Rad again felt a fever he had been suppressing all day. They were alone in a room where, by rights, there should also have been Dron, and the fact that there wasn't, that he and Nellie were in there alone together, unexpectedly swept away all the barriers he had been erecting. His body seemed to quicken, right to the tips of his fingers. His only salvation was to get back out just as quickly as he could. He withdrew from the room in such haste that he had to agree a time for meeting up with Nellie again when he was already out in the corridor.

To conclude his shower, Rad doused himself several times with cold water and felt thoroughly chilled. The shivering from cold was, however, preferable to that other feverishness.

Dron's trousers were, predictably, far too big for him. He and Dron were roughly the same height, but Dron was heavy-boned, portly, and round the waist the trousers had fifteen centimetres to spare. He had, however, no alternative. Rad tugged the belt through the loops provided, tightened it sufficiently to ensure the trousers would not fall down, and distributed the lurches over his loins as evenly as he could.

When Nellie saw him she could not help exclaiming, 'You look like a docker from the port of New York.'

'Have you never dined out with a docker from the port of New York?' Rad parried.

'I never thought I would need to.'

'Well you do now,' Rad said. 'What choice do you have?'

'I don't need any. This docker will do me fine.' She laughed again.

She did not want to dine in the hotel restaurant, or where they ate yesterday after Dron's departure, so they caught a songthaew to the city centre. The comfortable European-style restaurant where they had lunch on the day they arrived was etched in Nellie's memory as a bright, cheery, colourful spot, and she decided she would like to step into the same river twice.

They looked for the same river, circling round for forty minutes or so. Rad had no recollection of its name. Nellie thought she remembered it, but when they found the restaurant it was called not LL, as she had thought, but JJ.

'I have early-onset arteriosclerosis,' she announced chirpily when they were ensconced. 'Do you like the idea, Rad, of a woman with early-onset arteriosclerosis? In the prime of life but sclerotic! Can you imagine it? She can't remember today who she slept with yesterday, and by tomorrow will have forgotten who she slept with today. A useful sort of woman, don't you think?'

The little quips she came out with became increasingly blatant. Troy, so unconquerable in the past, stood now with its gates flung open. The night was approaching, and it was abundantly clear that he needed to take only one step, indeed even half a step, to find himself obliged to enter and take possession of the citadel.

Dinner came to an end, however, and Rad had contrived to let slip no hint that he had noticed the gates were no longer barred. In Nellie's place, he would have been offended. For him not to have noticed was simply not credible.

And indeed, Nellie was offended. As they waited for the bill she seemed to implode into aloofness; she became introverted, haughty, and now all that remained of her recent animation was the memory. 'Yes' and 'no' was as much as could be elicited from her.

As they returned to the hotel, the aloofness only became more marked. Now to extract a 'yes' or a 'no' would have been a major success: she said nothing, demonstratively not responding to him. The songthaew stopped by the hotel gate, Rad proffered her his hand and helped her down, went to the front to pay the driver, and when he got back, she was gone. From the darkness of the courtyard came the crunch of someone walking rapidly over the gravel. It was replaced by the tapping of high heels on the wooden decking of the verandah, and followed by a change of rhythm as Nellie began going up the stairs. Rad experienced painfully mixed feelings: of regret and jubilation. For heaven's sake, to turn your back on Troy when it had finally laid its riches at your feet!

He had been back in his room for ten minutes or so and just had time to brush his teeth when there came a knock at the door. It was firm and loud, and even if it had not been, he would have been sure it was Nellie. When he went over to the door, however, he said, 'Who is it?'

Nellie's voice came authoritatively from the other side of the door. 'Rad, open up. There is something I have to tell you.'

For a moment he hesitated. He knew it would be far better not to open the door, but how could he refuse?

Rad unlocked it. Before he could put his hand on the handle, it went down of its own accord, the door opened and, forcing him to retreat, Nellie entered purposefully. Indeed, she burst in. Her face was flushed with the same determination as had been evident in the firm, loud knock.

'Here is what I have to tell you …' she said, but did not finish the sentence. As purposefully as she had entered, she spun round, turned the key in the lock and came back to face Rad. She threw her arms round his neck; she clung to him and looked into his eyes; she sighed, 'Why are you playing the fool? Are you holding back because of Dron? He wouldn't! He wouldn't! Stop fooling! How dare you refuse me!'

She had changed, and was now wearing a silk terracotta-coloured dressing gown with dragons, not at all appropriate for flaunting outside a bedroom in the corridors of a hotel. The broad belt was loosely in place rather than tied, she had no bra or, perhaps, anything else under the dressing gown, and her breasts pressed with provocative submissiveness against him.

Rad's resistance crumbled. His hands were suddenly undoing her belt, opening the dressing gown, beneath which there was not a stitch! In an instant, the roughness of her pubis was searing his hand, her lips were teasing his mouth and, while one arm remained around his neck, the other hand was fumbling with the belt of his trousers. To no avail. She yanked: it did not yield.

'Can you take care of this yourself?' she said, relinquishing his mouth and taking Rad's hand from her burning bush. She impatiently moved it to his belt buckle. He got to work on the belt and she again threw both arms around his neck, again got to work on his mouth and, a moment before lapsing into inarticulate moaning, murmured with a snigger, 'Dron's fucking pants! He did this deliberately.'

A bucket of ice-cold water was thrown over Rad. Conjured by her words, the presence of Dron materialised in the room and stood there observing them. Or perhaps seeing nothing. Perhaps, like Gogol's Viy, he could see only if someone else raised his grotesque eyelids. But the mere fact of his being there rendered Rad impotent. He felt cloud nine rip beneath him and send him hurtling back to earth, where he landed with a splatter.

Nellie, leaning back, her belly pressed against his, asked in a shocked tone, 'What's happened? What's gone wrong?'

Rad took her wrist and unhooked her arms from his neck.

'Dron's trousers, you need to know, have nothing to do with anything. The belt is entirely mine.'

Nellie continued to look shocked, but now also baffled.

'Why are we talking about Dron's trousers?'

'Nellie! Nellie! Nellie!' Rad exclaimed.

He obliged her to unhand his person, took a step back, took the folds of her dressing gown and drew them together. He retreated some more, stepping to left and right as if describing a sine curve whose purpose was to distance him from her. But no matter what kind of curve he described there was no getting away from Nellie: the room was large, but almost its entire space was taken up by a huge bed with a mosquito net baldaquin. The bed could readily have accommodated a foursome in either direction. It organised the room's space and could, indeed, be seen as a room within a room, so that no matter what trajectory he might describe, the bed constrained it to pass straight along the x- or y-axis.

'Sorry, Nellie! You know what I'm here for. I couldn't look Dron in the face. Forgive me!'

Nellie stood in the same place by the door where he had left her and the folds of her dressing gown, unconstrained by the belt, had again parted to reveal the glowing body of a mature, childless woman. The only way not to stare would have been to screw his eyes up tight. Nellie could see him trying, and failing. A carnivorous smile played triumphantly on her lips. She moved to the bed and, without for a moment taking her eyes off Rad, with a quick, decisive movement, tossed up the gauze of the canopy. The next moment, the dressing gown shimmered from her shoulders to the floor and *la belle Hélène* lay before Rad framed, not in terracotta silk, but in all her natural seductiveness. The amphora of her thighs reduced Rad to a quivering jelly.

'Come hither!' she said, holding out her arms. It was not a request, not indeed an order, but a summoning. 'Shag my brains out, like you wanted to then at the Conservatoire, remember? Shag me black and blue. Fuck me. Now!'

Rad did not move, but mentally was at her side, inside her, but she again dropped him in the cold plunge.

'Forget about Dron,' she said enticingly. 'I know him. He even wants us to be together. He wants that. Forget him.'

'How can he want it?' Rad asked, not moving from where he was.

'Who cares? That's not your worry.'

'Perhaps he wants me to get you pregnant?'

Rad appeared to have hit the bullseye. Nellie's response was silence.

'Come here!' she summoned him again. 'Come, come to me!'

The Viy not only opened his eyelids: he pointed at Rad and commanded obedience to his will. They both wanted the same thing, but not under the death-dealing gaze of his eyes.

'Do cover yourself,' Rad whispered.

He turned and described a time-optimal straight line trajectory along the y-axis leading away from Nellie. In a corner of the room there was a back door to a terrace overlooking the river. It had a straightforward latch, which clicked loudly as he opened it. As vast as the universe, night stretched out beyond the doorway. Its coolness wafted over his face as his nostrils took in the bracing aroma of nearby water. In the middle of the river, its diesel engine chugging, a tug with a warning red lamp on its prow and dim light coming from its cabin dragged a barge as black as anthracite, its stern demarcated by another red light.

For a few endless moments, Rad stood looking at the river in front of him, but his awareness of the door's yawning maw behind him was unsettling: he forced himself to walk away along the terrace towards the restaurant. Not a light was on at the restaurant, and only in front of the verandah three dimly lit orange Chinese lanterns hanging from long poles inclined towards the river. Peace, tranquillity and a sense of the Creator's benevolence were in the air.

With a hideous whine, three or four mosquitoes launched a coordinated attack. Rad waved his arms to deflect them, and simultaneously heard hurried footsteps behind him. He turned and was stunned by a swinging blow to his ear. Before he could recover, an equally powerful blow afflicted his eardrum on the other side. He recalled the way, during his military training, his eardrums had been similarly assailed by a mortar fired next to him.

'Bastard!' Nellie exclaimed indignantly. 'Bastard! Bastard! Bastard!'

Rad, even before he was able to focus on her, managed to catch her hands and hold them in his own, averting another swipe.

'Nellie,' he murmured, 'Nellie, stop it …'

'Let go, you bastard! Let go!' She struggled to pull her hands free, overpowered and all the more furious because of that. 'Let go, you bastard!'

Rad did let go, and was immediately struck again, only this time the best she could manage was a slap in the face, loud but, after what had preceded it, an anticlimax.

'Bastard! Bastard!' she kept repeating in a strangled voice, as if unable to recall any more inventive term of abuse.

Now Rad said no more, only warily eyeing her hands, ready to intercept them again. Nellie, however, had exhausted herself. She flew at him, he stepped aside, and she hurtled past, the folds of her dressing gown now tied in place with the unyielding sureness of a mariner's knot. She sped across the square in front of the restaurant, the heels of her slippers resounding on the path leading through the garden shrubs to the stairs to the first floor.

His open back door glowed, framed by the doorway, like a mirage of sunlight in the nocturnal darkness. Rad wandered back and, without pausing in the doorway, closed it behind him. He relatched it and stood for a while, vacantly fingering the round knob on the end of the latch, his head hollow and empty. After Nellie's mortar rounds, his head felt like an iron cauldron that it would be best just to take off his shoulders and be done with. This was becoming a habit: he had disgraced himself with two women in succession and both had exacted payment in full.

When he finally got to bed, he found that the light from his open door had attracted, if not a regiment, then a full-strength platoon of mosquitoes, whose scouts had infiltrated the mosquito net, which had been left unsecured for a considerable time. To sleep was impossible: the whining of the mosquitoes drove him crazy, and for half the night Rad twisted and turned in his group-sex-sized bed, playing all four roles simultaneously.

When at last he fell asleep, he dreamed of Nellie. They were at the Horowitz concert in the Conservatoire and had just returned to their seats after the interval. Consumed by desire, he put his hand on her knee: she did not object or seem uninterested. She took his hand and slowly moved it up the inanimate coolness of her tights, up her leg, under her skirt, and suddenly she was not wearing tights. His hand was on her warm, living body, she had no panties on, and the smooth satin of her secret place, no less tumescent than he was himself, was in his hand. In front of everyone, he took Nellie by the buttocks and sat her on his lap, himself suddenly naked from the waist down, and what he so desired was happening. She was tight inside, like a passage leading to the centre of the universe, to its beginning, its birth, to the moment of the Big Bang. The audience around them, whether from embarrassment or because they were mesmerised by the music, ignored them as he and Nellie thrust at each other with wild abandon. All to the accompaniment of Chopin performed on the piano by Horowitz. Alas, no matter how he tried, Rad just could not remember the name of the piece.

He woke up when, hugging a pillow, he fulsomely erupted into the yawning emptiness of the bed, like a randy teenager.

CHAPTER TWELVE

The excavator was already at work. It lowered the jaw of its bucket into the water, bent its neck, gnawed off another piece of the bank and, raising the full bucket in the air, turned back its orange brontosaurian body. Its neck unbent, the bucket flap opened and heavy lumps of soil came tumbling out. The mound of excavated earth behind it had increased significantly over the three days. The air still retained something of the night's coolness; the gauzy haze on the river was not completely dispelled, but the sun rising behind the Sheraton looked as if it would toil no less diligently than the digger, and heat the air by noon to the temperature of a steam engine's firebox.

Rad ordered only a cup of coffee and, for fifteen minutes now, taking an occasional sip, had been watching the excavator. He deliberately sat facing it, with his back to the entrance in order not to see Nellie approaching. It would have been odd to look away as she came closer, and he did not want to see her, afraid of being unable to look her in the eye. That moment could be put off until she arrived and he had no option. She was bound to show up sooner or later, if not now, then in an hour's time. They were Siamese twins with a shared circulatory system. She had no way of getting away from him.

Nellie appeared when all that remained of his coffee, no matter how long he had stretched it out, was one final sip and the coffee grounds. He heard footsteps on the tiles and instantly recognised them. He knew it was her, but did not turn round, just picked up the cup and, tossing it back, took that last sip. The angle to which he tipped it proved overly acute, so along with the coffee he felt the disagreeable sediment of the grounds on his tongue.

'Good morning,' he said, when Nellie entered his field of vision.

She made no reply, silently pulled back her chair, sat down, made herself comfortable, and only then, looking him straight in the eyes, said,

'Good morning,' before adding, 'moral paragon.'

Rad deemed it expedient not to retaliate.

'What's doing with Dron?' he asked. 'Still busy?'

Nellie paused. The pause was, in effect, another pointed non-reply, with a repetition of 'moral paragon!' implied.

'All fixed,' she said eventually, and was again silent.

She was silent, and looked at him, in possession of knowledge he did not possess, affirming her superiority, demonstrating that it lay in her power to enlighten him or leave him to languish in ignorance. Rad, for his part, looked back at her in a childish contest to see who would blink first.

'And?' Rad caved in.

He had been afraid of not being able to look her in the eye, but it was her silence he succumbed to.

'Do you really want to know?' Nellie asked, as if that was not obvious from his question.

The barmaid appeared as if by magic. Her heels had clattered on the tiles but the sound only registered with Rad when she appeared at their table and said, 'May I offer you breakfast?'

Her pretty face was radiant with joy at the prospect of serving and pleasing them.

'You may, you may,' Rad said quickly, forgetting that Nellie had not yet ordered, as she was not slow to remind him.

'Are you assuming I will have the same as you?'

'Forgive me!' Rad exclaimed, throwing up his hands in mock horror.

Nellie discussed the menu with the barmaid in so much detail it seemed that was what she was planning to eat for the rest of her days.

'So, you do want to know?' she said, when the barmaid had gone.

Rad nodded affirmatively.

A nod was not enough.

'What is it you actually want to hear?'

'When he is coming back,' Rad said patiently.

'He isn't,' Nellie said with satisfaction.

She had every reason to relish the answer. It was entirely unexpected.

'And what does that mean?' Rad asked, disconcerted.

'What that means is that we are leaving.' Nellie let out her silvery laugh. 'We seem to have done everything here we are going to, don't you think? That being so, it would seem time to strike camp.'

'Wait a minute.' Rad suddenly flushed and, in spite of the chill in the morning air, felt hot. He took her announcement to mean that Dron had had to fly back with Chris to America and he would not be seeing him again. 'What's happened? What's up with Dron? Where are we going?'

'That is an interesting question, isn't it,' she said, giving him an arch look.

The barmaid returned with a collection of plates in her hands. She held them fanned out, and also the cutlery. It was a remarkable feat.

'Here you are!' she said happily, lowering the plates on to the table. 'Here you are! Enjoy!'

'Enjoy,' Nellie remarked, pointing to the plates in front of Rad.

'Nellie, tell me!' Rad demanded, feeling the throbbing of his heartbeat in his temples.

'Oh, moral paragons want to know everything, do they?' Nellie enquired. 'They make a rule of knowing everything? Like moral botanists.'

'Nellie!' Rad demanded. 'Answer, will you? If someone asks you a question, you should answer it.'

'Ooh, I'm so scared, I'm so scared!' Nellie gazed at him derisively. 'Do you want me to answer all your questions at the same time or one by one?'

The barmaid, setting out their breakfast, had the same serene, happy expression on her face. As she arranged their plates and laid out the cutlery, it seemed she could imagine nothing more engrossing in life.

'Enjoy!' she cordially wished them once more when the job was done.

She skittered away, and Rad was able to resume his conversation.

'What's up with Dron?' he asked. 'Is he all right?'

Nellie finally decided to relent.

'Nothing's up with your Dron,' she said. 'He's fine. He's waiting for us. We're going to the seaside, to Pattaya. Ever heard of it?'

'Why are we suddenly going to Pattaya?'

'I haven't the faintest idea,' Nellie said. 'There is evidently a reason. Don't you want to go to the seaside?'

'Why would I?'

Nellie paused for a moment.

'Because Dron is going there, and you'd better go too,' she said, picking up her spoon and fork and starting in on her breakfast.

'Of course I had,' Rad reflected silently. 'So when do we leave?' was all he asked.

'We'll finish breakfast and go to the airport,' Nellie said casually. 'You don't mind flying? We'll just take the next flight.'

'Fine,' Rad agreed.

'Only our seats won't be together,' Nellie said, narrowing her eyes at him. 'Is that all right? Can you bear that?'

'It will be painful, but I'll try,' Rad answered.

Nellie stopped narrowing her eyes.

'For me it will be a relief.'

In fact they were allocated seats together. When they checked in Nellie did not ask for them to be separate. The whole time after breakfast, while they were packing their bags, paying the hotel bill, travelling to the airport, queuing at the Thai Airways ticket counter, then waiting for the flight, they hardly exchanged a word. Only when something had to be decided or agreed, they agreed or decided it, and were again silent. Rad tried not to think about what had happened yesterday. He had decided Nellie was no use as an ally, but to have made an enemy of her was disastrous.

When they were in their places with their seatbelts fastened and the plane had taxied out to the runway, its engines roaring, shaking the fuselage, ready for takeoff but still waiting for the blessing of air traffic control, Nellie suddenly broke the silence.

'What made you so reluctant to give me a baby?' she suddenly asked.

Her tone now was quite different from her earlier tone at breakfast. It was the tone of an ex-lover for whom everything was firmly in the past, but with whom he was still close and who could talk with him about the most intimate things. This was a Nellie who had sinned with him so many times that the sin had ceased to count as such.

'You wanted a baby?' Rad ask cautiously, not wanting to frighten away this new Nellie.

'Yes,' she said.

'If it's purely about having a baby, my understanding is that in your situation you have many alternatives in America. They have sperm donor banks …'

Nellie interrupted.

'You mean, get syringed, like impregnating a cow?'

'Why choose that analogy?' Rad twisted his hands in front of him. The gesture did not actually express anything: he just wanted to add weight to his words, which at heart he felt they lacked. 'An analogy should bring out the essence, not the form.'

'The essence, the form,' Nellie aped him. 'When it's someone else's problem everything is much easier, isn't it?'

She was right. Rad had no answer. He was silent, trying to find a safe, diplomatic reply, but nothing came to him.

It was lucky he was not in too much of a hurry, because Nellie herself provided the answer.

'Actually, most likely, it will be the syringe in the end, from some anonymous bull.'

Rad came up with a good continuation.

'The main thing is, it will be your baby.'

'Of course,' Nellie nodded. 'By the way, if I got pregnant by you, Dron would kill you. Not in a duel, either. He's an excellent shot.'

There was a glaring contradiction between what she had just said and what she had been claiming in his bedroom last night. It did not, however, seem a good idea to point this out.

'To kill someone, you don't really need to be a good shot,' he remarked.

'He would have killed you as an excellent shot, with a single bullet,' Nellie insisted. 'If you were alive, you would be in his way, even if you lived on the other side of the globe.'

Rad felt an involuntary chill. Was she telling the truth? Did she believe what she was saying?

The aircraft engine roared at full power, the plane shuddered even more violently, before rushing forward and accelerating; Beneath the wheels the joints of concrete slabs tapped faster and faster until the plane rose into the air. The ground rushed away, turning into a three-dimensional model of itself, neat, tidy, toy-like. Nellie, in the window seat, leaned towards it, gazing down. When, a minute later, she turned back to Rad, a new thought was gleaming in her eye.

'What is there between you and Zhenya, then?' she asked. 'How do you feel about her?'

Rad had no idea who she was talking about.

'What Zhenya?' he countered.

'Wow!' Nellie exclaimed. 'What Zhenya? The one who helped you get in touch with Dron. Her father and Dron's were friends back in the old times.'

The penny finally dropped.

'Oh, Jenny,' he said.

'Yes, well, anyway, how do you feel about her?' Nellie repeated impatiently.

'Sweet girl,' Rad replied. 'She has some similarities with you.'

'Really?' It was not clear whether Nellie was pleased with the comparison or not. 'In what way?'

'In the radiance of her beauty and the brilliance of her intellect,' he said.

Nellie snorted.

'A wonderful answer. I only hope it's true.'

'Rest assured,' Rad averred.

'And what is there between the two of you?' Nellie had not forgotten the first part of her question.

'Nothing.' In a way, that was true.

'Li-ar!' Nellie chanted accusingly. 'She's so interested in you in her emails. If there was "nothing" she wouldn't be half so interested.'

Rad cursed to himself.

'My dear Nell,' he said, addressing her more intimately than usual. 'Zhenya, as you call her, put me on to Dron. That's all there is to it.'

'Li-ar,' Nellie chanted again. 'And you're wasting your time denying it. She's fallen for you. Do you really not know that? Why would she be so smitten if there was nothing between you?'

'And if there was something, why would that matter?'

Nellie treated Rad to the worldly wise look of an ex-lover whose ardour cooled long ago and who now harbours purely maternal feelings.

'Well, why don't you marry her? I can help. She's sweet, she resembles me and she's fallen for you. That seems a good start.'

'Yes, I really would like to marry her.'

'Well, what's holding you?'

'All that's holding me is how to persuade her to accept me.'

Nellie again treated Rad to her worldly wise look and seemed to be considering her response very carefully.

'Right,' she said finally, 'that's settled.'

The plane had reached its cruising altitude, the 'Fasten seatbelts' sign had been turned off, the Thai air stewardesses, their faces wreathed in caring smiles, rolled drinks trolleys the length of the aisles.

Half an hour later, the 'Fasten seatbelts' sign came back on and the plane began its descent. Then, as they were again belted into their seats in preparation for landing, Nellie launched a new conversation. As if in a hurry, while they were still alone together, there was something she really wanted to know but had never been able to ask.

'Look,' she said, 'just tell me: are you Jewish? Tell me the truth. I'm not anti-Semitic: I think you know that.'

'How amazing,' Rad said, taken aback by the question. 'Why the sudden interest now?'

'Well, partly because you have an un-Russian name. And your face. You don't look very Russian.'

'My face?' Rad repeated, as if that was the most important thing in what she had said. 'I don't know, I can't really comment on my face. As for the name, how many Jews do you know who get called "Slava"?'

Nellie appeared to be mentally running through a list of her acquaintances.

'No, I can't think of anyone, but what does that prove? Dron said you're Jewish, only different.'

Rad couldn't suppress a chuckle.

'And what is a usual Jew like? Rabinovich in a Jewish joke?'

Nellie burst out laughing.

'I know what you mean, but Dron has an instinct. I've said already, he has an animal intuition.'

'Is Dron a big authority for you?'

'He has authority over me,' Nellie replied.

'What did you mean when you said "partly"?' Rad asked. 'What is there apart from my name and my face?'

Nellie answered without a moment's hesitation.

'There is something about you that really is not Russian. Something not quite right.'

Rad felt a sudden urge to open up to her, to tell her about something he was used to not talking about, or laughing off. He felt suddenly trusting, as if they really had been lovers in the past, and had managed to keep alive their liking for each other. There could not be many women who, after last night's scene, would have forgiven him so readily rather than becoming a sworn enemy.

'As far as being Jewish is concerned, Nellie,' he said, 'I have to disappoint you. All I have to boast of is being one-eighth Western Slav. My great-grandfather was a Czech, one of those anti-Bolsheviks the schoolbooks call White Czechs. Do you remember your history? He fell in love with my great-grandmother and stayed on in Soviet Russia. In 1934 he was sentenced to forced labour, building the White Sea Canal to make him a real Russian, and they evidently succeeded. At least, in his grave his bones are a hundred per cent surrounded by Russian bones. My mother was an adult before she heard he had been Czech. Can you imagine the fear all that time? Well, anyway, I'm named after him. I sometimes wonder, of course, whether it all isn't just a family legend, but my great-grandfather's name was definitely Radislav, or I wouldn't have been called that, would I?'

He paused, and Nellie, who had not said a word during the story, exclaimed,

'What did I say?! Dron has animal intuition! Remember he asked you at the Conservatoire if you were Czech, and you said you were Jewish? Why did you do that?'

'I was winding him up.' Rad remembered that awkward conversation when they first met Dron during the interval. So Nellie remembered it too. 'It's not intuition Dron has: he's just good at thinking logically.'

'It's a flair,' Nellie insisted. 'Plus logical thinking, but first and foremost, it's a flair!'

The plane was landing. Nellie turned to the window and gazed avidly at the approaching ground which, as they watched, was being transfigured once more out of a model of itself into living reality. The wheels touched down, the plane hammered over the joins in the concrete. The roar of the engines, which had been surreptitiously beating his eardrums, suddenly tailed off, replaced by a hissing and rustling as the aircraft's speed was reduced to that of a truck. It turned off the runway and crawled across the airfield to the terminal buildings. Rad glanced at his watch. The flight had lasted precisely one hour and ten minutes, as scheduled.

When those around them were releasing their seat belts and standing up and Rad was about to follow suit, Nellie caught his shirt sleeve to keep him sitting down.

'I hope you won't say anything to Dron,' she hissed, as if about to bite him.

'I have no idea what I could have to say to him,' Rad said.

'Good,' Nellie said, relaxing her grip on him.

* * *

As they came through to the terminal, Rad and Nellie were met by Tony's laser-white smile. He shook Rad's hand and patted him matily on the shoulder.

'How are you feeling?' The mischievous look in his eyes showed he had not forgotten Patpong.

'How about you, Tony?' he asked in retaliation. 'Let's just forget Patpong, shall we?' was the implication.

'I am feeling great!' Tony exclaimed.

'And so am I,' Rad said.

'Where's Dron?' Nellie asked Tony. 'Is he not here?'

'Dron is not here,' Tony confirmed. 'He has a meeting. He is with Chris and Mike at the Regency Park Hotel. We will go to your apartment, drop off your bag there and go straight on to see them.'

'Regency Park has that Victorian restaurant we were going to take you to,' Nellie reminded Rad.

'And where will I be going with my bag?' Rad had banished the topic of Patpong, but it would not go away. As a result of his visit to Patpong, Rad was out in the street.

'You can sleep on our floor,' Nellie said with a laugh.

Her sarcasm was rapidly punctured when Tony said he had a room reserved for him at the Jade Pavilion, the hotel Chris had stayed at before. It was available, however, for only one night, but that would be enough.

'Tomorrow morning we will go to Pattaya,' Tony concluded his announcement. 'The hotel in Pattaya is all arranged, the programme is brilliant. It is going to be fun.'

Tony took charge of the wardrobe-like suitcase of Nellie and Dron, which until then Rad had had to deal with, and Rad collected his case from Nellie. They wheeled them out of the terminal.

In the car park, Tony's almost-limousine stood out among lesser cars the way a basketball player does in a crowd of ordinary human beings.

'Oh, Tony,' Nellie said, sinking into the rear seat, leaning back and stretching out her legs. 'Your colleagues must envy you your wheels. How do you deal with their jealousy?'

'My colleagues consider me very fortunate to be living like this,' Tony said, flashing her his dazzling smile. 'They would like to live like this themselves, but they do not have a friend like Dron.'

'Do you like Dron, Tony?' Nellie asked.

'What a question!' Tony exclaimed, probably exactly as Nellie had intended. 'I like Dron very much indeed! He is a brilliant guy.' Tony had moved off and was driving between the rows of cars out of the car park. 'And he has a brilliant wife who is a worthy match for him!'

'Well, Rad doesn't think Dron's wife is anything special.'

'What?!' Tony expostulated, glancing at Rad. 'Really?'

Rad was straining to make out what they were saying, and was less than eager to join in. He still found Tony's singsong English difficult to understand, and to join in what was no more than chitchat would have been tantamount to rolling boulders uphill. In response to Tony's question he just spread his arms and shrugged.

'There, Tony, you see? He doesn't think I am even worth talking about.'

It seemed to Rad that Nellie's needling of him was giving away the very secret she was supposedly desperate to keep. So, at least, it felt to Rad, and Tony too seemed to be picking up on something.

'You see, Nellie,' he said, 'we Thai people believe a woman has a role to play in life, and that a woman should not try to stop a man from being a man. European women want to turn men into their servants. As a Thai I do not like that.' Tony, now leaving the car park, drove out to the road and happily put his foot down. 'European men do not like it either. That is why they are so happy to marry Thai women.'

'Ah, I expect Rad just doesn't like the fact that I'm European,' Nellie responded.

Tony, taking his hands off the wheel, and turning to face her periodically, protested.

'No, Nellie, you are not European. I would say you are a Thai woman. You only look European, but inside really you are Thai.'

'Well, in that case Rad doesn't like the fact that I'm Thai,' she persisted.

Tony's unfailing smile showed signs of reproach.

'Rad, what you have done to Nellie?' he asked. 'I think you have made her sad.'

Rad was left with no option but to respond.

'Nellie is a Russian woman, Tony, and a Russian woman is probably a mixture of European and Thai. It is a dangerous mixture.' He had wanted to say 'explosive' but did not know the word in English.

Nellie finally noticed she had gone too far.

'How's your sister, Tony?' she asked, changing the subject abruptly, as if that was what she was really interested in and everything else they had been chattering about was neither here nor there. 'How's it going with that Swiss man? Has she managed to get him to Thailand yet?'

'Oh, it is not so easy.' Tony was suddenly looking serious. 'Unfortunately he is not a very young gentleman, and he does not have a very healthy heart. He does not want to come here. He is afraid of the heat. But my sister cannot go there. How would that look if she went there? And if he did not marry her, she would be disgraced. I do not want her to be disgraced.'

'Well, perhaps if he's not very young and not very healthy, your sister would do better not to think about marrying him.' Nellie clearly felt strongly about this. If she had chosen this topic at random, just to switch the direction of the conversation, she was now suddenly very involved.

Without turning to look at her, Tony waved dismissively.

'A man's age, if he has money, is no obstacle. Neither is his health. A Thai woman can make a man young again. Healthy, perhaps not, but by her side he will forget about his illnesses.'

'Could you send her to visit one of your other sisters in Europe and he could come to see her there? Then there would be no disgrace.' Nellie had got the bit between her teeth.

'Yes, I thought about that,' Tony admitted. 'The fare is very expensive, though.'

'Well, get your other sisters to help her buy the ticket.'

'Yes, I expect that is what we will have to do,' Tony agreed.

Rad was straining to understand their conversation, but not trying to join in. He looked out the window at the suburban landscape flashing by. It no longer had the magic of novelty. His eye registered here a vehicle repair workshop, everything inside it on full view to the outside world, there a lone palm tree in the middle of an empty plot with its crown a dishevelled mane, but this new familiarity had a magic of its own too.

As they came into Bangkok, the traffic jams began and the car slowed to a snail's pace. It took an exceptionally long time to drive up their own street. They were approaching from the other end this time, and when they entered it there were two schools, built on three sides of a spacious playground. It was the end of the school day, and the street was flooded with schoolchildren of all ages, boys and girls in white shirts and blouses; and jammed with the cars and motorcycles of parents who had come to take them home, and with the carts of the flying squads of street food traders who were doing good business. By the pavements, like a passing locust swarm, dozens of tuk-tuks reduced the traffic to a single lane.

'How lovely,' Nellie said, looking out the window at this white ocean of life. 'I'd love to be back now in seventh or eighth grade. Wouldn't you?'

The question, asked in Russian, was clearly addressed only to Rad.

'I don't go in for that sort of thing,' he said.

'Wishing doesn't do any harm.'

'I don't want even to wish. You should only desire the possible. Desiring the unattainable means turning a blind eye to reality.'

Nellie snorted.

'How boring!'

'No, it's just common sense,' Rad said, to stop her from discussing the issue further.

As soon as they entered the courtyard of Admiral Suites, the boy skipped out from its depths. It was the same wizened, elderly Thai with the figure of a teenager, in a black naval tunic, whom Rad had seen before. No sooner had Tony opened the boot to take out Nellie's wardrobe on wheels than the boy too grabbed the handle and pulled the suitcase to himself with such determination that Tony had to leave him to it. The case was plainly too heavy for him and the veins in his neck bulged, but he stubbornly hauled it out, and only gave the game away when he dropped it rather than put it down on the ground.

Rad and Tony stood waiting outside by the car but, a minute later, as if by prior arrangement, they exchanged a glance and got back into it to wait. The air conditioning had been on all the way from the airport and there was an invigorating coolness inside. The heat in the street bore down on them like a slab of concrete, and the special Bangkok smell of rotting fruit and exhaust fumes, which Rad had forgotten while they were in Chiang Mai, potentiated the effect of the concrete slab.

Together in the confined space of the car, Rad and Tony immediately felt awkward. They had not been alone together before, and were not sure how to behave towards each other.

'I understand, you and Dron are old friends,' Tony said, being the first to come up with a topic of conversation.

'Yes, very,' Rad said. 'Only we haven't seen each other for a long time, nearly half my life.'

'I understand that at the moment you have problems.'

'Unfortunately,' Rad confirmed.

Tony's dazzling smile lit up his coffee-coloured face.

'Dron will help you. Dron is an amazing friend. All that is needed is for him to see that you are also his friend. That you will do anything for him. Just as he will for you. If he sees that, he will help.' Tony had noticed Rad was having difficulty following him, and spoke in short sentences. 'He helped me so much. Nobody else could but Dron could. Yes, I worship Dron.'

Nellie reappeared beside the car, all pure, fresh radiance, as if there had been no rushed packing in the morning, no airport, no flight or car journey. She had changed and was wearing a provocative red and yellow dress with a plunging neckline, an open-backed semi-evening dress. She was every inch *la belle Hélène*, for the love of whom it was no sin to reduce diabolical Troy to a pile of rubble. The beautiful Helen was turning over her mobile phone in her hands.

'Tony, we'll go directly to the Regency Park,' she announced as she got into the car. 'Dron phoned and asked for us to do it in that order. Then, after the restaurant,' she touched Rad's shoulder, 'you can move into your Jade Pavilion. Chris will help you sort out any problems. As someone who stays there regularly he managed to organise a bed for you there.'

'It's all fine by me whatever order we do things in,' Rad said.

'I think so too,' Nellie concluded.

She was transformed from the Nellie of the past two days in Chiang Mai, and even from the Nellie he had known before. This was the Nellie he had seen during Chris's last visit: all Dron's, his faithful helpmeet, as devoted to him as a dog and, like a dog, prepared if necessary to bite and savage on behalf of her master.

* * *

Tony stayed outside the hotel to find a longer-term parking place. Rad and Nellie went in and were met by Dron, who, phoned by Nellie, was waiting for them in the lobby near the entrance.

'Where on earth did you get those trousers?' Dron asked incredulously. He had been about to hold out his hand to Rad, but changed his mind, took a step backwards and gave him a look of dismay. 'Are they too big for you or what?'

'Don't you recognise them?' Rad asked with a smirk.

Dron ran his eye over Rad again, stared at the trousers and recognised them.

'Mine, are they? What are they doing on you?' There was a note of jealousy in his voice.

'I gave them to Rad,' Nellie intervened. 'He didn't have a spare pair, and his were ruined when we were doing the rafting.'

'Well, what was to stop you buying a new pair?' Dron demanded, finally shaking hands with Rad but, judging by the fact that he was looking at Nellie, that was who the criticism was addressed to. 'Walking about looking like a tramp! My friends shouldn't be seen looking like that!'

'There was no time, Dron,' Nellie said apologetically.

'Have all the night stores in Chiang Mai disappeared? There's a hundred shops where you could have bought a pair of trousers!'

Dron was giving her a dressing down as if she was a negligent subordinate, and Nellie patiently took it as if that was precisely what she was.

'Come on, Dron,' Rad interceded. Yesterday evening and this morning's breakfast by the river at their hotel had revived and reinvented his connection with Nellie, and he didn't like the way she was being treated. 'Why get so worked up over a pair of trousers?'

'You keep quiet,' Dron silenced him. 'I'm not talking to you, so keep your nose out!'

'Dron, I understand,' Nellie said in her earlier contrite tone.

'I certainly hope so,' Dron said, looked again at Rad, and said, 'It's a fucking disgrace!'

Tony appeared in the doorway and Dron waved to him.

'Okay, let's go.'

The restaurant was on the first floor. It was a long, narrow room with no ceiling. To the sides, the hotel rooms rose in four tiers of open galleries, and it was only there, at a height of fifty metres above floor level, that the restaurant was covered in by an arched glass roof through which the light of heaven poured. The tables were arranged in only two rows, with a wide aisle between them, well away from each other. The luxuriant green leaves of palm trees in huge tubs screened the tables from each other, as if each was in a living green studio. There was dark brown wood panelling everywhere, solid, heavy, of unquestionably good quality. It immediately reminded Rad of the interior of the hotel where Dron and Nellie had been staying, only there the spirit of the Victorian era only hovered: this seemed to be where it lived.

Chris and Mike were seated at the far end of the dining room, at the last table. In front of them, like a flat casket of nielloed silver, the familiar laptop stood open. Both were staring so intently at the screen that they noticed the approach of Rad, Dron and Nellie only when all three were already upon them.

Mike jumped up to greet them, as if a spring in the seat had ejected him. Chris also rose promptly, but did so in an imposing and unhurried manner which reminded Rad of an ocean liner performing a manoeuvre on a great expanse of ocean. Next to the heroically proportioned Mike, Chris, although he was a substantial man with an athletic physique, seemed almost a boy. Even so, it was he who put Rad in mind of an ocean liner, while Mike, for all his size, suggested a pathetic little harbour runabout. He stooped, drew his head down into his shoulders, which he squeezed together, doing his utmost to seem smaller. Every aspect of his deportment conveyed a panicky obsequiousness. He greeted Nellie very formally, by her first name and patronymic. He would have liked to demonstrate the same deference to Rad but did not know his patronymic so, after a moment's hesitation, shook hands with him as 'Rad Esteemed-Fatherovich', having in the heat of the moment also forgotten the full form of his first name.

Chris, when greeting Nellie, kissed her hand.

'Nellie, you are, as always, enchanting,' he said with his triumphant American smile, and it was clear that he was more than sincere.

Stretching out a hand in greeting, his gaze fell on Rad's trousers. This too was clearly spontaneous.

'There, Dron was right. We meet again,' he said, recalling his departure from Bangkok when, out of politeness, he had said, 'Who knows, we may meet again,' and Dron, with a knowing smile, had remarked, 'You will, don't worry.'

'Dron foresees the future,' Rad said, 'and not only that.' The look on Chris's face when he saw his trousers told Rad everything he needed to know. Today Dron wanted to appear in Chris's eyes the very embodiment of Victorian respectability. This was why he had chosen the Regency Park rather than any other location for this meeting. This was why Nellie had emerged from her Admiral Suites practically in evening dress. Rad's trousers, bunched round his waist and bulging unpredictably, threatened to severely dent that image. Rad decided the best way to deal with the problem was to take the bull by the horns. 'If anyone is ever in trouble, Dron helps.' He decided to plagiarise shamelessly what Tony had said. 'You see?' He grasped the trousers and gave them a wiggle. 'I had to be here to meet you and my trousers were unexpectedly ruined. I could hardly turn up in shorts, and Dron, who was far away, by telepathy gave me the idea of wearing his trousers instead. Of course, they are a bit too big for me, but they are considerably better than shorts!'

Taking the bull by the horns worked very satisfactorily. As Chris listened to Rad, his smile grew broader and broader, and when Rad referred to turning up in shorts, he laughed out loud.

'So these are your pants!' he said, pointing at Dron. 'I was a bit surprised. "Dron always helps!" Even by telepathy! That's a great recommendation.'

How Dron was reacting Rad did not know, but Nellie, when he caught her eye, was looking at him gratefully.

Tony had evidently already seen everyone today. He was not involved in the conversation and stood quietly to one side radiating his matchless smile. When Chris laughed, however, he laughed too, and did it completely naturally, without a trace of servility or subservience.

Dron went to the table, turned the laptop screen to himself to see what they were viewing, and looked questioningly across to Chris.

'What were you checking? Any new questions?'

'No, no, Dron,' Chris responded, accompanying the words with a reassuring gesture. 'Everything is fine. Mike and I were just clarifying one or two things.'

Dron shifted his gaze to Mike.

'Clarifying?'

'Sort of, boss.' Mike was all grovelling subservience.

'Clarifying, or sort of clarifying?'

'Clarifying, boss, clarifying,' he rushed to make up for his blunder.

'Well, we don't need to advertise its presence here,' he said, indicating the laptop. 'Put it back where it's supposed to be.'

There was something hilarious about the haste with which Mike rushed to obey this command. No matter how hard he tried to shrink himself, there was no disguising his heroic proportions, and these, combined with his sycophantic submissiveness, were simply comical.

Mike turned off the laptop, closed it, retrieved from under the table the familiar black bag, and returned the laptop to its claustrophobic darkness. It was the same bag Rad had seen on the plane and in Dron and Nellie's room, and from that he inferred that this was the same laptop.

Mike put it away and zipped up the bag. He was about to put it back under the table when Dron stopped him.

'Fine,' he said, switching to Russian and holding out his hand to Mike. 'We'll expect you back as agreed. Get there and back here at the double, the sooner the better. If you get away tonight that will be good.'

Mike had a miserable, hangdog look. He had not expected to be dismissed so soon, or so unceremoniously.

'There aren't any Aeroflot flights this evening,' he muttered. 'It'll be tomorrow, but tomorrow I'll do my best, boss. If there's an empty seat, I'll have it.'

'Go tonight,' Dron said. 'Take a flight via Hamburg, London, Paris, whatever. *Poka!*' He withdrew his hand from Mike's.

Chris knew '*poka*' meant 'so long' in Russian. Hearing it, he came to life and his hand automatically performed the ritual motions associated with the word.

'*Poka*, Mike!' he said, proffering his hand.

Tony interpreted the situation from the gestures.

'Bye, Michael,' he sang as he performed the ritual handshake. 'We had fun together, eh?'

Rad and Nellie were not included in the ritual. The pathetic harbour runabout, after shaking hands with Tony, set sail for the exit so abruptly that they had to content themselves with a '*Poka!*' and a 'Safe journey' addressed to his departing back.

'Let's be seated!' Dron said, inviting them to the table.

They were one chair short, but the waiter was standing a short distance away with one at the ready, which he now brought up. In fact, he had two at the ready, but one was no longer needed.

The dinner was very sophisticated. They talked about everything under the sun, from the price of oil to the forthcoming trial of Michael Jackson, leaping from one topic to another with a joke to fit every occasion. They particularly liked Chris's George W. Bush joke.

'George Bush meets with the Queen of England. He asks her, "Your Majesty, how come you have such an efficient government? Can you give some tips?" "Well," the Queen replies, "the most important thing is to ensure you surround yourself with intelligent people." Bush says, "Great, but how do I know who around me is really smart?" The Queen takes a sip of her English tea. "Very simply. You just have to give them a riddle to solve." She rings her bell and in runs Tony Blair. "Yes, my Queen?" "Please answer me this question, Tony," the Queen says. "Your mother and father have a child who is not your brother or your sister. Who is it?" "It is I," he replies immediately. "Well done," says the Queen. Bush goes back to the White House and calls in Vice-President Dick Cheney. "Dick," he says, "answer me this. Your mother and father have a child but it is not your brother or sister. Who is it?" Cheney thinks hard, but then says, "I'm going to have to check this out. Let me think and get back to you." He runs to his advisers and goes round asking them all, but none of them can work out the answer. In the end he finds Secretary of State Colin Powell. "Colin!" Cheney yells at him, "give me the answer to this. Your mother and father have a child. It is not your brother or your sister. Who is it?" "It's me," Colin Powell replies instantly. Cheney rushes back to Bush, bursts in and shouts, "I know the answer. I know who it is. It's Colin Powell!" "You idiot!" Bush replies. "It's Tony Blair!"'

About why Chris was back in Bangkok and why, on the contrary, Mike was being despatched to Moscow, nobody said a word. Just once Chris's expression suddenly hardened, as if he had remembered something he had neglected to do. He told Dron he was going to need someone who spoke Japanese, and not just from anywhere but from here in Bangkok. Dron, looking very smug and with evident satisfaction, nodded casually and said, 'Oh, yes, I have just the person.' 'Would that be Bobby from the train?' Nellie enquired in her best tone of sophisticated insouciance. Dron's expression clouded for a moment: Nellie had no business interfering. 'Yes,' he said curtly.

They talked a lot about tomorrow's arrangements for getting to Pattaya. By car it should take two or two and a half hours. They discussed what time it would be best to leave to avoid the traffic jams, and whether in fact there was any such time. They wondered how much to take and which suitcases, to make sure they would all fit into the boot of Tony's car. Chris suggested they should give themselves extra space by renting a second car and Tony was offended: 'Is my car so small it will be crowded? I will fit everything in and we will travel in style. How can I put my friends in another car?'

The sky above the restaurant's glass roof gradually darkened until there seemed to be a black chasm opening up above them. The lights were turned on. When they finally left the restaurant, it was quite dark outside, but they still had the whole evening ahead of them.

Chris, who for the last half hour had been glancing at his massive rose gold wristwatch, announced that he had yet to visit the US Embassy today. Nellie said she was tired and would like to spend the rest of the evening at their apartment. Dron frowned and seemed about to object, but when he opened his mouth it was to say that he agreed with his wife.

'Can you take me to the embassy, Tony?' Chris asked.

'How could you doubt it?' Tony said, deluging him with his smile.

He had parked some distance away from the restaurant and would need to walk there. Dron and Nellie decided not to wait and just walk back to Admiral Suites.

'Can I have a word?' Before leaving, Dron took Rad's arm and led him back into the restaurant. Once inside, he pulled out his wallet. 'Go and buy yourself a pair of trousers.' He extracted two thousand baht notes but, after a moment's thought, took out a third and handed them to Rad. 'You might even buy two pairs, just in case.'

His first impulse was not to take it. He still had a little left over from the money Dron had given him earlier, but then he would risk being penniless again. In Dron's place, he thought, if he had invited someone, he would have given them their expense allowance on arrival, rather than dishing it out in dribs and drabs like alms to a beggar.

He took the money.

Chris did not get out of the car when they reached the Jade Pavilion.

'I hope you'll forgive me, Rad,' he said briskly, holding on to Rad's hand. 'I'm running late. You'll be able to sort everything out yourself, I'm sure. I gather we'll be meeting up more often now.'

The associative leap was easy enough to follow, but what lay behind his words was less clear.

'That will be great, Chris,' Rad said with conventional meaninglessness.

In the Jade Pavilion, on a board at the entrance, under the heading 'Welcome to the Jade Pavilion Hotel', was his name, set in magnetic letters. The boy, this time a hefty fellow in the Guards red uniform, took his bag as soon as he came in the door and then, keeping a polite distance away, accompanied him from then on. In the room he demonstrated with rapid, mechanical movements how and where to turn on the light. He turned on the air conditioner and showed how the television worked. Rad gave him twenty baht, which instantly stopped him, as if his motor had been switched off. He bowed, and the door closed behind him.

That evening he tarried in the multi-storeyed realms of the Emporium shopping centre by the Phrom Phong skytrain station until closing time. Dron had given him money to buy two pairs of trousers, so two pairs he bought. They were taken to a tailor to be hemmed for him and he went into one of the cafés, ordered a large cappuccino and sat over it for a long time, first on a bar stool, then, when a table in the far corner became free, he sat there alone. As soon as a thought came into his head, he dismissed it, as if by pressing the delete key. It was something he had learned to do in the course of the last few months, as, indeed, he had also grown used to feeling lonely.

In addition to the trousers, Rad bought himself a pair of swimming trunks, partly because he seemed likely to need them in Pattaya. That was eminently sensible. Partly, however, because he felt like doing something Dron had not told him to. That was less sensible.

CHAPTER THIRTEEN

Beach Road was like a pan of boiling water, only seething with people. Elderly couples in panamas and exotically designed ladies' hats were out strolling and looking very respectable. Dads, their faces careworn from the burden of providing for the everyday needs of their families, were taking mums for a walk. Single men and women with the same sleep-walking look in their eyes, were tacking in all directions as if in search of prey. Amoeba-like tourist groups, large and small, moved in the same direction. Cheerful, student-looking young people with backpacks of all colours winged like arrows through the crowd, as if fired from a bow. English, Thai, German, Japanese, and who knows what other tongues were all around. The street was opaque with the babel of voices and the roar of car and motorbike engines. Motorbikes were particularly in evidence, from sports machines you had to ride folded forward like a flash of lightning, to easy rider models with the front wheel so far ahead of the rest of the frame you had to lean back and drive it as if reclining in an armchair. In bars open to the street, at tables set out on the pavements beneath great parasols, sat Thais, Europeans, Chinese, Japanese, African Americans – the whole world, mocca coffee-coloured, white, yellow, black as coal, sipping fruit juice through a straw out of tall glasses, sipping tea and coffee from cups, and the same spectrum of colours was arrayed on the ribbon-like beach whose sand extended twenty metres from beneath the parapet of the embankment to the sea. Mocca coffee, white, yellow, coal black – although, of course, white European skin predominated. Many people were wearing shorts, to which Thai morality evidently had to turn a blind eye because of the economic importance of the resort.

The old fishing village had long turned its back on the past and was reaping the dividends of good fortune that had come its way.

The sea, receding from the mark where it quietly licked the sand to a sharply pencilled in horizon, lay in the chalice of a gulf of such improbable, saturated blueness that it seemed printed on Kodak's best photographic paper. Some 700-800 metres from the shore, several dozen yachts were pasted onto the photograph and the way they serenely blocked the gulf from one side to the other made the sea seem a continuation of the boiling pan of Beach Road: it too was doubtless alive with people.

Chris, shading his eyes with his hand and looking out at the parade of yachts sparkling white like the snow of Himalayan peaks, remarked to Dron,

'Perhaps he'll arrange the meeting on one of these beauties? That would be great in every respect.'

Dron, like Chris, shaded his eyes in order not to be dazzled by the blazing midday sun.

'Splendid idea,' he said, lowering his hand. He delved into his pocket and pulled out his mobile. It would be great in every respect. I quite agree.'

He moved away to a palm tree with coconuts ripening in clusters that was growing on the brink of the promenade, dialled a number and, looking out towards the yachts, again shaded his eyes and stood motionless as he waited to be connected.

'Who are they talking about?' Rad asked Nellie in Russian. 'What meeting? And what do the yachts have to do with anything?'

Nellie gazed at him with the motherly eyes of an ex.

'Why trouble yourself with that?'

Electromagnetic waves cut invisibly through the atmosphere, reflected from a satellite tethered by Earth's gravity to the site of its lonely vigil in space, were picked up by a terrestrial antenna, sped from relay to relay and somewhere, perhaps on the other side of the globe, perhaps only a few steps away, the phone Dron was calling came to life and invited its possessor to converse.

Dron, with his hand to his eyes and the phone to his ear, unhurriedly moved along the edge of the promenade towards another palm tree. His lips moved. He conversed.

'Nellie, this is driving me crazy,' Rad said, still in Russian.

'Don't worry,' she responded. 'Dron has forgotten nothing. It just means it's not yet time for a final decision, but he will make it, never fear.'

Dron, with the phone to his ear, gesticulating energetically, reached the further palm tree, turned and came back. Just before reaching the palm near which he had dialled, he stopped, took the phone from his ear, closed it and, shoving it into his pocket, came back to join them.

'Our order has been accepted,' he informed Chris.

Chris raised his hands appreciatively.

'Excellent!'

They had left Bangkok shortly after breakfast. The journey had taken less time than Tony expected and, having settled into their hotel, they had been boiling in the Beach Road cooking pot for twenty minutes or so, taking in their new surroundings. They needed something to do to get rooted in the life here and begin supping its juices, but it was too early for lunch and somehow they did not fancy just strolling along the boulevard, lowering themselves to the level of the family men with their better halves and the retired couples. They could have plunged straight in and sampled the sea, but nobody was prepared: Rad because he had not put on his swimming trunks before leaving the hotel, and the others because they had not thought to bring bathing costumes.

'I wasn't expecting to come to Pattaya,' Chris explained, spreading his arms.

Dron looked at Nellie.

'Why didn't we pack them?'

Nellie shrugged silently, as if to say, 'Is that solely my responsibility?'

'I just forgot,' Tony admitted with a smile, as if confessing to an innocent, and even rather sweet, transgression.

Only Rad, it transpired, was a paragon of foresight.

'How come you've got swimming trunks?' Dron asked in amazement. 'Did you bring them from Moscow?'

'I was given them free yesterday at the Emporium when I bought the trousers,' Rad lied.

'Were you really?' Nellie asked, almost believing him.

Dron suddenly flew into a rage.

'Nell-ie!' He switched to Russian. 'Credulity is a virtue of idiots. Isn't it obvious? He shoplifted them.'

Nellie's expression became distant.

'Don't be disgusting!' she said, turning away from Dron.

Rad felt guilty.

'Nellie,' he said, 'I do sometimes think ahead. I bought them yesterday.'

Nellie rewarded him with a vengeful look.

'You disappoint me. I thought you might at least have stolen them.'

Now Dron laughed. He liked Nellie's point-scoring.

'Nellie,' he said in English, 'suggests that we head for the nearest shop and steal ourselves some swimsuits.'

'Oh no,' Chris exclaimed in mock indignation. 'If you're going to steal, steal millions: for a swimsuit I'm happy to pay.'

Tony knew a large store nearby where there were enough swimsuits for the whole of Pattaya. After yesterday's visit to the Emporium, Rad was feeling an aversion to shopping and was entirely happy not to join them.

'Why don't I wait for you here?' he said.

They melted into the crowd and he was alone. He stood with his hands in his pockets, looking after them, then turned away, took a step and stopped, wondering what to do while he waited.

The girl who appeared at his side seemed to materialise out of thin air. One minute there was no one, and the next there she was. Actually, she was far from being a girl, although she dressed and behaved like one. Bearing in mind that she was Thai, she was probably well over forty.

'You want fabulous sex?' she said, so quietly that he barely heard it. Her lips seemed not to have moved, as if she was a skilled ventriloquist.

Rad took in her worn, spent face. It was inscrutable, emotionless, not a human face but a rubber mask stretched over a human skull. She could see Rad had heard and understood her, and waited impassively for his response.

'No,' he said curtly and, without uttering another word, she disappeared just as unnoticeably as she had appeared, dissolving into thin air.

Before he could move, he was assailed by a new vendor. Evidently his look of indecision as he stood there was triggering these attacks. This prostitute was less raddled than the first, but still far from young, and gave the appearance also of having no regrets about how life had steamrollered her. Looking at her, however, all he wanted was to be shot of her as quickly as possible. Her mastery of ventriloquy was no less than that of her predecessor, but she had a different catchphrase:

'Great sex. Want it?'

'Go away!' This time, rebuffing the approach, he allowed himself to be marginally more loquacious.

He roused himself, walked over and went down the steps from the promenade. His sandals filled instantly with sand. Shaking his foot at every step to get rid of it, he weaved his way between the sunbeds, deckchairs and canvas parasols stuck in the sand to the water and stopped just short of the surf line. The sea filled almost his entire field of vision, the horizon seeming to have risen and the yachts seeming to have come closer. For a moment Rad was ecstatic: he was standing on the shore of the Pacific Ocean! Not, of course, the open ocean, only an inland sea, even a bay, but still, these were the waters of the Pacific!

The moment lasted only a moment: the ecstasy which had penetrated as far as the membranes of his cells flowed past them, sterile, leaving no trace. It vanished like the girls on the waterfront, as if it had never been, as if he had imagined it.

Rad retraced his steps across the strip of beach, emptied the sand out of his sandals at the steps, climbed up to the promenade, crossed the boulevard and went into the nearest bar, which was almost entirely open to the street. He decided to spend the rest of his wait there to avoid any further soliciting, and also because he was thirsty. On the steps of the bar a notice announced in large letters, 'Happy hour! Beer 49 baht'. From what he had seen elsewhere, that was cheap.

A gaggle of young girls sat chattering at the bar. They had no food or drink in front of them and had evidently just come here to hang out and enjoy each other's company. Their conversation was interspersed with exclamations, laughter, jokey questioning; they were intoxicated with life and very much resembled a flock of chirping birds. When Rad came in, they turned as one towards him and, while he was ordering, waiting for his beer and paying for it, they watched him quite openly, but now in silence. When, occasionally, one of their number chirruped, the others immediately shushed her.

Rad took his beer, moved further away and sat at a table in the front row by the entrance in order to keep an eye on the street. He suspected nothing when one of the flock came over and asked if she might sit beside him. She was so unlike those two in the street, radiating such light and youthful freshness. 'You are sad,' she said. 'Why are you alone? May I help you?' It was only her eyes that gave the game away. They were empty. She really had not the slightest interest in why he was 'sad'.

At first Rad could not believe his own suspicions.

'May I get you something?' he asked.

'Only not noodles,' she said instantly.

No further confirmation was needed.

He could, of course, have sent her packing. What would she have done? Got up and gone back to join the other girls; but he suddenly felt so sorry for her it was impossible just to dismiss her.

'Whatever you would like to eat, you shall,' he said.

'Then ask them to bring the menu,' she prompted him.

She ate a dish of fried chicken with brown rice as Rad drank his beer, watching the street, looking at her, and seeing clearly the path she was destined to follow, from this sweet little chirruping creature to those toothless rat-like creatures on the boulevard. His feelings for her were purely paternal, as if he were sending her out to sail life's ocean, knowing what awaited her and powerless to give her a better lot than the one she had chosen.

His little bird ignored the fork and spoon that had been brought and adroitly attacked the food with a pair of chopsticks, glancing occasionally at Rad and, when their eyes met, giving him a quick, frankly pleased smile. Then she set about the food again. She ate in a purposeful, businesslike way, with a clear sense of entitlement to a good, substantial meal. The food, under a tacit agreement she believed they had made, since he was treating her to it, was part of her earnings and, if she had not yet completed her part of the bargain, she had every honest intention of doing so.

Dron and Nellie, Chris and Tony appeared when his bird-like companion was enjoying her coffee with ice cream. As he ordered her coffee, Rad had decided to round off his beer with a cup of Arabica, and no doubt the two of them, as they sipped their coffee, would have given the impression to a casual observer of a sweet couple who had just enjoyed a good meal together. The four others came to the place where they had parted, halted and began looking around for him. Dron and Chris were wearing dashing new straw hats with the brims cocked jauntily. Tony had on a new linen cap with a Union Jack badge. Evidently when they got to the store they had not confined themselves to the swimwear section.

Rad allowed himself a little fun at their expense, watching them going round in circles in perplexity and obviously arguing about whether this was the right spot. He took out his mobile and dialled Dron's number. Shortly afterwards, Dron reached into his pocket as his phone rang.

'Hello, behatted people,' Rad said. 'Looking for me?'

'Are you sitting up in a palm tree like a monkey gawping down at us?' Dron really did look up into the crown of the nearest palm tree.

'Look across the street, in the bar opposite you,' Rad said helpfully.

Dron followed the clue, lowering his head, probing the area with his eyes, looking for the place Rad had mentioned, and a moment later their eyes met.

'Oh, suffering catfish,' Dron said. 'Have you rented a girl or what?'

'I haven't, but I think she would like me to.' Rad glanced at his little bird. She was delightedly spooning coloured scoops of ice cream into her mouth and washing them down each time with a sip of coffee. She was totally absorbed in this activity, indulging in it to the full, and completely uninterested in whatever he was saying on the telephone, the more so because it was in some incomprehensible language. 'Just give me a minute. I'll settle up and come over to you.'

Dron waved disparagingly.

'Wait for me to come to you. Don't pay before I get there, so you don't get in a mess again.'

Rad did not argue.

'Fine,' he agreed.

Nellie, Chris and Tony, when Dron ended his call, said a few words to them, and headed across the street to the bar, stared at Rad with considerable curiosity, and Tony, flashing a big smile, gave him a thumbs up, holding the gesture until he was sure Rad had seen it.

The flock by the bar stopped chirping when Dron appeared, fluttered excitedly, then immediately froze, waiting to see what he would do next. Dron made straight for Rad's table, pulled back a chair, sat down, took off his hat and put it on the edge of the table.

'Nellie, incidentally, also bought something for you to hide your baldspot with. She's looking after you. I wish she looked after me so well.'

Rad was surprised.

'Nellie? For me?' He looked across to where Nellie, Chris and Tony were standing on the other side of the road. Nellie was holding her white knitted bag but nothing else. 'You're having me on?'

'Having people on is not part of my repertoir.' Dron fiddled with his hat on the table, picked it up and threw it back down. 'If something needs doing, I get on and do it, and come down hard. Did you get it on with her in Chiang Mai? Eh? I go off to Bangkok and you, in spite of my warning ... eh?'

Rad was inwardly jubilant that he could look Dron in the eyes with a clear conscience.

'No, Dron,' Rad said. 'And there was no need of a warning. In any case, if you had had any doubts you would never have left us there.'

'As if that was all I had to think about right then,' Dron said, fixing him with a cold-blooded gaze he had not seen before. Rad recalled Nellie's remark that he was a good shot. Dron seemed suddenly to notice that, besides them, there was a girl sitting at the table. He scowled across at her. She had just finished her ice cream and coffee, moved away the empty sundae dish and coffee cup, wiped her lips with a napkin, lowered her eyes and, with professional meekness, was waiting for Rad to continue the ritual. For a few moments Dron inspected her as if making an assessment, and then Rad again found Dron's gaze fixed on him. Now, however, it was the old Dron with his amiable, jolly gaze, the gaze of a man pleased with life, himself, and the order of the world. 'Here you are then, sitting with a chick,' he said. 'You don't waste any time, do you. Good for you. Want to take her?'

'No. This is purely accidental,' Rad was about to say, but then did not. Before he could open his mouth he read the subtext. Dron, who had been suspecting that he and Nellie had got up to something in Chiang Mai, had cleared him of suspicion, and he had his little bird to thank for that. For Dron, her presence at the table was a good enough alibi for Rad. If they had been making sweet music in Chiang Mai, Rad would hardly be consorting with a prostitute in front of Nellie. He would at least have tried to sneak away without anyone knowing.

'This isn't really a sensible time,' Rad replied. 'Later!'

'Later may not be possible,' Dron said.

'Why not?' Rad did his best to register baffled frustration.

'Well, only, of course, if you don't prioritise your own plans over the general plan.'

'No, the communal interest before all else,' Rad declaimed in the tone of a student taking an exam in Marxism-Leninism.

'Then settle up and let's go,' Dron said, taking his hat and putting it on.

He was telling Rad to do what he had been going to do anyway. Dron had not discerned any danger to Rad lurking in this bar. He had come over because it gave him an opportunity to air suspicions that had arisen from Nellie's behaviour in the store. It had turned out very well.

On top of the bill for food, the waitress demanded 200 baht from Rad for the dating service. She pointed to the little bird, who was sitting with the same professional air of meekness at the table waiting to move on to the next part of her job.

'Pay,' Dron prompted Rad in Russian.

Rad had been about to do so without needing to be prompted. He had, however, yet to get rid of the girl. Choosing his words carefully, Rad began explaining the situation to her when Dron interrupted.

'Beat it!' he said, staring at the girl. 'You are no longer required.'

The girl looked first at Rad then at Dron in consternation, unable to understand what was happening. She certainly had nothing against eating a free meal, but that was by no means the reason she had sat down next to Rad. She had money to earn.

'What? I don't get it!' she said.

'Just fuck off, will you?' Dron said without raising his voice.

'Sorry,' Rad added, wanting to soften the blow.

She finally grasped that she was being dumped. A grimace of contemptuous disappointment ran over her pretty young face, but she said not a word, got up and marched back to her flock, who had fallen silent at the bar. As soon as she was reunited with them, they exploded in a cacophony of cawing and cackling.

Rad felt sorry for her, well-fed but without any money for her family.

'Why were you so harsh with her?' he asked.

'It's the only way,' Dron said. 'What is she? Rubbish, dirt beneath your feet. Who is she and who are you? They have their lives and we have ours. If you have a use for her, use her, but then wipe your feet on her.'

The waitress came with the change. Rad took it, left a tip, and he and Dron immediately got up. As he passed the bar, Rad resolutely looked away.

As soon as they were outside, Nellie fished out a small white plastic bag and waited for them, holding it ceremoniously in front of her.

'It may interest you to know,' she told Rad with mock solemnity as they approached, 'that while you were forgetting all about us as you sloped about the hostelries of Pattaya, we were not forgetting about you.'

'At least, Nellie wasn't,' Dron interjected.

There had evidently been a contretemps between them on the subject.

The bag contained a hat the colour of ivory and the shape of a colonial helmet, without the chinstrap. Made of good solid material, it had a white linen lining and two small pockets with zips to the sides of the crown. It was a splendid hat, and Nellie had clearly taken considerable trouble over choosing it.

'My dear Nellie, I am most touched.' But for what Dron had been saying a moment ago, he would have kissed her on the cheek; under the circumstances he could only express his gratitude in words. 'May I put it on?'

'Why else would I have bought it?' Nellie asked ironically. 'I thought that was what would suit you best: neither a hat nor a cap.'

Rad gave Nellie back the plastic bag and put the hat on. Chris and Tony smiled expectantly, and then clapped.

'Top class! Splendid!' Chris exclaimed, and Tony again gave a thumbs up.

'Well, yes. Very good,' Dron gave his approval.

'Rad, we decided to go back to the hotel, get changed, and head for the beach,' Chris said. 'How about you?'

'I am at one with the will of the people,' Rad replied.

'At one with the will of the people,' Chris repeated, obviously taken by the expression. 'At one with the will of the people …'

It was a five-minute walk to the hotel. They made their way across a road full of speeding cars and motorcycles, followed Beach Road back to their soi, and began climbing it in their assorted hats, caps and colonial helmets.

Dron's mobile rang just as they were going through the glass entrance door of the hotel.

'Dron, that mobile phone is going to bankrupt you today,' Chris joked.

'I'm hoping it's going to do the exact opposite,' Dron said, not wholly in jest, as he took it out of his pocket. 'What you lose on the phone bill you gain in your bank account.'

He moved away from them to be able to concentrate on the call, and they settled themselves in capacious armchairs not far from the reception desk. Nellie did not let Tony sit next to her and asked Rad to do so instead.

'What's all this', she said in Russian. 'Hooking up with whores, are we? I'm choosing a nice hat for him while he's off cosying up to a prostitute!'

'Nellie, come off it!' Nellie was the last person who could make him feel guilty about that. 'I ordered a beer, she came, sat down, and asked me to buy her lunch. That's all there was to it!'

'Could you not have said no?'

'I could, but I didn't.'

Nellie was silent. She carefully adjusted the polite, casual smile on her face for the benefit of Chris and Tony, as if she and Rad were engaged in small talk about the weather.

'And what was that Dron said to you about not getting in a mess again,' she asked after a moment, 'just before he went over to you in the bar?'

'I have no idea what he was referring to,' Rad replied.

'You've already been renting girls here, is that it?' she enquired with a beaming smile.

Rad had no choice but to adopt the mien of one engrossed in a conversation about the weather.

'Nellie, Dron says a lot of things. It's just something he said.'

'Dron never just says something.'

'You flatter him.'

'I flatter Dron?' Nellie snorted. 'I don't think so!' She looked pointedly at the mark on his head where Lana had lashed out at him. 'Is that how you earned yourself that dent?'

'What an imagination!' Rad said. 'You really ought to take up writing romances.' He he stressed 'writing'. 'Have you never tried?'

Nellie found that undeserving of an answer.

'What kind of person are you?' she demanded, appearing to the outside observer to be admiring the climate. 'You turn down decent women and go running after streetwalkers.'

Rad did not have to work out a reply, because Dron's phone call ended the conversation, he snapped his mobile shut, and came towards them.

'Right,' Dron said as he approached, running his eye over everyone but addressing himself to Chris, as if reporting. 'A yacht it is, and not just any yacht – a mega. Complete with an evening's entertainment.'

'Excellent!' Chris said, leaping up as if ejected from his seat. 'A yacht is perfect. Issues can be talked through much better on a yacht.'

'But are we still going for our swim in the sea?' Nellie asked, with that same urbane smile she had worn while talking to Rad.

'Of course we are, of course we are!' Chris and Tony loudly proclaimed their fidelity to Dron's plans.

Rad kept quiet, really not caring one way or the other.

* * *

The songthaew taxis in Pattaya were not red, as in Chiang Mai, but dark blue, and their bodies were less like crates with tank slits along the sides for looking out, and more like carriages: high, with open space above the backs of the benches to the roof, which rested on round, shiny, nickel-plated rods. At the back, these rods turned into curved, nickel-plated handrails enclosing the saloon, and below them a grooved step was welded to the chassis. Up to four people could safely stand on it, holding on to handrails, increasing the passenger capacity by almost a third.

Rad and Tony were, however, the only two passengers in theirs. Beach Road had moved away from the shore, was no longer one-way, and had probably changed its name. There were buildings now on both sides, each either a shop, a stall or a restaurant. Each was brightly lit with advertising, which covered façades, climbed up to roofs, hung in banners over the street, and invited everyone to celebrate the Chinese New Year, which had either already arrived or was due to do so very soon. It seemed as if the early winter darkness which covered the earth at the time ordained did not apply to Pattaya, so bright was it. Almost as light as day.

'Look, look!' Tony shouted, pointing.

The taxi was speeding past a multi-windowed verandah above which a large, brightly lit hoarding proclaimed 'Restaurant Rasputin'. A yellowy-golden, crowned, double headed eagle seemed to light up like tongues of flame the familiar image of the bearded peasant, his slicked down black hair parted in the middle. Inside, the restaurant could be seen to be all but deserted, with only two fat men in white shirts sitting at the the bar counter with their backs to the street. Were they Thai, Russian, Japanese, German, American? There was no telling.

'Who do you think owns the restaurant?' Rad asked. 'Russians?'

The Rasputin was left behind them and new restaurants, Thai, Japanese, Chinese, Italian emerged from the fiery ocean, flashed past, only again to disappear into the depths.

'I think it is Russians. That is most likely,' Tony said.

'And what kind of customers do they attract with a name like that?'

'Whoever goes in.' Tony laughed. 'It has to be called something.'

Rad remembered being surprised, the day he arrived at the airport, by Tony's English name, until Nellie explained why Thai people all had nicknames. The man with the red Toyota, in comparison with which Tony's Toyota paled into insignificance, had a Thai name. His limousine was so aggressively red, Rad imagined that at speed the air around it would probably burst into flames as if lit by a match. When he introduced himself, the owner of the red Toyota pronounced his name so rapidly that Rad caught only the overall sound which, however, indicated that it had unambiguously Siamese roots.

'What is the name of our wise leader?' he asked Tony.

'Wise leader?' Tony did not immediately understand who he was referring to, but quickly guessed. 'Ah, our wise leader: His name is Mr Chert-thong-chai.' Tony repeated very distinctly, syllable by syllable the name of the owner of the vast red Toyota.

'Chert-thong-chai,' Rad repeated, doing his best to memorise it. 'But why is that a Thai name?'

Tony again did not understand, and Rad had to relay to him his own recently acquired understanding of the principles of Thai nomenclature. Now Tony respectfully, almost devoutly, raised his eyes towards the sky, as if what Rad was asking about touched on celestial concerns.

'The nickname a baby is given at birth is not the name that is entered in official documents.'

'But why does he not use an English name?'

'Our English name is also not the nickname we were given at birth. My nickname as a baby was Gung, "little monkey". We chose another nickname when we were students and thought it was cool for it to be English. Mr Chertthongchai does not need that. He uses his official name,' Tony said respectfully. 'He is a banker, a very big man. A man in his position must be called by his official Thai name.'

The reverence with which Tony spoke of Mr Chertthongchai made it clear why he and Tony were now bumping along in a songthaew rather than travelling like a fireball in the red Toyota. 'Sorry, Rad,' Dron had said when they were clustered round the hotel porch waiting for Mr Chertthongchai's arrival, 'we can't be packed into his car like sardines.' Tony's Toyota was in a car park a couple of blocks away. Rad and Tony had been on their way there, but had barely left the hotel when an empty songthaew came bowling along and Tony hailed it. Taking a taxi now could pose a problem with getting back, especially if that was late at night, as Rad pointed out before they got in. Tony pondered this, but only for a moment. 'Everything is going to be just fine,' he said, flashing a smile. 'Why carry on walking when we can ride from here.'

Thinking about this, Rad said,

'Tony, you are so carefree. You are so irresponsible, I can only envy you.'

'Oh!' Tony exclaimed, bestowing another of his smiles on Rad, 'Being serious just poisons your life. I look at problems through the wrong end of the binoculars. They are still the same, but much smaller.'

Rad was enraptured. It seemed simple-minded but breathed the wisdom of the ages.

'Tony,' he said, 'I really like you!'

This was the second time they had found themselves, just the two of them, together. The first had been yesterday in Bangkok, when they had been waiting in the air-conditioned car for Nellie. But the first time is awkward; the first time is about getting comfortable with each other, and to all intents and purposes this was the first opportunity they had had to talk directly to each other, heart to heart. Until now there had always been someone else nearby, three of them, or four, or five. Seeing that Rad had difficulty understanding his speech, Tony slowed down, pronouncing each word clearly, without Rad having to ask, because he wanted to help.

'You have a big problem in Russia, Rad?' Tony asked in response to his declaration of affection.

'Very big.' Rad decided not to be secretive.

'Stay with us in Thailand,' Tony said.

He really did look at life through the wrong end of the binoculars.

'What can I do here?' Rad asked.

'The same as in Russia. My friend lives on Phuket, an island in south Thailand. There is a big resort, many hotels. He writes to me that they need a sports club manager. They will invite people. Work is with foreigners, no need to speak Thai, only English. I can help you write the form.'

He seemed to have reversed not binoculars but a powerful telescope.

'What are you saying, Tony?' Rad could not resist a bitter laugh. 'I have a visa for only three months. When it ends, what then?'

'We will fix that, find a way. The visa is a problem we can solve. Only you will need to get your teeth whitened, like mine.' Tony grinned.

But now his teeth did not shine. They had left the ocean of bright lights behind them and all around was darkness. Ahead was the real ocean, extending beyond the parapet on the shore in an unbroken expanse of unredeemed blackness. Only in one place, as if the darkness had been damaged by a wave, some 300 metres from the shore a patch of light glowed invitingly. It was a sign reading 'Dolphin Seafood Restaurant'.

'I think we're arriving,' Rad said.

'I think we are,' said Tony.

The songthaew stopped.

They were at the shore end of a giant concrete breakwater which, putting a stop to the shoreline, disappeared completely into the darkness of the bay. Mr Chertthongchai's red Toyota flamed in the headlights of their songthaew. It stood ten metres in front of them by the breakwater's edge, and the headlights shone straight through it: the car was empty and there was not a soul to be seen.

'Let's catch up with them,' Tony said cheerfully, paying the driver.

The songthaew, enlivening the deathly emptiness of the breakwater with a final revving of its engine, turned and departed, leaving them enveloped in silence, and now total darkness. The only faint indication of the way forward was a greyness of the concrete slabs beneath their feet.

Rad and Tony caught up with their VIP group almost at the pier, against whose piles several small steamers were chafing. Dron, when he spotted Rad and Tony, grumbled, 'What took you so long? I was beginning to think we'd have to stand here waiting for you.'

He was on edge. This meeting with Mr Chertthongchai was evidently very important for him and Chris, and he did not want to cause the slightest inconvenience.

A large group of English-speaking tourists disembarked from a steamer which had just arrived at one of the quays from the Dolphin. A tall, grey-bearded man in golf shorts and socks, hearing Dron speaking English, stopped and waved a warning finger at all of them: 'Don't bother going to the Dolphin tonight. There's nothing doing. They promised a Russian show, but its been handed over to some bunch of Trimalchios!'

Dron gave a fleeting smile, nodded and said,

'Okay, okay. We'll steer clear of the Dolphin. You've persuaded us,' and added after a pause, 'We'll go for the Shark instead.'

'You're going for sharks?' The bearded man looked round at the bay. 'You're shark hunting? Are there sharks here?'

'Thanks for the warning, friend,' Chris said, coming to Dron's rescue. He patted the bearded man on the shoulder and prompted him to move along. 'We're not hunting sharks. Don't worry, it was a joke.'

'Could you tell who they were from the accent?' Nellie asked Rad, with a nod in the direction of the departing man in shorts.

'Of course not,' Rad said.

'Australians. They have a distinctive accent. When you've travelled abroad some more you'll get used to different kinds of English and be able to tell the difference.'

Popping up from behind the last of the Australian tourists, a young Thai appeared. He was wearing a white naval tunic and a black and white sailor's cap. The reverence with which he addressed Mr Chertthongchai verged on servility.

'This way, please,' Mr C said with a sweeping gesture when he had heard the sailor out. His movements, like his voice, were unambiguously imperious.

They went down the gangway to the steamboat and walked straight over it between the benches, to find that a luxurious cutter was moored alongside. This had soft white seats, and it was to this vessel that the sailor in the tunic led them. The moment they approached, the whole boat was flooded with light, and from below, helping them on board, a boy of about seventeen offered a steadying hand.

Tony, waiting his turn to step down onto the cutter, leaned over and closely studied its prow.

'Guess what the yacht is called!' he invited Rad, when they were already on board and milling in the aisle, sorting out who would sit where.

'How could I know that?' he asked, puzzled.

'The Golden Shark,' Tony enlightened him, laughing.

'How do you know?'

'I read it on the side.' Tony was bursting with satisfaction at having deciphered the meaning behind what Dron had said to the Australian. 'This is the yacht's cutter.'

The sea dog in his white tunic took his place at the wheel, looked back, and, receiving a nod of assent from Mr C, started the engine. The light went out in the boat and left only the dashboard glowing. The boy dropped the mooring ropes, pushed away from the steamboat, the engine roared, and the cutter started turning sharply away from the quay. A breeze blew over their faces with the tang of the sea. The boat, gathering speed, turned its stern to the shore, which was picked out by a line of coloured lights, and, sending great waves of spray into the air, sped into the darkness of the ocean ahead of them.

'This is the life!' Tony said. 'The ocean, a yacht. You can not beat it.'

After ten minutes, the illuminated coastline astern had been transformed into a narrow strip of light between the darkness of the sky and the darkness of the sea. The huge Dolphin Seafood Restaurant sign had merged with it and was indistinguishable, as if there never had been a floating restaurant in the middle of the gulf. Straight ahead, however, a new light source was growing steadily brighter, casting an increasingly distinct pathway of light on the water, and revealing more clearly the silhouette of a ship.

The searchlight beating down on them from above when they leapt from the cutter onto a ladder and climbed up was so bright it seemed as if a new sun had risen above the patch of sea where the yacht was rising and falling on the waves. To greet the arrival of the cutter, eight people were lined up on deck. Mr C shook hands with only one of them, who, like the sailor who had met them at the quay, was wearing a white tunic and a black and white cap. This was evidently the captain, and the man who met them at the quay the first mate.

Their tour of the ship took half an hour. The captain showed them the corridor with the cabins and, at his command, the steward opened and showed them round one and then another. After the cabins they were shown the cinema, then the swimming pool and, adjoining it, the fitness room with its equipment. The varnished wall bars, gleaming dully, invited someone to ascend them to the ceiling, which Tony duly did, his legs firmly together, rapidly and elegantly pulling himself up with his arms.

Descending in the same manner, he concluded his performance to general applause. 'And?' he looked at Rad. 'How about it?'

The wall bars beckoned, but not enough for Rad to be over-eager to repeat Tony's feat. Since everybody had turned to look at him expectantly, however, he could see there was no escape.

Pulling himself up to the ceiling, Rad switched hands and turned to face his audience, and held a straight leg raise for ten seconds, garnering applause even before descending back to ground level.

'You are a professional!' Tony exclaimed, putting an arm round his shoulders.

'Did you ever doubt it?' Rad responded.

The yacht's ballroom could have seated a regiment. The captain only accompanied them but did not enter. A table covered with a heavy white cloth stood at one of the shorter walls, leaving the rest of the space free. It was set for six people, with four on one of the long sides, and one at each end. The other long side was unoccupied, as if this were a high table on a dais, or alternatively, those at the table were the audience and the rest of the ballroom was a stage.

The food that was served could also have fed a regiment. One starter followed another. Plates were replaced, new cutlery brought, and the main course, American steaks ten centimetres thick, appeared only after forty minutes or so when they had no more room in their stomachs for starters and felt completely stuffed.

As the steaks arrived, Mr C rose with a glass in his hand and, surveying his guests with a look simultaneously ceremonious and imperious, declared, 'And now, a surprise! A surprise for everybody, but special for some. As most of my guests are Russian, the surprise is Russian. A Russian show!' he announced, raising his glass to Dron in salutation. 'A Russian show!' he repeated, looking at Nellie. 'A Russian show!' he said, not forgetting Rad. 'Cheers, your good health, Mr Chris!' He raised his glass to Chris. 'Cheers, Mr Tony!' he greeted Tony.

Dron, Nellie, Rad, and Chris in response took a sip of wine. Even Tony raised his glass to his lips. Mr C, however, having performed the European ritual of toasting, did not even do that. His teeth were not clean and white, like Tony's, or Esther's in Chiang Mai, or Bobby's, their companion on the train, but a more natural, slightly yellow colour.

'You don't suppose this would be the Russian show that Australian at the dock was talking about?' Nellie said quizzically, leaning towards Rad. He and Tony were at the ends of the table, and Nellie was on the long side next to Rad.

'If we are a bunch of Trimalchios, then I imagine it is,' Rad replied.

In obedience to a gesture from Mr C, one of the stewards hastily left the ballroom, and a moment later the door swung open again. First two men in decorative white high-collared Russian shirts brought in a drum kit. They were followed by two more, one bearing a guitar and balalaika, the other with a saxophone on his chest and a fipple flute in his hands. These, too, were in long *kosovorotka* shirts. Not white, however: one was blue and the other red. The red shirt was girdled with a blue cord, while the blue shirt had a red cord. One of the two who had brought in the drum kit installed himself behind it, while the other threw back the lid and seated himself at a piano. The man in the blue shirt held the balalaika, while the man in red had the flute. They exchanged glances, took a couple of steps forward and announced, not quite in time and with a sumptuous Ryazan provincial accent, 'The best Russian stars in Thailand! A Russian show!'

After this, almost predictably, the band struck up 'Kalinka'. At its first notes, three divas, followed by two macho men, floated in through the door. Unlike the musicians, the dance group were dressed entirely in the spirit of globalization: sparkling coloured bras and panties, sparkling shoes on gigantically high heels. The divas were crowned with colourful plumes; the men were in tightly fitting black trousers, displaying gluteal muscles like two medieval cannonballs, and colourful frilly shirts revealing their torsos and tightly knotted at belly button height.

Their hypothesis that they might be an audience and the ballroom a stage proved correct.

The divas did not dance with the machos, but paraded energetically to the music. They would stop, adopt some striking pose, and stand motionless for a few seconds before parading some more and again freezing into a *tableau vivant* with smiles of artistic inspiration fixed on their faces. Both divas and machos moved with excruciating awkwardness, having evidently failed to turn up regularly for ballet class. One of the machos was quite bald, in the very worst traditions of amateur dramatics.

'What a nightmare!' Nellie whispered, again leaning towards Rad.

When the 'Kalinka' routine was at last over, in order not to upset Mr C, they were obliged to clap enthusiastically. 'Wonderful! Just wonderful!' Dron repeated over and over again to his august table companion. Mr C sat with a face devoid of emotion, behind which, however, an exultant self-satisfaction could be divined.

'Kalinka' was followed by a spate of internationalism, the musicians playing something approximating to jazz-blues-rock, and the divas and machos performing something approximating to dancing. This went on for a good quarter of an hour and gave the impression that Russian shows really had succumbed to globalization. But then, suddenly, the international gypsy stuff gave way to poignantly familiar Russian gypsy stuff: their eardrums were ineluctably assailed by the heart-rending chord progressions of 'Dark Eyes'. The divas, now costumed in fulsome black and red skirts which they mercilessly shook from side to side, moved from one macho to another before forming two couples. This left one diva without a partner. Dancing a few steps on her own, she suddenly homed in on their table and, extending an inviting hand, summoned Rad to her side.

Probably this was part of the game plan in their routine at the Dolphin. They would drag a member of the audience into their ensemble, inviting the other spectators to identify with him and be entertained by the spectacle of his awkwardness and embarrassment. Out of the corner of his eye, Rad saw the perplexity on Mr C's face as he stared at the diva. That was the clincher, obliging Rad to respond positively to her challenge. He knew for a certainty that the distance between him and Mr C was infinitely greater than that between him and the showgirl.

The two other couples stepped back, giving their colleague and Rad centre stage. Rad took a look at his partner. Her broad Slavic face with its slightly snub nose rising above a thick layer of garish makeup was covered in beads of sweat. The smile, which she was still managing to hold, tugged at the corners of her lips. His partner, responding to his gaze, stared back at him and they broke into a waltz, cleaving to each other with their eyes even more inseparably than with their arms.

'Oh, you dance so perfectly!' the diva exclaimed, commending and encouraging him, and all with the same wonderful Ryazan accent, after they had made a few turns. This was a brazen lie: Rad had no delusions about his qualifications as a dancer.

'You flatter me, comrade,' he said in Russian.

His partner, dumbfounded, leaned back on his arm, her eyes as wide as saucers.

'Well, if that doesn't take the biscuit,' she said. 'My fellow countryman! What about the others?'

'Mostly, yes,' Rad confirmed.

'Oligarchs?' she enquired archly.

'Not all,' Rad said, having in mind primarily himself.

'But you?' his partner asked.

'I absolutely am not.'

'Oh,' she said. 'Right. So who's the oligarch?'

'Why do you ask?' he said, although the answer was clear enough.

'I might be interested.'

'He is unlikely to be.'

'We'll see about that.'

'Well, what exactly are you interested in?'

'Oh,' the diva said defiantly, 'girls can be interested in all sorts of things.'

Rad suddenly remembered articles and television programmes about hapless Russian girls who were lured to other countries with promises of mountains of gold, only to have their passports taken from and be turned into slaves.

'Perhaps you have a problem with your passport and can't leave Thailand?' he asked.

'What problem? Why would I want to leave Thailand?' she responded, her brow furrowed in disbelief.

'Perhaps someone's taken it away from you?'

'Oh!' She understood what he was talking about. 'No, I've got it safely here. I don't want to leave. Think now I'd want to go back to Russia? We just don't have anyone whose life we could make complete. Can you think of anybody? I and the girls would be only too happy to oblige.'

His diva was trying to milk the situation for all it was worth, to strike the iron while she had her hands on it, without waiting for it to be hot.

'No, my sweet,' Rad said ironically. 'They all already have someone to make their life complete. You'll have to keep looking.'

The diva came to an abrupt standstill, took her arms off him and moved back, obliging him to remove his arm from her waist.

'That's it,' she said. 'Good things come in small doses.'

In respect of the goodness of what she had offered, she was exaggerating shamelessly. Rad had experienced nothing positive while dancing with her.

Returning to the table, he was greeted with a volley of artillery fire worthy of an undetected spy returning from behind enemy lines.

'No problems with your trousers?' Dron enquired with an expression of sympathetic concern on his face.

'Rad, you did well, but the wall bars are definitely where you are best!' said Tony.

'It looked to me like she was trying to brainwash you into becoming her permanent partner. Am I right?' Chris asked with his most triumphant American smile.

Nellie said nothing, but demonstratively raised her hands high to clap him.

Only Mr C sat, the very epitome of inscrutability, like a statue of the Buddha, unmoving and unspeaking. His inscrutability was, however, no less expressive than Chris's smile or Nellie's applause.

'What were the two of you talking about so sweetly?' Nellie asked a moment after he resumed his seat. Her maternal tone was that of an ex-lover, watching with forbearance her lover's latest fling, but unable to remain entirely indifferent.

Rad noticed that Dron, sitting on the other side of her, was studiously pretending to be engrossed by the show, while in fact listening jealously to their conversation. He was again relieved that Dron had no cause for jealousy.

'She asked me to find her an oligarch to entertain,' he told Nellie.

'She never!'

'And when I declined, she sent me packing.'

Nellie laughed.

'Well, from here you looked very sweet, as if you were talking about Art.'

The show ended. The divas, the machos, the musicians, with their embroidered Russian shirts and their instruments, disappeared through the door and were reabsorbed by the universe. The half-eaten steaks disappeared from the table, to be replaced by tea, coffee, desserts and fruit. Then Mr C, Dron and Chris stood up. 'Try to get by without us for a bit,' Dron invited them.

Led by Mr C, Dron and Chris unhurriedly left the ballroom, and a sense of awkwardness immediately settled at the table. The three empty seats in the middle suggested desolation, even devastation.

'Shall we go for a stroll?' Tony asked.

Nellie thought this over for a moment, then resolutely got up.

'If you please …' she called to the senior steward, who was standing a little way off in a state of readiness to provide any service the guests might require. 'Take us up to the deck.'

Up there on the deck, under the perfect dome of night thrown wide open to the dizzying abyss of the moon and stars, with the lights of Pattaya a frail line on the far horizon, listening when they fell silent to the lapping of the water against the sides of the yacht, sagging in the deck chairs with their legs stretched out in front of them, Rad and Nellie were once again able to talk without constraint.

'What did you mean back at the quay when you said "when you've travelled abroad some more"?' Rad asked. These words, said so casually after Dron's conversation with the Australian, had been giving him no peace. There was something behind them, more than the simple message they contained.

Nellie turned her head towards him. By the faint light of the moon and stars dissolved in the darkness all around, he saw a twinkle of satisfaction in her eyes. She had been waiting for him to ask. She had cast her bait at the quayside, waited to see if he would bite, and he had.

'What did I mean about you travelling abroad?' Nellie repeated. 'I meant you will be travelling. Dron has made his mind up about you, and decided in your favour.'

Angels trumpeted in the realms of glory; the sound was pure and sunlit; the very harmony of the spheres rang out.

'How do you know?' he asked, holding back his jubilation.

'Just,' Nellie said meaningfully.

'Why hasn't he said a word to me?'

'Wait,' Nellie replied with the same meaningfulness. 'All in good time. You can see, he has other things on his mind at the moment.'

'But I've got a non-flexible return ticket for the very near future.'

'It really doesn't matter if you miss your flight,' Nellie said, and she seemed to be speaking with the tongues of angels. 'If your ticket expires you'll be given another one.'

Rad's jubilation nevertheless thirsted for exact knowledge.

'Why would I be travelling abroad?'

'It's a feeling I have. That's how your life is going to be.'

'Oh, well, something like Mike's?'

'Who?' She didn't know who he was talking about.

Rad reminded her about the giant with the laptop.

'No, of course not. I hardly think so.' Nellie seemed to recoil from her recollection of Mike. 'In fact, I'm sure. He's just an errand boy.'

On the other side of Nellie, Tony was sitting in a deck chair. He could hear everything they said, but they did not need to worry: all he would understand in their conversation was names, and Rad took care not to mention his.

'Tell me, though, your neighbour there on the other side …' he said, resorting to circumlocution. 'Dron helped him with money, did he? I know he helped him greatly, I just don't know how.'

'He helped him with money, of course, what else?' Nellie said ironically. 'My neighbour on the other hand is not only a great ladies' man, he's also a terrible gambler. He lost someone else's money and couldn't return it, but couldn't afford not to return it. That was his predicament, and Dron, literally, saved his skin.'

'And since then he's been Dron's faithful squire?'

'And why not?' Nellie asked in a superior tone. 'Thai people like to show gratitude. And in any case, it's no great burden for him. Quite the contrary. My neighbour on the other side earns very nicely when we're in Thailand.'

She paused, and Rad too was silent, hesitating to put a question he very much wanted an answer to. He needed clarity.

'So, I would also be something along the lines of a shield-bearer?'

'Why, don't you want the hassle? You just want to take and give nothing in return? The cash nexus presupposes an exchange.'

She was right, of course. Only what price would he have to pay in return for what Dron could offer?

'Forgive me for going on a bit,' he said, 'but why, this afternoon on the promenade, were you still asking me to be patient, when now you're saying Dron has already decided?'

'Because this afternoon I still had nothing to tell you. Do you think I'm playing games?'

Actually, no. Rad had no such suspicion. She was his ally, he had no doubt.

'I'm sorry,' he said. 'I was just putting two and two together. Yesterday, after the restaurant, when we were saying goodbye to Chris, he said, "We'll be meeting often now." Does that have something to do with what you've just told me?'

'Maybe so, maybe not,' Nellie replied quickly. 'Does it matter? Evidently Dron told Chris something yesterday that he's only just told me.'

She was his ally, that was for sure, and now he was so sure of it, Rad felt he could ask something that had been preoccupying him since he arrived but hadn't known how to find out.

'Can you tell me what Dron's business is? With Chris, I mean, in America?'

Nellie was entirely unfazed by the question, and it seemed he could probably have simply asked her on his first day in Bangkok.

'He is selling out our Motherland,' she said coolly, with the now familiar tone of irony. 'Selling Russia. Have you heard that expression? He is selling Russia's riches. How else can you make money?'

A newly topical phrase suggested a not very clever pun.

'Wholesale or retail?'

'Wholesale, retail, any way he can.'

'Excuse me for interrupting your conversation,' Rad heard Tony's voice coming out of the darkness. 'Does anybody knows if we are staying here overnight?'

'Tony,' Nellie said, rolling her neck on the back of the deck chair to face in his direction, 'I imagine that depends on the outcome of the talks they are having right now.'

'I would like to stay,' Tony said dreamily. 'I like sleeping on yachts, although I have to admit I have never been on one quite like this. Do you not think it is magnificent, Rad?'

'Magnificent, Tony,' Rad replied, unseeing, into the darkness.

The angels were blowing away at their trumpets, their angelic voices singing in highest heaven. How else could you describe the Golden Shark than magnificent?

* * *

Once again, now on this yacht with the predatory name which was placidly cossetting its great, sleek body in the still waters of the Gulf of Thailand at the entrance to the Bay of Pattaya, in a private air-conditioned cabin like a room in a luxury hotel, on a bed made up with the finest linen sheets exhaling the fragrance of unknown flowers and herbs, Rad was being tormented by an absurd nightmare.

He dreamed he was dancing with that showgirl, and she had surrounded the two of them with a halo of exotic tail feathers. Only, he was not leading her: she was leading him, clasping him to her with the relentless grip of a predator. They were dancing to the tune of the thieves' anthem, 'Taganka', salaciously played by the violin of a restaurant-style orchestra. They were dancing a foxtrot, with all its extravagant movements, its intricate progressions, steps and turns.

In the dream, he was a brilliant dancer. Everything came easily, he was graceful, incredibly nimble, and the sense of controlling his body gave him inexpressible pleasure. But it was galling that the woman was leading and, after a time, he could stand it no longer.

The showgirl resisted his attempts to reverse the situation and they came into conflict. Their dancing slowed and they began to sink, every moment getting deeper, to the ankle, to mid-calf, knee-deep.

He realised they were dancing on water, perhaps the same water of the Bay of Pattaya where, in real life, the Golden Shark was tugging at its anchor. In his dream, however, there was no yacht, not a single ship around, only the Kodak-blue expanse of the ocean and, far in the distance, that strip of coastline on the horizon.

He found they were not just dancing, but dancing in order to reach the shore. They had to dance their way there and be safe, but to do that they needed to dance at a fast and furious pace, because otherwise the water would not support their weight. They could have changed positions without losing speed, but his partner with her vulgar plumed halo would not give up her leading role. She would rather sink beneath the waves than give that up, and drag him down with her. She fought with the monomaniacal obsessiveness of a suicide bomber: having power over Rad was more important to her than life.

He gave in. He did not have the same desire for power as she had.

He gave in, and their dancing instantly regained its earlier tempo. They began rising back out of the water: now it reached only to mid-calf, then to their ankles, and now its ripples were gently tickling the soles of their feet.

'Fucking asshole,' the showgirl, who up till then had not uttered a word, breathed in his ear. Her voice was low and hoarse, the boozy voice of the streetwalker on Beach Road. 'If someone's leading you, give in. Do you think it's as easy on water as on dry land?'

'*Taganka! Your nights so full of fire. Taganka! Why have you been my ruin?!*' the violin shrieked as their foxtrot speeded up faster and faster. But where was the shore, why was it no closer? Why, to the four corners of the earth, was there only that rippling water tickling their feet?

'*Taganka! I endlessly come back to you. My youth, my talent lost within your walls!*' The wailing of the violin, the words of that despairing anthem of Russia's thieves reverberates in Rad, and he understands that if he does not find a solution now, does not decisively wrest the leading role from the showgirl, she will lead him further and further from the shore, dragging him out to a place from which no rescue will be possible.

Rad was waking, drifting out of sleep, drifting back, the dream returning. He was being carried by the nightmare showgirl, the dancing, out to the depths of the ocean, sinking, dancing again further from the shore, unable to find a way to reverse their roles, waking, falling back into sleep, the dream beginning all over again.

CHAPTER FOURTEEN

They breakfasted, not in yesterday's ballroom but in a buffet with a bar counter and two tables pleasingly positioned end-on to a wall with great, wide windows. There was a choice of American breakfast, Continental breakfast and Russian breakfast – hearty enough to see you through to evening.

'To see you through to evening!' Chris repeated, nodding approvingly as Rad explained to him what a Russian breakfast was.

His night on the yacht, enjoying the peace and tranquillity of the ocean, made Chris want his vacation to continue in the same way. 'Pattaya is hopeless,' he complained to Dron. 'It's noisy, it's crowded. It's no better than Bangkok. It would be great just to get away to an island somewhere.' 'Would it matter if it was not Thailand's most luxurious resort?' Mr C queried in response to Dron's request as he prepared to phone. 'It is high season, everywhere is full.' 'No problem,' Dron assured him. 'Any island.'

Mr C gave brief instructions over the phone and popped it back in his pocket.

'Everything is in order,' he said in English. 'Consider that your bungalows await you.'

Ten minutes later his phone came back to life. Mr C put the receiver to his ear, listened and looked at Dron.

'Ko Samed Island,' he said. 'Not close, but not far. One hour and a half further along the coast.'

'Fine,' said Chris.

'Fine,' Dron said to Mr C.

By the time breakfast was over, the cutter was at the side of the yacht, waiting to receive them. On the deck eight people, with the captain at their head, were again lined up, but now, instead of the spotlight, it was sunlight that mercilessly made Mr C's guests screw up their eyes. The ocean lay all around, a cyclopean bowl of sapphire rimmed by an exquisite horizon. Only in one place did the rough outline of distant land marginally detract from its otherwise total perfection.

Yesterday's sea dog in his white tunic and sailor's cap was waiting in the boat for them and, as they stepped off the gangway, gave each of them a hand, helping them down.

'I so love yachts,' Tony told Rad as they were leaving the cutter at the quay. 'Was it not magnificent!'

'Magnificent,' Rad repeated, trying to match Tony's enthusiasm. 'Does the yacht belong to Mr C?'

Tony's gesture indicated he could not be sure.

'I thought it probably was not. He is a big banker, but I think such a yacht is still in the future for him. He agreed it with someone out of respect for Dron. He has great respect for Dron.'

The problem of getting back to their hotel, which had exercised Rad and Tony yesterday, did not arise. Not because now it was day and the blue songthaews of Pattaya were constantly driving up to the breakwater, but because next to Mr C's red tiger Toyota was another chauffeur-driven limousine he had ordered, and which he graciously indicated to them.

An hour later everybody except Mr C, who had returned to his own life, was again sitting in Tony's capacious near-limousine and he, humming along to a tune picked up by his radio and relayed at low volume through the speakers, was cheerfully driving them to a town called Rayong.

It took them, as Mr C had anticipated, one and a half hours. The quay at Rayong was deserted, but several small steamers were bobbing up and down at two long wooden piers jutting out into the sea.

The island lay behind the concrete dyke of a great breakwater, and appeared a hazy, bluish eminence rising out of a plateau of blue. It took their little steamer forty minutes of leisurely chugging to get there, but as the island changed from greyish-blue to unambiguous green, and when individual trees and buildings on the shore and the yellow band of the beach leading down to the water became discernible, an equally unambiguous feeling came over them that they had come a long way and that here was a place quite separate from the careworn, routine life of the mainland. Here they could look forward to a different, unfamiliar, island life.

All this time Chris had been sitting between Dron and Rad on a bench, leafing through advertising magazines he had picked up at the hotel in Pattaya. In several places he scored something with his nail and bent the corner of a page.

'Listen, Dron,' he said when they had stopped at the first of the island's quays before setting course for the next, which was their destination. He looked furtively over to where Nellie was sitting a little way off and lowered his voice. 'Here's an advertisement for girls to pass the time with, and I guess it could be really boring on the island after a while.'

'You want to order a girl?' Dron checked.

'Well, look how much temptation there is,' Chris said, waving the fan of magazines in his hand. 'If I do, how would Nellie react? Will she be offended?'

Dron looked over at Nellie. She noticed and raised an eyebrow. He waved his hand to indicate it was nothing and turned back to Chris.

'Well, even if she does,' he said 'you don't need to worry. Unlike me, you're a free man, you have every right. Perhaps Rad here will keep you company. Will you, Rad?'

Rad instantly recalled yesterday's conversation at the bar when the chirpy young woman for whose meal he had paid had, unwittingly, done him a great favour. And now he was on his own.

'Who's paying?' he asked in Russian.

'I will,' Dron replied, also in Russian.

'I'll think about it,' Rad said.

'You'd better be quick.' Dron's clownish red nose sniffed the air. 'We aren't going to be here forever … Sorry, Chris,' he said, straightening up and returning to English. 'Just one or two Russian details to clear up. There's one thing I would ask you if you take a girl. May I?'

'Oh, sure.' Chris was all ears.

'Condoms,' Dron said confidentially. 'Don't forget the condoms. Do nothing without a condom.'

'Oh, Dron!' Chris was red-faced. 'If I do make up my mind to … I probably won't … just for the pleasure of some company …'

'As you will, Chris, as you will,' Dron continued in the same concerned tone. 'But even if it's only for company, make sure you have some with you, just in case.'

Their ship tied up. The quay was as deserted as the one they had left in Rayong, only in the shade under an awning, six Thai men and women, suntanned to an African blackness, were dozing on a bench near a heap of red and grey striped fabric bags, waiting, apparently, for there to be enough passengers for the next boat to sail to the mainland.

On the small, gravel-strewn square in front of the quay office several shops huddled together, a bar and an Internet café, all with brightly coloured, eye-catching signboards. There was also a motorbike rental business, spilling its gleaming, nickel-plated wares out onto the square. A dozen people in shorts, T-shirts, hats, caps and sunhats gave life to the area, bustling from one shop to another. Two bearded biker types, with black leather vests over their bare torsos and wearing red bandannas, rolled iron steeds out of the shop and revved their engines, discordantly filling the drowsy square with an entirely urban roar which hurt the ears.

From the road which led out of the square, a songthaew, this time fire-engine red like those in Chiang Mai but without a roof (which left it looking like a flatbed truck), drove into the square, drawing in its wake a cloud of dust. It did a U-turn and stopped. The driver jumped out and gestured invitingly. 'This way, please,' Tony urged them, like a hospitable host.

Their taxi drove them a few dozen metres down the road and stopped. The road forked to right and left, and directly ahead was woodland, in front of which an arch proclaimed, 'Ko Samed National Park'. Two men in beige uniforms, with caps decorated with a cockade and looking authoritative, approached the taxi and said something.

Tony gave an embarrassed giggle.

'Two hundred baht per person,' he said, 'for enjoyment of the national heritage of the people of Thailand. From foreigners, that is. Otherwise they do not let us through.'

'And how about you, Tony?' Dron asked, feeling for his wallet.

'I have nothing to pay because this is my national heritage.'

The tax gatherers received their due, one tore a sheaf of receipts out of a book, handed them up, and the driver, who had observed the proceedings in silence from the cab running board, ducked back inside, slammed the door, the engine rattled into life and the taxi moved on.

He took the left branch of the road, which was a mud track, only metalled here and there with clinker, and the truck left a cloud of sandy yellow dust hanging in the air behind it. The forest through which the road was winding thinned and the truck, bouncing over potholes, came out to the ocean. The road turned and followed the coast, with the sea on the left and the forest to the right, climbing up a rocky slope. Through gaps between the trees on the slope, groups of light green, brown or beige wooden houses could be glimpsed, sometimes close to the road, elsewhere quite far from it. They had balconies, most of them with a clothes line draped with towels, swimsuits and trunks merrily flapping in the ocean breeze. The houses were fifteen, twenty, thirty metres apart, each a separate little domain with its own territory, like a miniature stronghold. At the entrance to each new group of houses signs in Thai and English proclaimed, 'Bo Thong Hill Resort', 'Had Sai Kaew Resort'.

Twenty minutes later, key in hand, having dragged his case up stone-paved paths, Rad reached his bungalow. Steep concrete steps led up to a terrace with a round wicker table and two low wooden chairs. A folding deckchair was leaned against the wall. In a corner, by the door, was a large soft besom.

Inside, the house was dark because the curtains were closed. Rad pressed a light switch but nothing happened. He went in and looked around. The room was small: really only the size of two passageways. To the right was a dais, about ankle height above the floor, and this provided the base of the bed. Two pillows were provided, two blankets, and two sets of towels were stacked neatly on the pillows. Everything presupposed double occupancy.

The room was hot and stuffy. Rad walked along the edge of the dais to the air conditioner on the far wall and tried to turn it on. No luck, but the blades of the ceiling fan started turning. They moved so slowly the effect was minimal. Rad turned the air conditioner up a bit more, the fan stopped but the air conditioner did not come on. He turned it back to the previous position and the fan rotated again, slowly.

Rad opened a door in the back wall and found the toilet and shower. In there, oddly, the light was on.

He went back out to the porch and brought his suitcase in. Something crunched unpleasantly underfoot, and he found it was sand he had brought into the room on his shoes. The need for the broom in the corner of the terrace became apparent.

He went out again, picked up the besom and found a blue plastic dustpan under it. He swept the room, gathered up the sand in the dustpan and, without going down from the terrace, emptied it out.

Now, before returning to the room, he took off his sandals, left them outside the door, and entered the room in his socks. Without unpacking his suitcase, he fell face down on the pale blue silk coverlet, rolled onto his back and began counting the revolutions of the rotating fan blades. The five of them had agreed to meet for lunch at the resort office in half an hour's time, five minutes of which had passed. That left twenty-five minutes to kill.

* * *

Over lunch, which they took at the nearest open-air restaurant, they discussed their bungalows. Nobody's air conditioning worked, nobody's room light would go on, but everybody's fan and light in the toilet and shower did work. This suggested a pattern.

'They're saving on electricity.' Nellie was the first to hypothesise that the resort's owners were tight-fisted. 'During the day you don't need a light in the room, and the fan will use far less electricity than the air conditioner.'

'Especially if it turns that slowly,' Tony said with a laugh.

'Yes, the speed it rotates at is something else,' Chris chimed in.

'And during the day you don't really need air conditioning,' Dron contributed, 'because you should be sunbathing at the beach.'

'And communing with nature,' Nellie added.

'Which is what we are doing now,' Chris remarked, with an all-embracing gesture.

Tony, who had been the first to scoff at the resort's service standards, was also the first to suggest a plausible explanation for all this economizing.

'It is an island!' he said. 'They have to make their own electricity. I expect it is the same at all the other resorts. I expect they also have to save water. And by the way, it is best to buy drinking water, and not use water from the tap even to clean your teeth.'

'That's really great,' Dron said. 'Thanks, Tony, for painting such an apocalyptic picture. It could make us wish we'd stayed in Pattaya.'

'Enough!' Nellie stopped him. 'No apocalypse. I found out there's even an Internet café nearby.'

Dron laughed.

'Well, if there's an Internet café, it's not the apocalypse. We're within reach of civilization.'

Rad was not joining in the conversation. He was waiting for an opportunity to talk to Dron again, incentivised by yesterday's information from Nellie. The angels were silent, but celestial trumpets reverberated in his mind, notwithstanding the nightmare which had plagued him all night.

He was not listening to the conversation, and as his mind wandered he was the first to spot the squirrel. It was exactly the same as any squirrel in Moscow's Izmailovo Park or Sokolniki: red, with an earnest, slightly protruding muzzle and a bushy tail twice the length of its frisky little body. *Sciurus vulgaris*, he seemed to remember. It was running along a heavy electric cable which ran through the air like a tightrope, accompanied by other less heavy wires, from pole to pole. Its business-like certainty that it had every right to be running along this cable on a subtropical island was evidently in its genes.

'Look!' Rad said, pointing.

There was no difficulty seeing it racing along with its flame-coloured tail fluffed out against the background. It was as plain to see as a fire in the azure sky, burning in defiance of all scientific laws.

'It's a squirrel! A squirrel!' they exclaimed simultaneously. Nellie asked in surprise, 'Do squirrels really breed here?'

'Yes, quite amazing!' Chris said. 'Just like we have in the States.'

'And like we have in Bangkok,' Tony responded proudly. 'We have a lot in Bangkok. They must have been introduced deliberately.'

The squirrel ran along the cable to the next post, leapt into the air and landed on a branch swaying a metre away from this music stave of electric cables. The branch lurched precariously, as if to shake off its unexpected freight, but the squirrel was quicker. Its flaming tail cleft the air once more, and now it was scampering along a firmer branch. Foliage hid it from view, revealed it, hid it again. Another two or three flashes of ginger-coloured flame among green lace, briefer, fainter, and the squirrel was gone.

It was like a greeting from Russia, a reminder. A native, Central Russian squirrel here, a dozen degrees north of the equator: at home, living and, presumably, breeding!

'It's a small world nowadays,' Rad reflected.

'Yup, not big,' Dron said, and there was something in his voice and the way he looked at Rad that suggested the words might have more significance than was immediately apparent. It was as if he was telling Rad, 'Your move next.'

Lunch concluded with a joint decision to go swimming right away. Nellie tried to protest that swimming immediately after a meal was dangerous, but her objections were swept aside, even by Chris.

'To the sea! To the sea!' Dron, Tony and Chris chanted.

Rad was the last on the beach. His suitcase had not been unpacked. He had to unlock it, rummage through his belongings, put shirts on hangers, and by the time he got to the shore the others were all in the water, including Nellie. She was closer to the shore than the others, saw Rad and waved to him.

'Over here, over here! Come on in!'

The water was as warm as in Sochi at the height of summer, the sand firm and sloping gently.

'Hiya!' Tony waved to Rad. He had just swum back from further out and now stood in the water up to his chest, panting. 'How about a race?!'

Rad shook his head vaguely. He was not feeling competitive today.

'Wait a bit, till I'm ready,' he shouted.

'I need to get my strength back too,' Tony agreed.

Chris, in a bright orange swimcap, was conscientiously swimming the crawl in shallow water parallel with the shore, as if he were in a swimming pool: thirty metres in one direction, turn, thirty metres in the other. His face, with his mouth open for air, emerged from the water with the regularity of a metronome.

The only person Rad did not immediately spot was Dron. He was wearing goggles and constantly diving, spending almost all the time underwater and surfacing only for air. One time when he stood up to empty water out of the goggles, he saw Rad.

'Ah, you've made it!' he shouted and waded over. As he advanced, he took off the goggles and waved them. 'Want to take a look at the underwater world?'

'Dron, you promised me the goggles!' Tony yelled.

Dron stopped.

'Yes,' he said, 'I did indeed. You're second, then!' he told Rad.

Rad nodded.

'No problem.'

The goggles would save Rad from having to race him.

Dron handed them over when Tony came rushing across in a cloud of spray. Dron dipped his head in the water, grunted, brushed the water from his face and looked at Rad.

'I gather you might like to talk to me,' he said. 'Let's move over there out of the way, by those stones.'

The 'stones' were a pile of huge boulders, burnished by the waves to a glassy smoothness, which jutted twenty metres into the sea like a broad, jagged tongue. No one was swimming there, and if Dron had finally decided it was time for that conversation, then the tongue of rocks was as good a place as any.

Three metres before the rocks, Dron stopped. He floated on his back, closed his eyes and lay there a moment. Then, noisily flapping his arms, he sent a fan of spray into the air before again setting his feet down on the sand.

'No, I don't care who says what about this place, I really like it here,' he exclaimed. 'Those of us who have Soviet poverty as our baseline have nothing to complain about. What do you think?'

'You endured poverty in Soviet times?' Rad enquired, not without sarcasm.

'I did and all,' Dron chortled. 'So what if my old man was a deputy minister? You've seen where I lived. It was a hovel, not a home! Any third-rate state employee in the US lives better than that!'

'And if you compare it with Thailand?'

'Ah, well, Thailand!' Dron chortled again. 'Why compare it with Thailand? Wrong comparator. All I'm trying to say is that everything in life comes at a price. If you want a quiet life on an island, you pay in terms of amenities. That's something we ex-Soviet drudges understand. Don't we, Rad?'

What Rad understood was that Dron was warming up to being ready for the long-awaited discussion of his future.

'Understanding, Dron, is not the same as accepting,' Rad volunteered his newly-minted maxim. It was not, truth to tell, all that profound, but usefully filled in a gap in the conversation. 'Everything depends on the circumstances of the time and place.'

'The circumstances of time and place in the present instance are,' Dron informed him, 'that enquiries have been made about you. Apologies, of course, but it had to be done. I trust you will both understand and accept that.'

The information was not particularly pleasant, suggesting that someone had been rooting through his dirty linen, inspecting and sniffing. At the same time, it was only to be expected.

'I see,' Rad said. 'And what have they come up with?'

Throwing up his arm and cupping his hand, Dron hit the sea surface and propelled a sheet of rock crystal into the air. Rad dodged, but not quickly enough and was drenched with salt water.

'Your references, Radislav, are excellent!' Dron said. 'So good that I'm reluctant to believe them. They are unreal! You are a repository of almost every virtue!'

Rad pretended he was about to drench Dron in retaliation, causing him to jerk needlessly to one side. Rad gave a satisfied grin.

'Well, you've been sold a pup,' he said. 'I fall some way short of Jesus Christ, but I will repay your loan: that I promise.'

'You'll earn it,' Dron said, wagging a finger at him. 'You'll show us what you're made of. Is that fair?'

'How am I going to earn it? I hope you're not planning to turn me into a hitman.'

'May the heavens forfend!' Dron exclaimed, wincing. 'What sort of hitman would you make? No. Respectable desk work for you. A specialised white-collar job. Not something you're qualified for yet. You'll need to study.'

He paused, expecting Rad to request clarification, so he did.

'What sort of white-collar job?'

'A licensed insolvency practitioner, I think,' Dron replied. 'Someone who winds up failing businesses, an administrator. I'm not terribly up on the terminology.'

Rad lost the will to pretend to be about to splash Dron.

'You want me to become an asset stripper?'

'An asset stripper?' Dron repeated, looking puzzled. Then he said in English, 'Oh, an "asset stripper".' He had worked out the meaning. 'All these things you keep imagining: hitman, asset stripper. You'll wear a tie, drive a car. You're a mathematician, you've got the brains. You'll be coached and then, forward! Let's go out a bit deeper.' Dron sidled over the sandy bottom, paddling with his hands, to where it was less shallow.

A light swell coming from the sea had kept them shifting from one foot to the other and moving towards the shore. While they had been talking, they had moved several metres closer, so that the water, which had been up to their collarbones, now reached only to waist level.

Rad lowered himself and swam back those few metres with a leisurely breaststroke.

'But why me? I imagine there must be other people already qualified for that?' he said when they were again face to face.

Dron was in no hurry to reply, but then his eyebrows appeared to be playing a musical scale at great speed, reflecting the working of his thoughts and feelings and a determination to articulate them.

'Because other people don't have references like these. We need someone we can rely on, who is not going to let us down, for whom repaying a debt is a matter of honour. I take it that for you repaying a debt is a matter of honour?'

'Unquestionably.'

'That's why we need you,' Dron responded instantly.

The angelic voices which had sung in Rad's heart yesterday were mute. No trumpets sounded. The heavens which had been thrown open to reveal the realms of glory up above were firmly sealed and now no higher than a basement vault.

'I've heard about this profession,' Rad said. 'It's a sordid job. You're asking me to do something squalid, turning people out on the street, emptying their pockets …'

'Stop, stop, stop!' Dron interrupted. 'Have you any idea how many people would give their eye teeth to be offered this sordid job? And someone says, here, take it, the solution to all your problems, and you complain it's sordid! Well, I can only tell you, all business is sordid. You want to stay immaculate? Fine! Only don't squeal that you're poor and wretched. If you want to live half-decently you have to get down and dirty. Babies are not born to virgins. Don't you agree?'

'That virgins don't have babies?'

'With all of it, with all of it!' Dron almost shouted. They had done well to move over here to the rocks where there was no one to hear them. 'How much will your immaculate purity be worth when you're living in penury? There's nothing immaculate about poverty! Your purity's not worth a bent kopeck, not one!'

The angels on high, pierced by arrows fired from the earth, flopped headlong to the ground together with their broken celestial trumpets, like chickens sacrificed to human appetites.

'But what if I turn out to be a completely useless liquidator,' Rad said. 'What then?'

'You won't. There's no getting away from it,' Dron retorted. 'You've run your own business: you'll be a dab hand. It's not that difficult, and not that different either.'

A launch passing swiftly along the coastline raised a wake that rolled towards the shore and they had both, almost simultaneously, to jump up from the bottom in order not to be inundated.

The wave hissed over the rocks and passed on to the beach, their feet returned to the sand, and Rad hastened to resume their conversation ahead of Dron.

'I would be much happier if you could find me something different. You're right, I'm really a mathematician. I only managed a fitness club because that's how things turned out. Of course, I will have got a bit rusty over the years, but I did work in a bank. I could be a financial analyst. Something a bit closer to brainwork.'

Dron nodded.

'Why not? Of course. But right now what's needed is what I've told you. This is not something I've dreamed up. It's what will qualify you for backup, a 100 per cent guarantee that your gangland pals will hold off. What matters is that you'll be one of the team, not just a loner. You for all, and all for you. It will simply be impossible for what happened to you to recur. You can't defend your corner without power. Do you know why all those northern peoples, those Eskimos and Chukchi and Nenets, live in the Arctic Circle, in nightmare conditions, in icy darkness for half the year?'

He paused, waiting for Rad to ask.

'Tell me.'

'Because they've been squeezed out,' Dron replied with considerable satisfaction. 'And they were squeezed out because they were incapable of defending their interests by force. By bloodshed, if need be. Theirs and other people's. Preferably other people's. We need to economise with our own. A human being only has …' he chuckled, 'how much? Six litres.'

'Five,' Rad corrected him.

'There, you see? Only five.'

They had again drifted towards the shore, and again moved back out until it was chest high, Rad overcoming the resistance of the water and moving along the bottom, and Dron whipping up fountains around him, taking a few boisterous butterfly strokes.

'You really are such a Czech!' Dron said, getting back to his feet and harrumphing, as if the butterfly stroke had helped him remember what really mattered. 'I hit the nail on the head when I called you that!'

'Nellie told you?' Rad asked, although it was obvious.

'She did, she did,' Dron confirmed. 'That's why you're all at sixes and sevens, because you're Czech. If you live among Russians, you need to live like a Russian!'

'I'm not a Czech,' Rad said. 'That's complete nonsense. I'm a Russian. I've never even been to the Czech Republic.'

'That's irrelevant,' Dron interrupted him. 'Genes are what matter. Hide them as you may, out they pop!'

Rad remembered Nellie laughing at Dron when he said he was a Russian.

'Well, you live in America. Do you think you're still a Russian there?'

Dron narrowed his eyes for a moment before shaking his head.

'In America, I'm an American. Rad, I'm a rich man, and the rich, you need to remember, have no nationality.'

'You mean money is the nationality of the rich?'

A pleased expression lit up Dron's face.

'You know, I think you're right. There is such a country.'

'How do you get on with Chris? Are you relaxed with each other?' Rad asked.

'He doesn't live in Russia. If he did, who knows?'

Rad recalled now how, in Bangkok, after dinner at the Regency Park when Chris was hurrying to a meeting at his embassy, he had mentioned that they would be meeting often now.

'Am I going to be working with him?'

'Why do you ask?' Dron seemed instantly alert.

Rad explained.

'Oh, I see.' Dron found his explanation satisfactory. 'Yes, most likely. You know each other, you're in contact. Why not?'

'I'll be travelling abroad for meetings with him?'

'Yes, since you're already in contact, it'll be more convenient to use you than anyone else.'

Rad had no more questions. The loose ends had been tied up. Dron had filled in the background to what Nellie and Chris had said. That sordid little job would be only the beginning, his probation, making him one of the blood brothers. Then they would be in it together, he would be ever more deeply implicated in their affairs, the knot tightening. 'Round your neck,' a sardonic inner voice added.

'I can see you need time to take all this in.' Dron took a swing, intending to give Rad a soaking, but Rad beat him to it and drenched him instead. 'Wha! Wha!' Dron yelled, spitting out salt water. 'Quick response! With a reaction time like that, why does it take you so long to make up your mind? What's the date on your return ticket?'

Rad quickly subtracted the current date from the departure date.

'Six days from now.'

'Well, that's splendid,' Dron said. 'Take it easy. Relax. You won't in any case be flying back before that. You've got five days to think it over. Plenty of time.'

Without waiting for an answer, Dron turned his back on him and fell noisily on the water, swimming back to their party like a boisterous butterfly. With water streaming off his powerful torso, he took to the air, his arms bursting out of the water, describing a semicircle, and disappearing so that only the top of his head remained visible. A moment later and the torso was again rising, the arms again describing a semicircle: a hefty butterfly in flight.

Rad watched not without envy. He had always fancied the butterfly, tried to master it, and failed. He pushed off from the bottom and swam his boring breaststroke out to sea, keeping in sight the white wedge of a sail on the horizon. When he had swum seventy metres, he turned, but before going back, decided to dive and see how deep it was here. In this he did not succeed, because his hands immediately hit sand. He was over a sandbank. He stood up and the water reached barely halfway up his chest.

* * *

That evening, in a lie-down restaurant on the beach, reclining on sunbeds with soft, cloth-covered foam cushions and a headboard in the form of a triangular cushion, Rad discussed with Nellie the conversation he had had with Dron, adjusting the wick of an oil lamp placed between them. They had eaten, there was nothing to do in the bungalows, they had already done enough walking along a beach whose sand the sea had rolled as hard as asphalt and didn't fancy doing any more in the dark. So they continued to lie there, ordering beers all round, Tony choosing a non-alcoholic brand. They listened to the surf and looked out at the shimmering lights of boats on the horizon. Chris got out his smartphone and was going to check his email, but found the battery was flat. The Internet café was a seven-minute walk away, across the road and up a hill. He conferred with Dron and they decided to go and check it there. No sooner had they left than Nellie, moving over to the lounger next to Rad's, asked, as if she had just been waiting for an opportunity, 'Well, how did your talk go? I gathered you were finally going to have it over there by the rocks.'

Rad would have preferred not to talk to her about it, but that was impossible. Their new ex-lover relationship presupposed complete candour on his part.

'Yes, everything was as you said it would be,' he told her.

'How did I say everything would be?'

'You know, in terms of the price.'

'What, is he telling you you have to kill somebody?'

Rad could not help laughing at how similar their reactions were: his when he asked Dron about becoming a hitman, and now hers.

'No, there was no talk of outright murder.' For some reason he felt a need at this point to adjust the burner, lowering the wick a little to reduce the lamp's brightness, as if too much light was making it difficult to be open with Nellie. 'But certainly, in a way it did involve murder.'

'Stop it.' She pulled him up short. 'What murder? What are you going on about?'

'Killing factories and plants. Bringing them to the point of bankruptcy, putting them up for sale, buying them on the cheap and selling them at their real value.'

'So?' Nellie looked blank. 'That's just business, isn't it? Buying cheap and selling dear.'

Rad adjusted the wick again, increasing the flame as if now he needed to see her more clearly.

'You don't understand,' he said. 'Imagine I'm a doctor and you're my patient. I undertake to treat you and say, if you're to recover, I first need to pump all the blood out of you. Does that seem normal?'

'Ugh!' Nellie reacted. 'What horrible things you say. You mean, you're being invited to be that kind of doctor?'

'Clever girl,' Rad said, again reducing the flame. 'No flies on you, eh.'

'But there are other people doing that sort of thing?' Nellie asked after a pause.

'There are.'

'And you wouldn't want to?'

Rad gave a deep sigh. It came out before he could stop himself.

'It's not a question of whether I want to or not,' he said. 'I don't have much choice. The question is, am I prepared to do it?'

Now it was Nellie's turn to pause. Rad heard the sound of the sea lapping on the shore, the voices of people on the other loungers, the clatter of spoons and forks on plates. Tony spotted a waiter, drank the remains of his alcohol-free beer in one gulp and ordered another. Catching Rad looking at him, he smiled. Rad smiled back. The more he saw of Tony, the more he liked him.

'But you have no way out?' Nellie finally said. 'No choice?' she corrected herself.

'Well, I do, of course,' Rad said. 'I do have a choice and a way out. There always is.'

'Really?' Nellie was surprised. 'What kind?'

'Existential,' Rad said, again fiddling with the lamp wick.

'S-suicide?' Nellie stuttered.

'Of course,' Rad said. 'I'm telling you, you're a clever girl.'

'For heaven's sake!' Nellie exclaimed angrily. 'You talk such rubbish. Idiot!'

'I'm not saying anything,' Rad asserted, twisting the knob on the burner in the other direction. 'As is written in the Gospels, "*Thou sayest it.*"'

'What are you dragging the Gospels into this for?'

'My dearest Nell!' he appealed to her. 'Have you really not understood until today what way out, what choice I have?'

'Well, then, you don't have any choice!' she retorted. 'You accept Dron's offer and that's all there is to it. Then we'll see. Time will tell. If the worst comes to the worst,' she hesitated, 'if the worst comes to the worst,' she said firmly, 'you've got me. And if need be, I will be someone to be reckoned with.'

It sounded almost like a declaration of love. Rad, as he had on the day he arrived, was feeling like a gigolo.

'He didn't seem to feel you were someone to reckon with when he abandoned you with that sting on safari,' he was tempted to remind her, but that would have been cruel.

'Thank you, Nellie,' he said. 'I am immensely grateful.' A veneer of irony helped camouflage the emotion he was feeling. 'I have another five days before take-off to think about it, so …' He stopped, at a loss as to how to continue.

'What do you mean, "so …",' Nellie demanded, obliging him to answer.

'So, let's down the beer!' He raised his glass.

The waiter had just brought Tony his beer. He saw Rad raise his glass and took it to to be addressed to him.

'Cheers!' he called to Rad, raising his glass. 'Good health!'

'Cheers!' Rad responded. 'And to you!'

'And here we are again,' Dron said, looming over them.

At his shoulder, on the boundary between the light from the oil lamp and the darkness, Chris seemed a shadowy presence.

'Everything okay? Did you get your email?' Tony asked with an affable smile.

'Everything's worked out just fine, thank you,' Chris nodded.

'We received mail, we sent mail, Chris did and I did. We did all we needed to and more besides,' Dron said, sitting down on a lounger next to Nellie. 'By the way,' he said, 'Jenny sent an email to my address asking why you've stopped mailing her.'

'I'll see to it,' Nellie said. 'Perhaps even today.'

'Oh, today …' Dron grumbled. 'Am I going to have to go back there with you? You should get yourself a smartphone like Chris.'

'We don't need to go there specially.' Nellie's voice was the embodiment of angelic compromise. 'We can look in on the way back. Let's walk home along the road instead of along the shore.'

'That's more like it,' Dron muttered, recovering his glass from a hole in the sand and cleaning off the grains clinging to it.

'Over there, by the way,' Chris, lying down in his lounger, nodded towards the island's interior, 'there are hordes of mosquitoes. Here by the sea the breeze evidently keeps them at bay. It's wonderful here.'

'Oh!' Nellie exclaimed, 'how are we going to sleep? We'll be eaten alive!'

'No, we will not be eaten alive,' Tony responded, his voice full of smugness. 'I have taken care of that. I bought a special spray. We will spray the rooms and – no more mosquitoes!'

'Tony, you are a genius.' Chris seemed genuinely touched by his considerateness.

'Tony the Genius!' Nellie exclaimed.

'You can call me that from now on,' Tony consented, radiant with pleasure.

CHAPTER FIFTEEN

The Thai man selling shawls followed him from the café on an abandoned jetty, where Rad had stopped for a fruit juice. He had not been particularly thirsty, but liked the place and felt like passing time there. The tables were under a shelter built directly on a wooden platform forming part of the jetty, and a narrow wooden landing stage with rotting boards ran out into the sea. What looked like a fishing boat was bobbing on the waves just off the end of the landing stage. Several deckchairs were arrayed next to the café tables and Rad sat in one with his juice, turning it so that looking one way he could see the sea and looking the other way he could see the beach.

The Thai man selling shawls appeared when he looked at the beach. Perhaps they were not shawls; they could have been cloaks, or bedspreads, or used in any number of other ways. They were vivid lengths of silk-like material, blue, red, orange, green, with vivid pictures of dragons, palm trees, mountains, and sea dotted with yachts. They were folded several times over, draped on his arm, and he constantly held one out in front of him by the corners, like a torero displaying his cloak. For the role of bull he evidently needed tourists, and there were not many around. He was small, thin, and his height and general appearance made him seem more like a boy, but his face betrayed the fact that he was far from young, and his eyes had a haunted, hunted expression which made you want to look away.

But that was precisely why Rad could not take his eyes off him. It did not take the man long to notice, and immediately head towards him.

'Good thing!' he exclaimed, the English language clearly occasioning him difficulty. He contorted his throat, his palate and his tongue, but Rad still pretty much had to guess what he was saying. 'Good thing!' the man repeated, swaying the cloth in front of him with both hands, truly a torero enticing the bull to charge. 'Good thing!'

Rad, in some dismay, now carefully avoiding eye contact, gestured discouragingly.

'No, no. Thank you, no.'

'Good thing!' the man clucked again, looking ingratiatingly into Rad's eyes. 'Good thing!'

These seemed to be the only two words of English he possessed.

'No,' Rad repeated, turning away to look out to sea. He caught the bent straw sticking out of the glass with his lips and took a suck of juice. The bull, reluctant to charge the torero's cloak, was trying to oblige him to find another victim.

He finished the juice, summoned the waiter, paid and, to his relief, noticed there was no longer any sign of the vendor. The moment he stepped down from the jetty, however, his torero stood before him, having apparently sprung out of the ground.

'Good thing,' he said, waving the unfurled fabric alluringly and looking searchingly at Rad. 'Very good thing, very good thing!'

His vocabulary was more extensive than Rad had supposed.

'No,' Rad was about to say once again, but the man's beseeching eyes turned him inside out and rejection was stillborn.

'How much?' he asked for no reason he could imagine.

'How much' was evidently also in his vocabulary, and he quickly gabbled something. This might have been in English and might have included the price, but Rad did not understand it.

'I don't understand,' Rad said and made to leave, but the man grabbed his arm and began holding out his hand, showing the index and middle fingers. 'Five hundreds?' Rad speculated.

The Thai shook his head in negation and waved his hand showing the fingers.

'Two hundreds?' Rad suggested. 'Two hundred baht?'

'Yes, yes,' the Thai nodded affirmatively.

'Too expensive,' Rad shrugged and strode firmly past the vendor of shawls to continue his way along the island's coast road.

In truth, it was more a path than a road, and the fact that as he continued it began to resemble a track on which he encountered fewer and fewer people was entirely to his liking. He wanted to wander off into a wilderness where the only reminder of civilization would be his own machine-stitched clothing.

The vendor of shawls materialised in just such a spot, when Rad had turned off the road onto a branching, barely visible track which led abruptly upwards. The Thai evidently knew not only the paths of humans but even the trails of ants and had overtaken Rad on one of those. There he stood with a length of cloth unfurled, looking for all the world as if this was his registered place of business.

'Good thing!' his tormentor said provocatively, standing in the way of the bull he had selected.

He was incredibly persistent, belying the scared, put-upon look in his eyes.

'Too much', Rad muttered mechanically as he walked past.

When he reached the top of the hill, however, where his track, forcing its way through undergrowth, suddenly brought him out to a wide road metalled with yellow gravel, he again encountered the vendor of shawls.

'Good thing!' the torero cried, fluttering his cape in front of Rad. With excruciating effort, he squeezed the words out in a way Rad could understand: 'one-hundred-twenty.'

He had almost halved the price!

Rad submissively lowered his neck for the moment of truth, his resistance completely ground down.

His matador was holding a cloth depicting a dragon, drawn in pale grey on a saturated, cherry-red background. Rad took it. The man folded up the cloth, extracted a white plastic bag from a canvas bag at his shoulder, and tenderly coaxed the cloth into it. Rad took out his wallet and started sorting through his banknotes. He had several hundreds and fifties, but no twenties. He felt that was a sign. He took out a hundred, a fifty and then, after a moment's pause, another fifty. Perhaps when he asked for two hundred baht the vendor was expecting to be bargained down, but Rad could not bring himself to give him less. Five dollars for a work of art? How could he decently pay less than that?

When the vendor saw 200 baht instead of of the agreed 120, he shook his head and held out his arms to forbid such folly:

'One hundred twenty! Twenty!'

Rad took that to mean he had no change.

'That's okay,' he said. 'Two hundreds. Take it.'

'One hundred twenty! One hundred twenty!' the vendor kept repeating, as though Rad had insulted him.

Rad took the plastic bag with the shawl and thrust the money into the vendor's fist.

'Two hundreds,' he said. 'I want to give you.'

The vendor grabbed the hem of his shirt.

'No two!' he exclaimed very clearly, with a bewildered, hurt look. 'One hundred twenty!'

Rad finally understood. The man really did not have change, but did not want to take the extra eighty baht. He had lowered his price and wanted to receive the amount he felt they had agreed was fair.

It seemed the only way to get rid of him was to be extremely rude.

'Fuck off!' Rad yanked his shirt free from the man's hand. Since the vendor knew more than two words in English, he might understand that too. 'Just fuck off, will you?'

His bad language worked. The matador, having brought the bull to its knees, backed off and in a moment was nowhere to be seen. The undergrowth swallowed him up, leaving Rad alone on the road holding a shiny white bag.

He opened the top and peered inside. What was he going to do with this piece of cloth? It was the last thing he needed. He did not even know what it was for.

The road enticed him to continue his hike, but shortly afterwards came to an end. Or rather, it suddenly did a U-turn. It became much narrower, went steeply downhill for five metres or so, and ended in a sloping circle.

Rad continued down and walked to the edge of the loop. It was the end of the oecumene. Ahead was an abyss with tangled shoots of brushwood clinging to every crevice in the rock. There was no path here for man, neither ahead nor to either side. He had come to the end of the island, and the circle where the road ended was a kind of viewing platform. A good hundred metres below lay an improbable, Kodak-captured sapphire sea, its ripples sparkling in the sun and trimmed with a lacy ribbon of surf. It was brought to life by the no less incredibly white sails of two yachts, evidently at anchor twenty or so metres out from the cliff.

They were modest, two-sailed yachts, clearly no relations of the one on which they had been regaled by Mr C and, judging by their nearness to the island, it was quite possible that Dron, Nellie and Tony were on them right now. After breakfast, the three of them had called a taxi and gone somewhere on this side of the island for scuba diving. Dron and Nellie, it turned out, were avid divers, and Tony had also mastered the art. Dron thought it would be a good idea for Rad to go with them and take lessons from an instructor, but he had declined. 'I need to go for a long walk,' he said. Nellie and Tony started trying to get him to change his mind but Dron told them to back off. 'Let the man go for a walk,' he said, baffling Tony by adding, 'he's got some thinking to do. Isn't that right, Rad?' He peered quizzically at Rad. 'You're very perspicacious,' Rad replied. Dron chuckled, then lowered his voice to suggest, 'Or perhaps you'd like to keep Chris company?' Nellie heard. 'That I strongly advise against,' she told Rad with a furrowing of her brow. Dron scowled at her. 'And what makes you think you can advise Rad on what he can or can't do?' he said loudly. 'He's a free man.' 'I strongly advise against it,' she repeated with particular emphasis, as if not having heard Dron, and as if there was more behind what she was saying than might be obvious. It was a matter of a call girl. Chris had in the end phoned yesterday, placed his order, and today was awaiting delivery. 'I'll think it over,' Rad said, ignoring Nellie and addressing Dron. 'Remember, though,' Dron warned him, 'Chris won't share.'

For a time Rad stood on the clifftop, trying to see what was happening on the yachts, and peering into the water around them to see if anyone was diving there. He saw no sign of activity and so, taking in the breathtaking view for one last time, headed back up the road.

Speeding towards him with a deafening roar on a 750 cc Honda was one of yesterday's bearded bikers who had just arrived on the island.

Rad tore Nellie's gift off his head and waved it from side to side. The biker braked sharply, throwing up a thick cloud of yellow dust.

'What's up, mate?' he asked.

'Here is end of the road,' Rad warned, pointing behind him. He would have said 'cliff' but couldn't remember the English.

The bearded biker, still wearing a leather vest over his bare torso, gave him a cheerful grin.

'Oh, that cliff! Yeah, I know all about that. I've rode all the tracks here. Thanks for that. By the way, I'm looking for my pal. Haven't seen him, have you? He's a biker same as me, same beard, same leather vest. Looks like I've lost him.'

Rad could not tell whether the bearded man was British, American or Australian, but understood him perfectly, not like Tony. And as soon as he said 'cliff', Rad remembered the word.

'No, I have not seen your friend here,' Rad said.

'Fair enough.' The bearded man circled Rad, preparing to leave. 'Some bird again, I expect. Girls on this island are anyone's if you give them an airing on a bike.'

'Especially a bike as big as that,' Rad said, indicating his beast.

'Too true,' the biker agreed man-to-man.

He was about to turn the throttle and leave when Rad stopped him.

'I saw you when you and your friend were renting your bikes at the office. Do they have also not such big animals, just some ordinary motorbikes there?'

'That's what they mostly are.' A note of contempt was detectable.

'Could you maybe take me there, please?' Rad asked.

He had just realised what it was he needed. He needed to open up the throttle of a motorbike and immerse himself in speed, like a scuba diver going down into the sea. Scuba diving was beyond him, but a motorbike would be the next best thing.

'Get on,' the bearded biker nodded to the pillion. 'I'll drop you there.'

He was not wearing a helmet, and there was no spare helmet for a passenger. Rad tucked his shirt into his trousers, shoved his hat and the white plastic bag down his shirt front, and instantly felt the plastic clammy against his belly. He straddled the pillion.

'Hold tight!' the biker warned. He waited for Rad to grab hold of him and the Honda roared away.

The air lashed his body. His ears sang.

Ten minutes later they were at the square.

The biker's pal was indeed in the company of a girl of about thirty, of striking, southern Italian appearance, and was in the middle of the square, leaning against his motorbike, which was supported by its side stand. He and the girl were taking turns drinking from a plastic bottle with a label identifying its contents as lemon tea.

'Where've you been, you fucker?' he shouted at the biker who had given Rad a lift. 'We said we'd meet 'ere if we got separated!'

'And here I am,' the biker said with a wink to Rad.

Ten minutes later, Rad was rolling a light, dragonfly-like Suzuki out to the square from the open maw of the rental office. No documents had been required other than his passport, from which they copied the details, and his bungalow key, which confirmed the legality of his stay on the island. There was no mention of a driving licence, which would surely have been needed on the mainland.

The bikers had not yet left and, when they saw the size of Rad's motorcycle, their lips curled contemptuously.

'Oh, look, it's a baby bike,' said the one who had given Rad a lift.

'Yeah, that one's for Noddy,' his friend jeered.

The lady of southern Italian appearance said nothing, but her expression indicated she would have needed a microscope to notice a bike that size.

Rad was stopped at the arch reading 'National Park'. After some disputation, he gathered he needed either to produce a receipt or pay the fee for foreigners again. He looked in his wallet, but Dron had taken all the receipts when they entered the park and still had them. Rad showed them the key to his bungalow, but this was not the motorcycle hire office and it was not enough. Show a receipt, the tax gatherers repeated, or pay again.

Rad received a slip of paper in return for his 200 baht and was readmitted to the national heritage of the people of Thailand.

He rode along slowly, looking from side to side, sometimes stopping to take in a view which opened up, but an hour and a half was enough for him to travel the length and breadth of the island, neglecting only the ant trails. As he passed the café at the old, rotting quay, Rad spotted Chris in the company of his lady visitor.

Chris had clearly not stinted himself: the girl was extremely pretty. More than that, she was a beauty who outshone the Nicole Kidmans and Sharon Stones of the cinema screen. She sat by his side, gracefully moving her chopsticks from plate to mouth, a vision of such primness and placid respectability you could have sworn she was an ideal wife who had lived in matrimonial felicity with her European husband for quite some time.

On the way back to the rental office Rad stopped off at his bungalow and tossed the plastic bag with his purchase on the bed. All this time it had been pressed clammily to his belly. He emerged from the bungalow with a sense of a duty fulfilled, as if before he had only partly completed a job and now it was done.

It was past four o'clock and would soon be dark. He needed to hurry if he was to fit in a swim and take a shower. He needed to return the bike and get back as soon as possible.

When he rode back to the quayside square, a new landing of tourists from the mainland was trickling into it: young people with backpacks, elderly European couples, two young Thai couples, and a beefy, forty-year old, ginger-haired European with his own motorbike, ranking somewhere between Rad's dragonfly and the bikers' monsters. Then there was a young raven-haired, grey-eyed European woman, or rather, a girl wearing white jeans, a white blouse, and an elegant, broad-brimmed straw hat. She was clearly on her own, and looking around in some perplexity. Something in her appearance reminded him of Nellie, and Rad braked before reaching the rental office to look across at her.

There was an empty songthaew in the middle of the square, its driver hovering with an expression of agreeable anticipation at the back of it, ready to pack in as many passengers as he possibly could. The savvy young people with backpacks, who had been the first to spill into the square, immediately made for the taxi and piled in, taking off their rucksacks as they did so. The driver invitingly gestured to everybody else. One elderly Caucasian couple managed to squeeze on to the benches, together with a young Thai couple and then the taxi was more than full to capacity. An Everest of baggage filled the aisle.

The girl who reminded Rad of Nellie was still in the square. Unlike the others, she had made no attempt to get to the taxi. She stood there, holding on to the handle of a small, dark green Rongchang case and looking around.

Her eyes came upon Rad, focused on him, and at that instant Rad saw who she was.

It was Jenny. Either that, or the girl with the Rongchang suitcase was her exact double.

Before he could utter a word, however, the girl's face flushed with the joy of recognition and, trundling the bag behind her, she ran to him. Jenny it unmistakably was.

'Are you here to meet me?' she exclaimed, rushing towards him.

Rad decided against saying no.

'Well, hi,' he said. 'What brings you here? I heard you were complaining Nellie was not replying to your emails.'

'Well, she finally did,' Jenny said. 'Actually, I was supposed to come as a surprise for you. She promised she would meet me. I called her mobile when I landed in Bangkok but didn't get an answer, as if she had forgotten it somewhere.'

'She hasn't forgotten, she just doesn't have it on her today.' While Jenny rattled on, Rad remembered what Nellie had said yesterday at the restaurant, and that today, when Dron had suggested he might like to go off with Chris, she had twice 'strongly advised' against it. The mechanism behind Jenny's appearance in the quayside square became clear to him. 'She and Dron are away scuba diving. I don't imagine she took her mobile underwater. But I can see she explained in some detail where we are and how to get here.'

'In great detail,' Jenny confirmed.

Her face still lit up with joy made her look wonderfully sweet and touching. 'A charmer', Rad remembered categorizing her when they first met.

'So what happened? She sent you an email and you drove to the airport?' Rad asked.

'Something like that,' Jenny said. 'The plane was full, but as always someone failed to turn up and I got their seat. At this end everything was very straightforward. I got a two-week tourist visa at the airport and here I am. Oh!' she saw the make of the motorcycle which Rad was astride and her face broke into a smile of endearment. 'A Suzuki!'

For a moment Rad could not imagine what she found so endearing about the make of a motorbike, but a moment later remembered her little yellow car.

The songthaew, meanwhile, screeched, lurched forward, and obliged its passengers to grab their luggage which seemed eager to fall to the ground. It then rolled slowly out of the square.

'I'm not going to be able to fit you and that suitcase on this dragonfly,' Rad remarked.

'Why are you so ill prepared?' Jenny asked, still smiling.

'I'm completely unprepared,' Rad almost replied, but thought better of it.

'Don't worry,' he said. 'We won't be spending the night here. Hang on a minute while I return the bike.'

'I will,' Jenny replied like a well-behaved schoolgirl.

Rad came out of the office just as his bikers were riding back into the square like two brontosaurs, both now with an Italienne on the pillion. The girl of the biker Rad had stopped at the cliff was younger, but had a Roman nose.

'Our taxi has arrived,' Rad said, nodding in their direction.

'They're friends of yours?' Jenny enquired.

'All bikers are my brothers,' Rad informed her, undeservedly identifying himself with this special breed.

The bikers stopped and Rad's mate gave him a friendly wave.

'What, not saddled and you've already got a girl?' he asked approvingly when Rad came over to him.

'Yeah,' Rad said in his best biker voice. 'I need to get her back to my place. Can you help?'

Rad had inadvertently been right when asserting that all bikers are brothers. Two minutes later, Jenny's case was firmly attached to the pannier rack by durable rubber straps, *les Italiennes* had been deposed to await the return of their paramours, and Rad and Jenny had occupied their pillions.

At the National Park arch the motorbikes were stopped. The tax collectors went about their business with patriotic zeal. They were not interested in seeing the bikers' receipts, having checked them many times already. Who they were interested in was Rad and Jenny.

This time Rad had his receipt. He took it out of his wallet and showed it, then went to get the money to pay for Jenny: he had just 150 baht. His dragon shawl, his duplicated payment for entry to the island, his motorcycle rental had all been unplanned expenditure and he was skint.

Feeling as if his trousers had just fallen down in full public view, Rad had to come back to Jenny and ask her for the fifty baht he was short. She readily got her purse out of her shoulder bag and held it out open to Rad.

'How much do you need!'

The purse was stuffed full of thousand baht notes. Rad involuntarily asked, 'Why did you change so much?'

'Oh, well, when I was at the airport just after landing I took out quite a lot on my card, just in case.' She seemed puzzled that he should ask. 'Better too much than too little. I can always change it back into dollars.' She shook the purse: 'Help yourself.'

Rad checked through the notes. There were no fifties, only a twenty and the rest were all thousands. He took one thousand, gave it to the tax collectors, got the receipt and change and, adding to it his 150 baht, returned to Jenny. From her seat behind the biker she waved him off.

'Oh, I've already put everything way. I can't be bothered. Just keep it.'

Rad felt as if the trousers he had been struggling to hold up were round his ankles again.

'Here,' he said, waving the wad of notes at her and, after a pause, she moved her bag to her lap, unzipped it and dug out her purse.

'There's really no need for that, you know,' she said, taking the money, as if he had been rude to her but she was stoically forgiving him.

Rad had no answer. He sat behind his chauffeur and, leaning forward, shouted in his ear, 'Let's go!'

Within a few minutes they had arrived. The bikers, behind Jenny's back, simultaneously pointed to her and gave him the thumbs up before roaring off back to their Italian molls. Rad and Jenny were left standing, the two of them, on the road next to her suitcase.

'Now what?' Jenny asked, as if Rad had invited her here, here she was, and he seemed to be making a hash of her itinerary.

'Now, I think, we should go first to my bungalow,' Rad said. 'Is that all right by you?'

'It is,' Jenny consented, evidently satisfied with this part of the programme.

He took her case and, negotiating the twists and turns in the path, headed uphill. Jenny, he could hear, was right behind.

'You can roll it, you know,' she said when, at one of the turns, he transferred the suitcase to his other hand.

'It's not too heavy for me,' he said.

'You're very strong,' she said.

He glanced back. What was the significance of that?

'Your case is light,' he said.

'Really? I found it very heavy.'

'No,' Rad repeated, 'it's light.'

To the accompaniment of this meaningful conversation, they reached the bungalow, went up onto the verandah, and he opened the door, warning her she needed to take her shoes off before going inside.

'How democratic,' she said.

She repeated the remark when she had come into the room and looked around.

'I hope "democratic" is not disparaging,' Rad said.

'Oh, not at all. Purely descriptive,' Jenny replied quickly.

Rad went to turn on the air conditioner. The blades of the fan were immobile, and instead the air conditioner hummed and began directing a stream of cool air into the room, testifying to the fact that the island's administrators considered it to be evening and that it would soon be dark.

'I think …' he began, turning to Jenny, but stopped. He had been going to tell her that now it was getting dark Nellie and Dron would soon be joining them, and he was planning to go for a swim in the sea and she was welcome to join him, but Jenny was standing in the middle of the room with a look on her face which told Rad he should just keep quiet.

'Rad,' she said. 'why did you leave me?'

Without answering, he walked past her and banged the front door shut.

'Have you come all this way to ask me that?' he said from the door.

'To some extent, yes.'

He had never been good at knowing how to behave with women.

'My dear Jenny,' he said, 'my sweet, do you have any idea why I am here?'

'Yes,' she said, taking him aback.

How could she know? But then he saw how and why: Nellie. Well, that was probably to his advantage.

'If you know, then, what is there to explain? The last thing I needed were new romantic affairs!'

'Affairs?' she asked, hurt.

'I mean, affair,' Rad corrected himself.

'Affair?' she repeated, now sounding sarcastic rather than offended. 'But why didn't you tell me anything? Why did I have to hear everything from Nellie?'

'Well why, Jenny, should you know anything about it at all?' he said. 'You really didn't need to. It's a pity you do.'

'It's a great pity you thought that.' Her face, turned towards him, was full of reproach and indignation. 'You shouldn't have decided that. You had no business. No right!'

Suddenly she had her arms round his neck, her eyes looking into his. He could feel her breath. One of her bare feet was on his, but she seemed not to have noticed and he did not withdraw his foot.

'Rad, why did you not just tell me? Why?'

The best solution was to stop her talking, which Rad did. He took her lips into his, remembering the taste of them, their firmness, and a moment later one of his hands was firmly holding her narrow spine while the other was on the back of her head and he was squeezing her, both her feet now standing on his, to weld her to him.

He forgot about swimming in the sea.

'I need to take a shower,' he said hoarsely, tearing himself away.

'So do I.' Still standing on his feet, she arched back to look at him, her arms still firmly twined about his neck. 'Will you lend me a towel?'

'Everything here is for couples,' he said. 'I haven't touched the second set.'

'Were you keeping it for me?'

'Oh, of course.'

Listening to the sound of the shower behind the door, Rad realised why he had been fated to buy the dragon shawl from its put-upon but persistent vendor. Accordingly, when Jenny emerged from the shower holding a towel diagonally across her breasts, he was standing with the cherry-red shawl in his hand, like a bullfighter.

'Toro!' He flicked the cloth in front of her. 'Will you accept my humble gift?'

'How lovely!' She freed one hand and took the shawl from him. 'Turn round for a second!' she said. Half a minute later she announced, 'You can look now.'

Rad turned. Now the towel was draped only over her breasts and the shawl with the dragon was wound round her hips as a skirt. It made an amazing skirt: perhaps that was what it was always intended to be.

'Fantastic!' he said. 'Do you like it?'

'Very much,' she said. 'All I don't like is the thought that you bought it for someone else and now you've given it to me.'

'Not so!' Rad said, only with an effort restraining himself from unwinding her new skirt there and then. 'I just bought it and now, I find, I bought it for you.'

'Go on then,' she said, flashing her eyes at him. 'I'm waiting.'

He soaped himself at meteoric speed. He could not remember ever having washed so fast. It took just two minutes. Three at most.

When he emerged from the shower, the room smelt of perfume. To do it justice, it was delicately scented. The perfume was subtle, it was quiet music emanating from some source unknown, almost inaudible and yet, if it were to be taken away, the silence left behind would be deafening. It was still light outside, but already dusk in the room. When he went into the shower he had turned on the light, but now it was off. Jenny was lying on her back, covered with the sheet and with her arms folded over it.

Rad leaned over and, with one deft movement, whisked the sheet off her and into the air. She threw her hands up but made no attempt to catch hold of it. Her legs were crossed, and her pubic hair betrayed the fact that raven-haired Jenny's natural colour was mousey brown. It was shaved to a narrow strip leading down to her vulva. This was new to him. During their last encounter, at Serge's dacha, he had not had occasion to look. For an instant Nellie flashed before Rad's eyes, casting off her robe in his room in Chiang Mai. Nellie had proved unbarbered, displaying the rampant tropical jungle with which nature had endowed her. His unruly member, however, had no time for further speculation and comparisons. It had just one desire, which it was demonstrating with brazen impudence.

'I'm fresh out of chemists' goods,' Rad said, kneeling in front of Jenny and bending down to her breasts. 'How about you?'

'I have something,' she said. Her grey eyes looking up at him with tense anticipation. 'Under the pillow.' A moment later she said hesitantly, 'But do we need it? Have you been with anybody since ... us?'

'No,' Rad said without a moment's hesitation.

'Then, let's do without it,' Jenny said.

What was that supposed to mean: that she had not slept with anyone since him? That she had, but with protection? Rad stopped worrying. In these circumstances he relied on the woman. She was the one more at risk, and it was for her to choose. He had also stopped thinking. Jenny had one arm round his neck and his member in the other hand, which dutifully submitted to her direction. Jenny's legs were no longer crossed, she let him come in between them, and raised them higher and higher until he plunged into the abyss. 'A-ah!' they uttered synchronously, as if with only one throat between the two of them.

When they let go of each other, it was already completely dark in the room. Lights were on outside, the street lights were lit. Rad had a sense of blissful emptiness. That night in Serge's dacha had been extraordinarily ordinary, but what had just transpired was happiness. Albeit alloyed by confusion, because at times he had seemed to be sleeping not with Jenny but with Nellie. The awkwardness was compounded by Jenny's insistence on repeating over and over again, 'I love you! I love you!' to be followed a little later by, 'Do you love me? Do you love me? Tell me, do you love me?' 'Of course I do,' he replied, and he was not lying. Only was he addressing Jenny or Nellie?

'You must never run away from me again,' Jenny said a few minutes later, when they had resumed their separate identities. She rolled on to her stomach, threw a leg over him, and laid her head on his shoulder. 'I won't let you, not ever again!'

As she uttered these words, someone's mobile rang. They both jumped, but it was not Rad's. Cursing, Jenny quickly got up, stumbled to the chair where, covered by the dragon skirt, her clothes lay, retrieved the phone from her jeans pocket and said, 'Hello.' After that, she shuffled back to the bed and yelled, 'Well, about time too! Abandoning me and then asking how I am!' She moved Rad over and lay down on the side of the bed, indicating he should pull the sheet over her. 'Where am I?' she repeated, clearly for Rad's benefit and looking straight at him. 'I'm where I'm supposed to be. In just the right place.'

It was clearly Nellie on the phone.

'Tell her I saved you from a horde of savage bikers,' he said.

'Rad wants me to tell you he saved me from a horde of savage bikers,' Jenny repeated into the telephone.

Oho! Jenny knew how to dish it out.

'Nellie says congratulations on my arrival,' she told Rad, ending the conversation. She threw the phone to the far corner of the bed. 'They've just got out of their diving suits and say they'll be back in half an hour or forty minutes.'

'So we have plenty of time before they're back?' Rad asked, drawing Jenny towards himself. The news of their expected time of arrival suggested an invigorating way to occupy the interval. His unruly member was already making clear its desire to re-enter the Gates of Paradise.

'If the worst comes to the worst,' Jenny said, instantly hugging him in return, 'they'll just have to wait.'

* * *

They again had dinner at the lie-down restaurant on the beach. Again there were five of them, but with Jenny replacing Chris. From time to time, Rad caught Nellie looking at him, but there was no telling what she was thinking. As soon as he met her eyes, she looked away. She seemed to be surreptitiously scrutinizing him, as if expecting him to do something and trying to work out what it was. Jenny was snuggled up next to him and, from time to time, felt it necessary to take some morsel she judged particularly delectable from her plate and pop it in his mouth. 'Try this,' she said. 'It's delicious. This place is really not bad. To tell the truth, it's better than I expected.' The first time or two Rad allowed himself to be fed and then declined, but Jenny sounded so offended as she tried to persuade him that he gave in, and thereafter opened his mouth obediently. Several times his eyes met Nellie's during this process, and each time she looked away quickly.

Dron and Tony told them all about the day's diving. Actually, Dron did the talking and Tony ornamented his account with a variety of emotional exclamations.

'These Thais,' Dron said in English, either forgetting that now everybody except Tony understood Russian, or deliberately, in order not to leave him in the dark, 'Forgive me, Tony,' he said with a nod in Tony's direction, 'are worse than Americans. They made us pass a whole exam in scuba theory before they would let us dive. Everything in accordance with the regulations and no exceptions. It was crazy! They're true Americans. None of your Russian slapdash here.'

'Oh, no, no, no!' Tony exclaimed. 'No slapdash here!'

Dron feigned outrage:

'Quite apart from having to queue, as if we were in some Russian social security office, we even had to sit an exam! As if I'd never dived before!'

'There is nothing wrong with that! It is just normal!' Tony said with a laugh.

Nellie was reclining beside Jenny on the next but one sunbed to Rad. She laughed.

'We enjoyed the diving, of course we did. The path to our destination was long, but the joy of reaching it was all the greater.'

'Nellie, you understand the wisdom of the Buddha,' Tony put his hands together in prayerful veneration.

'Yes, on the ocean floor, contemplating those starfish …' Nellie replied, now entirely serious.

'Rad, I'd love to go diving,' Jenny said, looking at Rad.

He shrugged, at a loss for a response. She hardly needed his permission.

Tony came to the rescue.

'Jenny, you need special training before you can go scuba diving. You need to complete a whole course.'

'That sounds great!' Jenny said, looking again at Rad.

'No, Jen, don't start.' This time it was Dron speaking. 'We're quite likely to get called back to Bangkok any moment, just as soon as we get a message. Your money would be down the drain.'

'Oh, how much can it cost anyway,' she said. 'What's money got to do with anything?'

'Yes, the money isn't a problem,' Nellie was clearly, entirely deliberately, coming to Rad's rescue. 'It's just you wouldn't have the time.'

'After we've finished here we need to go and check our email,' Dron announced. 'Anybody other than me need to?'

Nobody did, but neither did anyone have anything against accompanying Dron to the Internet café.

'I'll be able to see where you emailed me my summons yesterday,' Jenny turned and said quietly to Nellie, so Rad would not hear. In reality, she was probably not much bothered whether he did or not. He did, but had, in any case, already worked that out. What he had not worked out was why Nellie had suddenly decided to summon her.

Jenny offered to pay the bill, and there was general agreement that she should be granted that right. Rad took no part in the decision: his wallet was virginally empty, as he was constantly aware, and if they had decided each should pay their share he would have had to beg from Jenny again.

Nellie and Jenny walked to the Internet café hand in hand, like two senior schoolgirls. Rad, Dron and Tony walked a few steps behind and

Rad, as he looked at them, thought that was a good comparison: there was something schoolgirlish about them. This, despite the fact that one of them had left that age behind a very long time ago. Now, as they walked side by side, her figure, no matter how admirable for her age, made that very obvious. Perhaps their schoolgirlishness was due to the fact that neither had had children, so that for both of them the most important thing in life was themselves.

'Listen,' Dron said to Rad, suddenly switching to Russian and interrupting the three-way conversation with Tony, 'I had no idea that you and Jen were so into each other!'

'How, into each other?' Rad queried.

'Well, so much that she just ups and flies here. It is, after all, an eight-hour flight from Moscow.'

Rad did not feel at liberty to discuss the subject of Jenny with Dron.

'What's eight hours. It's just a night's sleep. You go to sleep, you wake up.'

'Don't give me that,' Dron said. 'I know about these things.' He paused for Rad to respond, but he didn't. So Dron asked, 'Is she aware of your situation?'

'Does it matter?' Dron was charging into the intimacy of his relationship with Jenny, and everything in Rad protested against that.

'Yes, I would like to know,' Dron said. 'If she was aware of it, why didn't you just ask for help from her, given your relationship?'

No information was being divulged in his words. They were in a tightly sealed, non-transparent container, but the significance of the contents could be estimated from its weight, which was very considerable.

'Why do you think I should have asked her?' Rad responded.

'Well, because that was the nearest solution. Or did you really not tell her anything?'

'That's right,' Rad confirmed reluctantly.

'That's right!' Dron said. 'But, forgive me for asking, why ever not?'

Given the persistence with which Dron was trying to get an answer to that, Rad had a feeling that telling the truth might do him no favours.

'Well, self-respect,' he said. 'Will that do?'

'Self-respect?' Dron repeated. 'That sounds about right for you. But how about her father? Do you get along well with him?'

It was looking as if Jenny's father, although not mentioned up till now, was actually the main reason for Dron's quizzing of him.

'I don't know. I've never met him,' Rad said.

'Ah, I see,' Dron said. 'And why not? Does Jen not want you to meet him? Or he doesn't want to meet you? What's the reason?'

'It just hasn't happened,' Rad said.

They walked on in silence for a time. Tony was tactfully quiet, not intruding on their conversation with his Thai English; Dron was silent, perhaps thinking up his next 'why'; and Rad was silent. He had a few why's to ask Dron, but had little expectation of any straight answers.

They were just thirty metres or so by now from the Internet café, a shack with light streaming from its wide open door.

'Right,' Dron said, as if drawing a line under the conversation. 'I'll leave you to sort out your mess. It's your problem. My offer to you, at all events, stands. Make your mind up.' As if continuing the sentence, he turned to Tony, moving seamlessly to English as if it were still Russian: 'Tony, what is this? Everybody around you now has a woman. You're the odd man out. Time to put the matter to rights, don't you think?'

Tony laughed, pleased by the attention.

'All my women are in Bangkok, Dron. I'll do all right there.'

'Promise?'

'I promise, since that's what you want.'

Nellie and Jenny paused at the porch, stopped holding hands and turned to face them, waiting for the men to catch up. Before dinner Jenny had changed into loose, ankle-length slacks ('by Dior', Nellie noticed approvingly), an equally loose-fitting elegant blouse ('by Dior?' Nellie wondered and, checking out the label, confirmed with no less satisfaction that it was indeed); her shoes (Rad had noticed the label on the tread when she was putting them on) were also Dior, and her handbag, on a long double chain instead of a strap, which she had brought in place of the one she had arrived with, had a large, expressive 'D' monogram on the clasp. Everything about Jenny would have graced a model in an expensive glossy magazine, or could have been modelled on a model. Unlike Nellie who, for all her merits, bore little resemblance to a model. Rad did wonder who Jenny's father could be. Another tycoon like Dron's?

'Not coming up?' Dron queried.

'We'll just stand and wait for you here,' Nellie said, looking first at Dron, then at Rad to indicate she was speaking on behalf both of herself and Jenny. 'I'll get by today without my email.'

'Yes, I phoned Moscow to say I'd arrived,' Jenny said, looking at Rad. 'I don't need to confirm it by email.'

'Entirely up to you,' Rad said.

'Are you coming up, Rad?' Dron asked as he ascended the stairs. 'I notice you're a bit casual about email. Haven't seen you check it once.'

He was right. Rad had not once downloaded it. What was the point? There would only be the endless mass-mailings, which had probably completely filled his mailbox by now, so that all he would have to do was delete the lot.

He agreed nevertheless to join Dron.

'Yes, why not. I'll take a look.'

Standing back to let Tony go first, he climbed up to the porch.

Rad did not want to be left alone with Nellie and Jenny. How could he have behaved?

'We'll wait for you here and have a smoke,' Jenny called after him, in a tone that suggested it was only proper for her to keep him informed of what she would be doing in his absence.

'Sure. Have a smoke,' he responded from the porch.

There were plenty of computers free in the café. The three of them sat down at monitors and, severing all contact with each other, set out on their individual voyages.

His mailbox on Yandex certainly was packed, but not full: he had underestimated the resource. He wondered for a time whether he should just delete it all unread, or whether all the same he ought to sample some of them. He decided he would, since if he did not, there was absolutely no point in his being there.

He had been sitting at the computer for about ten minutes when he suddenly heard someone call his name. It sounded like a cry for help.

Rad glanced at Dron who, of the three of them, was sitting nearest the open door. He was peering at the screen, tapping his fingers on the table next to the keyboard and had obviously not called out. Rad looked at Tony who, at daunting speed, was battering away at the keyboard composing a message of his own. Everything about him indicated that he had not called.

Rad decided he must have imagined it and returned to the monitor, opened another email and was about to glance at the subject line when he sat back in his chair. It seemed to him that the voice calling him was Jenny's. But why, then, had neither of the others heard?

He quickly got up, walked to the door and stepped out on to the porch. After the bright light he could see nothing. Beyond the top step a chasm of darkness yawned.

'Rad!' Nellie's voice instantly called out to him in the darkness, as if his emergence had been expected, and indeed demanded.

The steps clattered under Rad's feet like a washboard.

'Nellie?' he called, peering at the silhouettes in front of him. There were three. 'Jenny?'

The third was the silhouette of a man, and – plunging into the darkness immediately made it permeable to sight – none other than one of the bikers, the second one who had been waiting for his friend in the square.

The biker was holding Jenny's arm at the wrist. When he saw Rad, he took a step towards him, but without letting go.

'Wotcha, Gregory Peck!' the biker said.

'Ra-ad!,' Jenny cried, endowing the sound of his name with a plea for help and echoing the voice which had roused him from the computer.

'Hands off!' Rad barked, inwardly readying himself to fight. 'Release girl!'

Somewhat to his surprise, the biker, after a moment's pause, let go of Jenny.

'No problem, mate,' he said, swaying towards Rad and enveloping him in a wave of beery breath. He seemed to have downed a full barrel, or at least a keg. 'We need to talk, mate, me and you. Let's 'ave a talk.'

'Okay,' Rad said, gesturing to Nellie and Jenny to go up into the café. 'What do you want to talk about? Let's do it.'

'Let's,' the biker agreed. 'You saw my girl? Sweet little thing, eh?'

'I don't know,' Rad said. 'What else?'

'She is, she is,' the biker assured him. 'You can check it out for yerself, mate. No problem. She likes you, says you look like the young Gregory Peck, and she's always fancied 'im. Get it? A fair exchange. I let you screw my girl, you let me try yours.'

Rad needed some way to turn the air blue, but had learned his English in a lecture theatre and had no sufficiently taboo linguistic resources. 'Fuck', of course, but that was his feeble best.

Lacking any more forceful expression, he told the biker to fuck himself.

That unoriginal suggestion was, however, enough to cause offence.

'Fuck you!' He swore back and, before Rad had time to think what was happening or duck, he got a punch in the face.

The blow hit his mouth and was evidently well-aimed: he immediately tasted something salty. Returning the compliment, Rad simultaneously took another punch to his face, holding out the promise of a spectacular black eye tomorrow.

Rad dealt a hook to the jaw: he was sober, while the biker was half seas over. It took the man off his feet, his head hit the road with a thump and he lay there motionless. Rad leaned over him: the biker was conscious, just stunned.

'Ra-ad!' Rad heard Jenny's voice, looked up and saw her standing on the porch alone. Nellie was not there but, before he had time to answer, they were all there: Nellie and Dron and Tony.

Dron and Tony lost no time coming down to join Rad. The biker was lying on his back at their feet, twisting with pain and looking silently from one to the other.

'You're a liability!' Dron told Rad. 'Was that really necessary? All we need now is for the police to get involved.'

'We need to leave,' Tony said, as if he had understood Dron's Russian. 'The lady who owns the café will not hesitate to call the police.'

'I'll just settle up and we're out of here,' Dron said, rushing back up.

Rad looked again to find a whole crowd in the lighted doorway. Well, four people at least.

The biker turned over and got slowly to his feet. He headed wordlessly down towards the road, but turned round after a few steps.

'You wait!' He pointed at Rad. 'I gave you a lift. I know where you live.'

Half a minute later, the engine of his Honda roared in the darkness, the headlight came on, the brake lights flashed. As he turned the bike, the headlight beam lit up the café for an instant, and he was gone.

Their way back from the Internet café to the refuge of the resort took twenty minutes. They walked quickly, almost unspeaking, only exchanging an occasional phrase or two, all the while listening out for the sound of an approaching motorbike. Rad's mouth was full of blood from a cut on his lower lip. It had evidently torn on the corner of a tooth. His saliva in the electric lighting of the street lights, when he spat it out, seemed completely black.

Without splitting up, all five of them went to the terrace of Dron and Nellie's bungalow. Nellie switched on the terrace light but Dron, who was inserting his key in the lock, told her to put it out.

'Blackout mode,' he said gravely.

'Oh, come on!' Nellie sniffed.

Dron shouted at her:

'What do you mean, "Oh, come on!"'

Nellie was silent.

Tony and Jenny stayed out on the terrace to watch the road, and Rad, following Dron and Nellie, removed his shoes and went inside.

'Go into the shower so we don't have to put the light on in here,' Dron instructed.

Nellie had hydrogen peroxide in her first-aid kit, disinfected Rad's cut and, after inspecting it, diagnosed the most imminent threat to his health as senile dementia.

'The important thing is, will it need surgery?' Dron asked from the room, where he was evidently following their conversation.

'I think we can get by without that,' Nellie replied, by now without irony.

'Well, I'm glad to hear it,' Dron said from the other side of the door.

Nellie put plasters crosswise on the wound, with the end of one of them coming over his lip, and Rad emerged from the shower room for general inspection. The first to inspect him was, naturally, Dron, who in anticipation had drawn back the curtains so that the electric light from the road filled the room. He peered at Rad and chuckled.

'A fitting end to our relaxing island break.'

'End?' Rad asked. 'Because of this incident?'

'Instructions by special courier from Moscow,' Dron said. 'We need to be back in Bangkok tomorrow afternoon.'

'The message came?' Nellie asked needlessly.

'Indeed it did,' Dron confirmed.

'Why didn't you say?'

'Other matters intervened,' Dron said, indicating Rad.

He seemed still to be blaming Rad for the incident, despite having had a full explanation of it on the way back from the Internet. Rad decided just to leave it at that.

'I'm glad we're going,' he said.

'You mean, getting shot of your fellow bikers?' Dron said.

'Of course.'

'We still have to survive until morning.'

'You'll have to apply your professional training,' Nellie said challengingly.

'I will,' Dron agreed.

Rad remembered Nellie identifying the Australian at the quay in Pattaya by his accent.

'I wonder what you think the nationality of my friend was from his accent?' he asked her.

'A hundred per cent English,' she said without hesitation.

'Oh, surely not.' He really did not want that thug to have been English. He had always been a bit of an anglophile, and it was hurtful to think the biker was a national representative of Great Britain.

'What do you mean, "Surely not"?' Dron jumped in. 'The British are a maritime nation, they ruled half the world. Don't forget that!'

Without parting, and without turning on the light, they sat on Dron and Nellie's terrace for three hours. They peered down to the road and listened to the sounds around them. Once or twice someone thought they saw or heard something, and then Jenny and Nellie took refuge in the room and locked the door, while Rad, Tony and Dron mounted a perimeter defence on the terrace. Every time, however, it proved to be a false alarm. Three or four times they heard the sound of an approaching motorbike. It became clearer, louder, closer, but each time rode on by. They were tormented by mosquitoes, and Tony ran to his bungalow to bring back a can of spray, but they were not in an enclosed space and the mosquitoes disappeared briefly, only to reappear. Respraying was required every few minutes.

By midnight they were all exhausted, no longer jumping at every rustle, no longer keeping watch on the road, and it was clearly time to turn in. Most likely, the bikers were on their own and had no reinforcements to call on. Perhaps, too, the biker who had given Rad a lift from the pier had declined to support his mate.

When Rad and Jenny got to the verandah of his bungalow, before he could get the key out of his pocket, she flung her arms round his neck and whispered ardently,

'Rad, I'm so sorry. Forgive me, forgive me! Does it hurt terribly? I'm so sorry!'

'What for?' he said. He was dog tired. This had been some day.

'For it turning out that way. We were standing there, and I just called out to thank him for giving us a lift from the quay. And he ... how could we have expected that?'

'Of course not. Don't worry about it,' Rad said. 'Let's get some sleep.'

'Are you angry with me?'

'No, not at all,' he said.

She wasn't going to let him off that lightly.

'There's something we have to talk about,' she said a moment later. 'Something very important, but we should probably leave it until tomorrow, do you think?'

What was it she wanted to talk to him about? Rad was not even slightly curious.

'Yes,' he answered mechanically. 'Tomorrow.'

She unclasped her arms from his neck.

'Open the door, please.' When he took the key out of his pocket and inserted it in the lock, she deftly slipped her hand into his trousers and quickly found her way to the powder keg. 'I hope, though, that you won't neglect me,' she said.

A minute before Rad was quite sure he would, but as he turned the key and opened the door, he was less sure. And by the time he was locking it from the inside, he had no doubt at all that neglecting her would be very unfair.

CHAPTER SIXTEEN

He felt like a guide, a Bangkok old hand, a master of its streets and its spirit. He and Jenny had come out of the hotel and were on their way to the skytrain when she asked, 'Why does Bangkok smell so bad? And what are those boneshakers on three wheels called? What are these little houses that are so small they look as if they're for gnomes?' And Rad gave her answers and explanations, exactly as Nellie had answered and explained to him on the day of his arrival. They would visit the same places he had visited with her: the Grand Palace, where else? Perhaps Jim Thompson's museum of village architecture.

'Why are there so many dogs in the street?' Jenny asked when they turned out of the alley as crooked as a crankshaft, which ran along the back of the white cliff of the Imperial Queen's Park Hotel, where they were now staying. They came out on to the broad expanse of Sukhumvit Road with its roaring cars, and immediately encountered whole colonies of lethargic, gingery-brown dogs, tearing at the suppurating patches of baldness in their groins. 'It's just unbelievable how many of them there are here!'

'I suppose nobody takes any care of them,' Rad said.

'That's because of the poverty,' Jenny said confidently. 'You don't find this sort of thing in rich countries.'

Perhaps she was right. There was nothing there for Rad to argue with. He just added, 'There are masses of dogs in Moscow, too.'

'Really?' Jenny asked after a pause, as if thinking back. 'I've never noticed them. At least, not in the places I frequent.'

Rad did not proceed with the discussion.

'Look,' he said, 'this park we are coming to has the same name as our hotel: "Queen's Park". Only it's open to the public.'

'Our hotel is open to the public too,' Jenny said. She raised a hand to her face and rubbed her nostril, just as she had when sitting on a bar stool at Serge's villa in Semkhoz. 'It's just that there are different levels of public access. That's how I would put it.'

'Maybe,' Rad said, allowing this conversation too to lapse.

The room at Imperial Queen's Park hotel had been reserved for them from Moscow. They arrived, gave their names and, yes, all booked, please come this way. All it had taken was a phone call from Jenny from the quay in Rayong when they got off the steamer. It was at last six in the morning in Moscow. On the way across, Jenny had found out from Nellie what hotels and serviced apartments were close to their Admiral Suites, and they came jointly to the conclusion that, if there were any rooms available, they were most likely to be at the Imperial Queen's Park Hotel. They had a suite of three rooms, together with a bathroom the size of a golf course. When Rad saw the rack rate at reception he could not help exclaiming in surprise. 'In Moscow this room would have been more than four times the price,' was Jenny's response.

They passed Queen's Park with its pond and found before them the tunnel-like staircase to the skytrain platforms.

'I love this,' Jenny said, squeezing his hand as if asking him to share her enthusiasm. As they left the hotel, she had immediately found his hand and put her own in it. Now, hand in hand, they really did seem to be climbing to the sky.

'Yes, it makes a very uplifting impression,' Rad agreed.

They climbed the stairs to the platform and were hit in the eyes by the advertisement on the gable of the multi-storey Emporium shopping centre with a woman's enormous face with purple eyelashes, like two great fans, which could surely have been used as wings with which to take flight.

'You know, this even looks like America, it's like Broadway,' Jenny murmured, gazing enraptured at the floating face with its eyebrows in the sky. 'Not entirely, of course, but still … Have you been to America?'

'I haven't had that pleasure.'

'I'd like to go to America with you.' She squeezed his hand again.

For a time they stood in silence, contemplating the Emporium's advertisement with its face poised for flight on purple eyelashes.

'Ra-ad,' Jenny called his name. She sounded breathless. 'Did you really hear me calling your name yesterday?'

'When?' Rad asked. 'What are you talking about?'

'Last night, at the Internet café.'

'Oh!' Rad understood. 'Yes, I did. That's why I came out so quickly.'

'But I didn't call out loud to you!' Jenny seemed to be admitting something to him she was afraid of admitting even to herself. 'Nellie can confirm it. I only thought your name …'

'We obviously have a telepathic link,' Rad inferred for her, with mock solemnity.

'It means we have, doesn't it?' Jenny said questioningly, excited and amazed. She turned to face him and gazed into his eyes. 'It must really mean that.'

Rad felt distinctly uneasy. That was what it seemed to mean, and he was actually prepared to concede the possibility of that sort of thing, although without all the mystical trappings, but … The question was, where was this leading?

'The train's coming,' he said pointing to where its square snout had appeared in the distance. He led Jenny to the platform edge. 'I need to initiate you into the secret of how to embark on the skytrain,' he said.

'What secret is that?' Jenny asked without any great show of interest.

'See how everyone's gathering in clusters?' Rad asked.

'That's just because they know where the doors are going to open.'

'Ah, but how do they know? Perhaps there's some kind of indication? Look around you.'

Jenny looked around herself.

'I don't see any indications.'

She paid no attention to the pattern of the line on the platform, and when Rad pointed it out, said, 'So simple. How boring.'

They changed trains at Siam, travelled on to National Stadium, and went out and found a tuk-tuk, repeating the route he had already taken with Nellie. The only difference was that now Rad was the old hand versed in the ways of Bangkok, and when the tuk-tuk driver delivered them at the white walls of the Grand Palace and was giving the change, it was correct to the last baht. 'Don't you need any help?' Jenny asked when he took out his wallet to pay. Rad shook his head. He was in funds. As soon as they arrived at the Imperial Queen's Park Hotel, he had stuck his debit card in an ATM near the entrance and withdrawn 100 dollars' worth of Thai baht. That left precisely $250 on the card to last for the rest of his life, but he dismissed the thought. He was not going to beg money off Jenny. He felt enough of a gigolo taking money from Nellie, even though it was Dron's.

There was a teeming crowd at the Grand Palace ticket office. There probably always was. Rad bought the tickets, and noted that today Jenny's feet too were inappropriately bare, albeit in Dior sandals. He hired a pair of socks for her.

'These are hideous!' Jenny exclaimed when he handed them to her. 'What on earth are they for?'

Rad explained.

'But I can't wear these!' Jenny seemed insulted by the very suggestion. 'I won't wear them! If you'd told me I would have brought a pair of my own.'

There were benches along the path leading from the ticket office to the palace entrance but they were covered, as if by flocks of birds, with people. Without replying to Jenny, Rad found a vacant space and sat down. She followed him.

'What are you doing?' she asked in puzzlement.

'I'll wait here,' he said, 'while you're looking for a shop to buy yourself a different pair of socks.'

For a moment Jenny continued to look puzzled, then her expression changed, indicating she was thinking hard. Then it changed again to a sheepish look of embarrassment.

'I'm sorry!' she said. 'Sometimes I'm such a bitch. Will you let me sit there while I put them on?'

Nothing had changed in the days that had passed since Rad was here with Nellie. The gold on the tented roofs of the stupas gleamed; the multi-tiered brown and green roofs of the numerous palaces, pavilions and gazebos shone, covered with the finest shingle, shaped like fish scales; the perfectly trimmed grass of the magnificent lawns seemed just to have shaken off the last drops of dew. Everything was washed and cleaned, burnished, renovated, there for the eye to dwell on and delight in. 'Wow!' Jenny exclaimed periodically in admiration. She had not forgotten, when doing her packing in Moscow, to bring along a digital camera, and Rad had constantly to take pictures of her: on the porch of the throne room, against a background of sculpted monsters from the *Ramayana*, next to the figure of the Emerald Buddha in the temple bearing its name.

On the porch of the temple, in an area by the lower steps, an old woman dressed in clean white clothes was giving a tall metal cup containing plastic sticks to anyone who paid her ten baht. A man who was given the cup went behind the old woman and knelt on a piece of yellow cloth spread before a small copy of the Emerald Buddha. He shook the cup in front of himself with both hands until one flew out, picked it up and went across to a nearby stand with a lot of pigeon holes. In these were stacks of long narrow slips of paper with printed text. He selected one and read it avidly.

'What's going on?' Jenny asked curiously.

The Bangkok old hand did not know. Either the woman had not been there when he had come with Nellie, or he had not noticed her. Rad stood a short distance away and observed. A minute later he had the answer. The sticks, he noticed, were numbered. The people shaking the cup took a slip of paper from the pigeon hole with the corresponding number.

'It's fortune-telling,' he said with a wry smile. 'Want a go?'

He had not so much been inviting her to have her fortune told as expressing a jaundiced view of what was going on, but Jenny was suddenly enthralled.

'I do! I do!' she exclaimed, and even clapped her hands.

Rad glanced at the piece of paper in the hands of a Thai who had just performed the ritual. It was, of course, printed in Thai script.

'No, you know, we won't be able to understand it,' he said, attempting to engage reverse gear, but Jenny was unstoppable.

'No, come on, come on. Let's do it, get the paper, and ask Tony to translate. It's so interesting. And you've got to do it too!' she demanded, when she saw Rad had only produced ten baht from his pocket.

Rad decided to humour her. She had conceded over the socks, so now he should go along with her on the future. He found another ten baht, gave the money to the old woman, got two cups in return and, slipping off his shoes, stepped with Jenny onto the cloth in front of the Buddha. The old woman folded her hands prayerfully in front of them, showing that, before proceeding to the fortune-telling, they should ask the Buddha's blessing.

'You're baptised though, aren't you?' Jenny said.

'Yes,' he replied shortly.

'And so am I now. Is it all right if we worship the Buddha?'

Rad remembered the four of them, Dron, Nellie, Chris and himself, visiting the temple of the Reclining Buddha at the next monastery along and, also on the porch, gilding the statues.

'Buddha is not a god,' Rad told her. 'And there is, after all, only one Creator.'

They knelt before the Buddha, venerating his teaching, picked up the cups again and started shaking them. This proved to be far less straightforward than it seemed. At Rad's first attempt a dozen sticks flew out, at the second, half a dozen, and success came only at the third attempt. Jenny took two attempts more than that.

'Here it is, the wonderful future!' she exclaimed triumphantly when, instead of a whole fan of sticks, just one fell out in front of her.

'Are you sure it is going to be wonderful?' Rad could not resist saying.

'I'll accept nothing less!' Jenny retorted.

Her number was 8; his was 15.

They took a single slip from the piles in the eighth and fifteenth pigeonholes. The lines of Thai were beautiful and mysterious in their complete incomprehensibility.

'Do you think our predictions will match?' Jenny asked, popping her slip of paper safely into her handbag.

'How could they?' Rad answered, understanding what she meant, but pretending not to. 'You have a number 8, and mine is 15.'

'No, I mean, will they fit together?'

'Well, they aren't a couple of docking spaceships,' he said.

He next took her to the temple of the Reclining Buddha to look at the gigantic, forty-metre statue. Jenny did not like it at all.

'It's like all those Lenin statues we had in Russia. It towers over you and scares you with its size. I don't like gigantism. I would never allow anything like that in my gallery.'

'You have a gallery big enough for a Lenin statue?'

Jenny missed the irony.

'Not in terms of height, needless to say, but lying down – why not? I have a big gallery.' Something like deference was to be heard in Jenny's voice when she mentioned the size of her gallery.

'But Lenin and the Buddha, my dear, that's two big differences,' Rad said, doing his best impression of an Odessan. 'One abandoned a palace: the other couldn't wait to get into one, and came a cropper. One perfected himself and never hurt anyone: the other was determined to perfect everyone except himself, and did nothing but sow evil.'

'Were you alive then, in Lenin's time?' Jenny asked querulously.

'Of course not.'

'And neither was I, but my father says Lenin was not at all the demonic figure he is made out to be nowadays. He was a normal human being and the kind of strict leader Russia needs.'

Rad felt no inclination to debate the merits or demerits of Lenin with Jenny at the foot of the Enlightened Buddha.

'Lenin was quite something, of course,' he said non-committally.

They came out of the temple, put their shoes back on and went down. At the foot of the stairs, the old Thai lady with a face like a ridged hose was sitting on a folding seat selling lotus flowers, a set of three incense sticks and a candle, and the booklets of gold leaf, just as she had been on his last visit. They didn't stop, however, to gild the Buddha. They were in a hurry now to meet Tony in the English park near the Grand Palace where people had been flying kites. Nellie had asked Rad if he wanted a go and he had declined. 'Some other time.' To which she had replied, 'There may not be another time.' An hour ago, as Rad and Jenny were leaving the Grand Palace, Nellie had phoned to say the three-way meeting between Dron, Chris and Mike was coming to an end. They had come to a compromise, and to celebrate she had reserved a table in a quite remarkable restaurant. So that they did not have to find their own way there, they would be collected by Tony.

Their shared predilection for punctuality brought Rad and Jenny to the rendezvous near the spirit house at the edge of the park a full quarter of an hour early. Examining the architectural features of the spirit house took two minutes and, when Rad stepped out from the shade of the trees on to the open grass and cast an eye over the park, nothing had changed.

Around the edge of the grass, groups large and small had spread cotton or plastic tablecloths and were enjoying a picnic. In the middle, fifteen or twenty people, mostly parents with children, were wandering over the grass flying kites. Not far away, the kite seller was wearing the same white T-shirt with portraits of the Beatles and was walking up and down in front of where he had laid out his kites in rows.

'What do you think,' Rad said looking at Jenny, 'should we fly a kite while we're waiting for Tony?'

Not anticipating any objection, he was about to head over to the kite seller when Jenny suddenly took his hand and stopped him.

'Wait,' she said. She was on edge, her expression solemn and portentous. 'I want finally to talk to you.'

Her expression portended wonderful news he would rather not hear.

'What is it?' he said. 'Why "finally"?'

'Because this is something very serious and I've had to pluck up courage.' She took his other hand, and now they were face to face, like a little boy partnered with a little girl to dance in front of all the parents at some kindergarten event. 'Tell me, only very, very truthfully,' she said, gazing into his eyes. 'I think you like me. You do like me, don't you?'

The music had started, she had taken the first step, and now it was his turn.

'I like you a lot,' he reacted.

'I agree to marry you,' she said. 'Of course, you haven't proposed yet, but why should I have to wait for that?'

'And I, as an honourable man,' Rad said, 'should now marry you.'

He was startled, stunned, gobsmacked. He mentally listed the synonyms as if listening to sentence being passed in an American court of law. There was no other way to describe how oppressive this felt.

'Looking at it in purely financial terms,' Jenny was continuing, 'our marriage would be more beneficial to you than to me.'

'Really?' Rad enquired mechanically. 'Why?'

'Because then I can ask my father to help out my husband, even if only prospective, rather than someone he knows nothing about.'

'Why didn't you just ask for help from her?' he recalled Dron remarking as they followed her and Nellie strolling hand in hand.

'You'll have to excuse me,' he said. 'Who exactly is your father?'

She hesitated slightly, as if in taking the last step she had made a faux pas.

'He works in the Presidential Administration,' she said.

'A big wheel?'

She seemed to stumble again.

'Yes. You could even say, very.'

'With a lot of influence?'

'Of course.'

Now Rad was out of step. So much so that he stopped dancing. The music was playing, but he just stood there and could not think which foot to move next to get back in time. He decided to trample straight ahead.

'So what do you know about my affairs that makes you think I need help?'

'That you've been had for a mug and owe 100,000 bucks.'

'Who told you that? Nellie?'

'Does it matter?' Jenny said. 'As if Nellie and Dron were the only friends we have in common.'

She didn't need to say any more. It was obviously Serge and Polina. Most likely, Polina. And Jenny was right, it made no difference.

'You don't think you're overplaying your hand?' Rad said. 'No matter who I am, why would your father come rushing to the rescue? He might decide instead that he needs to rescue you from me, some oddball with a fitness centre, gangsters on his trail, and a huge debt …'

Jenny interrupted.

'I'm not being overconfident. I'm a very careful person and my father knows that. I run my business well. It's profitable, even though running a gallery is high-risk. It's easy to slip up. I don't throw money about, as you may be thinking. I spend it wisely. My father is pleased with me and trusts me. If I ask him to help you, and we aren't just messing about, he will help.'

'Messing about'. That was some euphemism.

'Do you think I'm worthy of you?' Rad asked, trying to sound very serious. 'You said you would only marry a Jew.'

'I was wrong,' Jenny said, also seriously, and she, at least, appeared not to be play-acting. 'The moment I saw you – I'm an art expert, a good judge of faces … Yes, I would like you to be my husband. But you can forget the fitness centre this minute. I have no wish at all for my husband to be involved in that sort of business. You used to work in a bank and that's what you should go back to. In two or three years' time you'll be one of the top people.'

'You see me as a top person in a bank?' Rad said.

'Absolutely,' she confirmed.

'But I'll only get there with help from your father?'

'Naturally. How else? It's the way these things work.'

Rad looked at her agog. She was so sure of herself.

'In other words, you're proposing that I should become Daddy's totally under-the-thumb son-in-law.' He could feel the dance coming to an end. A few more steps and, '*Merci. Au revoir.*'

'Why under-the-thumb?'

'Because I would be living in my father-in-law's pocket and completely obliged to him.'

Jenny shook her head vigorously.

'I'm not suggesting you would live with my parents. I live quite independently myself.'

Rad did not reply. It was time for this dance to end. Fortuitously, the plaster on his lower lip started itching. He wondered how an astronaut on a spacewalk coped with an itch.

'Excuse me.' He could perfectly well have rubbed his lip with one hand, but took back both. This involved some effort, as Jenny was reluctant to let go. 'What do you say we fly a kite?' he suggested, patting his lip with the back of his hand and nodding in the direction of the kite seller. Without waiting for Jenny to agree, he walked away.

The salesman noticed Rad coming in his direction and a warm smile lit up his face. He squatted down and, in anticipation, began lifting his kites off the grass and talking rapidly in Thai, evidently extolling his wares.

Rad took the one the vendor handed him, paid twenty baht, and became the possessor of a long-tailed, highly ornamented red dragon about to soar into the sky on a line wound round an empty Coca-Cola can.

When he stood back from the vendor he found Jenny right on his heels.

'You didn't give me an answer.'

Her voice was tremulous and she looked as though she was about to burst into tears. Rad's hands were fully occupied, so he leaned forward and rubbed his cheek against hers.

'Go and buy one of those,' he said, indicating with his chin the cart of the balloon seller at the edge of the park.

Jenny looked at him intently, as if her eyes were burning, and seemed about to say something more, but didn't. Instead, she stroked one nostril with her index finger and walked quickly off to the balloon seller's cart. Rad watched her go. She had a steady, bouncy way of walking, her tight little buttocks wiggling prettily, and her slender figure seemed to be drawn heavenwards. There was a ten-year difference in their ages, not too much, not too little. For a long time yet she would still seem young, delighting him with her youth and unfading freshness. She was just right!

By the time Jenny returned, Rad had had a trial run with the kite. His baby dragon took to the air after just the merest run and, darting from side to side, shook its tail, climbed up and up, a real winged serpent whose element was the sky. Rad wound the string back onto the Coke can and waited.

Jenny came back and handed him the balloon without a word. He looked at her and she looked away. Rad took the balloon and tied it to the tip of the dragon's tail, let go, and the balloon, filled with a light gas, immediately rushed upwards, drawing the kite behind it, not needing any run at all to get it aloft.

'Take it,' Rad said, handing Jenny the drinks can with the string.

'What for?' she asked, finally looking at him. Her eyes still seemed to be burning.

'Take it, take it!' he said.

After a moment's hesitation, she did.

'Turn it, unwind the thread,' Rad told her.

Very reluctantly at first, Jenny began turning the can on its axis. The brash little dragon, its tail held erect by the balloon, crept higher and higher, and the higher it climbed, the more confident her hand movements became as she began to find it fun.

'I remind myself of Tatiana Larina after she sent her letter to Onegin,' she said when only half the string was left on the can.

'And does that make me Yevgeny Onegin?' Rad enquired.

'I hope not.'

'Let me have a go,' Rad said.

They passed the can back and forth to each other, letting the little dragon out to the full length of his lead, for a full ten minutes before Tony appeared.

'So here is what you are doing!' he said, flashing them that laser-white smile as he approached. 'We got here several minutes ago. It is lucky I decided to look for you in the park.'

'We' was Tony and Nellie. She was standing behind him, her expression understanding and approving.

'Now I see the kind of person you are,' she said to Rad in Russian. 'You didn't want to do it with me, but as soon as Jenny arrives it's all you want.'

Perhaps she did not intend the double entendre, but she could not have expressed herself more ambiguously. The ambiguity was apparent, however, only to the two of them.

'Want to hold it?' Rad asked cockily.

'Ooh, yes please. I'd love to join in your fun and games,' she continued. 'At least I can warm myself at someone else's fireside.'

'Fireside? Where's the fireside?' Jenny asked blankly, passing the can over.

'There isn't one,' Nellie replied robotically. She took the can in her hands like a steering wheel and moved it up and down, causing the baby dragon to flutter prettily in the sky. She had an expression of bliss on her face. 'The kite phenomenon,' she said. 'A sublimation of our mortal dreams of heaven: the body is earthbound, while the soul is in flight,' she declared biblically, speaking directly to Rad.

Rad could think of no suitable response. He did not think he had fully grasped her meaning, either because it was too profound, or possibly because there was none. He found himself wondering whether Helen of Troy was really very clever, or whether her beauty meant she had no need of intelligence.

Jenny was rummaging around in her handbag.

'Tony!' she said, producing the folded slip of paper foretelling her destiny. She held it out. 'Could you translate this?'

'Oh!' Tony flashed his smile at her. 'I see you do not find our ancient folk customs foolish. Let me see what I can do.' He took the paper, instantly becoming serious, read it and looked up at Jenny before beginning to translate. 'Your number is 8, placed between the auspicious numbers 7 and 9. That shows you are well provided for in life and that is your main good fortune. This protection does not, however, promise you a destiny without clouds. This coming year will be very important. You should not complain about life or try to turn it in whichever direction you wish. Life itself will give you what is needful for you. Follow the signs it gives and all that is in your destiny will come to pass.'

Tony stopped. He looked away from the piece of paper and handed it back to Jenny.

'Is that all?' she said, taking it back.

'That is all.'

'What a lot of nonsense.'

Tony laughed.

'Perhaps it is nonsense, perhaps not. Nobody can know.'

'But you, Tony, do you believe it?'

Tony rolled his eyes speculatively.

'I once went to a fortune-teller when I was very young, but then never again. I don't want to.'

'Why?' Rad asked, beating Jenny to it.

Tony wrung his hands.

'Because a lot of what was said coincided with my life. I do not want to know anything ahead of time.'

Jenny looked at Rad.

'Well, where's your piece of paper? Let's translate it.'

Without a word, Rad took the slip of paper out of his wallet and passed it to Tony. Tony again became serious, first running his eyes over the slip, then glancing at Rad before translating.

'The number you have been given tells that you are an exceptional person. You may achieve a lot in life, you may do a lot, but not everything depends on you. The problems you will face may prove too great, and you need to have the wisdom to understand that you should not try too hard to overcome them, but leave them and follow another way. You are at a turning on the road of life and your future depends on which way you go. Whichever way you choose will be right, but what you choose will decide your destiny to the end of your life.'

Rad listened and was shaken. 'A turning on the road of life', for heaven's sake! He took the paper back.

'Thank you, Tony,' he said.

Jenny had nothing to say about what she had heard. She looked at Rad. It was obvious she desperately wanted to comment on the prediction, but thought better of it.

'Nellie!' Rad called, thrusting the paper back into his wallet.

'Yes?' She turned.

'Shall we carry on flying the kite or be on our way?'

'No, there's no two ways about it. We need to go. Here!' She handed the can back to him. 'I'm here with Tony to bring you back in top form.'

'What does that mean?' Rad couldn't pass up the opportunity for a little more swordplay.

'It means, in a state where I find it pleasant to spend a few extra minutes in your company,' Nellie said.

For some reason, she said it in English, to blur the possibly provocative distinction in Russian between the more formal and the more intimate words for 'you'. Or was Rad imagining that?

He bit through the line with his teeth and, holding the kite by the end of its string, called Jenny over.

'Would you like to set it free?'

'Do you trust me?' she asked meaningfully.

'One hundred per cent,' Rad said.

'Then, so be it,' she said, holding out her hand to him.

Rad passed her the line and stepped aside.

A second passed, two, three ... Jenny stood with her arm upraised, hesitating to open her hand. It felt as if she was about to bestow freedom not on a coloured paper dragon but on a living being which for many years had been bowed down in captivity. Now the moment when it would be free was close.

'Go on!' Nellie prompted her.

'Let go!' Tony yelled.

Jenny looked round at Rad and released the string, which lurched heavenwards and the next instant was no longer visible.

Drawn upwards by the balloon, the kite gradually began to climb. The four of them stood with their heads thrown back, looking after it. Strangely, for as long as they could still see it, they felt they could not leave. As if their baby dragon really was alive, and to leave it being watched by other people after they had walked away would have been to commit an act of treachery.

Five minutes passed in this fashion, ten. The kite was tiny and you would no longer have known that it was hanging there like an inverted exclamation mark. But it was still visible, and they stayed there watching over it on its journey.

CHAPTER SEVENTEEN

A service was in progress in the Cathedral of the Holy Trinity and St Sergius. There were so many people it seemed impossible to push past, but flowing through the crowd, like the Gulf Stream in the Atlantic Ocean, was a trickle of those intent on venerating the relics of the monastery's founder. Nellie and Jenny made their way into it and were carried through the crowd, as if they had instantly acquired the right to oblige everyone to give them right of way.

'The last time I came here was with Rad,' Jenny said. 'A little over a year ago, in late autumn. I was baptised shortly afterwards.'

'Oh!' Nellie replied, surprised. 'Did he move you to do that?'

'I don't know, I'm not sure. I was probably just ready for it, but that's certainly how it happened. It was after I had been here with him.'

The stream carried them the entire length of the cathedral and brought them behind a high wooden screen. They passed along it and out to a dais where the reliquary reposed on a pedestal. The last time, she remembered, both she and he had only crossed themselves, but now, following the example of other people, she hurriedly crossed herself and kissed the silver casing of the reliquary without worrying about how hygienic that might be. More precisely, she did worry about it as her turn in the queue was approaching. She tried to persuade herself that the silver would act as a disinfectant, but was not entirely convinced. It was only when she found herself actually at the shrine that her doubts were suddenly dispelled, she kissed the shrine and felt no squeamishness as she did so. Nellie, she noticed as she came down from the dais, also bent down to the reliquary, brushed it with her lips and laid her brow on it, remaining like that for a few moments.

'I'm so grateful to you for dragging me here,' Nellie said when they were outside again. After the warm, clammy air in the cathedral, the fresh, frosty air of a still, January day caught in the throat like the fizz of champagne. Champagne there really would be later in the day, no doubt, to celebrate the Old New Year. 'It's such an unexpected feeling. I was saying good-bye, you know? We will emigrate and I really do not know when we will be in Russia again.'

'Is that not up to you?' Jenny asked.

Nellie looked nonplussed for a moment, but then said, 'No, not really, and Dron doesn't want to come back to Russia at all.' She circled her hands in the air, as if indicating a billowing cloud which represented the nature of Dron's wishes. 'He's got out of the way of living here and now you can't drag him back unless it's completely unavoidable. If he didn't have to be at this shareholders' meeting he wouldn't have come this time either.'

'But tell me, he was working for you-know-who, was he?' A tone of respectful admiration was clearly to be heard in Jenny's voice when she spoke of the profession she was hinting at. 'I keep saying to everyone, "Oh, this spy I know …" but actually I don't know for sure.'

Nellie knitted her eyebrows. Jenny had noticed in the past that she had a habit of raising and lowering them when talking about something she found distasteful.

'Who knows? Perhaps he still is,' Nellie said. 'Although officially he retired from all that a thousand years ago. Why "serve the Motherland" when you can travel abroad without needing all that?'

While they were talking, they had traversed the square and come to the rotunda marking the spot where, almost 400 years ago when the monastery was under siege by the Poles, a life-giving spring had appeared, only to dry up again when the siege was raised. The winter shadows, already very long, had lengthened even more while they were in the cathedral; the sun now fell only on the very top of the rotunda and the day was showing signs that, in an hour or an hour and a half, it would yield to night.

When they reached it they got up on the stepping stone, but after a moment Jenny asked Nellie in some embarrassment if they could go and stand on the other side.

'You see,' she said, as if hiding behind her apologetic smile, when they had moved round, 'when we were here before we stood just there, in that very spot.'

'We? You and Rad?' Nellie queried, although it was hardly necessary.

'Well yes, with Rad,' Jenny said. 'He talked so interestingly about miracles and faith, and how they are connected. He was so passionate about it. I just gazed at him in admiration.'

'What did he say? What exactly?' Nellie responded animatedly.

Jenny paused, then said with a chuckle,

'I don't remember exactly. I wouldn't trust myself to repeat it. Something along the lines that faith demands knowledge, and knowledge requires a miracle. Something like that. I only remember it was so interesting.'

'And after that you decided to be baptised,' Nellie said, but whether in jest or in earnest was unclear.

The look in Jenny's eyes as she looked back at Nellie was dreamy.

'You know, maybe that's right. Now I think about it, it is possible.'

Without another word to each other, they left the rotunda and went towards the way out of the monastery.

'So you don't know anything more about him?' Nellie asked some time later, cautiously and without looking at Jenny.

Jenny stroked the side of her nose.

'No. After he disappeared from the hotel he just vanished without a trace. I looked up his mother here, but she claims to know nothing either.'

'But he is alive?' Nellie interrupted.

'Yes, he's alive,' Jenny confirmed. 'At least, his mother says he sends her an e-mail every month, but without any specific information. He's alive and well, but as for where he is or what he's doing, she has no idea.'

Nellie raised and lowered her eyebrows. Jenny happened to look over and noticed.

'What he's doing there's no telling, of course,' Nellie said. 'But where he is is clear enough: he's in Thailand. His visa was expiring. There was only one day left on it. Where could he go without a visa? He's gone to ground, an illegal immigrant living the life of an illegal immigrant.'

'I sometimes think,' Jenny said suddenly, 'that he may have been deported back to Russia and he's somewhere nearby. We could be walking the same streets. What do you think? Could he have been deported?'

'What do I think?' Nellie repeated. 'I think it's unlikely. I think, taking everything into account, he had worked out some options. Or perhaps there was only one. He took the plunge – and vanished. Who in Thailand is going to bother searching for him? I think he had help from Tony. At least, Dron and I suspect Tony. Tony is saying nothing. He's as firm as a rock that he knows nothing, absolutely nothing!'

'As firm as a rock,' Jenny echoed .

'As firm as a rock,' Nellie confirmed.

They passed through the gates in the red brick wall girdling the monastery and found themselves in the square outside. It sloped from the gates down to a ravine with the river at the bottom of it. A free open space revealed itself to the eye, unencumbered by any building apart from a small church: a broad, restful view to be enjoyed and contemplated.

'I stood here with him then too,' Jenny said, 'and we went to that restaurant over to the left, across the road. Do you see it? The Russian

Innyard. And there I had lunch with him. It was so delightful. The Russian Innyard: can you see?'

'Right, that's enough about him.' Nellie took Jenny's arm, turned her round and led her firmly across the square in the opposite direction. 'Let's drive back. It's not warm enough for us to be standing here and it's time we were at the dacha. Dron and Serge are probably on their way already.'

'If they had arrived, I'm sure Dron would have phoned you,' Jenny said. She was reluctant to leave this place.

'I didn't say they would have arrived, I said they will be on their way,' Nellie replied.

Jenny's yellow Suzuki hatchback was parked only a hundred metres or so from the square, by a neat, single-storey McDonald's with clean, sparkling windows on Red Army Prospekt, which looked as if it had been transported here from the West where it belonged. They got into the freezing cold car, looking forward to the heat which would shortly fill the interior when they started the engine. The engine did not start at the first attempt. Or the second, or the tenth.

'What, has it frozen? Does it need a good old Soviet heater under it?' Nellie asked with a nervous laugh.

Jenny banged her hands on the steering wheel angrily.

'No, it's had something wrong with the electronics these last few months. Suddenly, for no reason at all, it just won't start. It's time for a change of horses. I realised that this summer. It was just so unreliable I didn't use it until the baby was born. I didn't want any nasty surprises.'

'So why haven't you changed it?' Nellie asked.

Jenny gave her that same sheepish smile she had had on her face when she asked if they could move to the other side of the rotunda.

'Well, for the same reason,' she said. 'He drove this car that time. You see, I know from the way someone drives a car what kind of person they are. It was the way he drives that finally did for me. I had felt it in him, but that was when I saw it.'

'Really? How curious,' Nellie said. 'So what was it about his driving?'

'Only, you'll have to forgive me if you think I'm being over-theatrical,' she warned.

'Yes, yes, you're forgiven,' Nellie prompted.

'He breathed such steadfastness and such serenity. I can't put it any other way. That is precisely how it was.'

'Steadfast and serene,' Nellie said. She was silent for a moment, as if inwardly weighing the words. 'Yes, I think that's right. That puts it well.'

They had naturally to wait for the breakdown truck in McDonald's. Jenny phoned her assistant at the gallery and told him to go to the garage and arrange for the car to be repaired when it was brought there. With that done, all that remained was for them to wait, and chat. Nellie asked Jenny about her pregnancy in great detail, about the birth, about how she had felt after it and whether she was breastfeeding. Jenny gave her all the answers, and felt she had changed places and now Nellie was the younger woman.

'Are you crazy?' she exclaimed, when Nellie asked if she was breastfeeding. 'You'd be tethered to the baby like a cow. *Merci!* And I want my breasts to keep looking like breasts!'

'Formula feeding?' Nellie asked.

'What on earth would I do that for? We don't have to re-invent the wheel when we've got the experience of centuries past – a wet nurse! Five hundred bucks a month and the problem is solved.'

'But you still have to find a wet nurse. We don't live in villages nowadays. This is Moscow.'

'No problem there either!' Jenny dismissed that with a wave of the hand. 'I just gave the health visitor from the clinic the 500 bucks and she brought me ten candidates by the hand. It was up to me to choose.'

Nellie brought her plastic cup of tea to her mouth.

'I gather the baby is his,' she said. 'Judging by the time. I'm sorry, don't answer if you don't want to …'

'No, why would I not want to? Of course it's his.' Jenny's voice was full of pride. 'It was absolutely the right time of month, and it was what I wanted. Admittedly, there was something I wanted even more, but …' She interrupted herself, her fingers moving in the air as if she was playing an invisible piano.

'What was it you wanted even more?' Nellie asked.

'Right, that's enough about him,' Jenny replied in Nellie's own words. 'For some reason we're talking too much about him.' Her feeling of unexpected seniority came over her and she asked something she would not have dreamed of asking in different circumstances. 'But, if you'll forgive me, why have you not had a baby? Is there a problem?'

'No!' Nellie replied instantly. She leaned across the table to Jenny and whispered, as if drawing her into a plot, 'I'm in my fourth month. You're the first person in Russia I've told about it.'

'Wow!' Jenny exclaimed in the same conspiratorial whisper. 'I was asking myself why you wanted to know all that stuff about my pregnancy and the birth!'

'Did you think I was just being nosy!' Nellie responded with a laugh.

Their conversation took off, so much so that when the yellow and black striped breakdown truck came to a stop right in front of the window they were sitting at, they only became aware of it when the driver phoned Jenny's mobile to say he had arrived.

Ten minutes later, they were free. The tow truck driver was given a generous consideration in advance, which warmed the cockles of his heart no worse than a bottle of vodka, and drove off with the toy Suzuki in the direction of Moscow. Jenny rang her assistant and asked him to be at the garage in an hour's time, and then did not have to worry about the car any more.

The sun set, the sky lost its depth, and a purple hue heralded the imminence of dusk.

Nellie and Jenny, seizing a moment when the streams of vehicles rushing towards each other had a gap in both directions, ran across to the other side of the road and started trying to flag down a car going to Semkhoz. They all sped heedlessly past, however, so the two women went down to a sad little park with a doll-like effigy of Lenin in front of the monastery wall where there was a bus stop. The road widened at that point, and buses and cars were constantly emerging from the roaring stream of traffic to pick up passengers.

The buses, when they reached the bus stop, were all privately owned minibuses. They drew up at the stop, dropped off passengers, took on others and immediately cast their moorings and were on their way. The route taxi with a number 55 on the windscreen struck Nellie as familiar. It seemed to her that when she and Jenny had driven away from Serge's villa that morning and were bowling through the village, a bus with that number had come speeding along the road in the opposite direction. Jenny had been concentrating on her driving; Nellie, as a passenger, had had more time to observe what was on the road.

'I think the 55 is going our way,' she told Jenny. 'Let's take that if it is. We'll be in the village in ten minutes and can walk on up to the house from there. The walk will be good for us.'

There was no telling when they would find a car to take them home, and the route taxi was ready and waiting, so Jenny unhesitatingly agreed.

'Does the 55 go to Semkhoz?' she asked the passengers getting off.

'Yes, yes!' several voices immediately replied.

Nellie and Jenny got in, slid the door to behind them, and the taxi moved off.

While Jenny was passing the money for their fares to the driver, she became aware that someone was staring at her, as if undressing her. Her observer was sitting in the front seat, facing the rest of the passengers. He was an old man who looked like a gnarled stick seasoned by time, and whose earth-brown face seemed sculpted from driftwood.

He had a trolley with two small wheels. The bag had been removed from it and in its place there was a large narrow-necked canister, the like of which Jenny had never seen in her life. It was blackened by time and firmly fastened on with an old rope, greasy and also blackened by time, which was wound round and round the trolley. As they drove alone, she again and again caught him staring at her. She would be talking to Nellie, forget about the old man, and suddenly be conscious that he was staring. She glanced at him to check, and he stared back, unabashed, unblinking, searchingly, as if groping her.

'How's Slava getting along?' he asked suddenly when their eyes met again. It was as if they knew each other very well, and he, tired of waiting for her to acknowledge the fact, had decided to make it public.

'I beg your pardon?' Jenny said coldly.

'Slava, Slava! What, have you forgotten him? Before New Year, November it must've been, I saw you together. He was driving you in some little yellow car.'

The little yellow car was undoubtedly her Suzuki, but what Slava could the old man have seen her with a year ago?

A moment later she realised who he was calling Slava.

'Do you mean Rad,' she asked the old man.

'Yes, yes,' the old man said, pleased. 'That's what he'd decided to call himself, but I called him Slava. That other name's pretty fancy, not Russian at all.'

'Jenny,' Nellie broke in. 'You know your way around here. Where do we have to get off?'

Their minibus was already driving through the village. It sped past the single-storey glass-and-concrete grocery store on the right, which was followed by a two-storey building which looked like a Soviet-era House of Culture drowning in the depth of a park.

'And stop here, here, just after the park, at the turning, will you?' the old man shouted, looking out the window and hastily turning himself towards the driver. 'I need out here! And so do you,' he said, turning round again, to Nellie.

'How do you know?' Jenny asked, peering uncertainly out of the window.

'Well, this is where Slava always got out,' the old man said, staring at her as if he knew some great, embarrassing secret of hers. 'Or is that not where you're going?'

'Right,' Jenny said, 'this is where we need to get off.'

The route taxi stopped, throwing everybody forward. Jenny got up first, pulled back the door and stepped down.

'Girlie, I don't know your name,' the old man called out, pushing his trolley to the door and preventing Nellie from getting out. 'Can you give me a hand here? I've got this damned hernia bulging and that can's got twelve kilograms in it. It's too heavy for an old man.'

There was nothing for it. Jenny silently grasped the rope tangled round the canister and lowered it and the trolley to the ground.

'Well now, thank you for that, you're a good girl, helping an old man,' he said getting out himself. 'Just like Slava. Slava always helped me too. "Here, Pavel Grigorievich," he would say, "let me help you with that!"'

Jenny thought it best to say no more.

Nellie stood at the door waiting for Pavel Grigorievich to get out of the way. She stepped down, slid the door to behind her, and the minibus, spewing churned-up snow from under its wheels, sped on its way.

'What is that you've got there?' Nellie asked, pointing to the canister on the trolley.

'Paraffin, of course. What else?' Pavel Grigorievich replied. 'We don't have your gas. How would we get by without paraffin? We do need to eat and drink, you know.'

'What, you mean you cook on a paraffin pressure stove?'

Jenny wanted just one thing, and that was for her and Nellie to get away from this old man as quickly as possible. She recognised where they were: it was the place Rad had got out of her Suzuki when they came back from the monastery that time, but she could not contain her surprise. It was unbelievable. Could it really be that it was not just somewhere in the back of beyond, but right here, next to where she was staying, that people were still cooking on paraffin stoves?

'What else do we have to cook on?' Pavel Grigorievich asked querulously. 'So we just have to get on and carry the paraffin back here. You can't stoke the stove up ten times a day, and if you use an electric hotplate it would cost you a fortune.'

'Right, Pavel Grigorievich,' Nellie said, bypassing him and walking towards Jenny. 'All the best to you. Nice meeting you.'

Pavel Grigorievich caught the sleeve of her fur coat.

'Well, but what about Slava? I haven't seen him around for a while? Has he gone off somewhere?'

He had caught Nellie's sleeve to stop them getting away, but the question was addressed to Jenny, and it was she who replied.

'Yes,' she said.

'Oh, dear!' Said Pavel Grigorievich, still holding on to Nellie. 'Has he gone far?'

'Yes,' Jenny said.

'Somewhere you can't see from here?' From his tone of voice it could be deduced that this was a joke.

'Yes,' Jenny said.

'Oh, dear, oh, dear!' Pavel Grigorievich sounded offended. 'You don't want to say. It's a secret! Keep your nose out, Pavel Grigorievich, none of your business.' He finally let go of Nellie's arm and was about to reach for the trolley, but stopped. 'Perhaps you could help me a bit more, girlies.' He seemed not to be talking, but almost chanting the words. 'It's such hard work heaving this trolley through the snow. See what little wheels it's got. They keep getting stuck. We are going in the same direction anyway. And you could take it in turns, eh? How about helping an old man?'

Jenny noticed that Nellie was about to agree, and had mentally already taken the handle to start dragging the trolley along.

'It's your problem – what's your name again? Pavel Grigorievich,' she said, heading off any temptation Nellie might have to agree. 'We have our hernias too. We're not supposed to carry heavy things. Good luck to you.'

Pavel Grigorievich's driftwood face was contorted with rage. He stepped forward quickly, and now it was the sleeve of Jenny's sheepskin coat he was clutching in his fist.

'You've got hernias? Why kind of hernias could you have? What heavy loads have you ever had to drag? Fucking little madams! Your hour will come. We'll string your men up, and you we'll screw till the jizz comes out your ears!'

'Let go! Piss off! Let go!' Jenny jumped away, tearing her sleeve out of his fist. 'You think you're going to fuck us? An old prick like you, with a hernia? In your dreams! You'd be lucky if you could get it up for your old woman!'

'Just believe me, your hour will come!' Pavel Grigorievich's mouth twisted in a vindictive grin. 'If we don't have the strength, we have sons, grandsons, and they'll take vengeance, for themselves and for us. It's the cat will weep the mouse's tears!'

Nellie and Jenny rushed away as fast as they could down the snow-covered road from the highway into the centre of the village, past the House of Culture in the depths of the dark, skeletal park, past the unexpectedly carmine-red replica church behind its arrow-head iron railings, and both of them were shaking. Behind them, in the still, frosty air increasingly infused with the dusk, they could hear the squeaking of Pavel Grigorievich's trolley, and no matter how they rushed, every step putting more distance between them and the old man, the scratching and scraping of its rusty metal grew not fainter but sounded all the sharper and more distinct.

'And to cap it all, you really were going to help him,' Jenny said when they were finally so far ahead of Pavel Grigorievich that the rasping of his trolley had become almost inaudible. 'I could see, just looking at you, you really were going to drag his trolley for him.'

'Don't remind me!' She emitted a strangled giggle. 'I felt so sorry for him.'

'Sorry?' Jenny exploded. 'You've completely forgotten in that America of yours what the Russian people are capable of. If the chips were down, he'd show you no mercy.'

'I had forgotten,' Nellie admitted, unable to restrain another giggle. 'That was some reminder.'

Their intention of enjoying a walk and taking in the beauty all around them was not realised. They hastened back to Serge's villa as if they had a strong tailwind behind them.

When they told Polina about the incident, she almost hit the roof.

'You must be crazy to take public transport! I haven't for the past thousand years. Altogether, I've been urging Serge to sell this house, make an effort and move to Millionaires' Row on Rublyov Highway. We need to live among our own kind.'

'But really, it is so lovely here, in every respect,' said Nellie. Their trip to the monastery had been wonderful and she wanted to stand up for this area which, until now, had been completely unknown to her. 'The scenery! And such forests all around. And the monastery so nearby.'

'So what if it's nearby!' Polina's excitability again caused her to nearly hit the ceiling. 'You can come and visit the monastery from Rublyovka, and don't have to live in a monastery!'

Nellie's eyebrows twitched.

'Well, yes. Living in a monastery might be overdoing it.'

'Of course it would. Who the fuck wants to live in a monastery?' Nellie's irony had passed Polina by.

While Nellie and Jenny had been visiting the monastery, the courtyard had filled with cars. Nearly everyone who was supposed to be coming had arrived, with the exception of the master of the house himself and Dron. 'They're on their way, on their way,' Polina said in reply to Nellie's enquiry of whether she had heard anything of Dron's whereabouts. 'Serge phoned just before you arrived,' she said, 'to say he was approaching the ring road. They'll be here in forty minutes or so.' Dron and Polina's husband had had some joint project today, an important meeting, and had planned to come back together after it.

'How did the meeting go? Okay?' Nellie asked.

'Yes, everything went splendidly. Couldn't be better!' Polina exclaimed. 'I can't tell you how grateful I am to you,' she said, taking Jenny's hand in both her own, squeezing and holding it for a moment. 'It's quite impossible to express how grateful I am to you for introducing Serge and Dron to each other. And us!' Letting go of Jenny's hand, she looked across to Nellie. 'Dearest Nellie, I'm so awfully glad that Jenny introduced us, awfully!'

'It was fated,' Nellie responded.

Half an hour later, Jenny found herself sitting at the bar counter with a martini in her hand in the company of the poet-artist who had been performing as Polina's star turn on the evening she met Rad, and who had been presented as dish of the day. Her guests were no longer treated in this manner to the poet-artist, who had been relegated to the standard menu and become a regular member of Polina's gatherings. The colourful check wool shirt, untucked in the fashion of the early 1990s, and the docker's canvas trousers he affected last year had been replaced by an entirely bourgeois dark suit, white shirt and bow tie, and he was now doing his utmost to appear as respectable as possible, although he had yet to expunge the hungry, wolfish gleam in his eye, and his apparently ineradicable morose expression.

'I am currently working simultaneously on a new cycle of paintings and a new cycle of poems,' the poet-artist was telling her, turning over in his hands a long, flat box of matches customised specially for Polina's soirees. From time to time he opened it, took out a match, twiddled it in his fingers, pushed it back in and closed the box. 'The paintings and poems are linked, so their themes complement and elaborate each other, as, indeed, do their images. This is my new concept of my inner world. A revelation of new depths, my new hypostasis. Of a creator in partnership with power. The creative will. There is nothing in this that could be described as positioning. Positioning always incorporates an element of intentionality; I would go so far as to say, artificiality. In my case it is the germination of a seed. The climate of the times calls for power. It breathes the desire for power. That fills me to overflowing. It fills me to overflowing and I open the floodgates. That is not a positioning, that is a discharge.'

'Discharge is a disgusting word,' Jenny interrupted him. 'So, you are turning yourself into a channel for festering pus. For excrement. Viewers and listeners are really going to want to bathe themselves in that!'

'No, you are using the word in its vulgar sense.' The poet-artist pulled a match out of the box, broke it, popped it back in and closed the box. 'A discharge is also an electric explosion of thoughts, feelings, states, in an unexpected direction, to a new level, the firing of a gun. In that other sense, "discharge" is the perfect term. You will sense that when you see the paintings of my new cycle. I look forward to welcoming you to my studio at your convenience.'

Jenny took a sip from her glass. Before that evening when she met Rad, she had been indifferent to martini, but now preferred it to anything else.

'Don't bother,' she said. 'You want to worm your way into my gallery? You'd be lucky, pal. If you aren't alive to the connotations of "discharge", you must be deaf to everything else. Don't you think?'

The poet-artist slid wordlessly from his bar stool, threw the matchbox on the counter and stalked away. Jenny turned to watch him go with acute satisfaction. She knew exactly why she had discharged both barrels at this charlatan. It was nothing to do with medical discharges. She had just taken an opportunity when it presented itself. Rad had disliked his poetry, and had produced a parody better than the original. He got it between the eyes because he wrote poems Rad did not like.

Within five minutes, the bristly-bearded poet-artist had been replaced by a young shaver with chubby cheeks and a curiously louche and brazen expression.

'Your name is Jenny,' he said. 'Don't try to deny it.' He took her glass from the counter, sniffed it and put it back. 'Martini. The drink of James Bond.'

'And not only him,' she said.

'Of whom else?'

'There are other worthy people in the world.'

'You are referring to yourself?'

'On this occasion, no.'

'Do I need to pour myself a martini, to be worthy?'

'Worthy of what?'

'You,' the young thing exclaimed, staring at her so lustfully it seemed the fly of his black jeans must be about to burst at the seams.

'Well, pour yourself one,' she said. 'Take a chance. The citadel is not locked and bolted.'

She was not at all averse to flirting with this rude boy. And perhaps, time would tell, to do more than just flirt. She liked him. So young, and already so very wicked.

The boy went behind the bar, helped himself to a bottle of martini, took a glass, unscrewed the bottle, filled the glass, screwed the top back on and replaced the bottle.

'To your beautiful citadel, Jenny,' he said, inviting her to clink glasses.

She liked the ambiguity of his toast, too. She had, of course, set it up, but he had taken advantage of it quite neatly.

'And what is your name, Mr Bond?' she asked.

'My friends call me Bob,' he replied suavely.

'Robert, I take it?'

'Boris, but Bob to my friends.'

'Splendid, Bob.' She took up her glass and clinked it against the one Bob was still holding in the air. 'And you can call me Jenny. Feel free. I don't mind.'

She seemed to have found her company for the evening, as long as she could pace it right.

'Jen!' Nellie called her, beckoning from the other end of the room. Dron and Serge were standing next to her, so forty minutes must have passed. The programme Polina had prepared could be expected to begin at any moment. That Polina would have prepared one there could be no doubt, as there could be no doubt that it would include a highlight and a dish of the day. 'Jen, over here!' Nellie waved again.

'Guard my martini,' she told Boris-Bob, 'and don't lose sight of me.'

'I'd sooner lose my life, Jenny,' Bob called after her, rather cleverly.

Jenny crossed the living room, kissed Serge, kissed Dron. A strange iciness was coming from them and their cheeks were stone cold. Why could that be if they had been travelling by car?

'What have you been doing outside?' she asked. 'Smoking? No, you don't smell of tobacco.'

'Jen, you are spy material!' Dron said. 'I appoint you to my residency.'

'Is he joking?' Jenny asked, looking at Nellie.

'Yes,' Nellie nodded. 'He doesn't have a residency. I told you.'

'My cover is blown!' Dron put his hands up. 'Exposed and unmasked! I surrender. Jen, Serge and I have a surprise for you outside. Come and admire it. It is, after all, the Old Russian New Year. A time-honoured Russian tradition.'

'Pagan!' Nellie snorted.

Serge was standing nearby, listening to them, and seemed impatient. His expression, unlike that of Dron, was tense and anxious.

'Jenny, I'd like a word,' he said, finally managing to get a word in. 'What was this incident today? Something to do with paraffin, Polina was saying. I want to hear about it from the horse's mouth and here you both are. Tell me what happened.'

'Oh, Serge, it really was just nonsense,' Nellie said, evidently repeating what she had been saying before Jenny appeared. 'Really, nothing to get stirred up about. Jenny and I are over it. It was a piece of nonsense, not worth talking about.'

'No, it's not nonsense.' All the lightness had gone out of Serge. Jenny had never seen him so grim-faced, quite the Man of Steel. 'I need to know everything about this. It's essential. I live here.'

It would have been just too embarrassing to tell Serge everything Pavel Grigorievich had threatened, but between the two of them they did manage to convey the essence of the incident. As they continued, the furrows left his face and he became quite his old self again.

'There, Polina was just putting the wind up me,' he said, when Jenny and Nellie finished their tale. 'I thought it was something really serious. It is just nonsense. Let's forget all about it.'

Now, however, Nellie was a bit hurt that he seemed not to be sympathizing with them enough over the ordeal they had suffered.

'Well, yes, but … I have to say, Serge, this is all a very bad sign. What if suddenly … all right, so he's just one old man, but he really did say, they have children, and grandchildren.'

'No, it's nonsense,' Serge repeated. His face was completely back to normal. His expression was relaxed and complacent, as if he had achieved Nirvana and the affairs of this world could no longer affect him. 'If, as you say, suddenly something kicked off, then I can tell you, now is not 1991 when there was no one to defend the Soviet system.

'Now people have property. They won't just let that be taken off them. Now, if the riffraff try to start something, without a second thought they'll make the bastards bleed. They'll crush them like lice.'

'It's actually nits people crush,' Dron interjected with a chuckle. 'Lice have to be extricated.'

'How do you know that?' Nellie asked, looking at him startled.

'Personal experience, believe it or not,' Dron said. 'At the Military Translators Institute there was a fellow from somewhere out in the sticks. Don't know how he found his way in there. He came back one time from leave, louse-ridden. Before they worked out what was happening, half the regiment was scratching.'

'The animal!' Serge exclaimed with that relaxed, smug look on his face. 'You were lucky it was only once.'

Dron chortled.

'Luck had nothing to do with it. Pediculosis in a military university, and not just any old one at that! The command were furious. They didn't wait until the next exams to fail him. They found some pretext and booted him out to serve as a conscript and repay his debt to the Motherland.'

'Quite right too. People need to know their place,' Serge said approvingly.

Jenny was finding all this talk of lice and nits just too disgusting and decided to get the conversation back to the surprise she had been promised.

'What's the surprise?' she asked, addressing herself to both Dron and Serge. 'Why have you been outside? Do we have to wait long?'

'No, not long at all,' Serge said. 'I'll just check the programme with my wife, whether it's now or later.'

'Right now, right now!' Polina popped up, waving her hands in the air. 'If everything's ready, then right now. Ladies and gentlemen!' She jumped up on to a chair and clapped her hands. 'Put on your hats and coats and everybody outside! Everybody outside! A surprise! I promise you won't regret it!'

The surprise was a fireworks display. The part of the courtyard not taken up by parked cars was now occupied by rockets, single, double, triple, in clusters, which Dron and Serge had readied for launching. All that remained was to light the blue touchpaper, retire, and admire their fiery flight.

Boris-Bob turned up next to Jenny holding her glass of martini, which had been refilled to the brim.

'I've been guarding it,' he said. 'Fancy some?'

Jenny took a sip and handed it back to him.

'Carry on, sentinel.'

'May I drink from it?' Bob asked, already raising the glass to his lips and, without waiting for her reply, sipping from it.

Jenny liked that. It was sexy.

'Bob,' she reprimanded him, 'that is my glass and my martini. You are supposed to be guarding it, not drinking it.' She removed the glass from his hand and took another sip, the glass finally vicariously bringing their lips together. 'Guard it!' she said, giving it back to him.

The first rocket hissed, thrusting a trail of fire down into the snow before taking off. A second rocket hissed and took off, a third, a tenth. Then it was time for the doubles, the triples, and the clustered artillery. The courtyard echoed with booms and bangs; red, blue, green and purple rockets hung and hovered, danced and dazzled in the sky. In no time at all everyone was ready to party. Polina knew how to get things going.

Standing close to Jenny, Bob took her hand in his and began touching her fingers one by one. He left them and moved up to her wrist, only, a little later to creep back down to her fingers. He was young but knew his stuff.

'Down, boy,' she said.

The silence after the noisy demise of the last of the fireworks left them deafened.

'Wow!' Polina shrieked, jumping up on to the porch and raising her hands in the air. 'The Old New Year begins! Everyone inside! Everyone inside! What's in store? Wow!'

'Wow! Wow!' shouted all around, coming to life again and starting to move in the direction of the porch. 'What have you got for us, Pol? Pol, give us a peek behind the curtain!'

'There's a time for everything! All in good time!' Polina exclaimed, bouncing up and down on the porch like a spring.

Jenny reached out a hand towards Bob and instantly felt the coldness of glass awaiting her fingers. She took a sip and returned it.

'Permission granted, sentinel. Avail yourself.'

'With the greatest of pleasure,' Bob said, raising the glass to his lips.

'Jen!' she heard Serge calling. He was not following the stream of people into the house but standing to one side of the porch, holding a folded sheet of white paper in front of him. Dron was at his side. Since they had come back from Moscow they had been inseparable. 'Jen, look, Dron and I have thought this over,' he said when Jenny reached them. 'Whether to tell you later or now. We're going to have to tell you some time, and, anyway, we've decided it's best to get it over with now.'

Jenny had no idea what he meant. She had never before seen Serge at a loss for words.

'What is it?' she asked. 'What are you talking about?'

'Here,' Serge said, handing her the sheet he was holding. 'Read this. I received it today. It's not addressed to me: it was forwarded. Read it. You'll understand what's happened.'

Puzzled, Jenny took the paper and unfolded it. The railings on the porch were throwing a shadow, and she stepped to one side so nothing would prevent the light from falling on the sheet.

It was the printout of an e-mail. 'From: To: Sent: Subject: Folder:' Was it for her? The next moment, however, as she was wondering about that, her eye caught Rad's surname. It was in the 'From' box. And also in the 'To' box. Only in the 'From' box the email address was hotmail.com, and in the 'To' box it was mtu-net.ru. Jenny looked down at the text, which was in English. 'Dear Mother …' Was he writing to his mother? 'Please forgive I could not write before I see computer first time only today.' Jenny looked at the signature, certain she would find his name there, but the letter was signed with a completely unknown name, long and with the letters so strangely combined that she could not immediately read them: 'Sumana Chaiwongthong'. In front of the name were three English words, two of which she knew. The middle word she had never encountered before.

'What does "inconsolable" mean?' she asked, looking up at Serge and Dron.

'Too sad to be comforted,' Dron explained.

Jenny was shaking. She was shaking more violently even than when she and Nellie had been racing along the road with the sound of Pavel Grigorievich's squeaking trolley in their ears. The sheet of paper in her hand was trembling. She tried to stop it but could not. The letter was something to do with Rad, and evidently contained bad news.

'What is this?' she asked, shakily handing the sheet back to them. 'I can't make head or tail of it. Read it to me. Tell me what it says.'

Serge and Dron looked at each other. 'You do it,' Dron's look appealed to his new-found friend.

Serge took the letter, shook it open and was about to read, but changed his mind, folded it again and handed it to Dron. He took Jenny's hands in his.

'Jen,' he said, 'it tells us Rad, it turns out, was living on Phuket. That's an island on the west side of Thailand, in the Indian Ocean …'

'I know what you're going to say,' Jenny said, afraid to look at Serge. 'And he got caught up in that awful tsunami just before the Western New Year. Is that it?'

'Yes,' Serge confirmed. 'He was working as a sports manager at one of the hotels. He was at work that day and, well …'

'Well what?' Jenny said quickly. 'Has he been drowned?'

'He's missing,' Dron said, butting in. 'Of course, quite a lot of time has passed, almost three weeks, but they are still finding survivors.'

Jenny wriggled her hands to make Serge let go of them. She had stopped shaking, outwardly at least, and her hands were no longer trembling.

She pushed her hands into the pockets of her coat. She felt awful, looked about her and saw Bob hovering nearby clutching her martini. She beckoned him over, took the martini and drained it. She handed back the glass, saying nothing, and waved him away.

'Well, what's that bit about the inconsolable widow?' she asked, turning back to them. 'Had he got married there?'

Dron butted in again.

'Just a detail. Tony's sister. I phoned him today and found out.'

'But he said he had no idea where Rad was.'

'That's what he said, but I put the screws on him and he came clean. I remembered the name of his sister. That's the signature at the end of the letter.'

'And it was addressed to Rad's mother?'

'Yes,' Serge said, taking over again. 'She forwarded it to me. We've kept in touch this past year.'

Jenny felt she needed another martini. She looked around but there was no sign of Bob, who had cleared off. 'I drank all the martini,' Jenny reflected.

She turned up her coat collar, pulled it tight at the front and hugged herself, as if the shivering was not coming from inside her.

'Almost three weeks,' she said, looking from Serge to Dron. 'Do you think there's really any chance he might still be found alive? But then, why would that woman call herself his "inconsolable widow"?'

Serge glanced reproachfully at Dron.

'Dron wanted to make it easier for you,' he said, turning to Jenny. 'Rad is dead. It says so in the letter. I'll give you it. You'll read it there.'

He was going to hand her the letter, but she did not take it.

'What for? Whether he's only missing or dead, he hasn't been there for me for almost a year now.'

The door into the house opened and Nellie and Polina came out on to the porch. They were no longer wearing their outdoor clothes.

'Serge! Dron!' they called, before seeing the three of them down there. 'Jenny, you're there too! What are you doing? Everybody's waiting for you!'

'Well, Jenny, that's it,' Dron said. 'Forgive us. You can imagine, we'd have preferred not to be the bearers of such news.'

'What are you talking about down there?' Polina shrieked from above. 'Come inside. You can finish talking about whatever it is in the house!'

'You go in,' Jenny said to Dron and Serge. 'I'll stay out here for a bit. Don't wait for me.'

She could see they were hesitating, reluctant to leave her alone but also not wanting to stay there, not knowing what to do or say.

'Go on, go on,' she shooed them. 'You needn't worry about me. I'm not going to do anything stupid. I'm a single mother now, my son needs me.'

'A single mother!' Dron snorted.

Her flash of humour gave them leave, they went up on to the porch to their wives, and the door slammed shut behind the four of them.

* * *

A few minutes later, Nellie came out again, this time wrapped up warmly. She came down to the courtyard but did not find Jenny there. She was not in the parking area or in the shadow of the outbuildings. Nellie was about to go back inside to raise the alarm, but then thought to look out in the road. The bolt on the gate was pulled back. She went outside. Jenny was standing, with her arms folded, in the middle of the road where it was darkest, where the nearest lamps no longer cast any light. She had her head held back and was gazing up at the sky. Nellie ran to her, although there was no need. She heard the footsteps, lowered her gaze and waited. When Nellie reached her, she said, 'What a bastard, eh?'

Nellie was perplexed.

'Who!'

'Him, of course, him.' Jenny's voice was emotionless, as colourless as if it had been bleached with hydrogen peroxide. 'Fancy preferring some wretched Thai woman to a Russian!'

Nellie felt something like a twinge of jealousy. Not for Tony's sister, who she knew really could not be described as wretched. Rather, the jealousy was for Jenny, and she had been meticulously suppressing it ever since inviting her to join them on Ko Samed.

'It wasn't a woman he ditched,' Nellie said.

'No?' A tinge of interest appeared in Jenny's colourless voice. 'Who then?'

'This country.'

'Oh, this country.' Jenny's voice was flat again. 'You've ditched this country yourselves, and if things get bad, I'll ditch it too. Only not for Thailand. What's a country? It's not a person.'

'Is that what you read in the starry sky just now?' Nellie asked. She could not think what else to say.

'The starry sky is silent,' Jenny said. 'It just helps you get your own mind straight.'

Around a bend in the road the figure of a man appeared, lumbering unsteadily towards them. He was wearing a heavy jacket which made him look square. It might have been quilted against the cold, or a sheepskin. On his head was a large fur hat, and he had what looked like felt boots or soldiers' boots on his feet. He was obviously local.

'Let's go back into the house,' Nellie said urgently as the burly, bear-like figure approached.

'Yes,' Jenny agreed immediately. The sight of this primeval figure in the deserted street gave her the same sense of unease as Nellie.

They hastily went back to the gate, skipped through and heard it lock behind them, but even though they were now in a secure area, they made for the porch no less hastily, as if propelled by a tailwind. All they wanted now was to be inside the house again, where it was warm and light and they would be surrounded by their own kind. In there, nothing terrible could happen. It was safe, secure, invulnerable, and it was the only place where life was worth living.

CONTENTS

CHAPTER ONE 5

CHAPTER TWO 19

CHAPTER THREE 45

CHAPTER FOUR 60

CHAPTER FIVE 82

CHAPTER SIX 98

CHAPTER SEVEN 123

CHAPTER EIGHT. 148

CHAPTER NINE 172

CHAPTER TEN. 190

CHAPTER ELEVEN 202

CHAPTER TWELVE. 240

CHAPTER THIRTEEN 258

CHAPTER FOURTEEN 282

CHAPTER FIFTEEN. 298

CHAPTER SIXTEEN 320

CHAPTER SEVENTEEN. 333

Dear Reader,

Thank you for purchasing this book.

We at Glagoslav Publications are glad to welcome you, and hope that you find our books to be a source of knowledge and inspiration. We want to show the beauty and depth of the Slavic region to everyone looking to expand their horizons and learn something new about different cultures and different people, and we believe that with this book we have managed to do just that.

Now that you have got to know us, we want to get to know you. We value communication with our readers and want to hear from you! We offer several options:
– Join our Book Club on Goodreads, Library Thing and Shelfari, and receive special offers and information about our giveaways;
– Share your opinion about our books on Amazon, Barnes & Noble, Waterstones and other bookstores;
– Join us on Facebook and Twitter for updates on our publications and news about our authors;
– Visit our site www.glagoslav.com to check out our Catalogue and subscribe to our Newsletter.

Glagoslav Publications is getting ready to release a new collection and planning some interesting surprises — stay with us to find out more!

Glagoslav Publications

Office 36, 88-90 Hatton Garden

EC1N 8PN London, UK

Tel: + 44 (0) 20 32 86 99 82

Email: contact@glagoslav.com

Glagoslav Publications Catalogue

- The Time of Women by Elena Chizhova
- Sin by Zakhar Prilepin
- Hardly Ever Otherwise by Maria Matios
- Khatyn by Ales Adamovich
- Christened with Crosses by Eduard Kochergin
- The Vital Needs of the Dead by Igor Sakhnovsky
- A Poet and Bin Laden by Hamid Ismailov
- Kobzar by Taras Shevchenko
- White Shanghai by Elvira Baryakina
- The Stone Bridge by Alexander Terekhov
- King Stakh's Wild Hunt by Uladzimir Karatkevich
- Depeche Mode by Serhii Zhadan
- Herstories, An Anthology of New Ukrainian Women Prose Writers
- The Battle of the Sexes Russian Style by Nadezhda Ptushkina
- A Book Without Photographs by Sergey Shargunov
- Sankya by Zakhar Prilepin
- Wolf Messing by Tatiana Lungin
- Good Stalin by Victor Erofeyev
- Solar Plexus by Rustam Ibragimbekov
- Don't Call me a Victim! by Dina Yafasova
- A History of Belarus by Lubov Bazan
- Children's Fashion of the Russian Empire by Alexander Vasiliev
- Boris Yeltsin - The Decade that Shook the World by Boris Minaev
- A Man Of Change - A study of the political life of Boris Yeltsin
- Asystole by Oleg Pavlov
- Gnedich by Maria Rybakova
- Marina Tsvetaeva - The Essential Poetry
- Multiple Personalities by Tatyana Shcherbina
- The Investigator by Margarita Khemlin
- Leo Tolstoy – Flight from paradise by Pavel Basinsky
- Moscow in the 1930 by Natalia Gromova
- Prisoner by Anna Nemzer
- Alpine Ballad by Vasil Bykau
- The Complete Correspondence of Hryhory
- The Tale of Aypi by Ak Welsapar
- Selected Poems by Lydia Grigorieva
- The Fantastic Worlds of Yuri Vynnychuk
- The Garden of Divine Songs and Collected Poetry of Hryhory Skovoroda
- Adventures in the Slavic Kitchen: A Book of Essays with Recipes
- Forefathers' Eve by Adam Mickiewicz
- The Time of the Octopus by Anatoly Kucherena

More coming soon...